A HALL OF FAME
Historical Novel ™

THE CONQUEROR'S WIFE

NOEL B. GERSON

ace books

A Division of Charter Communications Inc.
A GROSSET & DUNLAP COMPANY
360 Park Avenue South
New York, New York 10010

THE CONQUEROR'S WIFE

An ACE Book

Produced by Lyle Engel

Published by arrangement with Hall of Fame Romantic-Historical Novels, Inc.

2 4 6 8 0 9 7 5 3 1
Manufactured in the United States of America

Marriage is an evil that most men welcome
—MENANDER

THE
CONQUEROR'S
WIFE

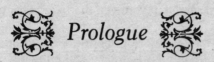 *Prologue*

"FATHER, I will not marry a bastard!"

The songs of troubadors and traveling gleemen pictured Lady Matilda as the epitome of all loveliness and charm, but Count Baldwin, watching her as she stood at the window of her bower, her fists clenched and the color high in her face, thought—and not for the first time—that she was a recalcitrant, narrow-minded vixen. He shifted his weight in the heavily padded chair that had been installed in her chamber for his comfort and fingered a band of embroidered gold that encircled the front of his tunic of dark red wool. Whenever Baldwin was disturbed the feel of precious metal soothed him, and as he was the wealthiest man in Christendom it was not difficult for him to find solace.

"Please be reasonable, Matilda," he said in the deceptively calm voice he usually reserved for his more intricate dealing with his own Flemish wool merchants.

"I'm always reasonable."

There were times when the Count wondered whether she was really his daughter or whether she had been sired by Beelzebub. In ten and a half centuries of the Christian era no father had ever been subjected to such defiance. It was his own fault, in a sense, and the knowledge that he had allowed her too much freedom

1

and was now paying the penalty made him no happier. "I urge you to look at this matter from a practical point of view."

"That's precisely what I'm doing." Matilda turned and smiled serenely, and as always when she was pleasant she appeared far younger than her twenty-one years.

"Do you want to lose your heritage?" In his growing agitation he began to twist the emerald ring that sat on the little finger of his left hand. "If you'll behave like an adult, you and your brother will inherit the wealthiest independent county in Europe, but if we arouse William's anger and he decides to invade us, I shudder to think what will happen."

Matilda's smile broadened and her green eyes sparkled. "Why not use a little of your wealth and hire an army of mercenaries to defend us, Father?"

"Against William?" Gripping the arms of his chair, the Count pulled himself to his feet, but in spite of his upset he carefully smoothed the folds of his calf-length tunic. "If I had enough money to hire every landless knight on the Continent—which I don't—William would cut through them as easily as he sliced that goat cheese at supper last night. You've got to face reality, Matilda. He can be a very dangerous man. Look at his record. Do you realize he pacified Normandy when he was no more than nineteen? And that since then he's conquered four counties and a duchy? The Normans are our neighbors, Matilda, and if those wild men attack us, we're lost. Even the King of France has made a treaty with William, so who are we to stand up to him?"

"He's still a bastard," she replied with supremely feminine lack of logic.

"And you're too good for a bastard, even for the most

powerful general of our age, the greatest military genius since Charlemagne, or perhaps even Julius Caesar. You think well of yourself!"

"It so happens that I do."

There was, of course, sound cause for Lady Matilda's high self-regard. Tall and slender, with long, wavy red hair and clear features that reflected intelligence and strength, she had been courted as much for herself as for her father's gold. Ever conscious of her place in the world, she stood regally in her graceful gown of pale green silk, and it was no accident that even her clothes bore the mark of her individuality. The dress, which fitted snugly to her waist, was trimmed with a band of gray fur straight down the front; other ladies used only bits of the fur, which was imported from Siberia at exorbitant cost, but Matilda, who set her own styles, could afford to indulge her whimsey. Her enormous sleeves, which began at her elbows and hung below her knees when she held her arms at her sides, were her sole concession to orthodox fashion, but even these she wore because she considered them attractive and not because others did likewise.

Her assurance was too much for her father, and he advanced toward her across the bower, impatiently kicking at the rug he had imported for her from Persia. "There are times," he said, "when I'd like to whip you."

Matilda laughed musically. "It's a little late for that, I think."

"Yes, unfortunately." Baldwin stopped short, stung by her ridicule, as she knew he would be. "I'm too civilized a man to thrash the mother of children who are three and four years old."

"Gerbod is five, Father."

"All the more reason for you to remarry, then. He'll

be a grown man himself before we know it, and you'll be too old. You've been widowed for two long years now, Matilda. Aren't you ever going to remarry?"

"When the right man asks for my hand, I shall certainly accept him." Hoping to end the discussion, she reached into a voluminous pocket at the side of her skirt, an innovation of her own invention, and drew out several sheets of parchment containing a portion of the Book of Job, which had been loaned to her by the monks of the monastery located just outside the Lille town walls.

At the sight of the paper Baldwin's anger flared anew. "It's indecent for a women to know how to read!" he cried. "And your hair, look at your hair!"

"What's wrong with it?" Matilda murmured, touching a long lock with her fingertips.

"Respectable matrons wear it braided and tied on the tops of their heads, and you know it. It's wrong for you to wear it loose like a maiden."

"As we both realize from this long and fruitless discussion, Father, I'm not a married woman."

"You certainly aren't! And that puts you under my direct jurisdiction." The Count's eyes blazed triumphantly. "So I order you to marry Duke William of Normandy."

"Don't be absurd. Under the papal bull of 1041— no, it was two years earlier—His Holiness ruled that a widow may marry whom she pleases."

"And it definitely doesn't please you to marry William, even though he's come here from Rouen for the express purpose of making you his bride. And your one reason—even though you know the hazards involved for us—is that he's illegitimate."

Matilda put the parchment back into her pocket. "Oh no," she said brightly. "There are other reasons."

"Name them. And I wish you'd stop wearing silk. Be good enough to remember that the wealth of Flanders comes from our wool."

"There's one of the reasons, Father. His mother is baseborn. She's the daughter of a wool carder, I believe."

"She's the daughter of a tanner." The Count raised his voice for the first time. "William told us as much at supper last night. He seemed very proud of his mother. He spoke of her with great affection, and that's more than I can say of my daughter's feelings for me."

"I really wasn't paying much attention to what he was saying, if you must know. He smells of the stables, and I spent the better part of supper trying to avoid him."

"Yes, you avoided him because you were so busy simpering at that Englishman. I saw you, and I'm afraid William saw you too."

Matilda drew herself up haughtily. "Lord Brihtric is a gentleman. He's cultured and suave and refined, and I forbid you to speak of him in the same breath as that crude Norman lout."

Baldwin retreated rapidly to his chair and sat down hard. "You're in love with the Englishman?"

She pondered the question for some moments, her lips pursed and her eyes thoughtful. "I think the relationship has the potential of considerable development."

The old man shook his head. "Brihtric is a casual guest who has stopped off for a visit with your brother on his way home from Rome. And surely you can't be serious. Surely you couldn't prefer an obscure nobleman from a remote, half-pagan land like Cornwall to the bravest, ablest——"

"When Brihtric learns that I'm not like the rest of my

family and that money isn't all important to me, he'll become interested in me."

Her father could only gape at her. "I'll be damned," he said.

Matilda shrugged her shapely shoulders. "I'm not competent to judge, one way or the other. But if the problem bothers you, I suggest you take it up with your confessor. I can only tell you that I'll be damned before I'll marry the Norman."

Duke William paced up and down the length of the main hall of the Lille palace. Always restless indoors, he was even more impatient than usual, for he knew that a decision regarding his own future was being made upstairs and it bothered him that he was not exerting a direct hand in the shaping of his destiny. It was one of his firmest beliefs that throughout his twenty-five years he had been in control of his own fate, and to a large extent his conviction was justified. Ordinarily William shaped events more than they changed him.

Being handicapped at the moment, he was somewhat less than himself. In any case, a measure of Lady Matilda's criticism was justified: there was a faint aroma of the stables about him, although that of the harsh liquid soap he used each morning to shave his face was stronger; and he was undeniably the son of a tanner's daughter, Harlotte, whom he had installed in a quietly luxurious home of her own on the seacoast.

But he was the son of Robert the Devil, Duke of Normandy, too, and he had fought for his birthright when, at nineteen, he had come out of the hiding imposed on him twelve years previous when his father had died on a pilgrimage to the Holy Land. And he had wrested his duchy from the lawless barons who would have deprived him of it. He had been fighting ever since.

It was small wonder, then, that he looked like a soldier, for he knew no other life. His bronze, acorn-shaped helmet, with its Norman noseguard pushed up, rode on the back of his massive head, its chin strap hanging unfastened. His broad shoulders and thick chest filled his tunic of supple leather, which hung to his knees, and his stride was so long that its narrow skirt was slit at the sides to allow him greater freedom of movement. His tight-fitting breeches of unbleached wool revealed his muscular thighs and his long, sturdy legs were encased in knee-high leather Norman pedules, or sock boots. As it was warm in the hall, his short cloak of rough, black wool was open and was held together by a strap across his chest, which left his sinewy arms unhindered.

In a sense his arms and hands were the keys to his character. Although he had come to Lille on a social visit for the purpose of matrimony, his left forearm was nevertheless encased in a padded leather half sleeve, which was customarily worn by Norman knights on the battlefield to prevent chafing by their heavy shields. And with his right hand he fingered his wide leather belt, into which was tucked a unique dagger of his own design, a weapon with an extra, curved blade that swept out sideways from the hilt and gave the dagger the appearance of a miniature battle-ax. He wore no or-namentation, no trimming, no gold.

His dark eyes were clouded, his chin jutted out, and occasionally he touched his firm lips with the tip of his tongue as he lifted his head in the direction of Lady Matilda's bower. Now and again he glanced at his companion, Seneschal William Fitz Osbern, who sat with one leg thrown over the arm of a chair. But the

Seneschal, William's principal lieutenant, was careful to keep his own lean face expressionless and was directing his gaze into the fire blazing in the hearth. Fitz Osbern, a six-foot warrior of great repute in his own right, was dwarfed by his master and was no match for him in physical strength. Besides, having spent the past ten years at William's side, he could sense the Duke's explosive mood.

"I'll wait a few minutes more, that's all," William said flatly. "Then I'll go up to the wench's room myself and demand an answer."

Fitz Osbern hooked his thumbs into his double-strapped leather belt, so made in order to accommodate the twin daggers he wore at his hips, and carefully considered his reply. "I wouldn't, if I were you," he said at last.

"Why not?" William demanded, halting before him and rocking back and forth on his heels.

Fitz Osbern, who was a married man, spoke in a tone he would have employed with a child. "A woman," he said, "is not like a fortress. She can't be taken by direct assault. You've got to woo her gently. You've got to use art and cunning and subtlety."

"That's a lot of rubbish." William took off his helmet, wiped perspiration from his high brow, and ran his fingers through his short, dark brown hair. "You make courtship sound like a campaign, Fitz Osbern."

"Exactly."

"Not in my experience. Every woman I've ever known——"

"Every woman you've known has been a camp follower. Matilda is a great lady. There's a difference."

"She's an attractive wench." William relaxed a trifle and grinned speculatively. "Every report I had on her stressed her beauty, but I was surprised all the same, I was willing to marry her to tie Flanders to me by peaceful alliance, but I wasn't expecting to enjoy the experience. Now I'm actually looking forward to being married to her. And don't laugh."

"I'm not laughing, William."

"Good. Because I like her. And I imagine that after I've broken her to my ways I'll even love her." The Duke resumed his pacing, clapped his helmet back onto his head, and gripped his dagger by its plain leather handle. He looked much as he did in the field the night before a battle, or in his great hall when he was forcing a new policy down the throats of his once-unruly barons.

Fitz Osbern had not achieved his position through subservience, and he held his ground stubbornly. "I don't think Lady Matilda is the sort of woman who can be tamed."

William's laughter reverberated against the walls. "I've tamed Anjou, Maine, and Brittany, and I've twice beaten France. I don't think a woman whom I can carry in one hand is going to cause me any problems."

"You assume she'll agree to marry you." There was no humor in the Seneschal's voice, even though William refused to take him seriously. "I was watching her last night, I tell you, and she had an expression around her mouth that reminded me of my wife. It's just possible that she won't have you."

"It's also possible that marriage has softened you, Osbern." The Duke hated to be contradicted. "You sound as weak as a Frenchman. Since when has a female had the right to decide what she will or won't do? Besides, no woman in her right mind would refuse a duchy, and Matilda seemed sane enough."

It was useless to argue with his liege lord, Fitz Osbern knew, but no Norman ever surrendered until he had fought to the last. "I wouldn't be surprised if she's had proposals of marriage from other reigning dukes. As I recall, there was a rumor last year that Felix of Lorraine——"

"I suppose she's rejected kings, too!" William's patience snapped and his voice became harsh. "Maybe you've forgotten that my cousin has promised that England will be mine after his death, but I assure you that Matilda's father remembers it! You should have heard him last night. Did Edward swear on oath when he offered me his country? Who were the witnesses to the pact?"

He paused for breath, and at that instant his ears, made sensitive to remote sound during his childhood years of forest dwelling, caught the gentle tapping of soft leather on stone, and he took up a position near the foot of the winding stone stairs before Count Baldwin reached the ground. Fitz Osbern, hoping he appeared more casual than he felt, tried to observe the amenities. "We've just been talking about your palace, Lord Count," he said genially. "There are a few traces of our Norman architecture here and there, but obviously you found your model elsewhere."

"Yes, as a matter of fact, I did." Baldwin crossed the hall slowly, absently shuffling through the rushes that covered the hard dirt floor. "I once visited Norway and admired the royal palace there, so King Harold Hardrara was kind enough to send me his own builder when I decided to put up a bigger house for myself."

The mention of Harold Hardrara was unfortunate, Fitz Osbern thought. The Norwegian monarch was reputedly the fiercest soldier on earth, and William had often expressed the desire to meet him in individual combat. And this was not the moment to arouse dormant jealousies. "Your position here at the top of a hill is perfect for defense," the Seneschal of Normandy declared, "but we've been amazed that you haven't built a castle. With stout walls and buttresses, a broad moat and no more than three towers you'd be impregnable. If you'd be interested, I'd be pleased to send you one of our builders from Routen or Bayeux."

"Thank you, but there's no need for a castle here," Baldwin replied hastily, betraying his nervousness by laughing, then catching his breath. "Flanders is a peaceful land, and we don't anticipate being attacked—by anyone."

William could not restrain himself any longer. "Well?" he demanded in a loud voice.

No one needed to ask what he meant. Fitz Osbern sat upright and Count Baldwin sank into his heavily padded chair that stood on a dais at right angles to the hearth. "You've fortunately never had occasion to know that my daughter is a headstrong woman," he said, not quite daring to look the Duke in the eye.

William mounted the dais in a single step and stood close to his host. "You mean she rejects my suit?"

"I wouldn't put it so bluntly, Your Grace. You recall meeting Bishop Aram last night at supper, the papal envoy? Well, my daughter spoke to him late in the evening about your offer, and the Bishop expressed the opinion that the Church might not look with favor on such a union. Naturally he couldn't define final policy without word from Archdeacon Hildebrand in Rome, but as he's one of the Archdeacon's principal assistants, I think we can take his views as being more or less authoritative. And he's virtually certain that Hildebrand would oppose the marriage on the grounds that a united Normandy and Flanders—which we'd be for all practical purposes, don't you agree?—would be too strong a force and would upset the whole balance of power in this part of the world. I dare say," he added apologetically, "that the ambassadors of France and the German Emperor have seen this step coming and have worked against our mutual interests by poisoning the minds of the Holy Father and of Archdeacon Hildebrand against us."

"The King of France and the Emperor may go to the devil," Fitz Osbern said bluntly, smashing his fist with such force on the arm of his chair that the wooden peg holding it to the body was weakened.

William was already thoroughly conversant with the complexities of the international situation, and his full attention was caught by a more personal aspect of the matter. Clapping a hand on his host's shoulder, he stared at Baldwin incredulously. "Do you mean to tell me," he roared, "that you permit a female to discuss affairs of state with papal envoys? You let a mere woman meddle in something that's none of her business?"

The Count smiled feebly. "My daughter is a most unusual woman, as I've tried to indicate to you."

There was a long, uncomfortable silence, and William's eyes grew stormy. When he spoke at last, his voice was thick with anger. "A woman who can find only a flimsy excuse to refuse a marriage with the Duke of Normandy is more than unusual. She's a fool." Turning abruptly, he walked out of the hall.

Baldwin twisted the fabric of his long sleeve. "The excuse was mine, not Matilda's. I hoped it would soften the blow. She never bothers to justify herself."

Fitz Osbern, who was frowning, said nothing.

"Do you think, Lord Baron, that William will declare war on us?"

"I don't know." The Seneschal stared at the arch through which his master had departed.

"I'm willing to sign any reasonable treaty that will bind our two lands in friendship." Baldwin, sick with fear, tried to rise but could not. "I'll do anything in my power to preserve the peace between us. I'll——"

"The choice isn't yours, Lord Count. And it's useless trying to guess what William will do. When he loses his temper he's unpredictable. And he's lost his temper."

A short, heavy rain, the first of the spring, drove the people of Lille indoors, but then the sun reappeared, and although the roads were muddy the merchants and artisans, craftsmen and vendors and traders hurried out again to complete their day's business. The narrow, winding streets were soon crowded with busy citizens, and their devotion to duty was unexpectedly rewarded when they saw an unusual procession making its way from the church in the center of the town to the palace on the hill. Lady Matilda rarely ventured into Lille, and for that reason, perhaps, she was cheered enthusiastically on her infrequent appearances.

She had chosen to attend Mass at the church instead of in her father's private chapel, and she and her ladies made an exceptionally pretty and appealing picture as they rode slowly, graciously accepting the plaudits of a people starved for color and glamour. Lille was rightly proud of the realm's first lady, for she was a striking figure on her white mare. The long skirt of her delicate blue silk dress was looped up for riding and revealed her magnificently embroidered lavender undertunic. The hood of her lavender cloak was thrown back, showing a circlet of pearls at the crown of her head, her thick braids of hair fell over her shoulders, and over her right wrist was a gold strap holding a prayer book. Everyone who saw her agreed that there was no lovelier princess anywhere.

And her entourage did her full credit. Her ladies, all in soft silks, flowing cloaks, and fluttering veils, their costumes of pale yellows, blues, and pinks resembling wild-pea flowers, represented the essence of feminine grace. And the one man in the party, whom those tradesfolk who dealt at the palace identified as the English Lord Brihtric, was even more gaudily attired than the ladies. His soft, high orange felt hat matched his linen tunic, which ended in a very full, swirling skirt ten inches above his knees. He wore a short, emerald green cloak, and green linen strips wrapped spirally up his legs served as stockings. Soft leather shoes of shiny black were the same shade as his sword scabbard, and Lille gaped at the outlandishly attired foreigner; in Flanders only the jesters at the courts of the mighty dressed like peacocks.

Matilda, who had been out of sorts after her unpleasant interview with her father earlier in the morning, enjoyed her reception and was in no hurry to return home. She decided she would have to make it her business to come into town more often: the people deserved to see her, and these demonstrations helped to consolidate the family's popularity. She suffered no false illusions over today's act of defiance and realized that there might be difficult times ahead, so the more she could do now to win the support of her father's subjects, the more united would Flanders be in the event of trouble.

That trouble thrust itself at her far more quickly than she had suspected it might, however. Her first inkling that something was amiss came when she saw the pedestrians in the street ahead scattering, running into alleyways and houses. Then, as she rounded a corner, a devastating apparition loomed directly ahead of her, and her mare halted of her own accord and pawed the ground nervously.

A man mounted on a heavily armored black stallion was advancing toward her, and for a moment she did not recognize him. His bronze helmet was buckled in place, and his long nose-guard hid his face. Over his leather tunic he wore a long coat of scalelike chain mail that immediately identified him as one of the notorious Norman "fishmen," and in his left hand was a kite-shaped, five-foot shield of steel, so heavy and cumbersome that he had to support at least a part of its weight with a broad strap that looped around his shoulder. A pair of seven-foot, steel-tipped lances sat upright in a socket at the horse's flanks and the rider carried a battle sword in his right hand, a long, double-edged weapon that only a barbarous giant could wield effectively.

The people of the Flemish capital, who had heard tales of the terrible Normans for years, were certain that an invasion had begun, but Matilda knew better. As the monster approached her she realized that Duke William Bastard was about to exact a penalty for her refusal to marry him.

He turned his horse so the animal blocked the narrow road, then he dismounted, laid his shield across the pommel, and slipped his long sword into a noose at the side of the saddle. Pushing up his nose-guard, he walked slowly toward Matilda. To her amazement he was smiling, but a single look at his eyes told her he was not amused. Never had she seen such naked violence in the expression of another person and she was certain that he intended to murder her. The fleeting hope crossed her mind that Brihtric would come to her aid and that one of her ladies would have the presence of mind to summon help from the garrison. There were at least two thousand Flemish troops stationed in the town, and no lone man, not even a Norman, could expect to escape unscathed if he assaulted her in the streets, in broad daylight.

Then she forgot everything but William as his huge hands closed around her waist and he lifted her from her saddle. She had expected brutality, and his touch was so gentle that she was utterly confused. His left arm swept under her legs and she found herself being carried across the road as easily as though she weighed no more than a baby. Her face was only a few inches from William's and she looked at him, then hastily averted her gaze. The frankness of his hostility frightened her, but the coldness of his rage bewildered her. He was indulging himself in no insane tantrum; whatever he was doing to her had been carefully planned, and every move was deliberate.

Matilda was vaguely aware of the white faces of her ladies, and Brihtric was a blur somewhere in the background. She could see people staring at her from doorways and windows, but no one cried out, no one dared come to her assistance, and the strange quiet that had descended added to the unreality of the experience.

William stopped, bent forward and lowered Matilda to the ground. Before she quite knew what was happening he rolled her slowly in the mud and slime at the side of the road. Still handling her with infinite care so she was not physically injured, he methodically turned her first one way, then another, until her clothes, her face, and her hair were filthy.

"When you come to know me better, you'll learn that I always get what I want," William said, his voice curiously free of bitterness. "And whether you like it or not, madam, you're going to marry me." Bowing to the girl sprawled at his feet, he strolled back to his horse and mounted. Then he snapped down his nose-guard, picked up his sword and shield, and rode off at a leisurely pace in the direction from which he had come. And he did not bother to look back as he disappeared from view.

Matilda's humiliation was so deep that she was beyond tears as she struggled to her feet. Lille would remember her disgrace for generations to come, Flanders would share her shame and the rest of Europe would laugh at her; in almost no time traveling minstrels would be entertaining noble lords and ladies with scurrilous songs about the fall of the haughty Lady Matilda. And, worst of all, she realized that William had chosen the most effective of all possible means of retaliation against her. There was no need for him to wage war against Flanders, as he undoubtedly knew; her father would willingly grant the Normans concessions without end in order to keep the peace. And just as she had rejected him for purely personal reasons, so he had elected to strike back in kind with the most penetrating weapon that could be directed against a lovely woman: ridicule.

She looked less than lovely as she lurched toward her horse, her clothes wet, her hair straggling, and her face smeared with dirt and refuse. The other members of her party, seeing her move, began to recover from their shock and Brihtric dismounted and came to her side. Matilda was barely able to refrain from striking him across the face with her muddy hand.

"Why didn't you help me?" she asked in a low, contemptuous voice.

"It's a hanging offense to attack a reigning duke when he's on a visit of state to a foreign country. If I'd touched him your father would have had me swinging from a gibbet before sundown. And he'd have been right.

Please remember that I'm only a guest in Flanders myself."

Matilda laughed hysterically. "You were afraid you'd sully those pretty clothes."

"No gentleman likes to become involved in a street brawl," Brihtric said distantly.

"No lady enjoys it either, but I seem to have become involved." Matilda shoved him aside, mounted her mare, and, holding her grubby chin high, started off down the twisting road. The ride home seemed endless.

The little castle that Robert the Devil had built at Eu, facing the Flemish border, was cold even in summer, and the thick stone walls tenaciously held in the chill. Even the bridal chamber on the second floor was damp, and the new Duchess of Normandy shivered and wished she had included a few woolen dresses in her trousseau. Methodically brushing her long hair as she sat before a small table, she thought that her dressing gown of thin white silk might be appropriate for a wedding night but it was all wrong for Eu.

It would be pleasant, she reflected, to warm herself beneath the covers of the bed on the far side of the room, but she could not; if her bridegroom found her there when he came upstairs from the wedding banquet, he would believe she was no more than a brazen wench. So she brushed her hair all the more vigorously, and tried to shut out the sounds of revelry rising from the great hall below. Judging from the steadily increasing roar, the merrymaking would continue all night, and she sighed. When she and the other ladies had withdrawn an hour previously, the great nobles of Normandy and Flanders had already been eating and drinking, mostly drinking, for the better part of the evening. Men, it was plain, were all alike.

Her father had been glassy-eyed, her brother's speech had become thick and only semi-articulate, and most of the Norman barons had been the worse for wear too. It occurred to her that she was ignorant of her bridegroom's condition, for she hadn't paid that much attention to him. To be more precise, she had studiously avoided even looking at him, which was the most effective way of hiding her resentment of him. If he hadn't taken her for granted, if he hadn't ruthlessly pushed through their marriage in the face of her opposition, if he had bothered to court her or at least to treat her with respect, she might not feel as she did now. It was unfortunate and sad to contemplate, but only four hours ago she had become the wife of a headstrong, stubborn, self-opinionated boor.

Of course, she had to admit to herself, though to no one but herself, she did find him attractive. There was something magnetic about his assurance and she could not help but respond to his ruthlessness. He wasn't handsome, in the sense that Brihtric was handsome, but she could not deny the appeal of his masculinity. And there was something in his character, too, that frequently reminded her of a small boy, and while she knew that he would be outraged if he gleaned even an inkling of her feelings, she liked to think of him as being little and rather dependent on her.

As a matter of fact, she told herself, he did need her, and with her help he might become more than just another ruler of a duchy that stood out among its neighbors merely because it happened to boast a strong army. It was all to the good that William had already proved his abilities as a soldier, but she would teach him that through the more subtle arts of diplomacy he could become a great man. And she would rise in the world with him.

On second thought, there would be no real necessity for telling him of her ambitions for either of them; he was a bear, and bears could be tamed. Matilda held her left hand out in front of her, and held it vertical so she could examine the new jewelry that adorned it. The solid band of plain gold on the ring finger did not interest her, but the heavy, gem-encrusted signet ring on the index finger was significant to her, and she admired it at some length. The ring bore the coat-of-arms of Normandy and was an elaborate feminine version of one the Duke wore; jewelry, as such, meant nothing to the new Duchess, but the crest was the symbol of her future, and as she gazed at it she told herself fiercely that there was no height she could not attain.

Whatever William's reasons for marrying her might have been, she could not truly regret the bargain, for through him the daughter of a mere count meant to make herself the first woman in all of Europe. The Norman signet would be the key to glory and, even more important, to power.

"You like your rings, do you?"

Startled, Matilda looked up at the sound of the deep voice, and saw the Duke standing in the arched entrance; he was watching her closely, and his enigmatic expression baffled her. His actual presence made her feel less sure of herself, but she tried to smile as she hastily drew the front of her dressing gown closed. "I admire them very much. They're lovely rings, both of them."

"They ought to be. I'd hate to tell you what I paid for them."

He had no breeding at all, Matilda thought. "Please don't," she said firmly.

William moved slowly into the room, and his rolling walk again reminded her of a bear. He stopped a few feet from her and stood gazing down at her. "The ceremony wasn't too bad, was it?"

She wished he would stop rocking back and forth on his heels; the gesture made her nervous. Then she realized that he was ill at ease and was trying to make conversation, so she grew calmer. When she dealt with others she was almost invariably in command of the situation, and it pleased her that William, in spite of his impetuous and highly unusual wooing, seemed to be a trifle afraid of her. "I enjoyed the ceremony very much," she said brightly.

"I told the archdeacons I wouldn't stand for any nonsense. I've gone to weddings that lasted for hours, but I was damned if mine would."

"Do the archdeacons usually obey your requests?" She was impressed but made an effort not to show it.

"Naturally." There was a faint note of wonder in William's voice, then he grinned. "In Normandy one person gives the orders and everyone else obeys them."

Matilda wondered whether his comment was deliberately barbed, but her face remained bland. "I see."

"Not yet you don't. But you will." He chuckled as her cheeks became pink.

There was no longer any doubt as to his intent, Matilda thought. He was reminding her in the clumsiest possible manner that he was her lord and master, and her back became rigid.

"Come here," he said, and when she did not move he reached for her, placed his huge hands around her supple waist, and drew her to her feet.

"Please." Matilda could only hope that he had not

drunk too much. She looked up at him: his eyes were clear and there was no more than a slight and not unpleasant odor of spiced wine on his breath. Everyone else had been drinking a heavy brandy, and his unexpected temperance surprised her. But, following her preconceived plan, she turned away from him so he would not see her admiration.

Her resistance stimulated William, and he pulled her roughly to him and kissed her. She struggled, but he put one hand at the back of her head and with the other held her firmly, so she was helpless. His ardor increased, but it cooled a little when she did not return it, and at last he released her. "What the devil! I'm not going to eat you!" His eyes were puzzled and his tone was angry.

"Aren't you? I wasn't so sure." It annoyed her to hear her voice quaver. At all costs, she thought, she would need to keep secret, now and always, the effect William had on her when he touched her.

"You have spirit, Matilda. I like that." Again he extended his hands, but this time he deliberately slid them inside the front of her dressing gown and began to fondle her.

His approach was an affront to her dignity, and although his caresses aroused her, she steeled herself and stood unmoving, her shoulders back, her head erect, and her hands hanging at her sides.

Never before had William known such an unresponsive woman, and his temper was a match for his pride. He let his hands roam for another moment or two, and when she still did not stir, his eyes became dark. "What's the matter with you?"

"Nothing, I hope," Matilda replied sweetly, silently grateful that he had moved away from her. Had he continued to make love to her, she knew she would have lost all semblance of self-control very quickly.

"Then you don't like me." It was a hard, flat statement rather than a question.

"That's not true. I consented to marry you, didn't I?"

"Because you had no choice, that's why."

"Oh, really." She forced herself to laugh and hoped it sounded natural. "I wouldn't have suspected it, but you're terribly naive."

Not quite knowing what she meant, he began to feel unsure of himself and his anger increased. His last desire at this moment was to fence with her. She was ravishing, and he wanted her, desperately. Never one to mince words, he cut through the preliminaries and struck at once at the heart of the matter. "You're my wife, Matilda. And I'm going to bed you. Now."

She held her breath for an instant so he would not see her palpitation. "If you insist, my lord."

Her seeming serene humility was too much for him. "Of course I insist. What kind of a man did you think you were marrying?"

"I didn't know, but I hoped you were a gentleman," she said, so softly that he could scarcely hear her.

"I'm the Duke of Normandy!"

"So your signature on the marriage register indicated." Matilda knew that she was bending him to her will, and she discovered that she liked the feeling. "I wonder if you happen to know who I am?"

"The most contrary wench on earth!" He was dimly aware of the fact that he was shouting and that the guests below in the great hall might hear him, but he didn't care.

"First let me tell you who I am not," she said, emphasizing each word. "I am not one of the camp followers with whom you've so obviously associated. I am not a trollop to be taken when it suits your pleasure and then discarded when you have no further use for me. I am a lady. And I insist on being treated with dignity."

William tried to laugh, but the effort was a total failure. "Yes, Your Grace," he said with heavy irony.

To Matilda's astonishment tears came into her eyes. She was horrified, and felt certain that she was destroying all she was attempting to accomplish. No man could tolerate the sight of a weeping woman, and, even worse, she would look her most unattractive if her eyes and nose became red. Unless she could stem the flow, William would no longer want her, and the prospect disturbed her more deeply than she had imagined possible. She seemed to be learning things about herself tonight, and it stunned her to realize that she urgently wanted him to think her lovely and to desire her at all times.

Once again his reaction was the opposite of what she had anticipated, and it began to dawn on her that, far from being simple, he was an extraordinarily complex man. He picked her up so gently that she hardly knew she was being lifted off the floor, and he cradled her in his arms almost as one would a baby. Then he kissed her with infinite tenderness, and Matilda was unable to think coherently.

The time for talk was past, and William, his instinct unerring, had chosen precisely the right moment to act. As he lowered Matilda to the bed she slid her arms around his neck and clung to him joyously, possessively. Her last conscious thought, before the wave of their rapture overcame her, was to wonder for an instant whether her design had been successful. Submitting to him eagerly, she did not and could not know which of them had conquered.

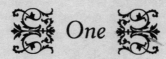

One

THEIR GRACES were quarreling again in the family dining chamber, and the atmosphere in the adjoining kitchen outbuilding was tense. The hand of the principal cook trembled as he removed a leg of lamb from the spit and sprinkled it with herbs; when the Duke was aroused he frequently found fault with the meat. And the unfortunate churl who was to serve the meal tugged anxiously at his long woolen tunic as he examined it for spots; when the Duchess was annoyed she was often sharply critical of the servants' cleanliness.

The great hall of the castle, which stood just beyond the dining room, was deserted save for the sentries of the household guard who stood at the entrance, their faces impassive. The children's tutors and nurses kept their young charges out of reach of parental wrath; the officials who had been waiting to see the Duke decided they had urgent business elsewhere, and the Duchess's ladies found that pressing matters required their attention in their own bowers. In nine tempestuous years everyone in the castle had learned how to become invisible when a storm was raging.

As usual, William's voice was dominant, and he thumped the heavy oak table for emphasis as he addressed his wife. "I won't tolerate your interference," he shouted. "You're making a mockery of Norman justice."

"You exaggerate, dear." Matilda studied the cuff of

her green silk overdress, and only the brittleness of her tone betrayed her own turmoil, for she looked calm and relaxed as she smiled at William. "I've never spoken a single word when you're passing legal judgments, and you must admit that I stay inconspicuously at the rear of the hall.'

"Inconspicuous? In that dress?"

Her eyes widened as she examined her gown. Its only trimming consisted of bands of cream velvet sewn with hundreds of tiny seed pearls, which she wore at her neck, hips, and as cuffs on her wide sleeves. The pale blue undertunic that showed at her throat and wrists was modest, her hair was caught loosely in a net of gold threads knotted with small pearls, and she knew the effect she created was one of dignity. "Some men," she said, emphasizing each word, "would be pleased their wives still had the figures of young girls, even though they'd borne several children."

"Don't change the issue." The Duke paused as the manservant entered and stood at his side. He examined the smoking meat carefully, cut off a thick slice with his knife as the churl held the lamb by the bone, and he started to eat before speaking again. William never permitted a marital dispute to interfere with his appetite, although he was more apt to be critical of what was set before him during an argument.

Matilda, secretly relieved that he seemed to be enjoying his dinner, daintily took some of the meat and placed it on a piece of coarse-ground wheat bread. "I'm afraid I don't understand your complaint, dear."

"You never do when you're in the wrong." Before they were through, William thought, he would lose his temper; he had never yet convinced Matilda that he was right, and mere logic was useless. Only when he bellowed at her did she really listen to him, and even then he suspected that she clung stubbornly to whatever views she might be defending. But he would try once more. "You jeopardize my authority by your facial expressions. Each time I pronounce sentence in a case, I discover that everyone in the hall is looking at you, not me. And in each case you indicate by a frown or a smile or a smirk whether you think my judgments are wise or stupid. It's harmful. And it's frustrating!"

While Matilda tried to frame a reply, a churl appeared in the rounded arch that led into the great hall and interrupted her train of thought. Irritated, she glared at the wretch, who paled, but it was William whose anger exploded first. He was convinced he had made a point that Matilda could not answer, but the stupid churl was distracting her and the thread of argument was lost. "Get out!" the Duke said, and picked up a silver tankard of mead.

The servant did not move, however, and an instant later the tankard crashed against the wall only a few inches from his shoulder. The frothing beer splattered him, but he ignored his discomfort, having expected worse. "Your Grace," he said in a quavering voice, "a messenger has arrived from Count Guy of Ponthieu and begs for an immediate audience."

"His Grace doesn't grant audiences while he's eating," Matilda interjected firmly. The rule was one that she herself had made to provide some measure of privacy at mealtimes; when she had first been married to William, it had been his custom to conduct the affairs of Normandy at table, from his bath, and even from his bed. She had changed all that and she had no intention of permitting a lapse into bad habits now.

Her stand, however, produced a result opposite to that which she wished. The Duke smiled and leaned back in his carved oak chair. "Send the messenger to me," he directed the bewildered churl, who promptly backed off. "Guy of Ponthieu," William continued, turning to his wife and grinning more broadly, "is a loyal vassal, so I owe his messenger every courtesy."

"You're dipping your sleeve into your bowl."

"Then stop having these damned trailing sleeves made for me."

Matilda knew that on this subject, at least, her position was unassailable. "It's bad enough that you insist on wearing a leather tunic as though you were out in the field campaigning. You simply can't wander around looking like some poor thegn who has been out tilling his land. I'm glad I remember that you're a reigning duke, even if you don't."

William wouldn't admit that he was in error, and if he couldn't distract her, he was sure she would mention the embarrassing incident of two years previous, when an envoy of his cousin Edward of England had mistaken him for a soldier of the household guard. She reminded him of the occasion whenever she had an opening, and he was certainly handing her one now. "You give me no chance to forget my rank," he said hastily.

At that moment the messenger entered, bowed to the Duchess and dropped to one knee before the Duke. "Greetings from Count Guy to his liege lord," the youth intoned, surreptitiously straightening his black skullcap.

"Never mind the formalities," William said, ignoring his wife's disapproving nod. "What word from Guy of Ponthieu could be important enough to make my meat grow cold?"

"Two days ago a terrible gale raged up and down the coast, Your Grace—"

"That gale also struck here. Rouen was not spared, so

any damage that Guy suffered was doubtless less than our own." William hated to part with money and was not going to show charity to an indigent count who literally should have put aside funds for a rainy day.

"A ship was wrecked on our shore, Your Grace, and Count Guy made seventeen of her passengers prisoner. Some were richly dressed, and though they tried to conceal their identity——"

"Ah, ransom!" William interrupted, brightening.

"Yes, Your Grace," the messenger said eagerly, forgetting his awe of the great man. "One in particular should bring an enormous ransom. When Count Guy threatened him with torture he admitted that he's Earl Harold of England."

There was a stunned silence, and both the Duke and Duchess stared at the young man. Matilda was the first to recover. "Earl Harold Godwineson?"

"Yes, Your Grace."

"You're sure?" she persisted. Harold Godwineson, England's premier earl, was the actual ruler of that country, for Edward the Confessor and his wife, Edith, who happened to be Harold's sister, did not concern themselves with temporal matters, and Harold had already secured earldoms for three of his younger brothers.

"Very sure, Your Grace," the messenger replied earnestly. "Two seamen in the party were put to the rack, and they insisted to their last breaths that their leader is Earl Harold."

Matilda's green eyes grew thoughtful. "Why would Harold of England sail from his homeland with such a small party? Where was he going?"

"I—I don't know, Your Grace." The messenger had heard it said that Matilda of Normandy had a mind as keen and quick as any man, but he was unaccustomed to such sharp questioning from one so lovely, and he felt confused.

William promptly came to his rescue. "All that matters," the Duke said expansively, "is that my rival is delivered into my hands. My greetings to Guy of Ponthieu. If he'll send Earl Harold to me, unharmed, I shall pay any ransom—out of my own coffers—that Guy demands. Any within reason, of course. But if Harold does not arrive safely within the next two days, I'll hang Guy of Ponthieu by the thumbs in my dungeons. Take my word to your master." He was still smiling pleasantly.

"At once, Your Grace." The messenger jumped to his feet and departed before the Duke could reward him with the customary coin.

"Well." William chuckled and reached for his tankard. Even when he saw it was not there he was not shaken out of his good humor. "Steward," he shouted, ignoring the bell that Matilda always wanted him to use for the purpose. A servant appeared, and William addressed him genially. "Get me another mug of mead. The one I had met with a slight accident."

He glanced at his wife, but she showed no reaction to his words; indeed, her thoughts seemed to be far away.

"Well, my dear," he said jovially. "It was only last week that you urged me to send agitators to England to arouse the people there against the son of Godwine. I'm certainly glad I refused."

"You were very wise, darling." Matilda scarcely heard him and sat with her chin cupped in her slender hands, her food untouched.

"So he had designs on the throne of England, did he? He hoped to put himself into a position to succeed Cousin Edward, did he?" William lifted his new tankard to his lips with enjoyment, then brought it down on the hard wood of the table with considerable force. "That's what I'll do to the mighty Earl Harold!"

Ordinarily Matilda would have protested that he was marring the furniture; now she did not notice. "You were right to insist that Count Guy send the Earl to you. No one of lesser station could be his host. It wouldn't be proper."

"Oh, I'll be quite proper, never fear. And so will you. We'll both go through the motions of welcoming an honored guest. And then there'll be an accident that will end Harold's ambitions once and for all time."

"An accident?" She simply wasn't concentrating on what he was saying.

"That other mug of mead I was drinking spilled—by accident."

Matilda regarded him coolly. "Harold might be more useful to us alive than dead," she said slowly.

The very idea was so ludicrous that William laughed. "Impossible," he replied, then chuckled again, unable to believe that she was serious. But when he saw that she failed to respond, his humor drained away. "I know you like to think of yourself as being well informed on what goes on in the world, my dear, but it's obvious that you know nothing of the state of affairs in England. Cousin Edward is a good man, so good that he's a fool who'd let an upstart earl rob him of his country and me of my promised heritage. I met Harold when I visited England, remember. He's shrewd, he's strong, and he's the sort men will follow. But you know all this as well as I do, Matilda. It was you who were so worried about him last week!"

She nodded, and the fire in the hearth played on the copper of her hair. "Yes, darling. He's so dangerous to us that his value is all the greater if he's alive."

William's mind was made up, and he had no desire

to prolong the conversation. "Satisfy yourself with your household and your children, madam, and leave the world to me." Even as he spoke he realized that nothing else he might have said would have been so incendiary.

However, although he could predict an enemy's move on the battlefield with uncanny accuracy, Matilda was still an enigma to him. "All I really care about is that you have the world, dear," she said gently. "And I won't be satisfied until you're crowned King of England."

He saw through her subterfuge immediately. "That was an eloquent little speech, but the thoughts behind it were muddled, Matilda." Finishing his meat, he reached out to a large, round cheese and cut himself a chunk. "What you meant to say, I'm sure, is that you won't be satisfied until you're crowned Queen of England."

She smiled at him sweetly. "Of course, darling. The notion is hardly a new one. We've discussed it many times."

"You mean you've dinned it into my head until I'm sick of listening to you. For the last time, England has no queens. Look at Lady Edith—she has no title, and she doesn't want one. She's happy just to be Edward's wife."

"I'm happy being your wife," Matilda murmured, the softness of her speech belied by the way she thrust her pretty chin forward belligerently. "Nevertheless, I still want to be Queen of England. And please spare me the rest of the argument. I know it by heart. Canute's wife wasn't Queen of England. Edmund Ironside's wife wasn't Queen of England——"

"And William of Normandy's wife won't be either," he concluded, then added as an afterthought, "I might find after I become King that the people of England are ready for a change. In that case I'd be willing to consider the possibility."

Matilda's poise deserted her for the first time since she had sat down at the table. "Be good enough to spare me your pious rhetoric about the people of England. I'll need nothing but your approval for me to become Queen, and you know it!"

"I've got to become King first," William said scornfully. "And to end all possibility of doubt in the matter, I intend to remove Harold from the lists as a rival. The subject is closed, and I want no further interference from you!"

"I never interfere!" She pushed back her chair and stood. "I've been a great help to you, and you ought to be big enough to admit it."

"All right. I admit it," he said wearily. "Now if you'll just keep in mind that Edward's promise to me doesn't include you, we'll have no more trouble."

Matilda pretended she had not heard him as she walked from her end of the long table to his. Her pattens, thick wooden soles with high heels which she wore over her soft leather shoes, clattered on the stone floor, but she was accustomed to their sound. "There's just one thing more I want to say, dear, and I wish you'd listen to me."

The Duke looked down at her feet and frowned. "Must you wear those damned things in the house?"

"They improve my ankles." She couldn't admit that she used the pattens to make her appear taller and that she was always conscious of the difference between her height and William's. "Now, what I want to say—"

"There's nothing wrong with your ankles. I like the way they look."

"Thank you, dear. William, have you thought of the repercussions at other courts if Harold dies while he's our guest? Paris is aching to blacken your name, the Bretons hate you, and the Burgundians are afraid of you. And our relations with the Vatican haven't been stable for very long. If you kill Harold you'll be known as the Black Duke. You'll be painted as the worst villain——'

"As I've been called William Bastard all my life, I'm not sensitive to unpleasant names. They've never hurt me yet."

"No, but an alliance of all our enemies could ruin us." She put a hand on his shoulder.

It was always difficult for William to think clearly when she touched him, and he rose abruptly. "My foes will unite at their peril!"

"At our peril, you mean. You can't beat the whole world, you know. And where do you think Harold was going when he was shipwrecked, have you stopped to think of that? Ponthieu is near Brittany, isn't it? So the answer is plain." When he would have turned away from her, Matilda caught the front of his tunic. "He was en route to Paris!"

His attention was caught at last, and he gazed down at her thoughtfully. "You think so?"

"It fits, doesn't it?" The Duchess spoke rapidly, earnestly. "We know that King Philip would do anything he could to crush us——"

"But his regiments run from the field when they see the lion banners of Normandy." William laughed contemptuously.

"Exactly. So he's looking for friends who will help him. And Harold is his natural ally. If they can dispose of you, Harold can take the throne of England without opposition and Philip can absorb Normandy into France."

He ran a hand through his short hair, which was

prematurely sprinkled with gray. "They've got to dispose of me first, Matilda, so I'm going to act before they do. Not even Philip can make an alliance with a ghost."

Matilda, who had thought she was making progress, stamped her foot in exasperation. "Just open your mind long enough to let me explain—"

"No!" William's dark eyes became hard. "I hate to say this, madam, but you give me no choice. There are times when I think my wife is my worst enemy!"

She was stung, and tears came into her eyes. "You can't mean that."

"I do mean it." He hooked his thumbs in his wide belt and glared at her. "Do you remember your first public appearance when I brought you here as a bride? You had your page announce you as Duchess of Normandy, Countess of Flanders and—what was the phrase that caused all the trouble?—'protectress of England.' "

"Must we drag all that out again?" she asked dispiritedly. "You're as bad as your mother. Every time we see her she weeps because the Church didn't recognize our marriage for a few years."

"Leave my mother out of this." When he was really upset he spoke softly, and his voice was barely above a whisper now.

Matilda chose to ignore the danger sign. "You brought up the subject. I didn't!"

"No, of course you didn't. You don't want to be reminded that you always lose your head and go too far when you aren't bridled. Naturally my mother was hurt. Suppose the Church refuses to sanction Gerbod's marriage when he finds himself a wife. And when Robert grows up, how would you feel if Rome wouldn't grant recognition to his marraige? You'd cry your eyes out—just as my mother did."

"I hope," Matilda said icily, "that I'd have the good sense to do what I did in our own situation. I'd set about correcting a mistake. And you have a remarkable memory. All you ever remember are the things that put me in a bad light. Who was it conceived the idea of sending Abbé Lanfranc to Rome, I'd like to know? I did!"

"Yes, yes, and he performed his mission successfully," William said impatiently. Whenever he backed Matilda into a corner she managed to bring Lanfranc, their spiritual adviser and his close confidant, into the conversation, and she invariably contrived to make it appear as though she and the priest held identical views. It was one of her most irritating traits. "But what you can't seem to understand is that he wouldn't have had to go off to the Vatican if you hadn't first created a problem."

She sighed and looked at him pityingly. "I marvel at your inability to see beyond the end of your long Norman nose. The Abbé came away from Rome on the friendliest of terms with Archdeacon Hildebrand, didn't he? And you know what Lanfranc told us. Hildebrand will be the next pope. It won't hurt us to enjoy good relations with the Holy Father, will it? Will it, William?"

Her ability to justify herself, to shift blame, and maneuver herself into a favorable light had once been amusing; now it was maddening. "It's no thanks to you that Lanfranc is close to the Archdeacon. He deserves a little of the credit himself."

"Abbé Lanfranc deserves a great deal of credit," she replied smoothly. "But it so happens that he's grateful to me, too. He's said so many times—and in your hearing."

William would have brushed past her and gone into the great hall, but she blocked his path. "What in the devil has all this to do with Harold of England?" he demanded.

Matilda could not resist a triumphant smile, although she knew she should have concealed her satisfaction at his inability to answer her argument. At moments like this he seemed as naïve as a child to her, and she believed it was her duty to guide him through the intricate maze of relations with other countries. No one person could possibly be endowed with all of the essential qualities of leadership, she thought; and this man whom she had so reluctantly married might be the greatest general of his age, but he was utterly lacking in the subtlety that was a primary requisite of diplomacy. If they were to achieve more than fleeting renown, if they were to make a deep and lasting imprint on history, she would have to lead him and prod him toward that glory which they could only fulfill together.

"If you'll treat Harold with care, dear," she said slowly, trying hard not to sound condescending, 'you can win the greatest victory of your life. Try to see this whole situation like a campaign." How clever, she told herself, to put the matter in military terms that he could grasp. "Imagine yourself preparing for a decisive battle, the biggest you've ever fought, and—"

"I'll prepare for a battle in my own way, thank you." William had heard enough, and he spoke with finality. "I'm not going to coddle a man who'd deprive me of my legacy. I'm going to deal with him precisely as he'd treat me if I fell into his hands. Within a day of his arrival here there'll be an accident, and Harold will be dead."

He took hold of Matilda by her waist, and, as in all their physical relations, his touch was gentle, almost delicate. Lifting her into the air, he set her down to one side, out of his path, then walked with a sure, determined stride into his great hall.

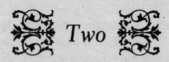 *Two*

IN ALL THE YEARS Matilda had lived in Normandy, Rouen Castle had depressed her; in her mind it was a fortress, not a home, and she was always glad to get away from it, even for a little while. Now, as she mounted her mare in the entrance hall, she felt her spirits rise, and she smiled at the members of her entourage who were waiting for her outside on the path that led to the stables. And when she caught a glimpse of her own Green Court, surrounded by graceful stone arches, she felt still better. She recalled vividly how appalled she had been when she had first married William and had discovered that this dwelling of one of the mightiest lords in Christendom had been no more than an armed camp. She had been so discouraged that William had humored her and had allowed her install her Green Court, and had himself supervised the planting of oaks and maples there. In those days he had been anxious to please her.

Of course she had gone too far when she had insisted that the kitchen greenyard was a waste and an eyesore. On a practical basis she had been right, for the soil was poor, the carrots and beans grown in the yard were small and tasteless, and the stench of rosemary, the one plant that flourished, was overpowering. She had not realized—then—that the produce garden had been started by William's mother during the years she had lived here with Duke Robert, but she would never forget William's fury when she had ordered the offend-

38

ing patch torn out and cobbled. The garden was still there, to be sure, but she saw it only twice a year now, when William's mother came to Rouen for her semi-annual visit. It was some consolation to Matilda to know that her mother-in-law thought no more highly of the vegetable plot than she herself did, but Lady Harlotte never dared to express her opinions and always thanked her son for keeping it. Such an attitude was as weak as it was stupid; Matilda had no use for spineless women.

Her escort of soldiers ranged themselves in front of her and four of her ladies, who were accompanying her, took up positions behind her. Waiting for them to take their places, Matilda glanced over her shoulder at the castle itself and immediately wished she hadn't. Her hatred was probably sinful, but she could not help thinking of it as a prison. Its heavy stone walls were ten feet thick, its windows were high and narrow, and its buttresses of solid masonry which became huge towers overhead dominated the entire countryside. Beyond all else Matilda loathed being made to feel insignificant.

The young lieutenant who would lead the cavalcade approached the Duchess and saluted politely. "Your Grace is going out for a little airing?"

"No, I'm paying a call on Abbé Lanfranc. We'll take the country road."

The officer coughed discreetly. "I wouldn't advise it, Your Grace."

"Why not?" she demanded, bristling. "Our progress would be slow if we rode through the town. Too many people are abroad in midafternoon."

"Robbers held up a party on that road two days ago, Your Grace."

"Two days ago? You're new to us, aren't you, young man?"

The lieutenant heartily wished himself elsewhere. "Yes, Your Grace. I was transferred to the household garrison only last month."

"I thought so. If there was a robbery two days ago, Duke William undoubtedly hanged the villains yesterday. We'll take the country road." Matilda smiled brightly, the officer blushed as he hurried to his horse, and the caravan got under way.

They rode slowly through the gate set in the great wall, and as they moved in single file across the drawbridge Matilda made a mental note to remind herself to have the scum cleaned off the top of the moat water. With warmer weather approaching the moat would have to be kept clean or the odors that floated up to her bower would become unbearable. William, of course, was indifferent to such minor inconveniences, and she sometimes wondered if he was even aware of them.

The sentries on duty outside the castle drew to attention and Matilda nodded to them, then realized that they were looking not at her but at someone behind her. Following the direction of their gaze, she saw that the interest of these youths had been drawn by her daughter, and she felt pleased. Gundrada was a sweet girl and would soon blossom into a lovely woman. At this moment she looked considerably older than her twelve years, and after studying her briefly Matilda knew why.

Gundrada was wearing a green silk dress which complemented her free-flowing hair, which was a shade lighter than her mother's deep copper tresses. And Matilda had to suppress a smile: the dress was William's doing. He spoiled his stepdaughter, and from the very first had treated her as though she were his own child.

The party increased its pace as it made its way down the hill from the castle, but Matilda, deep in thought, paid no heed. William, in spite of all his faults, was really a good man, as kind as he was hot-tempered, as generous as he was stubborn. The love he gave without stint to Gundrada, Matilda knew, was really a reflection of his feeling for her, a feeling he seemed incapable of expressing freely or adequately. From the beginning there had been barriers between them, and only when William made love to her was there real concord. The excitement of passion was gratifying, but to Matilda it was a poor substitute for the deep bonds that were supposed to unite a husband and wife.

Perhaps, she thought pensively, the clergy was wrong in preaching that a man and a woman could live together in real amity. If her own experience were any criterion, and she had no other standard, perfection could no more be attained in marriage than it could in any other phase of living. The notion was comforting, but it didn't fit facts as she knew them, and she stirred in her saddle. Matilda believed that she was a realist, and she had to admit that most of the couples whom she knew seemed satisfied with their lot. The relationship between Fitz Osbern and his wife, Adela, was remarkably harmonious, and even that uncouth bear, Roger Mont Gomeri, one of William's most trusted generals, was happy with his wife, Mabel. Of greater significance was that Mabel seemed to be at peace too, but it was impossible for Matilda to understand how a woman of taste, wit, and refinement, qualities that Mabel had in abundance, could live with an oaf like Roger.

Trying to examine her own marriage objectively, Matilda could see that the great disruptive force was the tension that grew out of nowhere whenever she and William were together. If only they didn't quarrel so much; if only there weren't some hidden devil in each of them that set off sparks even when they discussed non-controversial matters! She wondered briefly if she should discuss the difficulty with Abbé Lanfranc; he was William's confessor as well as her own, and if anyone could help, he could. However, she decided, she could not afford the luxury now, when affairs of real importance were pending. If William carried out his rash threat against Earl Harold, he might lose England, so personal problems had to be ruthlessly put aside. What was more, Matilda told herself, once she and William sat on a joint throne in London, it would not matter if they argued from morning until night.

The sun was warm as it filtered through the budding branches of the fruit trees that lined the side of the road, and Matilda unfastened her cape. Her ladies followed her example, and when she caught a glimpse of Gundrada she remembered that she had a duty as a mother to perform and beckoned to the girl to ride beside her. "I see you're wearing a new dress," she said.

"Yes, Mother. Father gave me a bolt of cloth and two of your needlewomen made it for me last week." Gundrada looked at her mother anxiously. "Do you like it?"

"It seems to be a finely woven silk."

"Father sent to Lyon for it," the child said proudly. "It's the first gown of imported material I've ever owned. I think it's lovely."

"Yes, it is. Lovely."

Something in Matilda's tone made Gundrada's eyes widen. "You aren't—angry or upset because Father gave it to me instead of——"

"Certainly not!" The very idea was shocking to Matilda. "I was merely wondering whether it's an appropriate costume for a visit to Abbé Lanfranc. Wool would have been more suitable."

"Would it? You're wearing silk, Mother."

It occurred to Matilda that Gundrada sounded more

like her stepfather every day. And she was particularly annoyed because she had chosen her own gray dress with great care. Its only ornamentation was a trimming of gray Siberian squirrel fur at the neck and on the long cuffs; the sole touch of color was at her wrists, where the red of her *chainse*, or undertunic, showed, and she had thought she was striking precisely the right note for a visit to a cleric. "When you're a matron," she said severely, "you may wear what you please."

"Oh." Gundrada was crestfallen. "Father said he was giving me the material because you had never been allowed to wear silk when you were a girl, and he knew how badly you always felt."

Matilda's irritation increased; whenever William made a gesture toward her, it was always indirect and hence lost its potency. "That was very thoughtful of him. But I'm sure he wouldn't approve of your wearing it this afternoon. However, what's done is done and there's no turning back."

There was no joy in Gundrada's face, and her eyes, so like her mother's, were tragic. A sense of guilt assailed Matilda, for she knew she had made more of an issue of the matter than it deserved. William was to blame, of course; his recalcitrance regarding Harold of England was enough to drive her out of her wits.

The remainder of the ride was passed in silence. Gundrada fell back and rejoined the other ladies, and they, sensing the Duchess's mood, did not dare to converse even in whispers. At last the party arrived at the monastery and school of St. Etienne, a collection of one-story gray stone buildings in the shape of a cross. A friar escorted the ladies into the refectory while the guards watered their horses at a trough outside the main entrance. It was unusual for the Duchess to come to St. Etienne, as Lanfranc usually journeyed to Rouen Castle to conduct Mass and preach a sermon in the chapel there three times a week, so most members of the faculty found excuses to wander into the refectory and pay their respects to their Duke's lady. All of them were keenly aware that William Bastard had never ceded to the Vatican his right to promote his own clergy, and everyone knew he had made his half brother, Odo, Bishop of Bayeux when the boy had been only twelve. For that matter, Lanfranc had been an inconspicuous priest until the Duke had created him an abbé, and those who were ambitious made it their business to impress themselves on the Duchess's consciousness.

Finally a lay brother brought word that Lanfranc would receive her, and he led her to the open arched gallery on the south side of the main building, a pretty walk adjacent to a flagged courtyard with a stone sundial set in its center. As Matilda stepped out of the building into the gallery, she caught sight of the Abbé, and she paused. He had not seen her, and he stood leaning against the base of an arch, staring out into space. He was only a year or two older than William, but his thin body looked frail in an ankle-length black chasuble bound with a plain leather belt. His lean, ascetic face was inscrutable and Matilda wondered, not for the first time, what he might be thinking.

She liked to tell her intimates that she was afraid of no man, but the boast was untrue: Lanfranc, who had an uncanny ability to read other people's minds, frightened her. And although she was not superstitious, she sometimes had the uneasy feeling that he possessed magical powers. Occasionally, when he fastened his black, unnaturally bright eyes on her, she felt an almost irresistible urge to giggle and needed to remind herself forcibly that he was no more than an unprepossessing little man who owed his present position to William.

She had first met him when he had performed the marriage ceremony that had united her with William, and even though he had been her friend and confessor in the years since, she had never been truly at ease with him. His alien manners and his unorthodox career made him strange, she liked to tell herself, but she knew that his background was only one of the reasons he seemed remote and unfathomable. Neither she nor anyone else would ever learn the inner secrets of his nature, she knew, for Lanfranc, rarely talked about himself and never mentioned his hopes or ambitions.

William had told her that the Abbé had studied to be a lawyer in his native Pavia, and had actually practiced the profession in several Italian towns before turning to the priesthood. He had drifted to Normandy to open a school, and had first come to the young Duke's attention when he had taken a post as household chaplain to Lord Herlwin of Conteville, the amiable nobleman who had married William's mother and raised her to the rank of lady.

The relationship between the ascetic priest and her husband was a curious one, and Matilda resented it. They understood each other completely, often achieving a meeting of minds after exchanging only a few words, and Lanfranc's ability to bend William to his will was in part responsible for Matilda's faint suspicion that he might be a wizard. Certainly it was true that he was the only human being in Normandy who could stand up to William when the ducal temper exploded, and only last year, during the most recent war with France, Matilda had heard Lanfranc address William as no other man dared. Norman troops had pillaged two towns across the border, looting, burning and raping, and the Abbé had given his noble master a fierce tongue-lashing. Amazingly William had stood with bowed head, twisting the end of his cloak in his hands and looking all the world like little Henry, his youngest son. He had accepted the rebuke without a word, and thereafter the Norman army had scrupulously obeyed the humane rules of warfare.

Staring now at Lanfranc down the length of the gallery, Matilda prayed that he would help her. If she could convince him that she was right, he might be able to persuade William to let Earl Harold live. She started forward, and Lanfranc, becoming aware of her movement, looked up. He smiled faintly and waited for her to come to him, then lifted his hands so she could kiss the pontifical ring that he wore in his capacity as Auxiliary Bishop of Rouen, a title William had conferred on him just this year.

"I was expecting you," he said.

Startled, Matilda gaped at him. "I sent no advance word that I——"

"I needed no word." There was a suggestion of amusement in his eyes. "News reached me this morning that a rather distinguished gentleman is languishing in Ponthieu, and I've just heard that he will soon be your guest."

The feeling grew in her that he was indeed a necromancer. Then Lanfranc's smile broadened, and she felt as foolish as a maiden. "You always manage to keep informed, don't you, Father Lanfranc?"

"Well, news occasionally finds its way into this remote corner," he admitted.

"Then I suppose you know all about my latest dispute with William."

"Disputes between you and William are no longer news. Shall we stroll up and down? It's a trifle chilly if we stand here. Or perhaps you'd rather go indoors."

"No, thank you. I don't want anyone to hear us, Father Lanfranc."

"Ah, then you haven't come to confess. I thought you might be feeling remorseful." He glanced at her obliquely.

"No, I feel no remorse." She heard him sigh, but ignored the sound. "I'm in the right, Father. William wants to kill Earl Harold, and I'm opposed to it. I've come for your help."

"Murder is one of the most vicious of crimes," the Abbé agreed. "I'll preach my sermon on it at High Mass next Sunday."

"That may be too late." Matilda was a little abashed to realize that the moral aspects of William's intended deed had never entered her mind. But that was something she could never admit to the priest.

Lanfranc immediately read her mind. "You have a practical reason for seeking my help, of course."

"How did you know?" She felt suddenly cold and moved into the sun.

He did not reply for a moment, and when he spoke he answered her question with another. "What would you do with the son of Godwine who stands between William and the English throne? Would you keep him a prisoner at the castle, or——"

"Certainly not!" Matilda's indignation was genuine. "Such an idea never crossed my mind!"

"I'm glad one of my flock is acquiring Christian virtues," Lanfranc murmured, making it clear that he was not taking her statement at face value.

"It strikes me that if we can persuade Harold to swear allegiance to William as his overlord, our claim to England will be totally unopposed," she said crisply.

The Abbé stopped pacing and looked at her sharply. "There are times when I think the Lord almost intended you to be a man," he said, half to himself. "What was William's reaction to your proposal?"

"He wouldn't listen to it! He was furious because I wouldn't agree with his own barbaric notion! Believe it or not, Father, his idea of brilliance and cunning is to have Harold meet with an 'accident.' He wouldn't see we'd be giving our enemies all over Europe a rallying cry. And when I tried to tell him my plan he shouted me down. I suppose I ought to be accustomed to his abuse by now, but I can't stand by idly and let him miss a God-given opportunity."

"Remember the commandment that the Lord gave to Moses!" Lanfranc raised his voice for the first time. " *'Thou shalt not take the name of the Lord thy God in vain; for the Lord will not hold him guiltless that taketh His name in vain.' *"

Matilda was annoyed with herself. She had obviously impressed the Abbé and had felt almost certain he would lend her his support, but her blunder might cause him to withdraw. "I'm sorry," she said, humbling herself as she would to no one else.

"We like to think we live in an enlightened age, but perfection is too much to expect from anyone, I'm afraid." He tugged at the long tongue of his belt and looked out at the sundial. "Your idea is excellent, Matilda, as you know."

She lifted her head eagerly. "Then——"

"But you'll have to pay a heavy price for its acceptance."

Bewildered, the Duchess could only look at him. Some members of the clergy were not above requesting nobles to build them new churches or to add new sections to their monasteries in return for special favors, but Lanfranc had never shown the slightest interest in material wealth. "What is the price, Father?" She could feel his eyes on her, prying into her.

"Your marriage."

"I don't understand."

"What do you want most in this world, Matilda? Do you want to be a loving wife to a loving husband, or——"

"You know as well as I do that I love my husband!" she interrupted angrily.

"—or is it your goal to see yourself crowned Queen of England?"

"I'm a good wife. And I also want to be Queen of England. I don't see what one has to do with the other."

"Apparently not. Come with me." Lanfranc led her to a stone bench in the courtyard and they sat down together. "You like to think of yourself as a logical woman!"

"I am a logical woman!" Thoroughly confused, Matilda glared at him. He admitted that her idea was excellent, yet he seemed to be preparing to talk her out of it, and she was on the verge of despair, although she did not show it. If Lanfranc blindly supported William, she would be without hope.

"William is a logical man. So you should be able to thrash out any problem between you. But you don't."

"Of course not." She no longer bothered to be diplomatic or polite. "You men use only logic. But mine is tempered by another quality."

"And what is that?"

She had the feeling that the Abbé knew precisely what she was going to say and that he was deliberately maneuvering her into a trap. "My femininity!" she declared belligerently.

"I've heard you refer to your instinct. Is that what you mean?"

"Yes. My logic is guided by my instinct. But you still haven't told me the price——"

"I was coming to that." Lanfranc clasped his thin

hands over a bony knee. "If your instinct is sound, you realize that you're losing William."

"But that's absurd. He's never as much as looked at another woman, and he never will."

"Can you only lose him to another woman? What of his work, his expanding realm, his army? You saw your father bury himself in his treasure chests, Matilda. And I warn you that, by persisting in the tactics you employ with William, you're separating yourself from him by a wall higher than that of the castle."

"Just what are those tactics?" she demanded aggressively, not letting him see she was afraid there was some truth to his accusation.

"You impose your ideas on him, you impose your mind on him. And he resents your interference."

"Interference! Now you sound like William."

"What else would you expect him to call it, Matilda? Until he married you he was responsible only to his Maker. He trusts his own decisions, and, loving you, he wants to trust yours. But when they conflict with his—and remember that he doesn't think in the same way you do—he begins to doubt. William of Normandy can't doubt himself. If he does, he's doomed. And he knows it."

Matilda caught only a glimmer of what he was saying, but the import of his meaning was clear. "You're telling me that I must close my eyes while he murders Harold."

"Persuade him to accept your plan if you must. But keep in mind that if he does, he may resent you all the more. Look back on your quarrels with him and you'll find that virtually all of them are a direct result of your——"

"My interference!"

The Abbé shook his head sorrowfully. "Not long ago I loaned you the copy of St. Paul's Epistle to the

Ephesians that Brother Jode illuminated. Either you haven't read it or else you haven't taken it to heart. Do you by chance remember his admonition to walk with all lowliness and meekness, with long-suffering, forbearing one another in love?"

Matilda stood, and was disturbed to find that she was trembling. "If I didn't love William, I wouldn't bother! If I didn't care about him I'd let him kill the Earl instead of making certain that England will be his!"

Lanfranc continued to sit and looked up at her in gentle reproof. "His, Matilda—or yours? You've spoken too often in the confession box of your desire to be Queen to fool me now."

"Then what would you have me do, Father? Shall we throw away this magnificent chance because I have a normal ambition to——"

"It isn't my place to say whether your ambitions are normal. And it isn't my place to advise you."

"William ought to be grateful to me!"

He stood, shrugged, and tugged at his robe. "That isn't for me to say, either. You ask for my help, and here is what I offer you: don't be hasty. Think the matter over, and your own conscience will tell you what to do."

The interview was at an end, and Matilda felt utterly frustrated. "I'll do as you've bidden me," she said wearily.

"Then you'll be sure to find the right answer for yourself. And Matilda—remember that William was a man of some consequence long before he married you."

"To be sure," was her parting retort, "but thanks to me he's more now than he ever was!"

William moved down the pink granite steps of his dais, took his place at the long oak table that stood

beneath the windows along the west wall of his great
hall, and looked at each of his principal lieutenants in
turn. Fitz Osbern lounged comfortably in a padded
chair, with one leg cocked over the arm, and his eyes
were shining. Roger Mont Gomeri, a black-haired
giant whom the Bretons called "The Butcher," and
with good reason, showed no emotion whatsoever. The
Duke's own half brother, Robert of Mortain, Harlotte's
elder son by Lord Herlwin, who had only recently been
admitted to the Council, was the only one who betrayed real excitement. He had spilled a few drops of
mead on the table, and was rapidly sketching a design
with the liquid.

"Well?" William demanded. "You've heard the
situation. I'll listen to your suggestions."

Mont Gomeri was the first to reply. "You've directed
me to meet the damned Englishman on the road with
an escort of a cavalry squadron and an infantry battalion. Is that right, William?"

"It is."

"Then there's no problem." Mont Gomeri's deep
bass voice rolled down the hall and was finally muffled
by the bright wool tapestries, depicting scenes of the
Duke's triumphs, that lined the walls. "I'll dispose of
him and all whose who are with him. Never mind the
details; just leave them to me. I've gone boar hunting
once or twice in my lifetime." He laughed coarsely.

"Osbern?" William's face was impassive.

"I say we wait until Harold gets here," the Seneschal
replied slowly. "In the late evening, when his vassals
are either drunk or in bed, we'll coax him into the
rough green yonder on some pretext or other. We could
tell him we want to show him the outer wall—
something like that. The English are very lax in their
defenses, you know. When I was there I saw only

wooden palisades and little moats so shallow that a horse could wade across them. So Harold will be anxious to inspect a castle that's really impregnable." Fitz Osbern paused and stared up at one of the high, deepset windows; he was never impetuous, and when he presented a scheme it was thorough and complete. "Once he's out there in the dark, whoever is showing him around can move away from him. Then someone up in the southwest turret can drop a boulder on him. The incident can be accomplished very quietly and neatly, and it can easily be made to look like a mishap."

"Robert?"

"I claim the honor of killing Harold by my own hand!" the young man said eagerly. "It's my right of kinship." The Baron of Mortain looked first at Fitz Osbern, then at Mont Gomeri, challenging them, yet hoping they would not accept the gage and insist on precedence over him.

William took a long draught of mead. "One other suggestion has been made to me. Before I convened this meeting of the Council, I had a visit from Odo."

"And what does the good Bishop think?" Mont Gomeri did not bother to hide his contempt for the younger of the Duke's half brothers.

"Of himself, naturally," Robert interjected.

Fitz Osbern, who concentrated on one subject at a time, was annoyed. "We aren't here to discuss Bishop Odo. I doubt if any plan he could devise would be a match for mine, but it might have some slight merit. What does he suggest, William?"

"I present his thoughts to you without comment from me. In Odo's ecclesiastical opinion, all Englishmen are heretics. So he wants me to turn Harold over to him, and Odo will try him for sorcery."

"No!" Mont Gomeri roared, smashing the table with

a mailed fist for emphasis. "Harold is mine!"

"I disagree!" Robert was on his feet. "As William's blood brother I insist that the right to dispose of him is mine."

Fitz Osbern continued to dangle a booted leg over his chair arm. "My idea is the only sound one. Just because Odo is an idiot is not reason——" He broke off as the Duke leaned forward in his seat.

"Yes, Odo is an idiot," William said. "And so are the rest of you. The reasons we can't hand the Earl to Odo are obvious. And it's equally plain that your schemes—all of them—are worthless."

His barons stared at him, daring him to prove them wrong.

"If any of you had stopped to think about this matter, you'd have realized how complex it is. Where was Harold going when he was shipwrecked in Ponthieu? Probably to France—to form a secret alliance with Philip. Granted that we have the best army and the finest generals in the world, we still can't fight everybody at once. Remember that we're surrounded by enemies. The Bretons are afraid of us, the Burgundians hate us and the French mistrust us. They're all looking for an excuse to band together against us.

"And if we follow any of the ideas that have been presented here this afternoon, we'll be in for real trouble, as sure as the earth is flat.

"Do you want me to be known as Black William? That's what they'll call me, and they'll all descend on us at once."

"Let them come." Mont Gomeri spat on the floor.

"France, Burgundy, and Brittany. I'm not so sure," Fitz Osbern murmured. "And of course there'll be an uprising in Maine the day a general war breaks out against us. I have to keep two of our best divisions there as it is."

"Exactly!" William's voice rose, and he made a short, chopping motion in the air with his right hand. "So we won't waste time. Hear my decision. Roger, you'll bring the Earl safely to me or I'll have your own skin in return. Escort him by way of Bayeux, Caen—all of our big towns—and give the people every opportunity to see him and to know he's being treated with courtesy under the Code of Nobles. If he tries to escape, of course, you might have to bring him here in chains, but that's another matter. I want you to take young Gerbod with you as your personal equerry. When word drifts back to England that my own stepson was in the escort party, even Harold's closest supporters will know that we treated him with honor."

Mont Gomeri, speechless, gaped at the Duke, sure that he had taken leave of his senses.

"Osbern," William continued, "I charge you with personal responsibility for Harold's safety while he's my guest. And Robert, you'll see to it that no harm comes to any of his vassals. We'll give a great banquet for him, and we'll entertain him as no man has been entertained here since my father was host for a week to the German Emperor. The old one who was poisoned by his nephew."

The Seneschal was too good a soldier to object, and he nodded his head, even though his expression made it clear that he was obeying against his best judgment. Robert, to whom discipline was anathema, flushed but was wise enough to remain mute and sat scowling at his hands.

"No effort will be spared to show Harold the best of Norman hospitality," William declared emphatically. "Meanwhile, during the week or two that he's here we'll prepare a ship to take him back to England. And when he leaves us, we'll present him with gifts, all of us. Osbern, the Arabians in your stables are the best I've ever seen. I'm sure you'll want to present the Earl with a stallion as a token of your esteem. Roger, your wife and her women are marvelously adept at needlework and weaving. I have no doubt that Mabel will be pleased to give the first noble of England a tapestry to take home with him. And Robert, your collection of weapons is growing cumbersome. It will make you happy, I know, to present Harold with a Norman sword—possibly the one I used in the ceremonies when I created you a baron. The jewels set in the hilt are very costly, so it will be a fitting gift to a great earl who already holds East Anglia and Essex and Kent in his own name."

There was a deathly silence and no one moved. William's barons did not dare look at each other for fear their expressions would reveal their conviction that he had truly gone mad.

"I hear no cheers of approval." The Duke sat back in his chair, hooked his thumbs in his belt, and suddenly he laughed. "Perhaps this will satisfy you, then. After Harold has left us and we've shown the world that Normandy has no better friend, he'll be struck down in a tragic, unexpected accident. Perhaps his party will be set upon by robbers while riding to St. Valéry or some such seacoast place to embark on his voyage. Or it might be preferable if sea rovers sink him after he's begun his voyage. It doesn't really matter, of course. That's a petty detail that can be settled at any time. What's important is that no stigma be attached to us. No one will ever be able to blame William of Normandy for the death of his honored guest."

The Council relaxed.

"Brilliant," Fitz Osbern said enthusiastically.

"I couldn't have thought of a plan like that if my life depended on it," Mont Gomeri declared.

"Brother William, I'm proud of you!" Robert of Mortain cried.

The Duke waved aside their compliments with a self-deprecating hand. "Not at all, not at all. I merely use what little intelligence the Lord gave me," he said modestly.

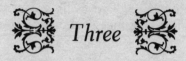

Three

A RAW WIND from the hills blew in through the uncovered windows of the L-shaped ducal bedchamber on the second floor of the castle, and Matilda, wide awake and chilly, huddled under the good Flemish blankets of pure white wool. The canopy of the bed billowed and rippled in the breeze, and the Duchess told herself that the lions of Normandy, embroidered at the head of the bedstead must be shivering; she could remember joking about the lions, but that had been long ago, and she no longer found the conceit humorous. William insisted on fresh air at night, and she had never been able to persuade him that the heavy tapestries hanging on the walls should be drawn across the open windows.

She had no real grounds for complaint, of course. When she had first come to Rouen as a bride, the chamber had been little better than a stable, and she had made so many changes in it that William often said he felt like a stranger in it. But in spite of his faultfinding he enjoyed the improvements she had made, she told herself smugly. He would be lost without the pitcher of watered wine that stood on a little table at his side of the bed, and he liked the innovation of bed sheets so much that he had taken them into the field with him on his last two campaigns. His clothes were no longer scattered all over the room but were neatly arranged in a carved cupboard of cherry wood, where he would find them in the morning, and she had often noted that he never sat on the hard walnut bench that he insisted on keeping in the chamber, but always chose one of the padded chairs instead. If he ever stopped to think of all she had done to make the castle more comfortable, he would be grateful to her.

That, however, would be asking for too much, she thought bitterly. Like lesser men who failed to appreciate their wives, he took her for granted and treated her like a housekeeper. Propping herself on one elbow, she looked down at him. His face was serene in sleep, which irritated her, and the sound of his deep, even breathing annoyed her even more. He had no right to throw off his cares like this, as though a problem of momentous importance didn't exist.

The wind cut through Matilda's thin nightdress and she drew on her pink wool robe, then slipped her feet into brocaded, soft leather shoes, and walked across the rushes scattered on the stone floor to a chair on the far side of the chamber. William's exasperating calm, his ability to slumber at a time of crisis disturbed her so much that she could not devote herself to essentials until she had removed herself from him.

Abbé Lanfranc would be pleased if he could see her now and realize how upset she was over his advice. His words had run through her mind constantly since her visit to the monastery of St. Etienne this afternoon, but she was no nearer a solution than she had been when she started her homeward journey. And she was actually sorry that she had gone to see Lanfranc; before he had spoken to her she had been sure of herself, sure that the stand she had taken was right. Now she was badly confused, and she could almost sympathize with William's violent anger when he could not solve a dilemma; she could not tolerate indecision either.

She became restless, sitting in the dark and brooding, and without quite realizing what she was doing she began to wander around the room. The rushes whispered under her feet, and after several minutes William stirred. "Is that you, Matilda?" he asked, not opening his eyes.

"Yes, dear." She longed to discuss the whole matter with him now, but knew better. William was never in his most reasonable frame of mind in the middle of the night.

"Are you ill?" His voice was thick with sleep.

"No, I'm fine," she replied softly.

There was a long silence, and when he nestled into his silk-covered pillow of goose down, she thought he had dropped off again. "Why are you up?" he asked suddenly.

"I wasn't sleepy."

The Duke yawned noisily and buried his face in the pillow. "Ridiculous! Everybody is sleepy at this time of night."

She had to bite back a retort, which left her with nothing at all to say.

"Come back to bed!" he commanded grumpily.

Matilda walked to a chair, making as little noise as she could, and sat down.

"Did you hear me? I told you to come back to bed, madam!"

"Yes, dear." Swallowing her resentment, she obeyed.

When William felt her presence beside him he muttered something unintelligible, turned over, and promptly went to sleep. Matilda moved as close to her edge of the bed as she could and stared at the wall, her body rigid. How typical of him, she thought, and what a child he really was. He believed that he needed only to issue an order and his whole world would immediately fall into place in accord with his wishes. He never took anyone else's desires into consideration, and it certainly never crossed his mind that he might be wrong.

He treated all of Normandy like a unit of his army that he could move or halt, maneuver or deploy at his will. And the least significant member of that army was his wife, who had given him children, improved his habits, made him comfortable beyond his wildest dreams, and had, in the bargain, often piloted the duchy through the treacherous waters of European statecraft.

It was too much to hope that William would recognize her achievements, Matilda thought, but Lanfranc had deflected her from her course with his irrelevant talk about marriage and love. Her duty to William, to Normandy, and herself was plain: regardless of the cost she would have to persuade William to let Earl Harold live. Her mind made up at last, she smiled to herself and fell asleep.

When the Duke awoke in the morning, he was faintly surprised to find that his wife was already up and out; as a rule she continued to sleep until she heard him stamping around the room. A churl brought him a silver basin of warm water and he shaved quickly with his army razor and soft yellow soap, then dressed methodically while humming a bawdy marching song popular with his troops. Brilliant sunshine streamed in through the windows, and he was tempted by the idea of taking his falcons into the fields south of Rouen, but after a slight struggle he rejected the notion. He had scheduled a meeting of his tax advisers for this morning, and he conscientiously put thoughts of personal pleasure aside. His work came first.

His inclination was to increase the tax on the merchants of his towns, who had enjoyed unprecedented prosperity during the past year, but he was reluctant to act until he studied a financial census that had been made for him. His nobles were all urging him to raise the merchants' tax, of course, but that was to be expected. The more others paid, the lighter would be their own burden.

He was still thinking about taxes when he came down to the private dining chamber behind the great hall, and there another suprise awaited him: the family was already assembled, which was highly unusual. As a rule one or another of the children was tardy for the one meal they shared each day with their parents. He bent over Matilda and kissed her absently, then made his way to his own place at the head of the table, answering each child's good morning greeting in turn.

"You look very pretty today," he said to Gundrada, who was dressed in a pale yellow silk gown. "So do you, milady," he added to six-year-old Adelize, whose sky-blue linen dress matched her eyes and showed up her long, flaxen hair. Both girls beamed at him, and he turned his attention to his sons. "Robert, sit straight! William, stop fidgeting!"

Robert Short-Hose, the eight-year-old heir to the duchy, jerked erect and was rewarded with a paternal smile. He was dressed today in a tunic similar to his father's, but in brown wool instead of leather; he wore high boots like the duke's instead of a small boy's low shoes, and in his belt was a small blunt-edged dagger which had been made for him by the castle armorer against Matilda's will and better judgment.

"Aren't you attending classes with your tutor this morning, Robert?"

"No, sir. The Seneschal is taking me hunting."

The Seneschal, William thought grimly, would not go hunting, but there would be time to break the news to the boy later. If he himself had to attend the tax meeting, Fitz Osbern would be there too. Matilda was about to speak, but at the same instant she and her husband saw that a small jar in front of four-year-old William was wobbling precariously. The little boy, aware that he and his property had become the center of parental attention, reached for the jar, but too late. Before he could touch it a frog leaped out, jumped to the floor, and disappeared among the rushes. There was a shocked silence, and everybody looked at Matilda, whose inviolable rule it was that no pets could be brought to the table, her husband's mastiffs excepted.

To the entire family's amazement she burst into laughter, then, reaching out, she affectionately tucked her son's white linen shirt into his wool breeches. "Where did you find that beast?" she asked pleasantly.

The boy grinned, relieved that he was not going to be punished. "I fished him out of the moat. Adelize helped me."

"You know your mother's rule," the Duke said severely, but Matilda interrupted him.

"No harm has been done, dear," she declared sweetly.

He looked down the table at her sharply. Ordinarily, although she knew he disliked scenes at breakfast, when he was trying to organize his day, she would have dismissed the offending child from the table. It crossed his mind that something rather strange was in the air, and now, really noticing Matilda for the first time, his suspicion was strengthened.

She had dressed with care in a plain *bliaud*, or tunic, of heavy white silk, trimmed only at the neck and cuffs in green, and around her waist was a belt of gold links, a prize of war he had brought her several years ago. Her hair was dressed in the style he liked best, and hung loose to the middle of her back, with one heavy lock over her left shoulder, rippling over her breast to her waist. And William could not resist pushing his chair back and peering at her feet under the table. His guess was confirmed: she was wearing soft-soled green leather slippers, and her wooden pattens were nowhere in evidence.

Straightening, he pretended to concentrate on his first course of roasted chicken. He was pleased at the pains Matilda was taking to make this morning's meal harmonious, but he knew her well enough to realize that she never did anything without a motive. He picked up a drumstick and glanced at her; she was smiling at him blandly, and he decided that two could play the game.

"You're beautiful this morning, madam," he said.

"Thank you, dear. I always try to look my best for you."

"If I didn't know that you're the mother of this brood, I'd swear you were younger than Gundrada. Closer to Adelize's age, maybe."

The children laughed at their father's unexpected joke, and their noise drowned Matilda's reply, which satisfied William, as it gave him more time to think. He knew she had gone to see Lanfranc the previous afternoon, but as she had said nothing last night about the visit, he had assumed that the Abbé had discouraged her absurd idea of keeping the English earl alive. Now he was not so sure, and he wanted to give her no opportunity to open the subject again.

She tried to say something, but he interrupted her hastily. "Why isn't the baby here? He's old enough to have breakfast with us."

"Certainly, William, if you wish." Matilda nodded to a maidservant who stood in the arched entrance. "Summon Baron Henry to the table," she ordered, then turned back to her husband, her face innocent. "Of course we aren't all here this morning. I was told that Gerbod has gone somewhere on a mission for you." She made the remark as a flat statement, but the lift in her voice at its end indicated that she was questioning him.

The Duke chose not to interpret it in that light. "I'm ready for the next course," he announced to no one in particular.

There was an immediate bustle in the kitchen, and in a moment two menservants entered with large, steaming bowls. William sniffed the fragrance and temporarily forgot his suspicions in his delight at being served his favorite dish.

"*Dilligrout!*" he shouted, and the children echoed his cry.

Then he saw Matilda take a portion, and his last doubts vanished. She definitely had some scheme in mind or she would never demean herself to touch *dilligrout*, a Norman peasant dish which she loathed but which he learned to enjoy during the long years of his impoverished childhood and adolescence when he had been forced to hide from his enemies.

It had always annoyed him that his wife thought herself too good to eat the concoction, and although she had protested vigorously that its taste simply did not appeal to her, William was unable to believe that anyone could fail to enjoy it. A stew whose principal ingredient was oatmeal, it contained chunks of garlic- and spice-laden sausages, strips of salted beef, onions, and carrots, and William was never content to eat less than three helpings.

The children had inherited his taste, he was pleased to see, and even Gundrada, who was not of his blood, was eating heartily. He thought of calling Matilda's attention to the fact, but changed his mind when he observed that she, too, was eating with apparent relish. He knew from long experience that when she was determined to quarrel, even the most innocent remark would serve as a cause, and he had no intention of becoming embroiled this morning. Besides, it was impossible for a man to be in a bad mood while eating *dilligrout*.

"William," the Duchess said, and from her tone, so free of guile, he knew that something was coming and braced himself. "I wonder if you'd settle a point of dispute between some of my ladies and me."

"If I can," he replied cautiously. "I know a great deal about many things, but I'm no expert on matters of the bower." He winked at Robert Short-Hose, who smiled politely in return. The jest was too adult for the boy, and only Gundrada laughed.

"Oh, it has nothing to do with women," Matilda said. "It's something you must know more about than anyone in the world. We were discussing the Code of Nobles yesterday——"

"I see." In spite of himself he was amused. "Robert, William, listen to your mother and take heed. When you're older you will wonder what ladies talk about while they sit sewing in those rooms filled with tapestries and silks and frills. Now you know. It's the Code of Nobles, no less." He chuckled and helped himself to another bowl of *dilligrount*. "Which Code are you asking about, dear, the West or the East?"

"I didn't know there was more than one." The Duchess was obviously bewildered.

"The Turks and Persians and the other barbarians of the East have their own Code," William explained condescendingly. "It seems to be quite effective in a primitive way, although it lacks the refinements—naturally—of the Code used by the more civilized nations of the West. Now, what was it you and your ladies couldn't agree on?" He was happy to see that the children, who were usually absorbed in conversations of their own, were all listening.

Before Matilda could reply, little Henry was brought into the chamber, wrapped in a blanket of fine wool mesh. The nurse, who should have known better, carried him first to his father, and at the sight of this virtual stranger the baby began to scream. There was no sound quite as jarring to William as that of an infant's wail, but Matilda came to his rescue at once.

"Remove the Baron," she directed, and the nurse withdrew.

Henry had been the inadvertent spokesman for the other children, who did not dare express opposition to their parents, and they exchanged sly grins, then stiffened in anticipation of the inevitable maternal rebuke. But Matilda had other things on her mind this morning.

"I know so little about the Code that I'm afraid this will sound stupid to you," she said to William calmly, as though there had been no interruption, "so forgive me. But what happens when a knight or a noble takes an oath of allegiance to an overlord—and then breaks his oath?"

"I'm afraid I don't understand you," William answered, frowning as he wondered what obscure point she was trying to make.

"Mother! I know!" Robert declared eagerly, then intoned the ritual, " 'An oath of allegiance to an overlord is an obligation freely given on honor.' No knight ever breaks his oath, Mother."

"The boy is right." William helped himself to a

cimnal, a potato-flour biscuit which was brown and hard on the outside and soft on the inside.

"I'm sure he is—in theory," Matilda said gently. "But suppose, for instance, that Fitz Osbern broke his oath to you——"

"Impossible. There's no more devoted man in the duchy than Osbern. In fact, all of my barons are loyal. Not one of them would raise his hand against me."

"I'm showing my ignorance, I know, but you're the vassal of Philip of France, dear. Yet you've fought two wars against him."

"That's a different situation, completely different." William spread goat's cheese on his *cimnal.*

"Oh? Why is that?" Matilda's green eyes were round.

"Philip is only my nominal overlord. I've never actually performed the ceremony of swearing an oath of recognition before him. If I had, then I wouldn't be able to fight against him. That's why I've always refused his invitations to visit Paris."

"It's becoming clear to me now," Matilda murmured. "You may leave the table," she told the children, who had lost interest in the conversation and were becoming restless.

"I hope that settles the problem for you," William said expansively. He saw that she seemed satisfied and told himself that his suspicions had probably been unfounded. In the future he would try to give her the credit she deserved when she made an effort, he concluded, leaning over the side of his chair and bestowing kisses on Adelize and Gundrada as they left the room.

"It does and it doesn't," Matilda sighed.

"But I've just told you——"

"I know you have. But the ladies and I just went round and round yesterday, and I don't know any more now than I did then, really. So have a little patience with me."

"I'm being very patient," William assured her, and meant it.

"I can best explain by taking an imaginary situation—something that could never actually happen in Normandy. Do you follow me so far?" They were alone in the dining chamber now.

"Go on."

"Suppose you had a vassal lord, a count, perhaps. Or better still, an insignificant lord of a manor. Let's say he became dissatisfied with his lot and rebelled against you. What would you do?"

"I'd put him to death, of course. You know that as well as I do, Matilda."

"But would you have the *legal* right to execute him?"

"You know I do only what's legal!" He was proud of his record as a lawmaker and a dispenser of justice, and no one in Normandy was more scrupulous than he himself in cloaking every act in the righteous armor of legality.

"Then an oath breaker would be an outlaw, wouldn't he?" she asked ingenuously.

"That's right. If your imaginary manorial lord should escape from me—something that would never happen in real life, you understand—he'd be more than an outlaw. He'd be a complete outcast from society. No other noble would take him in. Even his own brothers would be forced to disown him under the Code, or they'd be guilty of his crime too."

"And the Church feels the same way?"

"To be sure. There isn't a priest in Christendom who would give sanctuary to a breaker of an oath of allegiance. A man who swears vassalage to an overlord and then deserts him is the most miserable creature who exists. He's even lower than that frog your son brought to the table." William took a little spiced wine, the only beverage he ever drank at breakfast.

Matilda sat unmoving, seemingly absorbing his words. Then she lifted her head, and when she spoke there was a new note of strength in her voice. "How wonderful it would be, then," she said slowly, "if Earl Harold could be persuaded to swear an oath of allegiance to you. Then he and all of his house and all his vassals would have no choice but to support your claim to England when King Edward dies."

There was a long, stunned silence, and William gripped the arms of his chair so hard that his knuckles turned white. Then he shoved back his chair violently and began to pace up and down the room, his eyes clouded, his chin low. Finally he stopped beside Matilda. "Was this the idea you wanted to present to me yesterday?"

"Yes, dear." She thought that he might strike her, but she did not cringe.

He resumed his pacing, but his powers of analysis seemed to have deserted him. He discovered that he was dwelling more on Matilda's infernal cleverness on leading up to her point than on her suggestion itself, and that was wrong. Although he hated to admit it, her plan was very much worth his consideration.

Watching him, Matilda decided to press her argument. She knew he concentrated hardest when he paced and that he disliked interruptions, but she had already dared so much that there was little to lose now. "Your enemies would be dumfounded," she said gently. "They'd be left without an argument against you. Even Philip wouldn't know what to say or where to turn."

"Quiet, madam." He did not look at her.

"As for the English, all opposition to you would collapse. All the resentment we've been told has been aroused at the idea of a foreign king would die stillborn if the premier Earl acknowledged you as his master."

"Quiet, I said!" William glared at a manservant who started into the chamber to clear away the breakfast remains but who hastily backed out again.

"Of course, dear."

There was silence for a time as he wrestled with the problem. "I must say," he declared abruptly, "that your idea is audacious."

Audacity, she knew, always appealed to him.

"And it's cunning. My God, its the most cunning scheme ever devised. If you weren't my wife, if I didn't know, I'd swear you were an emissary of Beelzebub."

"I'll take that in the way I'm sure you intended it—as a compliment," Matilda said, forcing a light laugh.

"The more I examine it from every angle, the more perfect it seems." William halted again, near her.

"Thank you, dear."

"In fact, it's so good that I don't trust it."

"Don't be superstitious, William." She knew immediately that she had said the wrong thing.

"Superstition be damned! My feeling is against it! Suppose something goes wrong?"

"In that case," she murmured, "you could always revert to your original plan."

William fingered the hilt of his double-pronged dagger. "Yes," he said, "I could." Suddenly he lifted Matilda to her feet and laughed, and if there was an undertone of misgiving in his voice they both ignored it. "All right," he said, "I'll try it."

He kissed her, hard. The fingers of Matilda's right hand dug into his shoulder and with her left she caressed the nape of his neck. When they broke apart, she was breathless; to her surprise, William was looking at her somberly.

"If this plan miscarries," he said, "may the Lord have mercy on your soul."

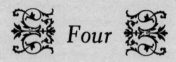 *Four*

THE TENSION in the great hall of Rouen Castle was almost unbearable as the overlord of Normandy, his nobles, and their ladies awaited the arrival of Earl Harold. Every man present had long been looking forward to the day when he would accompany his liege to England and be granted estates far more extensive than those he already held; every woman had long dreamed of holding court in her new English manor house, and on a scale impossible to achieve here at home, where custom and tradition limited pomp, curtailed ceremony, and forced every lady and her husband to bend their knees at the ducal court instead of receiving the homage of their inferiors at their own. To the Normans England was the Promised Land, but Harold was the Pharaoh who would keep them from it if he could, so it was bewildering to have gathered here to honor him.

No baron, no court, no lord or knight thought of acting otherwise, however, and those ladies whose hearts rebelled kept their own counsel. William had decreed that the Englishman was to be received with dignity and in friendship, and no one was foolish enough to disobey the ducal command. Although the Norman gentry were proud of the reputation they had achieved for individual independence and zealously guarded their personal rights in their dealings with the world and each other, they were practical men and women and it did not occur to them to flout their master's will. It was common knowledge that a dark corner of the dungeons beneath the castle was piled high with the bones of unrealistic nobles.

There was little conversation, the men tugged at their fur-trimmed tunics, the ladies straightened their silk gowns, then rearranged them again, and everyone kept watching the principal entrance to the great hall. Even the most provincial lord of a manor from an obscure country seat deep in the interior knew that the meeting of his Duke and the ambitious foreigner would be a historic moment. Occasionally someone murmured a few words to his neighbor, but the atmosphere more closely resembled that of the hour before a battle than it did a reception for a distinguished guest. Now and again a baron glanced at Normandy's overlord, who was seated in a massive oak chair on the top of his pink granite dais, but he seemed preoccupied, so it was more prudent to turn away from him and avoid his gaze.

William fingered his plain, circular crown of iron, the symbol of his rank and power, and hoped that for once it would not give him a headache. He had put it on too soon, having donned it when a messenger from Roger Mont Gomeri had arrived with word that the escort party was approaching the city, but that had been almost an hour ago and the iron crown was becoming increasingly uncomfortable. William shifted slightly in his seat and tried not to crease his ceremonial robes, which he loathed. The last time he had worn them had been at the christening of his son, Henry, and he certainly wouldn't have taken them out of his cupboard today had not his nobles appeared in full regalia. He felt an active dislike for his floor-length cloak of scarlet silk, which was trimmed with emeralds, sapphires, topazes, and rubies, and his cloth-of-gold tunic, edged with a hem of black sable, always reminded him of the costumes worn by strolling players. Whenever he was attired in his finery, he felt ill at ease, almost as though he were playing a mummer's part; he had made himself master of his duchy and of the lands that bounded it wearing armor, and only when he was encased in steel did he feel at home.

He would have liked nothing better than to greet Harold in armor, but he had only himself to blame for his oversight: by the time the idea had crossed his mind his vassal lords had already assembled and it had been too late. In a sense, of course, it was Matilda's fault, for he usually left the details of rituals in her hands, and she invariably thought in terms of her own pleasure rather than of his peace of mind. He looked at her now as she sat, one step below him and to his left on the dais, and it seemed to him that she was the one person in the great hall who was actually enjoying this time of waiting.

She had an instinctive love for the dramatic, he told himself; issues meant nothing to her, and she courted excitement for its own sake. He suspected that she saw the present scene solely as a tableau that she could later recapture on a tapestry, a pretty picture of an event in which she was a major figure. The real significance of Harold's arrival, the grim struggle for power that would ensue, and the harsh threat of necessary violence that hung over the great hall were of cloudy, secondary importance to her. All that mattered to her was that she was on glittering display. But that would suffice if only she would be content to receive homage for her beauty and charm and would leave the stresses of the world of affairs to men who understood such things.

Looking at her, William thought that she more than lived up to her obligations as a wife and as a duchess;

she was more regal, more radiantly alive than any other lady in the room, and she was well aware of it, yet the knowledge apparently did not satisfy her. Her bearing was that of a queen as she sat erect in a dress and undertunic of deep blue velvet with a wide band of ermine outlining the neck and huge pockets at her hips. And even William, who liked to think of himself as being indifferent to women's clothes, appreciated a colorful touch of her own creation, the trimming of the ermine with its own black tails. But, he reflected, she had gone too far in wearing a circlet of gold filigree set with diamonds and pearls around her head. To Harold and his party the coronet would look like a crown, and her impatient eagerness irritated him. William did not believe in prematurely advertising his strength or the disposition of his forces to an enemy.

A trumpet blared somewhere in the distance, the sound of horses' hoofs was heard, and the crowd in the great hall stirred. The Duchess, her eyes shining, smiled brilliantly, the lords of Normandy struck poses of pretended nonchalance and their ladies quickly dropped sheer veils over their faces. Only the Duke did not move, but those who knew him best saw a white line form along the contour of his jaw; they noted, too, that although his hands were seemingly relaxed, his fingers were slightly curled. The Lion of Normandy was ready to spring.

The first to enter the great hall was Matilda's son, Gerbod, who carried his chain mail easily in spite of his youth as he walked quickly up the long chamber and dropped to one knee at the foot of the dais. "Lord Duke," he said in a voice just changing from soprano to baritone, "Baron Mont Gomeri has been true to his charge, and craves indulgence to bring your guests to you."

"Let them come in." All rituals were a waste of time, William thought; one of these days, when he had the chance, he would draw up a new code that would dispense with needless formalities.

Mont Gomeri and his officers appeared in the entrance, bowed to the Duke, and joined their ladies. William noted out of the corner of his eye that Matilda was frowning faintly, and he could barely repress a grin. The dust of the road was still thick on the boots of Roger and Gerbod, and the Duchess's sense of propriety was disturbed. She would never understand that to a Norman nobleman duty came before appearances.

Several people started to talk at once, then all conversation ceased as a striking figure appeared, followed by his retinue. The Normans were big men, but of all those gathered for the occasion, only William himself was as tall as Earl Harold, only William had shoulders as broad and legs as long. Harold stood for a long moment just inside the arched threshold, and the company was immediately impressed by his arrogance. His deep blue eyes were proud, he held his massive head high, and his attitude was that of one who was accustomed to giving commands, not taking them. The warriors in the throng immediately recognized a kindred spirit, the politically minded sensed that he was a man of guile as well as strength, and the ladies, aroused by a magnetic virility which they had heretofore seen only in their own Duke, took a new interest in the proceedings.

The Normans stared at Harold, and he in turn coolly surveyed them. Very few of those present had ever visited England, and to the others he was like a being from another world; every detail of his appearance was closely and critically scrutinized. He wore a huge thumb ring on his left hand, his long blond hair touched his shoulders, and his upper lip was covered by a thick mustache, which disgusted the clean-shaven Normans. Every soldier noted his armor and thought it inferior to the local variety: it consisted of solid iron plates sewn to a padded linen tunic which stopped at mid-thigh, and it looked cumbersome. On his head was a dome-shaped helmet of the kind the Normans had discarded fifty years previous, and the two small protective plates which hung over his ears would certainly be a nuisance in battle. His round shield was incredibly small by local standards and was made of wood instead of iron, with only a few brass hoops to strengthen it; however, it did have a huge, sharp point rising out its center, so it might be useful.

The Earl's sword, which had a curving hilt and hung from a loop on his broad leather belt, was so short compared to those worn by the men-at-arms in the assemblage that they privately thought it was a mere decoration, not a weapon. But everyone was awed by his mighty battle-ax, an instrument of death that had gained renown throughout Christendom. It was almost as tall as Harold himself, and its razor sharp steel head measured one and one-half feet from the blade at one side to the rounded, clublike protrusion on the other. No man who had ever ridden to battle could fail to appreciate that ax.

William's first reaction as he looked down the great hall was one of dismay; like Harold, he should have worn armor for this meeting. Then, conquering his feelings, he studied his adversary and, although his hatred for the Earl burned deep, he could not help but admire the man. Harold had no inkling of the fate that might be in store for him here; indeed, for all he knew he might be set upon and slaughtered before he crossed the chamber. But there was no fear in his eyes and no hesitation in his step as he moved slowly into the great hall, and with the wisdom of a true leader he ignored the lesser creatures; his eyes met those of his host and thereafter he looked at no one else.

Men of equal rank did not bow their heads or bend their knees to each other, and the Norman duke and English earl were of roughly the same status, but the visitor could not afford to stand on protocol and the crowd happily waited for him to abase himself. To their astonishment William gave him no opportunity to bend his back before the ducal throne. Rising swiftly from the chair, he draped his cloak over his left arm, descended from the dais, and walked toward the Earl with his right hand outstretched.

"Welcome to my home," he said loudly. "Welcome, Lord Earl."

A flicker of surprise showed in Harold's eyes, but he mastered it as he extended his own hand. "My thanks, Lord Duke," he replied, his accented French harsh. "It is good to be here after so many tribulations."

They clasped hands, then each gripped the shoulder of the other, and the courtiers saw that they were approximately the same height. They moved together to the dais, and there Harold promptly demonstrated that the English, contrary to rumors, were not barbarians. Removing his helmet so deftly that his hair remained smoothly combed, he dropped to his knee before the Duchess, and when she graciously extended her hand to him, he pressed it to his lips.

"Your Grace," was all he said, but there was something in his voice, perhaps its timbre, that caused shivers to travel up a score or more of feminine spines.

"Never have we looked forward so eagerly to the arrival of a guest," Matilda decided, and no one who heard her could doubt her sincerity.

"Your kindness overwhelms me," Harold replied, rising and trying to conceal his bewilderment. He was endowed with a vivid imagination, but this warm reception was the last thing he had expected, and he was wary as he glanced first at his host, then his hostess. "Permit me to present the members of my party," he added, hoping to gain time to think and trying to feel his way.

It was customary for the host to request the presence of inferiors or to keep them waiting, and Matilda bridled at the Earl's calm usurpation of ducal authority. It was obvious that he gave directions as naturally and unthinkingly as did the Duke, and it never crossed his mind that one of his orders might be countermanded. William, aware of his wife's irritation, told himself that now perhaps she would begin to realize the mettle of this man who until now had been no more than a bloodless chess pawn in her mind. "Bring them in, Lord Earl," he said heartily. "We bid them welcome, too."

The Normans gaped as the Earl's vassals and retainers trooped into the great hall, and some of the ladies blushed at the appearance of these savages, whose attire they considered indecent. The worst offender was Harold's young brother, Wulfnoth, who was a year or two older than Gerbod, and several of the gentlemen who had made pilgrimages to the Holy Land were heard to mutter that he was dressed like a dancing girl in the harem of a Saracen. He wore a tunic of light blue linen with a short, full skirt which revealed his tight yellow breeches, and his full, swirling cloak was of blue and yellow silk squares. His stride was manly, however, his voice was deep, and his handclasp was firm. Patently the English were a strange breed and could not be fitted into convenient categories.

The other yellow-haired Saxons were attired as out-landishly, and seemed to be totally unembarrassed by their immodest tunics. As soon as their liege had presented them to the Duke and Duchess, they made themselves at home, and when William called for mead to be served to all, they drank with gusto, matching the Normans mug for mug. In short order they were exchanging bawdy jokes with the men, flirting with the ladies and behaving as though they had lived here all of their lives. And within a few minutes the Normans dropped their suspicious reserve and began to enjoy themselves too.

But the little group on the dais was more subdued, and although Matilda was smiling and William and Harold were grinning, the veneer of etiquette was thin. The Earl summoned his brother to join them, and addressed a remark to the youth in their own language. William tried to hook a thumb into the nonexistent belt of his cloth-of-gold tunic as he looked hard at Harold, then at Wulfnoth. "As I don't understand English," he said carefully, "I'll appreciate it if you'll speak only French."

"Certainly," the Earl agreed. "But I'm surprised. I'd have thought that you'd have made special efforts to learn our tongue." His voice was bland and his eyes showed no expression. "Do I assume that you have no liking for it?'

"Not at all," William replied in the same tone. "I have a great admiration for the English language, and I object only to its abuse by the people who speak it."

Only Wulfnoth laughed.

There was an awkward pause until Matilda filled the breech. "We hope," she said sweetly, "that your plans are such that you'll be able to stay with us for a time."

"My plans are already realized, Your Grace," Harold declared, lying glibly and turning to the Duke. "It was my intention to visit you, and I sailed from England only for that purpose."

"Then the wind that cast you ashore on the coast of Ponthieu was favorable," William said heartily, revealing only by a very slight narrowing of his eyes that he didn't believe a word of the tale.

"It wasn't a wind I'd have chosen, but it did bring us here."

"Yet your retinue is remarkably small for a visit of state." A note as hard as the granite underfoot crept into William's voice.

"I don't believe in pomp, and I've been told that you don't either." Harold allowed his gaze to linger for a long moment on the dazzling jewels of the Duke's cloak. "I've found there's no problem so great that it can't be solved by two men who meet each other face to face."

"Agreed, Lord Earl!" William realized that his wife was about to interrupt, but he gave her no chance. "I hope you're not implying that you and I are plagued by any problems."

"I know of none," Harold said quickly.

"Nor do I." Any member of William's council would have recognized his hint of menace.

Harold was not insensitive to it either. "Your land and mine live in peace together. I've come to see you in the hope that by growing to know each other better we can perpetuate the friendship of England and Normandy."

"Our countries are bound by many ties," William said, and paused to let the significance of his words take root. "You'll stay with us for a time, then?"

"We're in your hands, Lord Duke." Harold's smile broadened, but his eyes were humorless.

"So you are," William assented carelessly. "It's therefore my duty and that of my lady to insure that you enjoy yourselves in Rouen. If anything pleases your fancy, ask for it and you shall have it. If anything disturbs you, it will be removed. We Normans don't take our duties as hosts lightly, and when you return to England we want all of your memories of this visit to be happy ones.'

The Earl and Wulfnoth exchanged a surreptitious glance, and the boy, less expert at the art of dissembling than Harold, could scarcely hide his astonishment. He had been positive he would be killed on his arrival here, and he was stunned by the warmth of William's welcome. Harold, however, was not to be bested in a duel of words. "I'm sure," he said, "that all England will join with me in singing your praises—when I return home."

No useful purpose would be served in prolonging the conversation, so William nodded affably and then beckoned to several of his barons, who approached with their wives and were duly introduced to the guests. The talk became general, Harold related the story of his shipwreck, and Wulfnoth explained to several of the younger people that his brother's principal earldom, East Anglia, was almost as large as Normandy. The boast, which happened to be true, was received skeptically but politely. The Duke and Duchess remained with the group for a short time, then Matilda touched her husband's arm and they drew apart, moving to the far edge of the dais.

"I was right!" Matilda said in a low, exulting voice. "Did you see the look he gave his brother when he was trying to persuade us that it was his intention all along to come here?"

"I saw it." William continued to watch Harold over the top of his wife's head.

"It's just as I suspected. He was planning to set up an alliance with Philip. But he's trapped now, William. We can do with him what we please—and he knows it."

"He knows we can kill him. But if I'm any judge of character he'll resist your scheme, just as I would if his position and mine were reversed." Matilda tried to object, but William shook his head. "Look at him right now. You see how they hang on his words, how they smile when he smiles and frown when he frowns? Only a handful of men like that appear in a century. He's the sort people follow, so he's dangerous. Don't underestimate his strength."

"Oh, I don't," Matilda replied, and smiled. "But I'm not worried. I know that in a contest you're stronger than Harold."

"Yes, I am," William said heavily. "I've got to be."

When the guests sat down to their first meal in the great hall, a surface amiability assumed by men who were determined to behave in a civilized manner toward each other created an atmosphere that was tolerable if not pleasant. All of the Englishmen, even those who did not deserve the honor, were seated above the salt, and although a few long Norman noses were temporarily disjointed, no one of consequence really objected to the gesture. Only one incident marred the early part of the meal, and as Harold was as embarrassed as his hosts, no harm was done.

The first course was a rich stew of beef, venison, and goose, cooked in wine, and when the steaming bowls were placed in front of the hungry nobles, Wulfnoth, the Earl's young brother, made an adolescent blunder. Sniffing at his dish, he peered at it suspiciously, and remarked to no one in particular, "What's in this?"

Matilda, thinking him guilty only of bad manners,

told him the ingredients, but Wulfnoth was not satisfied.

"Is that all?" he persisted. "Are you sure that's all?"

William, who was the first to guess what the boy had in mind, ignored the questioning and tried to continue a conversation he had begun with Harold, who was seated in the place of honor on his right. "Strange as it may seem," he said, "I find that Italians are the best falcon trainers. I know that most people prefer Spaniards, but I have two Italians on my staff. I wouldn't be without them."

"Italians," Wulfnoth declared loudly, spearing a chunk of meat with his knife and then letting it splash back into his bowl, "are also expert poisoners."

There was a shocked silence, and several of the Norman barons began to mutter under their breaths. The polite veil of convention having been ripped away, the situation was explosive, but the Duke was equal to the emergency. He laughed loudly, as though Wulfnoth had made an excellent joke, and then he deliberately took a large mouthful of the stew. "Every land has its own customs, I suppose," he said slowly. "I don't know how you feel in England about these things, but here we have a very low opinion of anyone who resorts to poison. Personally, I believe in being direct. If there were someone I wanted to put out of the way, I wouldn't waste good cold steel. There's nothing like it."

"Quite true," the English earl agreed, glaring at his brother. "Steel for my enemies—and a birch rod for young boys to teach them perspective."

Everyone except Wulfnoth laughed, and several people started talking simultaneously. Normans and Englishmen vied with each other in attempts to be friendly, and for the next two hours the party enjoyed the superb repast the Duchess's cooks had prepared.

Vast quantities of wine were drunk during the meal, but the trouble began when the last course had been finished and large flagons of brandy were passed down each side of the table. Harold, who had poured a generous quantity of the liquor into his cup, suddenly jumped to his feet.

"A toast!" he shouted, and everyone present looked at him. "I propose that we drink to the health of the King!"

There was a moment of tense silence, which Fitz Osbern broke. "Here in Normandy," he said quietly, "we always drink first to the health of our own ruler."

'To William!" Roger Mont Gomeri cried, and without waiting for anyone else gulped down his drink.

Harold remained on his feet and continued to hold his cup poised in front of him. His arm was steady, and no one but Matilda, who had been watching him closely all evening, realized how much wine he had consumed with his meal. "A king stands higher than a duke!"

Mont Gomeri rose, and his thick fingers curled around the hilt of the knife at his belt. "You'll drink first to William of Normandy if I have to slit your throat and pour the brandy into the opening!"

Every man at the table reached for his weapons, one of the ladies screamed and the sound of curses, both Norman and English, filled the air. Mont Gomeri, who had been seated four places down the table from the Earl, rushed at him, dagger raised high, and only the intervention of the Seneschal prevented the spilling of blood. Fitz Osbern threw his full weight against the side of his fellow baron and Mont Gomeri, losing his balance, staggered, bumped into a small serving table loaded with pitchers of wine and fell to the floor.

Meantime Harold had drawn his own dagger and

had started toward his antagonist, but William, whose
instincts rarely failed him in a moment of crisis, came
up behind the Earl, caught his wrist, and tried to
wrench the blade away from him. Harold, thinking he
had been attacked from behind, began to struggle with
his unseen assailant, and by the time he half turned and
recognized the Duke, he had already landed a solid
punch with his free hand on the side of William's head.

Harold was too incensed to realize that William's
sole desire was to disarm him and restore order. Growl-
ing inarticulately, the Earl made a supreme effort to
break the grip of the other giant and William, seeing
the wild gleam in his eyes, suddenly knew that he
himself was in mortal danger. Harold was past reason,
and would plunge the dagger into him, regardless of the
consequences, unless he managed to keep his hold on
the Englishman's wrist. It was even possible that
Harold knew precisely what he was doing: he had been
given a perfect opportunity to rid the world of the hated
Norman who stood between him and the throne, and if
he himself survived, he could always claim, with some
justice, that William had attacked him first.

It would be easy enough, the Duke knew, to summon aid; a single shout would bring a score of guards to
his assistance. But the last thing on earth he wanted was
help, either from his soldiers or from his eager nobles,
for he was desperately afraid that in the melee someone
would kill Harold. And if the Earl should die now,
literally at the table of a host whose hospitality was
automatically assumed to include complete protection
of the life and health of a guest, the repercussions
would turn all of Europe against Normandy. William
could hope to succeed to the throne of England only if
Harold emerged unscathed from this unfortunate fight.

And, the Duke told himself as he called to his barons

and ordered them not to interfere, he had to keep his own skin whole in the bargain.

Harold, straining with all his might, loosened the clasp of the fingers that clutched his wrist, and in desperation William threw his free arm around the other's head. They wrestled briefly, crashed to the floor, and rolled over and over as they struggled for possession of the dagger. And while they fought, silently and intensely, all other activity in the great hall ceased. Lesser men forgot their lesser hatreds and watched in awe as the two greatest men of the age pounded and pummeled each other like a pair of peasants quarreling over the ownership of a hog.

Several of the Normans would have intervened, but Fitz Osbern, who was as keenly aware of the delicate problems involved as his master, held them back. And the English, although they would have liked nothing better than to come to the aid of their leader, knew they were badly outnumbered and prudently refrained.

Had an outsider been privileged to look in on the scene, he would have sworn that the calmest person in the great hall was the Duchess of Normandy. Matilda continued to sit, and she was actually smiling, as though the violent scuffle between her husband and the Earl was no more than an entertainment that had been devised for the amusement of the guests. No one could have guessed how much the effort to maintain a semblance of composure cost her, but she knew she could not give in to her feelings. If she showed signs of hysteria, the entire party would be thrown into a panic, and many men might die.

William, of course, was unaware of the reactions of anyone but his opponent, for he had to concentrate his full attention on Harold. The Earl struck savagely, repeatedly with his free hand, and the blows stung

William's face and made his body ache. But he did not
for an instant again relax his grip on the Englishman's
right wrist, no matter how hard he was jarred by the
other's punches. And, worst of all, he had to keep his
own temper in check, for he knew that if he lost it they
would indeed battle to the death.

It would have been no trick to disarm a less powerful
man, but Harold's strength was equal to his own, and
after several minutes of accepting bruising punishment
without giving like in return he knew that only a mira-
cle would prevent the murder of one or the other unless
he acted quickly.

He had not engaged in such undignified combat in
many years, but in his youth, when his inheritance had
been at best dubiously remote, he had often been
forced into rough-and-tumble fights, and he called on
his memories of those days now. Locking his long legs
around Harold, he squeezed with all of his might, and
the more the Englishman struggled, the more pressure
he applied. Harold, who had been brought up in the art
of gentlemanly combat, knew nothing about wrestling
as it was practiced by the common man, and eventually
even his great strength began to ebb.

The pain was excruciating, every breath was an effort, and finally, in spite of his stubborn determination,
he felt his fingers open. The dagger clattered to the
stone floor, and suddenly the pain was gone. William
relaxed his hold, and as he scrambled to his feet he
picked up the weapon and hurled it into a far corner of
the great hall with exaggerated vehemence, so no one
could mistake his intent. Then, not pausing to catch
his breath, the Duke snatched a brandy cup from the
table.

"To the King of England!" he said hoarsely, and
drank.

Harold, who stood slowly, looked bewildered, but as he gazed at his host a sheepish grin spread slowly across his face.

William immediately called for another goblet, and when a servant started to bring it forward he took it from the man and himself handed it to Harold. "To the Duke of Normandy, long may he prosper!" the Earl cried, recovering his equilibrium and at least some part of his dignity.

The cheers of Normans and Englishmen echoed and re-echoed against the stones of the great hall, and William threw an arm around the shoulder of his distinguished guest. "I must have my armorer make you a real dagger," he said. "Maybe you'd enjoy having one like mine, with two blades."

"Thanks very much, but I'd rather you taught me that leg grip." Harold smiled ruefully, but brightened when a servant refilled his cup.

When he drank, everyone else followed his example; the guests simultaneously made the discovery that the evening's exertions had made them thirsty. It appeared as though a long night was ahead, and as the ladies made ready to withdraw, the major-domo sent to the cellars for more brandy. However, Harold had the good sense not to prolong the occasion and risk a new flare-up, for he knew that both his followers and William's, having already been aroused, would respond to the slightest spark. And so he quickly finished his second cup, announced that the day's journey had made him sleepy, and after a graceful speech of thanks to the Duchess for a delicious meal he went off to bed.

His retainers took his hint and followed within a few minutes, leaving the Normans alone in the great hall. The footsteps of the last of the Englishmen could still be heard on the stairs when the barons began to damn the guests, but William, shaking his head in mock sorrow at their folly, silenced them. "My lords," he said, "your shortsightedness amazes me. When you objected to toasting the King first, you were stupid. Why? Because, after Edward the Confessor goes to his Maker, the King of England and the Duke of Normandy will be one and the same person, that's why."

The barons rarely tried to anticipate their Duke's moves, having learned early in his reign that he was unpredictable and that he set his own patterns rather than follow those laid down by others before him. But even the barons were surprised at the friendship that developed between William and Harold of England. Fitz Osbern, who knew his master better than did the other nobles, propounded the theory that there was a natural affinity between these two great men, and he seemed to be right. William and Harold were cut from the same cloth: they made decisions immediately where lesser beings hesitated; they were seemingly careless of their personal safety when out hunting together, repeatedly risking their lives in sending their horses over obstacles or plunging through treacherous bogs. Most sane men were endowed with a natural sense of caution, but William and his guest ignored every rule yet emerged unscathed from trials of daring and endurance that would have broken the bones and exhausted the bodies of ordinary mortals.

Strangely, neither William nor Harold was actually reckless in spite of the sense of competition that goaded them. When the Duke entered a thicket armed only with a short lance and emerged with the carcass of a wild boar, his every move was carefully calculated. And when Harold successfully attacked a timber wolf with a long knife, he knew precisely what he was doing. These two had supreme self-confidence in their own judgments: they knew themselves and their capabilities, and they acted accordingly. This, perhaps, was the secret of their achievements and the source of their courage, or so Fitz Osbern argued.

Effect was more important than cause, however, and the Norman nobles were elated when William proposed that an afternoon be devoted to knightly trials of strength and Harold instantly accepted the challenge. Here at last was a clear-cut opportunity for the Duke to prove that his prowess was greater than that of the foreigner, and every lord made it his business to be present as a spectator.

The weather was perfect for the little tournament: the sun was hidden behind deep clouds and so would not shine on the armor of those taking part in the jousts, and while the day was warm, a cool breeze blew from the north, to the infinite relief of those who would be encased in armor. The games opened when three of Harold's thegns engaged in a spear-throwing contest with three Norman commoners, sergeants of the Duke's household guard, and while this mildly diverting spectacle was in progress and spear after spear thudded into a wooden target, the audience filtered up to the battlements overlooking the rough green of the castle.

The ladies and gentlemen were in high spirits, having dined on a variety of roasted meats which they had washed down with strong wine, and there was a holiday mood in the air as they good-naturedly jostled each other for places of vantage behind the stone wall. Among the last to arrive was the Duchess, who was conspicuous in a gown and veil of light gray silk. A servant brought her a high chair, and as she sat several of the nobles and their wives started toward her, hoping to watch the tournament at her side. But they fell back as an unexpected figure appeared on the battlements and joined her. Abbé Lanfranc seldom wasted his time on frivolous pursuits and he was known to disapprove of jousting matches, which in a sermon he had once called a barbarian practice. And so there was immediate speculation as to the reasons for his presence, and although many guesses were ventured, no one hit upon the truth. Lanfranc, like everyone else, was eager to watch two invincible giants pit their skill, their valor, and their strength against each other.

The spear-throwing contest ended, and the Seneschal, after studying the results, pronounced the visitors the winners. There was a polite smattering of applause, then interest in the proceedings became somewhat greater as Gerbod and Wulfnoth, each lightly armored and each carrying a padded lance, rode out into the field mounted on geldings. Neither boy had yet been awarded the spurs of knighthood, and although Harold's brother was a little older than William's stepson, they were about the same height, and were therefore considered to be fairly matched.

The Seneschal dropped the gage of battle, and the boys charged toward each other, their enthusiasm for combat compensating in part for their lack of experience. Matilda bit her lower lip and closed her eyes; then the crowd roared with laughter and she opened them again and saw that Gerbod was at the north end of the rough green and Wulfnoth was at the south. Each had missed in his attempt to strike a blow.

They charged again, and this time Wulfnoth's lance scraped against Gerbod's shoulder but did no damage. On the third try Gerbod touched the young Englishman's helmet and the crowd, making no attempt to hide its partisanship, shouted its approval. When two knights entered the lists, it was customary for them to fight until one or the other was sent sprawling, but it had been prearranged that the boys were to be given no more than four attempts, so each was determined to emerge the victor in the final charge. They cantered toward each other at full tilt, shouting disparagements at the tops of their young voices; in their exuberance they forgot that knights were required to maintain silence.

The geldings approached each other and the viewers on the battlements pressed forward. As the horses drew parallel the riders thrust their lances at each other; Wulfnoth missed his target, but to the crowd's delight Gerbod landed a solid blow and unseated his opponent. A great cheer went up, but an instant later it changed to a groan, for Gerbod had overreached himself, lost his balance, and toppled to the ground too. Although he was technically the victor, he had disqualified himself. Fitz Osbern, grinning broadly, carried the traditional silver cup of mead onto the field; the boys picked themselves up off the ground, clasped hands, and quickly drank the cup. Then, laughing together, they left the green, and more than one observer noted that their friendship seemed as firm as that of their distinguished older relatives.

The audience's mirth subsided when Lord Ednoth, the ranking noble among Harold's retainers, rode out on a bay stallion and was followed by Hugh de Grantmesnil on a similar mount. Both carried long, padded lances, both were dressed in full armor, and from the moment they saluted each other it was evident that two veteran warriors had entered the lists. When the Seneschal's gage fell, they attacked each other crisply, and their cool savagery aroused the spectators to a frenzy of excitement. Both riders pounded tirelessly up and down the field, thrusting relentlessly at each other with practiced skill, and the crowd on the battlements completely forgot its dignity. Only Matilda and Lanfranc remained silent; the Duchess averted her gaze, still unable after all these years to find any pleasure in primitive Norman sport, and the Abbé, his eyes sad, smiled a trifle wistfully as he watched the fight.

The battle seemed endless, but at last Ednoth unseated his rival with a particularly vicious thrust. Hugh de Grantmesnil was stunned and lay on the ground unmoving until his churls rushed out into the field and helped him to his feet. And the crowd, which had been very silent, suddenly remembered its breeding and cheered the winner.

After the cup of mead had been drunk and the two knights had withdrawn, a tremor of excitement ran through the throng. Matilda, her face drained of all color, looked anxiously at Lanfranc beside her, and he touched her hand to soothe her. She had insisted, both to William and to herself, that he was superior to Harold, but now that the moment of actual trial was at hand, her confidence vanished in a panic of doubt. She, no less than William, recognized in Harold a man of extraordinary talents and strength, and she dreaded the consequences if he should emerge as the victor on the rough green today.

It was William's proud boast that no man had ever vanquished him in combat, either real or simulated, and Matilda knew that far more was at stake today than the wreath of oak leaves that was awarded to the winner of a jousting match. If William should be defeated the blow would be too great for him to bear, Matilda thought, and in that event he would surely return to his original plan and have Harold put to death. As she had long ago learned, he lost his perspective when his masculine conceit was in jeopardy, and she could only pray now that his self-esteem would not be damaged.

Had she been given a voice in the matter, this trial would never have taken place, but it had been arranged without her knowledge, and she was helpless to intervene.

The first on the field was Harold, and although none but his own little band bore him any love, he made such a splendid appearance that the Normans could not refrain from applauding him warmly. He was dressed in full armor but was bareheaded; he carried his dome-shaped helmet on his lap and held it fast with his strange little English shield. And in his right hand he carried his terrible battle-ax, its cutting edge padded. He was riding a huge white stallion from his host's stables, and the beast, accustomed to William, responded magnificently to Harold's firm touch too.

The Earl moved at a stately pace across the field, approached the battlements, and raised his battle-ax in salute to Matilda, who forced a smile to her lips as she bowed to him. He did not know that if he won today, he would probably die, and she could not tell him. A wild shout from the spectators startled her, and she looked up to see William ride out onto the rough green, and at the sight of him her confidence returned; he was surely a figure to inspire such confidence.

His conical helmet, complete with long nose-guard, was already in place, and his body was encased in a knee-length, belted tunic of chain mail, the flexible armor that looked like scales and caused the Normans to be known as "fishmen." In his left hand he carried his shoulder-high kite-shaped shield of iron as easily as though it were a toy, and in his right was his mighty double-edged sword, its blades carefully wrapped in strips of cotton bound in linen. His black stallion slowly circled the field, and William finally drew to a halt beneath the battlement and raised his sword to Matilda.

Her part in the ritual was now expected: she was to drop him a token that he could carry, and she removed her wimple, or veil, from her head. Then, on sudden impulse, she kissed it before letting it fall, and the crowd boomed its approval. William caught the fluttering square of silk on his sword and tucked it into his wide belt. He turned slightly in his high-pommeled saddle and grinned at Harold, who smiled at him in return. And Matilda felt a sudden stab of jealousy as she realized there was a side to William she had never known and could never know. He and the Englishman were enjoying a rapport from which she was eternally excluded. There was something in the character of men that eluded her, and she could not define it; she knew only that this moment before they joined in combat was painful to her but that they found keen pleasure in it.

Harold donned his helmet, he and William saluted each other gravely and silently, and they rode off to opposite ends of the field. Fitz Osbern appeared at the edge of the green carrying a long lance to which was affixed a multicolored streamer of silk. He lifted it high over his head and a hush fell over the assemblage, then he thrust it toward the ground and the spectators sighed. The trial by combat had begun.

The two stallions walked quietly toward each other as the great warriors took each other's measure. Unlike their juniors neither William nor Harold favored a blind, headlong charge, and, like the seasoned captains they were, each sought to find a chink in his opponent's defense. Harold held his small, round shield at arm's length, and its value immediately became apparent to the soldiers on the battlement: although it offered less protection than the Norman shield, it could be used as an offensive weapon, and its sharp center spike made it dangerous.

Harold's battle-ax was raised high in the air as he rode, but William carried his sword across his pommel, and to anyone unfamiliar with his style he looked as though he had no intention of fighting. But Harold was not fooled; he was prepared as the mounts closed in on each other, and when William suddenly lashed out with the great blade he caught the blow neatly on his shield and at almost the same instant struck with his battle-ax. It landed with shattering force on the chain mail covering William's shoulder, but the Duke did not flinch and there was no change in his expression.

Now, before the Englishman could shift his position, was the time for a deft counterstroke, and the sword cut through the air and landed with such impact against Harold's armor that the sound reverberated against the heavy stone walls of the castle. The Earl was thrown off balance, but he was a superb horseman and not only kept his seat but parried with his shield, thrusting it at William while he took a better grip on his battle-ax.

They circled each other slowly, raining blow after blow on each other, taking the brunt of the attack on their shields when they could, quietly absorbing the punishment with their metal-clad bodies when they could not. Smaller men, weaker men would have wilted, and even the barons in the audience, all of whom had suffered mercilessly in real campaigns and in trials of strength, wondered how these incredible warriors found the stamina to continue. Shield crashed against shield as they closed in, and William's sword darted in and out with such speed that the spectators had difficulty in following its movements. To their astonishment Harold used his great battle-ax as though it were a sword, despite its great weight, and he, too, displayed the nimble dexterity of a magnificent artist.

Twice William was in danger of being thrown to the

ground, and three times Harold was almost unseated, but both men recovered again and again, then returned to the attack with renewed vigor. Roger Mont Gomeri, who had been a professional soldier since the age of seventeen, was heard to mutter that he had never witnessed so extraordinary a performance, and Richard Fitz Warren, who had killed more than a score of enemies in combat, kept blinking, unable to believe that he was actually witnessing the scene that was taking place.

It was significant to the onlookers that neither the Duke nor the Earl lost his temper; each maneuvered coolly, attacking when he could, defending himself when necessary. The Norman feinted and the Englishman blocked him, the Englishman tried to trick his opponent into shifting his guard, but the Norman anticipated him. Rarely had two fighting men been so well matched, and as the duel wore on it became clear to both as well as to their audience that it no longer mattered which of them won—the accidental breaking of a shield strap or a rock under a horse's hoof could settle the affair one way or the other, and all that counted was that they were equal in ability, in cunning, and in courage.

Eventually the horses grew tired of the noise and the incessant jarring, and when they showed signs of restlessness their masters drew apart for a moment. The day's surprises were not over, and the spectacle that followed was one that would never be forgotten by those who saw it. William suddenly removed his helmet, dropped it to the ground along with his sword and shield, and dismounted. A film of perspiration covered his face, but he was grinning broadly as he walked stiffly toward the Earl. Harold uttered a loud cry of joy, threw down his battle-ax and shield, and then removed his own helmet.

As his was the more cumbersome armor, he could not dismount without help, but when several of his retainers started out onto the rough green, William waved them away and himself gave Harold a hand. They embraced, then pounded each other happily on the shoulders, and the crowd saw that both were laughing. It was plain that they had enjoyed the trial even more than had their audience, and now, on William's initiative, they were content to let the battle end in a draw.

Matilda, to whom every second of the fight had been an agony of fear and suspense, turned indignantly to Lanfranc, her eyes flashing. "Look at them!" she said bitterly. "One or the other of them will become the most powerful ruler in the world, yet they risked their lives in a senseless demonstration and now they're hugging each other like blood brothers. Do you wonder why I despair, Father Lanfranc? William hasn't once stopped to consider all that's been at stake in this absurd mummery, and now he's behaving even more like a thoughtless, impulsive little boy! I'd expect such conduct from his sons, but when the Duke of Normandy acts like a child, it's intolerable."

The Abbé regarded her at length before replying. "Apparently it has never occurred to you, Matilda," he said tartly, "that it would be good for William and good for Normandy if you gave your husband some of the compassionate understanding that you save for your sons. It would even be good for your marriage."

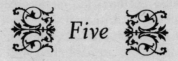

Five

MATILDA'S SANCTUARY was her bower, a large, un-usually light chamber on the third floor of the castle, located between the guest rooms and the children's quarters. When she had first come to Rouen it had been William's armory, as it had been his father's before him, but she had noted its windows, which were much the largest in the building, and she had promptly convinced her husband that he needed more space for his trophies and weapons and had moved him elsewhere. No one had told her that the bower, which was located directly beneath the roof, was cold in winter and hot in summer, but, having made up her mind, she refused to change it and professed to be indifferent to the extremes of temperature there. Her ladies hated the chamber, however, as their disposi-tions if not their skins were more tender than Matilda's, and any girl who was chosen to join the Duchess for her midmorning sewing hour considered herself unlucky.

Lady Charlotte, the eldest daughter of Roger and Mabel Mont Gomeri, who had been attached to the suite of Her Grace for a year, was certain that the fates no longer smiled on her, for this was the third time in a week that she had been selected as Matilda's compan-ion, and, even worse, she had been forced to reject an offer from the charming Baron Robert of Mortain to walk with him in the garden. She therefore concen-trated on her own thoughts and paid scant attention to the Duchess's remarks as they worked together embroidering a new banquet cloth.

"The jousts yesterday are proof that I'm right about men," Matilda said, jabbing her needle through the thick linen. "They like to believe themselves to be thinking, rational beings, and they don't even know their attitude is a sham."

"Yes, Your Grace," Charlotte remarked absently.

"They substitute action for contemplation, and they can't understand that a wild charge on the back of a horse is far less effective than a careful plan that can often be achieved with a quiet word. Do you understand me, Charlotte?"

"Yes, ma'am. But all men aren't like that." Charlotte was positive that no one could be more reasonable than Robert of Mortain.

"They are, all of them." Matilda had rarely been more emphatic. "I know what you're thinking, but you're wrong. Husbands are the very worst. Once you've been wedded and bedded, a man simply won't bother to listen to your opinions."

Charlotte blushed and turned away in an attempt to hide her crimson checks. "My father always listens to my mother," she protested.

The Duchess smiled. "So he does, but Mabel is a very remarkable woman, you see." She refrained from adding that Roger could always be influenced by a pretty face and that his wife had the good fortune to be beautiful.

"She says the same thing about you, Your Grace."

"That's sweet of her. I don't know that I deserve the compliment, but I try to do my duty." Matilda sighed and glanced out the window, past the castle wall to the green fields beyond. "It isn't easy, just as it won't be for you when you marry. Men like to believe they must coddle us, but they're actually the ones who need to be humored. Unlike us they're impulsive, and they instinctively justify everything they do, especially their mistakes. Oh, how they justify! But you don't dare tell them they're wrong. If there's anything that drives them wild, it's a blow at their masculine invincibility. The only way they can be persuaded to do what's right—and to rectify their errors—is to flatter them until they think your ideas are their own." Someone stood in the rounded frame of the arch and Matilda looked up idly, then stopped speaking as she saw her husband.

Something, she felt sure, was amiss. William was always uncomfortable in the bower, claiming that the very atmosphere made him feel awkward, and came here no more than twice a year. And one look at his tense, glum face confirmed Matilda's guess. "Well, dear," she said cheerfully, "this is a surprise. I thought you had gone into Rouen to settle a shipowners' dispute of some sort."

"I'm leaving shortly." The Duke glanced first at his wife, then at her lady in waiting.

"You may leave us, Charlotte."

The girl, happy to escape, curtsied low and fled. Baron Robert might be riding to town with his half brother, but there would still be time for a brief stroll in the garden.

William walked into the room, and as he took in Matilda's appearance his sense of depression increased. She had no right to look so self-possessed and lovely when he was disturbed. As a rule it pleased him to think that his wife was attractive, but her dress of soft pink silk annoyed him. He decided that what bothered him was its extravagance; its wide neck was edged with knotted lace made of pure gold thread, and a band of the same gold lace was closely fitted around her waist. And even her hair was braided with gold thread. Although he had remonstrated with her many times, she could not or would not understand that the coffers of Normandy, unlike those of Flanders, did not overflow.

"It's all your fault," he said.

Matilda picked up her embroidery again and smiled blandly. "May I know what I've done?" she asked sweetly.

"It's Harold, of course. I like him." William stood with his feet wide apart and buckled his belt a notch tighter.

"You've made it evident that you like him, but I fail to see what that has to do with me." Matilda knew better than to point out his inconsistency to him, but she could not remain silent. "You've gone hunting with him practically every day since he's been here. I haven't. And it was you who arranged for the jousts yesterday."

"He fought well." There was genuine admiration in William's tone. "I'm proud of my barons. They're good warriors, every last one of them. But not even Fitz Osbern or Mont Gomeri could have stood up to him. Harold is a real man, Matilda, not a chess pawn."

"So I gathered. You both seemed quite pleased after battering each other almost senseless."

"I'm glad you understand, and my apologies for thinking you wouldn't. Now you see why I've got to return to my original plan."

Matilda, aghast, dropped her needlework and jumped to her feet, and at the moment she looked more like the Flemish girl who had defied William than a regal duchess. "You can't mean it!"

"Of course I mean it," he said peevishly. "I know men, I know human nature, and I know how soldiers react when they're subjected to pressures. Your little scheme would have been effective enough if we'd been dealing with an ordinary person. But Harold is a leader, a great leader, and he has more courage than anyone I've ever met, on the battlefield or off. He'd laugh at me if I asked him to swear fealty to me."

A sense of panic assailed Matilda, but she kept her voice calm. "You don't know that, and you won't until you try."

"Woman, please use what little intelligence the Lord gives to your sex! If I speak to him, he'll be forewarned. He'll talk to his retainers, and then look at the situation I'll face. I won't be able to kill him without doing away with all seventeen of his followers as well. Even you will admit that would be too much!" William's face hardened and he spoke with finality. "So that leaves me no choice. I'll have to arrange an accident. It will take place after he leaves, precisely as I planned it from the first."

Matilda did not remind him that his actual scheme had been crude; now was the moment to practice the advice she had given to Charlotte. "I must admit that most of your decisions are very wise and farseeing, dear," she murmured. "And if I've made a mistake I'm certainly anxious to atone for it. But I still don't know what I've done wrong."

"You persuaded me to adopt your scheme. If I'd gone ahead in my own way from the start, I'd never have become friendly with Harold. Now it's far more difficult to have him killed."

"Is it? Why?" She forgot to modulate her tone.

"I've just told you! Because he's my friend!" Her inability to grasp simple principles baffled William as much as it annoyed him.

"Do you mean to say," Matilda demanded, "that you would murder Harold in the name of friendship rather than ask him to become your vassal?"

"In the first place," he retorted loftily, "I object to your loose use of the word 'murder.' When the future of a nation is at stake, as it is in this matter, what I must do becomes politically expedient. Murder is a personal crime committed in passion, but I can't expect your feminine mind to grasp legal complexities. Any more than you can understand my second point. I've told you repeatedly that Harold has become my friend, yet you can't see there's a principle at stake."

"Would I recognize the principle?" Her voice was dangerously soft.

"No woman could. The honor of a man is involved here. And it happens to be my honor."

Matilda wanted to tell him that every word he uttered was rubbish, that honor was a concept men adopted or shed at their convenience. But again she remembered what she had said to Charlotte about male vanity, and she took a deep breath. "You can't expect me to know as much as you, dear." She paused until William reacted as she thought he would, then she spoke swiftly. "But I am certain of one thing. If I were to broach the subject to Earl Harold for you, if I were to suggest to him, very casually, that he might want to accept you as his liege lord——"

"Absolutely not!" William's firm baritone voice reverberated against the stone walls.

His wife continued to smile at him. "Why not? It seems very logical and sensible to me——"

"I don't care what seems reasonable to you and what doesn't!" William's limited store of patience was exhausted. "I forbid you to interfere in any way, do you understand?"

"I don't care for your unfortunate choice of words, I must say!"

"Whether you like it or not is irrelevant. You're not to meddle!" The Lion of Normandy stamped out of the bower, and every servant in the castle could judge his mood by the sound of his boots on the stairs.

Matilda continued to sit very quietly, and a stranger, looking at her, would have said she was reposed. Without quite knowing it she had acquired William's habit of appearing her calmest when she was seething. She might have been inclined to obey her husband's strict injunction had he not used the word "meddle," but she would have no respect for herself if she bowed cravenly to his command. Let him mistakenly consider her intellect inferior, if it pleased him, but she could not abide his imperious condescension, as though she were a menial. However, she wished neither revenge nor recognition, and she expected no apology. When they sat together on the throne of England, they would both know that her wisdom had brought them there; that would be balm enough for the insults she had been forced to endure.

She looked up to see Lady Charlotte hesitating in the entrance, and something tentative in the girl's attitude annoyed her. "Yes?" she asked sharply.

Charlotte, satisfied after an exchange of tender glances with Robert, was anxious to relate the details to her friends in the household. "I presume Your Grace will have no further need of me this morning?"

"You presume wrong." There was no change in Matilda's expression as she added, "Find Earl Harold and ask him if he'll be good enough to attend me."

"You'll receive him—here, Your Grace?" Charlotte was startled.

"Yes, of course."

"As you wish, ma'am." The girl's face was wooden. "I'll give Earl Harold your message."

"Wait!" the Duchess called sharply. "You'll do more than that. You'll accompany him, and you'll remain with us the entire time he's here!"

Matilda watched disapprovingly as the bewildered lady in waiting retreated. Until today she had always dismissed the gossip about Mabel Mont Gomeri as mere maliciousness, but now she was not so sure. The very idea of entertaining Harold alone shocked Matilda, and she could not help thinking that Charlotte might have inherited a set of flexible values from her mother. Obviously the girl would bear close observation in the future.

The immediate present, however, required complete concentration, and Matilda demurely covered her slippers of gold-embroidered silk with her skirts, then deliberately brought one thick braid of hair forward over her shoulder. Ordinarily she did not care too much for this style of hairdressing, in which the other braid was wound around her head like a coronet, but it had its uses, not the least of which was to remind a man that he was in the presence of a married woman. And Harold, judging by all that was said of him, needed to have his memory jogged.

It was common knowledge in the courts of Europe that he enjoyed a relationship of a dubious nature with a notorious creature, Edith Swan-Neck, the daughter of his principal butler, and it was Matilda's theory that a man who showed no respect for one woman felt none for any. Only recently she had heard that two young English earls, Edwin and Morcar, who were brothers, had tried to consolidate their positions by arranging a marriage between Harold and their sister, Aldyth. And Matilda had applauded the natural reluctance of Lady Aldyth to throw away her life.

Not that the Norman nobles didn't take mistresses;

Matilda knew better than that. But they were sufficiently sophisticated to conduct their affairs in the open, unlike the sanctimonious and barbaric English, who hid an inamorata under the transparent name of "handfast wife." And Harold was even worse than most of his countrymen, for it was rumored that the woman Edith had borne him several children.

Matilda began to regret the impulse that had led her to send for the Earl, and she realized that if William had been less dictatorial she would not have dared to take the initiative into her own hands. However, there was no way to rescind the invitation now, for footsteps sounded in the corridor and Harold stood in the door.

His hostess tried to smile at him, but she could not; although she believed herself to be broad-minded, the English style of dress was positively lewd. Over a plain white linen shirt the Earl wore a tunic of unbleached wool, and even though it was trimmed with a band of silver braid across his chest and another around the hem, even though the buckle of his wide leather belt was made of engraved gold and set with rubies, his thigh-length tunic was embarrassingly short by Norman standards. Matilda tried to excuse his appearance but could not, for the over-all effect he created was crude. Certainly no Norman gentleman would think of binding wool hose with crisscrossed leather thongs, nor would any truly highborn guest blatantly and unnecessarily advertise his peaceful intent by letting the leather sling strap for his dagger dangle empty from his belt.

Harold's manner, however, was as suave as that of a minister of state at the French court. He bowed, eyed the Duchess attentively, and murmured, "Every time I see you, Lady Matilda, I'm reminded again that your reputation as the loveliest woman in all Europe is deserved."

It was presumptuous of him to call her "Lady Matilda," as the privilege was reserved by custom to one's equals, and the Duchess did not place a mere Earl, no matter how powerful, in that category. His words had a salutary effect on her, however, and her sense of nervousness vanished. "You're very kind to pay me this visit, Lord Earl," she said sweetly. "You and I have had so little opportunity to know each other that I thought this morning would give us the perfect chance. Won't you sit down? And Charlotte," she added firmly to the lady in waiting, who was about to slip away, "you'll join us, I'm sure."

Harold took the adjacent chair and Charlotte sullenly threw himself onto a stool near the entrance. "We missed you at the banquet last night," the Earl said.

Matilda thought it would be impolitic to tell him that she abhorred the drinking bouts that invariably followed jousting matches. She had attended so many similar affairs, and the pattern was always the same: the men made spectacles of themselves as they fought their mock battles again, verbally, and she usually retired early with a headache caused by the raucous shouts and laughter of the warriors. "I was indisposed, I'm sorry to say, or I certainly would have joined you. I've been anxious to congratulate you on your brilliant exhibition. It thrilled me."

"I did my best, of course," he replied modestly, "but I don't mind telling you what I'd confide in no one else. Your husband inspired me, Lady Matilda. What a magnificent fighter he is!"

"He says the same of you." Matilda's feeling of dominion increased, and she sat back in her chair, allowing her long sleeves to droop almost to the floor.

"Well. I've never had a compliment that I treasure more highly." Harold's responses were polite but his blue eyes remained wary; he had been accurate when he had referred to Matilda's renown as a beauty, but he had said nothing about the reputation she had also acquired for cleverness, a name surpassed only by that of Archdeacon Hildebrand, the principal administrative assistant to the ailing Pope in Rome.

"The deeds you and William performed yesterday will never be forgotten, I know," Matilda said, trying to sound enthusiastic. "Why, I was told at breakfast this morning that the minstrels have already composed three different ballads about your jousting match." She paused for a catch of breath. "Together, you and William are positively invincible."

As she had known it would be, the conceit was pleasing to him. "Yes," he said quietly, "I'm sure that together we could destroy any enemy. But I'm afraid we'll never have the chance to prove it. Who would dare to incur the wrath of Harold of England and William of Normandy?"

"No one, to be sure," Matilda said, and smiled. She did not fail to note that the Earl had mentioned his own name before that of William. Her husband would have bristled had he heard the remark, but she simply became all the more determined to put this self-satisfied foreigner in his place.

"Someday William and I might travel together to the Holy Land," Harold continued. "Between us we'd drive every infidel there into the Sea of Galilee." He grinned boyishly, then spoiled the effect by stroking his mustache.

"Oh, there's no doubt you'd be successful," Matilda declared blandly. "But I doubt that you could interest William in a journey to the Holy Land. His father died there, you know, and he has no desire to see the place.

As a matter of fact, his fighting days are behind him, more or less."

"Really? How very fortunate." Harold raised his eyebrows slightly.

"No one wants to make war against him. No one would be so foolish. Philip of France is too weak, the German Emperor is too sensible, the Duke of Burgundy is too lazy." The Duchess's green eyes were alert beneath sleepy lids, and she pursued her point relentlessly. "And of course the bond that ties William to our dear cousin Edward of England is firm for all time."

Harold shifted in his chair and tried to look unconcerned. The conversation was veering into a channel he would have preferred to leave unexplored, but he didn't know how to silence this loquacious woman. It was a novel experience to discuss affairs of state with one of her sex, and Matilda was unquestionably unique, but he wished she was occupied with her own dreams and was paying no attention to her elders. So he contrived to look innocent and said, "Your land and mine will always be friendly. There's no reason they shouldn't, Lady Matilda."

"Exactly so!" she agreed, and her tone was so vibrant that Charlotte looked up for an instant. "And I can't tell you how happy I am to hear you say it, Lord Earl. You've given the lie to all those who have been trying to spread vicious rumors!"

He knew now that she was leading him somewhere for a specific purpose, and he tried to end the subject. "I learned long ago to ignore rumors," he said flatly. "If a man in my position listened to every whisper, he'd waste his substance."

"I'm inclined to agree with you—up to a point."

Matilda fingered her thick braid absently. "But poisoned talk can do a great deal of harm. I'll give you a perfect example, Lord Earl. You've undoubtedly heard a good many accounts of the last war that my husband was forced to fight against Philip of France. Do you know why that war was waged, and why William had to administer such a severe whipping to the French?"

"Well, I—no, I can't really say I'm familiar with the details." Harold thought that in spite of her great beauty she was bloodless; water as chilly as that which tumbled down the mountains into Northumbria's river Tweed flowed through her veins.

"It's a sad story, really," the Duchess said blandly. "We kept hearing rumors that King Philip was determined to crush William. Our common sense told us that the King of France was far too intelligent to embark on a stupid campaign, but every traveler from Paris brought us the same story, until finally William had no alternative but to act in his own defense. And so you see," she added slowly, emphasizing each word, "a man in your position can't be too careful, Lord Earl."

Consideration of the delicacy of his situation occupied Harold's mind to the exclusion of almost everything else, and had ever since he had been shipwrecked on the Norman coast. "I'm always careful," he said, trying to fence but not knowing what weapon this infernally adroit woman was using or where she would strike.

"I knew you were. After all, Lord Earl, you're a civilized man in every sense of the meaning." It was almost impossible for Matilda to conceal the rising note of triumph from her voice. "That's why I feel positive you'll want to do everything in your power to end these nasty rumors that you hate William and want to harm him."

Even an ordinary guest would have had to observe the amenities, and Harold was no ordinary guest. "Naturally I'll be glad to do anything in my power. If you'll be kind enough to tell me who my detractors are, I'll face them and——"

"Oh, they won't come out into the open. That sort never does." She pretended to ponder the problem at some length, then looked up at him, her green eyes innocent. "A public ceremony of some kind would certainly silence all of our enemies, wouldn't it? For example, you might swear an oath of allegiance to William."

"Yes, I might." Harold turned deathly pale, instantly aware of every nuance of her deadly suggestion. He had no illusions about the snare that had been set for him, and he realized there was no escape from it. The worst he had feared had now come to pass, but he was helpless and he hated the Normans with all of his strength and all of his weakness.

A single glance at his face was enough for Matilda to recognize the magnitude of her victory, and she knew that anything more she might say would be unnecessary and anticlimactic. "Such things are really beyond my ability to decide, of course," she declared brightly, dismissing the subject with a wave of her dainty hand. "After all, I am only a woman."

When William returned to the castle from Rouen, his wife was in their bedchamber, dressing for dinner, and he came straight to the room. The dust of the road was thick on his boots, but when a maidservant who was helping the Duchess approached him to wipe them off, he glared at her so fiercely that she backed away and fled into the corridor. The Duke rocked back and forth on his heels, but Matilda, who was slowly combing her long hair, seemed blithely unaware of his mood.

"Well," he said.

"Did you settle the dispute in town to your satisfaction, dear?" She began to twist three long strands into a braid.

"You disobeyed me, Matilda. You held a long conversation in your bower with Harold after I left today."

She could not hold back the laugh that bubbled up in her. "Don't tell me you've had people spying on me, William! Not after all these years!"

"Spying?" His rage became explosive. "It was hardly necessary to spy. At least six people told me about it by the time I crossed the drawbridge!"

"Oh? Then I suppose you know what was said." Matilda smiled to herself as she finished the braid.

"I'm not interested!" he shouted. "I distinctly ordered you not to meddle, but you defied me! You——"

"William dear, I'm sure you will be interested. Harold will swear allegiance as your vassal."

"——were told not to interfere, but——" He stared at her as though she had struck him. "What did you say?"

"You heard me, dear." Matilda approached him and took hold of his tunic sleeves. "Harold will do as we wish. You should have seen him when I hinted to him that it would make your friendship permanent. No, I more than hinted. I suggested. And I assure you that he wasn't concerned with any code of honor. Harold is a realist, William. He knows he has no choice, and I could see that he's been expecting something like this from the very first. So we've won."

"May I go straight from this earth to heaven without spending a single day in purgatory," said the Duke of Normandy, who rarely thought about his soul and never concerned himself with theological questions regarding the Hereafter.

"Your mistake, darling, was to think of him as being as noble and sensitive as you are," Matilda said soothingly, placing her head against his chest. "There's no one like you anywhere, but you judged Harold by the standards you apply to yourself, simply because he's something of a leader and knows how to fight. But he lacks your qualities, just as every other man does."

William said nothing. He was torn in two directions at the same time, a feeling that was not new to him in his relations with Matilda. She was right about Harold and he knew it, even though he would not be satisfied until he spoke to the Earl himself. Yet he could not bring himself to compliment Matilda for her perspicacity or her deft handling of a situation that would have been too difficult for even his most trusted advisers. She deserved punishment rather than praise, for her disobedience of his direct order had been flagrant and deliberate. And even as he secretly rejoiced with her, he felt hopelessly frustrated.

He knew only one way out of this most husbandly of dilemmas, and, lifting her face, he kissed her with a passion that gave him an outlet for his turbulent emotions. It was a natural consequence that Their Graces of Normandy arrived late at the dinner table.

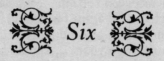 *Six*

NEITHER HOSTS NOR GUESTS found it easy to make conversation at dinner, and the atmosphere was distinctly strained. The English, who were sullen, showed little appetite, and while the Normans ate with their customary gusto, they had little to say except when they tried to compensate for their unnatural silence with short bursts of forced hilarity. Only the two principals in the drama seemed more or less at their ease; William ate his veal with relish, and Harold, who was seated on his right, consumed large quantities of roast crane, an English delicacy that had been prepared in his honor, and he behaved as though he had no cares.

The urbanity of the Duke and the Earl was remarkable, and they discussed such diverse subjects as the welding of armor, the collection of taxes from townsfolk, and the advisability of permitting anyone other than the clergy to learn reading and writing. The tenor of the small talk that flowed between William and Harold in no way indicated that the future of a kingdom was at stake; the strain was greater on the Englishman, of course, and even Matilda, who sat opposite him, had to admire his poise. As she watched him she could not help but wonder if William would have behaved as magnificently had he been trapped in a similar situation, and although she promptly squelched the thought as disloyal, she knew that her husband was not the only truly great man present.

At last the meal drew to an end after several rounds of

stiff and meaningless ceremonial toasts, and even those who dreaded the inevitable were somewhat relieved when William invited Harold to tour the castle with him. The issue that hung between them would surely be resolved by the time they rejoined the company.

The two giants mounted the stairs arm in arm, chatting companionably, and after a routine inspection of living quarters, in which neither was particularly interested, they spent more than an hour in the armory. There the question of the succession to the English throne was momentarily forgotten as they enthusiastically balanced and tested swords and maces, spears and knives and lances. William presented his guest with a new Norman shield, kite-shaped and made completely of iron, and while he admitted that it was cumbersome, he laughingly insisted that it was vastly superior to the English variety.

Then, as they started back down the stairs to the great hall, he suggested a visit to the cellars. "My steward looks after the wines," he said, "and frankly I wouldn't know one from another. But I thought you'd like to see my dungeons."

"I've heard quite a lot about them," Harold replied.

"Have you?" William was pleased. "I've spent considerable work on them, you know. If I do say so, I don't think you'll find a more modern prison anywhere."

Two servants who were stationed at the heavy oak door that led to the lower regions of the castle lighted torches, and the little group made its way to the cellars down a winding stone staircase. Harold commented politely on the architecture, as English houses, even those of the nobility, were built only above the ground. But his remarks were rather absent-minded, and his smile was forced when they were joined by William's chief jailer, an unshaven man who wore a coiled whip around his waist like a belt. The party wasted little time on the cells used for commoners or on the cramping chambers, tiny rooms in which a prisoner could not stand erect, for these rooms were like those to be found almost anywhere. And the stench of the inmates discouraged close inspection.

But William called a halt in a large chamber which had large chaining rings set in the walls on one side and a pair of stone whipping posts on the other. "This is one of my own innovations," he declared modestly. "Prisoners over there can watch others being punished. It's a very effective means of persuading the closemouthed to talk. Isn't that so, Bertrand?"

The jailer shook his head enthusiastically. "Like I always tell His Grace here, I never seen anything like it. They're anxious to talk after a little while. They'll say anything you want them to say!"

"I can have a set of plans drawn up for you, if you'd like," the Duke offered.

"Oh, I'll remember this," Harold said.

He was shown other special chambers, too, including a room with rings in the walls and the main torture hall, which was equipped with every scientific device from a body press to the latest turning-wheel rack. William lingered so long over each instrument that the servants had to light fresh torches, and it was some time before they came out into the corridor again. Finally they paused before a heavy iron door, and at the Duke's order his jailer threw it open.

"This," William said proudly, "is a cell that's completely different. It's for the highest nobility—no one else. Notice that it has a fresh pallet on the floor for sleeping purposes. And see how small and light the chains are. They were wrought by my own ironsmith. I happen to believe that a man of standing deserves better treatment than the peasantry."

"Very thoughtful of you," Harold muttered.

"Would you care to step inside and examine the fixtures more closely?"

"Oh, I can see perfectly from here."

The door was closed again and they started back up the corridor; the jailer was dismissed and they were about to return to the ground floor when William again halted. "There's one more room I want you to see. It isn't unusual in any sense, but as long as we're here we might as well make the tour complete." He led the way to a chamber lined with tables on which foot and hand screws of iron and wood were placed.

"The Scots use this sort of thing, I believe," Harold said, making conversation. "King Malcolm is very fond of instruments like these."

"You don't say." William stored away the information in his mind, then absently twirled the handle of a thumbscrew. "My wife tells me that you and she had a very pleasant little talk earlier today."

"Yes, very pleasant. She's charming."

"Nice of you to say so." William twisted the thumbscrew until it shut, then opened it again. "She says you'd like to pay me the compliment of swearing allegiance to me as your overlord." His voice was calm and even.

"Yes. I would." Harold matched his tone.

"I couldn't accept the gesture unless it were voluntary, of course. You know that. In my experience—and I'm sure you've found the same thing—an oath given grudgingly is no oath at all."

"There's no question in my mind," Harold said slowly, "about the value of the oath that I'll take."

They stared at each other steadily in the light of the flickering torches, and neither looked away. Each knew what was in the other's mind, and each made his own private evaluations. For a long moment there was no sound but the crackling of the burning rushes and the steady drip of water that had seeped through a wall of the dungeon somewhere. Finally William broke the silence. "Let's go upstairs, shall we? It's so damp down here that I think a cup of mead will do us both good."

So many Norman nobles came to Rouen to witness Earl Harold's oath-taking that the castle chapel proved to be too small for the purpose, and preparations were made to hold the ceremony in the great hall, the only chamber large enough to accommodate the multitude. The household staff worked feverishly for three days under the Duchess's supervision, and the results were startling: the austere and cavernous hall was transformed as if by necromancy into a place that was warm and almost intimate. Huge curtains of deep red silk were hung over the walls and were studded with sprays of white lilies and green fern, the rushes were swept out, and other cloths of dark green silk were spread over the floor. Red velvet covered the steps leading to the dais, and the Duke's chair, which in the minds of his followers was now virtually a throne, was freshly gilded.

Great pains were taken in the construction of the twin altars that would be used in the ceremony, and these were placed directly in front of the dais, at the base of the steps. Made of wood, they were boxlike structures which rested on flat, highly polished base stones. The stones and the sides of the altars were painted in red, yellow, and green, and had been made to look like Norman arches, and on the top of each was a miniature replica of a church with arched windows. Embroidered altar cloths of heavy white silk were draped down the front of each box, where Harold would stand, and the observant noted that the Duke himself devoted a surprising amount of attention to the making of the altars.

Only William and a few of his most privileged associates were present in the great hall at dawn on the day of the ceremony, and no one else was even aware of the surreptitious arrival of two monks from the monastery of St. Etienne, who carried linen-wrapped bundles which they handled reverently. Whatever their business, it was concluded in a few minutes and they departed; William returned to his bedchamber, where he made so much noise shaving and whistling tunelessly that he awakened Matilda, and the others who had been with him found their own ways of killing time.

At last all was in readiness, and the crowds began to gather. The first to arrive were the novices from nearby monasteries and convents, all in white. They took places beneath the high windows, a choirmaster stood before them and they began to sing; they were to chant until the actual ceremony itself began. The ladies of Normandy drifted in, some wearing dresses in soft shades of rich silk, others in embroidered wool gowns that swept the floor. Without exception their sleeves were graceful and trailing, some as long as the hems of their *bliauds*. The ladies took careful note of each other's attire, but no one else would pay much attention to them this morning, for the occasion was one in which the men would be all-important, so they remained inconspicuously in the background, near the wall opposite the windows.

There they were eventually joined by the Duchess Matilda, whose arrival created something of a stir. Only then did the ladies realize that her chair was not on the dais and that she, like they, would be a mere spectator. No one knew from her quiet smile and firm step that she was angry and humiliated, and not even her closest friends were able to guess that she had spent long, futile hours trying to persuade William to give her a more prominent post. It was ironic that she, the chief architect of the scheme that would blossom today, had to content herself with a role in which she would share none of the glory.

Nevertheless she looked regal and lovely in a flowing gown of heavy white silk, trimmed at the neck, down the entire front, and on the wide, sweeping sleeves with dark brown miniver. Flowing from her shoulders was an emerald-green cloak, which trailed the floor in back and was also trimmed with miniver. A circlet of gold and emeralds rested on her brow, and encircling her throat was a magnificent necklace of emeralds, the most expensive gift William had ever given her. He had presented it to her after she had given birth to Robert, and it was her most prized possession.

The ladies curtsied to her, and she nodded graciously to them, then serenely moved to the center of the group and stood in the front row. There was some genteel scuffling as several of the more pushing gentlewomen tried to inch near to her, but she pretended to be unaware of their maneuvers. Nothing, her attitude indicated, must be allowed to spoil the solemnity of the occasion, and the ladies promptly took their cue from her. Even some of the maidens who had been whispering animatedly to each other fell silent.

The lesser nobles marched into the great hall in a body, swords at their sides, knee-length cloaks in rich but sober blues, greens and browns flowing from their shoulders. Next came the counts, their cloaks fur-trimmed, each wearing on the forefinger on his left hand the carved ruby ring that was the symbol of his rank. Earl Harold's entourage crept into the chamber almost unnoticed, and their short tunics of blue-gray seemed less outlandish today. Perhaps their wrapped hose, which blended with the rest of their attire instead of contrasting garishly with it, was responsible, or possibly the Normans were by now accustomed to seeing them.

Only Harold's brother, Wulfnoth, stood out: the color was high in his face, his eyes were unnaturally bright, and anyone who cared to study him carefully could see that he had been weeping. But he carried himself with the dignity of a man, the sword at his side was the property of his brother and he kept his hand on its hilt as a subtle reminder to his hosts that more than a ceremony might be required to settle the problems that vexed Normandy and England.

The formation of the onlookers created a center aisle down the length of the great hall, and the spirit of the occasion was such that it rather resembled a nave. This feeling was heightened when the chant of the novices grew louder and the clergy arrived. Led by Archdeacon Gilbert of Lisieux, the priests moved in stately procession, and the guests bowed their heads. Archdeacon Gilbert, in his private life a mild and inoffensive man, looked nothing short of magnificent, and was the most splendidly arrayed person in the assemblage. His miter was of white silk, edged and crossed with orphreys, or braids, of red wool and silver thread, and as befitted his exalted rank of cardinal, his cassock, his dalmatic, or outer tunic, and his cope were red. In his hand he carried a crozier, a pastoral staff as tall as he, of carved wood with a cross on the top.

Directly behind the Archdeacon came three bishops, all in black silk cassocks and white linen albs and surplices, or tunics, lace-trimmed and embroidered. In the center of the trio was Bishop Odo of Bayeux, Duke William's half brother, whose small black eyes took in every detail of the gathering. Odo was young, but his face was heavy and he was already developing a paunch; no one in the duchy, it was said, was his match as a glutton.

Next came Abbé Lanfranc, who as an auxiliary bishop was entitled to wear robes other than his simple black habit, but no earthly event was sufficiently important to him to cause him to change into more ornamental attire, and only a small silver cross that hung by a slender chain from his neck relieved the solid black of his costume.

Bringing up the rear were representative Norman priests from every part of the country, all in black silk cassocks, black copes, and ankle-length white linen albs, and all bareheaded. The Archdeacon offered a short prayer before each altar and then moved to the foot of the dais, where he was joined by Abbé Lanfranc. Odo's face mirrored his annoyance over the preference being shown to someone of lesser rank than he, but there was nothing he could do to alter the arrangements. Not even a bishop who was related to the Duke by blood dared to object to any honors William cared to bestow.

The great barons were the next to arrive, and everyone was impressed by their solemnity; everyone felt the majesty of the enormous power they wielded. In the forefront was the Seneschal, wearing his heavy gold chain of office and carrying a gold mace. Directly behind him, keeping step with each other, were William's small sons, Robert and William, then came the warrior barons, each holding a naked ceremonial sword in his right hand. The boots of these mighty men trampled the cloth of green silk on the floor, but they did not know it, and if they had they would not have cared. Each was a law unto himself in his own domain; pride and arrogance, intelligence and strength and cunning were written on every face. The barons were the masters of the earth, and well they knew it.

But even they bowed their heads low as their liege lord made his entrance from the dining hall, attended only by his stepson, Gerbod. William mounted the dais slowly, sat, and arranged his ducal robes; he had refused Matilda's pleas to have new clothes designed for the occasion, and wore the same scarlet silk cloak and cloth-of-gold tunic he always donned for state occasions. On his head was his plain crown of iron, and as always he shunned any sword that he could not actually use. The double-edged blade that Gerbod carefully laid across the arms of his chair was familiar to his nobles, for they had seen him carry it in battle.

William looked slowly around the hall at his subjects, and there was no joy in his face. He appeared older than a man just past his mid-thirties, and to those who stood nearest to him he seemed tired. His eyes rested for an instant on his wife, then he smiled faintly at Lanfranc, but he singled out no one else in the crowd. Finally he raised his left hand to silence the novices, and there were those who detected a curious reluctance in the gesture. The very idea was absurd, of course; no one could imagine any valid reason why he would not be pleased to see the ceremony performed.

"Who stands sponsor to the candidate?" he asked, not bothering with preliminary ritual.

The Seneschal stepped forward out of the ranks of the barons and threw back his fur-trimmed cloth-of-silver cloak. "I do, Lord Duke," he declared.

"Baron William Fitz Osbern, Seneschal of Normandy, presents a candidate for Norman knighthood," William said, hurrying through the familiar formula. "If any man deems the candidate unworthy, let him stand forward."

No one moved.

"Seneschal, you may present your candidate."

Fitz Osbern walked slowly down the aisle to the entrance, turned, and came back. Ten paces behind him walked Harold, currently Earl of Wessex, Earl of East Anglia, Earl of Gloucester, and Earl of Hereford, the first prince of England. On his head was a narrow coronet of beaten gold and he carried himself with the dignity of a king. Even his clothes emphasized his wealth and majesty: his knee-length white linen tunic was heavily embroidered in gold thread and jewels, his gray-blue mantle was clasped over one shoulder with a large sapphire and his black stockings were cross-gartered with pure gold braid. Naturally he carried no arms.

He was pale but composed, and his blue eyes revealed no emotion whatsoever as he walked very slowly down the aisle. He turned first left, then right, and he studied the faces of the Norman nobles as though trying to engrave them in his memory. And only when he saw his young brother did the lines of his mouth soften for a moment. It was strange that at no time did his gaze rest on William, and the Duke did not look at him, either, but seemed to be peering at a spot directly above his head.

The throng was very quiet as Harold reached a point between the two altars, and when he halted there someone sighed. William, who had apparently been lost in thought, roused himself. "Seneschal, who is your candidate?" His voice was husky.

"Harold." The one word sufficed, and Fitz Osbern resumed his place in the line of barons.

Archdeacon Gilbert took a single step forward, and at his direction the Earl placed one hand on either altar, and his hands, unlike those of lesser men, were steady. The Archdeacon intoned the brief oath, first in Latin, then in French, and finally, as a special concession to the knight-to-be, in English. And Harold repeated the words in each language; like William's, his voice was slightly husky.

"I, Harold, do swear my allegiance unto death to William the Norman. From this time forth and evermore so long as I live I do freely declare myself his vassal. And my vassals, through me, shall be his vassals. I do take this oath freely, and may my right arm wither if I do break it."

The novices began a new chant, and Harold's hands fell to his sides. He moved slowly toward the dais, and at the base of the steps he paused, removed his coronet, and handed it to the Archdeacon. Then bareheaded, he mounted to the top step, knelt at William's feet and placed his hands palms upward in a gesture of submission between the Duke's. Softly now, almost inaudibly, he repeated the oath.

William raised the sword; it trembled slightly as he touched the Earl with it, first on the right shoulder, then on the left. "I, William the Norman, do accept your pledge of fealty." Not many in the assemblage could hear their liege's voice. "And I do swear to you that I will protect you as my vassal. Rise, Knight Harold."

The Earl stood and moved to William's right. Both men seemed to be relieved that the oath-taking was completed. Then the Duke, in a typically impulsive gesture, rose and handed the sword to Harold, hilt forward. The Englishman grasped it, and for a breathless instant it appeared as though he would strike William down with it, but the moment passed when Archdeacon Gilbert moved to the nearer altar and celebrated Mass.

At its conclusion the entire gathering joined in the singing of a *Te Deum*, and at that juncture the ceremony, had it followed normal procedure, would have been finished. But, to the surprise of all but the handful who had been privy to the secret, William moved down from the dais to the altars and beckoned to Harold to join him there. They stood side by side for a moment, then William reached out and with his own hands whisked away the altar cloths. The crowd craned and shuffled in an effort to get a better view as the Duke pointed slowly at the altars, and a fortunate few saw that the boxes were hollow and that in them were a number of small, open caskets of gold and silver.

"Look well, Harold," William said in a loud, deep voice. "Look well and see that you have sworn your oath on the sacred bones of saints!"

A low murmur traveled through the assemblage, and Harold looked stricken, as well he might. Of all the hundreds gathered in the great hall, only William and Matilda, together with Lanfranc and a few of the priests, were not superstitious. To all of the others, Harold among them, an oath taken on saints bones were inviolable, and anyone rash enough to break such a vow would bring swift, certain punishment down on his head.

William, who had been opposed to the ceremony from the start, was taking no unnecessary chances. He had often taken to the field against men who had previously sworn fealty to him, and his own sense of honor had permitted him to make war against Philip of France only because he had never gone through the formal motions of swearing that he was the King's vassal. Hence he knew from long and bitter personal experience that a man was likely to break his word when it conflicted with his own best interests. No one in his right mind would turn from an oath he had taken on the bones of saints, however, and, judging from

Harold's reaction, William's strategy had been a brilliant one.

The Earl ran his hand inside the collar of his tunic as though it choked him, his eyes became glassy, and he shifted his stance, moving his feet wide apart so he would not stagger and fall. Several members of his entourage hurried forward to help support him, but he recovered in time to wave them away, thus salvaging his own dignity and that of the ceremony. Archdeacon Gilbert, himself superstitious, felt sympathetic toward the Englishman and clasped him by the shoulder after returning his coronet to him. Harold showed his true mettle as he placed it back on his head, for he quickly mastered his emotions and his hands were once more steady and his face impassive.

The crowd became quiet again, not knowing what to expect. But Harold disappointed his audience by making no response to William's revelation, the Duke returned to his dais and everyone knelt for the Archdeacon's blessing. The ceremony was at an end, and all but the highest-ranking nobility filed out to the green, where they would be served cold roast pork, mutton stew, mulled ale, and other light refreshments. The barons and their wives, along with a few favored counts and the clerical leaders remained in the great hall, of course, and everyone followed custom by offering congratulations to Harold, who accepted the good wishes with no outward display of hostility or rancor.

Matilda, who had known nothing of the placing of the saints' bones in the altars, wanted to tell her husband how much she admired him, but she had no opportunity to speak to him privately, as several ladies hovered near her and William, who had descended from his dais, was deep in conversation with some of his nobles. She looked around the hall for Lanfranc, but he had quietly disappeared, so she made her way to Harold. The crowd parted for her, and she held out her hand to the Englishman.

"My felicitations, Lord Earl."

"Thank you, Lady Matilda."

Deep hatred boiled beneath his cool façade, and Matilda recognized it instantly. She admired his control, but she was angry too, as she knew beyond any shadow of doubt that his continued use of the familiar salutation was intended as a deliberate insult. He was William's vassal now, and as such should address her as "Your Grace." He would regret his insolence, she promised herself: when she became Queen of England he would be the first of her subjects to kneel at her feet. But in the meantime she would not give him the satisfaction of realizing that his blow had struck a tender spot.

"It's good to know that you've become one of us and that you and we have an understanding."

He bowed slightly. "We've understood each other from the day of my arrival."

William, who had just made arrangements to dispatch a number of Norman agents to England with the news, joined them at this moment. He removed his iron crown, grinned in relief as he handed it to Gerbod, and then gripped Harold by the upper arm. "You and I must devise a simpler system for this sort of thing," he said. It was unnecessary to add that he was anticipating the day when English nobles by the score would swear fealty to him.

"I'll see what I can do." Harold's face gave no indication of his meaning.

To William victory was its own reward, and he took no pleasure in gloating over those whom he defeated, so he decided to change the subject. "I've just received a gift of a new pair of falcons, and I'd like to try them out." He was aware that Matilda resented his continuing informality to someone who had now become his vassal, but she knew nothing of men, and he ignored her. "Let's try them out and spend the day hunting tomorrow, shall we?"

"There's nothing I'd like better," Harold replied, his voice tinged with just the proper shade of regret. "But I think I should start to plan my return home. My brother Tostig has been acting as my deputy, but he has his own lands to worry about. And as you know—even better than I—no one can successfully govern even a small district from a distance."

Matilda was surprised at Harold's ungraciousness, but William had known that the unwilling guest would be anxious to leave Normandy as soon as possible. "It occurred to me that you'd be anxious to look after your affairs," he said, "so I've already given orders to have one of my own ships prepared for you."

"You're very kind, William, but there's no need to put you to all that trouble," Harold declared firmly. "I'm sure there are any number of ships I could rent or buy for my purposes."

The Duke, feeling uncertain of those purposes, was adamant; he had no intention of allowing Harold to proceed with his original plan and travel to Paris. "It's no trouble at all. And I wouldn't be that inhospitable. You shall sail in one of my own vessels, manned by my own crew."

"And," Matilda added, "I shall see to it that only those foods you like are placed on board for you. We'll spare no effort for your comfort."

"Or your safety," William said. "I suggest you sail from Bayeux, and then travel straight across the Channel. It's the most convenient route to Winchester. That is, I assume you intend to go to your own capital?"

"Yes, I do." Harold found it extraordinarily difficult to fence with a man who knew his mind as well as he knew it himself. There was sure to be a terrible storm raised by his nobles in England when they learned he had become William's vassal, and he would need to put his house in order in Winchester, the principal city of Wessex, before he dared proceed to London.

"I'll accompany you to Bayeux myself, then, and we'll ride with a full regiment of my best cavalry. I want to take no chances on any accidents befalling you on the road." William spoke with great sincerity, for he meant every word.

Harold looked first at the Duke, then at the Duchess; a good general always knew when to retreat. "Your kindness and your thoughtfulness overwhelm me." He, too, meant every word.

Matilda took her husband's arm, and the guests, realizing that the private conversation had come to an end, approached and joined in the talk. The Earl was loquacious, laughed and joked with anyone who spoke to him, and showed great aplomb as he ate various delicacies that were offered to him and drank a rare brandy distilled by the monks of a remote monastery in Montdidier. Matilda was charming and effervescent, and few present had ever seen her in such rare good humor. Her cheeks were slightly flushed, her eyes sparkled, and even beauties who were ten years her junior looked wan compared to her. It was natural that she should rejoice, for her scheme had been completely successful, down to the last detail, and she was positive that no obstacle now stood between William and the crown of England.

The atmosphere became increasingly gay as the spirits flowed freely, and only William himself failed to enjoy the festivities. He felt restless, and when Matilda upbraided him for being gloomy, he could not tell her why he was depressed. Actually he could not admit even to himself that he felt desperately sorry for Harold.

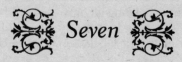 *Seven*

AUTUMN WAS the Norman air, the harvest had been reaped and the fruit gathered, and the world was peaceful and prosperous. Major problems were nonexistent, minor disputes were settled quickly and easily, and Duke William found himself bored. So his thoughts naturally turned to military defenses, and he spent most of his time at his permanent encampment some ten miles from Rouen Castle. Here he drilled his troops, conducted mock war exercises and justified his activity by explaining to his wife that unless he kept his men busy they would hire themselves out as mercenaries to foreign rulers and the best army in the world would be no more. Knowing nothing of such matters, she was in no position to protest.

One sunny afternoon William and his seneschal, who shared his dislike for indoor confinement, took a company of foot soldiers into the field and proceeded to conduct a series of experiments. It had long been the Duke's contention that his peasants' efforts were wasted in battle and that the technique of surrounding each mounted knight with a cordon of infantry served no useful purpose. Troops, he said, had value only when they could strike a concerted blow, and, to prove his point, he had armed the company with bows and arrows two weeks previous and had given orders that the men were to learn to use the weapons.

The soldiers had protested, as was to be expected; no one who had become expert in the use of a modern lance wanted to return to an ancient weapon that had

134

long ago been discarded as obsolete. But William, wise in the ways of military affairs, had let the men grumble, and gradually they had discovered that their bows were strong, their arrows firm, and that they could consequently achieve rather startling results. Even a beginner could fire an arrow much farther than he could throw the most perfectly balanced spear.

William and Fitz Osbern lined up the company in a double row at the edge of a wood, facing an open pasture, and at the far end of the area they erected the usual targets, crudely painted wooden likenesses of Saracens on horseback. The company's officers, young knights who had been awarded their spurs within the past year or two, retired discreetly into the background, having learned like their colleagues that it was best not to disturb the mighty duke and his powerful seneschal when they were at play.

"The formation is clumsy," William said. "Those in the first line block the men in the second."

"We've been through this before." In the field Fitz Osbern behaved like his master's equal. "An enemy would ride down a single line in a few moments. We've got to have two in order to maintain a steady rain of fire."

"Yes, I suppose you're right." William paced up and down while the troops waited patiently. "You say they've practiced the operation with the front rank on one knee?"

Fitz Osbern nodded, and the Duke approached the nearest soldier, took his bow and a sheaf of arrows from him, and then squinted at the distant targets. No other reigning ruler was on such familiar terms with his troops, but no one in the company was surprised; as William so often said, he never expected his men to perform any feat he could not accomplish himself. He dropped to his bare right knee, indifferent to thorns and brambles, fitted a shaft into the bowstring, and let fly. His arrow soared high over the wooden target and he was satisfied.

"We'll try it," he said, rising. "Obviously a unit will need many weeks of diligent practice before it can perfect its aim from such a position, but the idea had possibilities."

At Fitz Osbern's command the company fired a rain of arrows at the target, then another, and both commanders grinned. "A regiment of archers," the Seneschal said, "could turn aside a full squadron of knights."

"You may be right." William wanted to agree, but remained cautious. "It would depend on the armor of the cavalry and the striking power of the arrows. But make no mistake—I'm not discounting the effect on the riders. I think even my enthusiasm for battle would be dampened if I had to face a hail of arrows. Let's see what damage has been done to the targets."

He and Fitz Osbern strolled up the field, and as they studied the painted boards they discussed the advisability of increasing the weight of the arrows. They were so engrossed in their conversation that they failed to notice the approach of a cavalcade until the party of newcomers was almost upon them. Then William glanced up, and to his annoyance saw his wife, surrounded by an escort. He started toward her at once, glowering, while Fitz Osbern, after waving to the Duchess, tactfully walked back to the soldiers.

A military encampment was no place for a lady, and in all the years Matilda had been married to William she had visited him in the field no more than once or twice. Hence it surprised him that she had come here, and her costume actively annoyed him. She had not bothered to change into riding clothes, and the soldiers, William noted, were staring hard at her; although their boldness irritated him, he really could not blame them. It wasn't often they were privileged to see a beautiful woman in a violet silk dress with black lacing that ran around the neck and down the front of her bodice to her waist.

Matilda knew better than to appear before soldiers in a gown that might be suitable enough in the castle but that here, in the open, was nothing less than provocative. He intended to speak his mind to her as soon as he helped her dismount, but she looked once at his face, knew what he would say, and therefore gave him no chance.

"I hate to disturb you when you're busy, dear. But a messenger arrived from England, and I thought I'd best bring you the news myself. I didn't even take time to change my clothes, I was in such a rush." Matilda smoothed her skirt, adjusted her light cloak, and managed to present a charmingly incongruous picture.

"What's the news from England?" William demanded, forgetting everything else.

"There has been a split in the house of Godwine!"

"Oh?"

"Apparently Earl Tostig has been furious ever since Harold took the oath to you. They've been arguing for months, and Tostig turned Northumbria into a citadel. Harold's supporters urged him to put Tostig under arrest, and apparently that's what he intended to do, but Tostig slipped away, and——"

"What do you mean, he slipped away?" Women, William told himself, could never impart information concisely.

"He fled to Norway, and King Harold Hardrara has given him sanctuary. More than that. He's given Tostig a command in the royal army."

"Did the messenger tell you what disposal has been

made of Northumbria?" William could not help but think in terms of England as though it were already his.

"Yes, Harold has given it to one of his other brothers, Gyrth, I believe." Matilda spoke rapidly; she was concerned only with essentials. "In Norway——"

"Never mind Norway! You say Harold has made one of his other brothers Earl of Northumbria. What has King Edward been doing? Hasn't he had any voice in the partitioning of his country?"

Matilda resented his tone. "According to the messenger, your cousin no longer has any interest in earthly matters. He spends all his time in West Minster, just outside London, supervising the building of his new church and abbey."

"The sooner he's buried there, the better it will be for us," William said, so deep in thought that he was unaware of the brittle edge that had crept into her voice. "The better it will be for England, too. Naturally. The sons of Godwine take everything in sight, and it may be no easy matter to dispossess some of them so I can reassign the earldoms." Suddenly he laughed. "However, don't worry about such matters. I'll take care of them at the proper time. In the meanwhile you've brought good news, and I'm grateful to you." He had forgotten all about her inappropriate attire.

"Good news, William?"

"Certainly! We have one less son of old Godwine to vex us. Tostig will rot in Norway, where he can do us no harm, and whatever hold Harold still has is weakened. It's very bad for a family when brothers fight," he added smugly, flattered that he had been the cause of the dispute. "Now if you'll pardon me, Matilda, I have a great deal of work to do before sundown." He was about to say that unless she left he might be late for supper, which she hated, but that would only precipitate a quarrel. And he had no desire to ruffle her; the news was excellent and she had inconvenienced herself to bring it to him personally.

Relations between them had been unusually peaceful ever since Harold's departure for England, and there was no reason they should not continue to be calm. In fact he had been congratulating himself of late, for he believed that he had tamed her at last and that she was content to accept a role in the background, as befitted a woman. Her presence here in the field at this moment confirmed his view that she was only trying to be helpful, and he thought that not many wives would have gone to so much trouble. It would have been so easy for her to send the messenger to him and dismiss the whole matter from her mind, but she had dropped whatever she had been doing; he beamed at her. Perhaps he had been a trifle abrupt in saying he had to return to his military experiments, so he decided to amend his remark.

"You know, things are so quiet these days that you might think about going off to the house on the Isle of Jersey for a few weeks next month. We can go alone, and we'll take only a skeleton court with us. What do you say?"

A long-absent but familiar spark of contemptuous anger in her green eyes startled him. "I say you're the most shortsighted man I've ever known."

"See here, I've just invited you——"

"Oh, I appreciate your invitation, William. You know that. But we can't afford to go anywhere these days. I was afraid you'd miss the whole significance of Tostig's flight, and you have. That's why I had to bring you the news myself!"

"Precisely what have I missed?" he demanded self-righteously.

"You know Harold Hardrara's reputation. He's an unscrupulous scavenger, and he'd like nothing better than to take England for his own!"

William stared at her incredulously. "You don't suppose I'm afraid of a Norwegian, do you? Of course he'd like to be master of England! So would every other penniless adventurer in Europe who sees a rich peach dangling from a branch!" He paused for breath and pointed across the field at the idle archers. "There's my answer. England belongs to me, and Harold Hardrara knows it. Do you think he'd be fool enough to risk a war with my 'fishmen,' Matilda?"

"They aren't 'fishmen' now. They're only wearing plain wool tunics," she replied with typical feminine logic.

"Archers can't possibly wear armor," he said in growing irritation. "And that's beside the point!"

"It certainly is! The Norwegians haven't taken in Tostig because they like him, and he hasn't gone to them because he wanted to see their country. Why didn't he come to you for protection, do you suppose? Normally a man in his position would have come to you. Aren't you his future overlord?"

She could confuse Beelzebub, William thought; the reason Tostig had fought with Harold in the first place was because he was opposed to the idea of England being ruled by a Norman-born monarch, but it would be useless to explain mere facts to a woman who saw danger in every shadow. "Go home, Matilda," he said brusquely.

She was so aroused that she probably did not hear his command. "Tostig and the Norwegian have made a pact. Anyone with a little sense can see that. They intend to invade England together and claim it for themselves."

William laughed heartily and shook his head at her.

"You amaze me. Who is Tostig? A discredited young noble without a home, without more than a handful of personal retainers. Where is his army? You forget a few essentials, Matilda. King Edward is still alive, and anyone who attacked his realm would be branded as an outlaw by the Holy Father in Rome. And when Edward dies, Harold—who has immediate control of the country—is pledged to support me and my legitimate claim."

"But——"

"Stop daydreaming simply because you have nothing better to do! Neither the Norwegians nor anyone else will dare take to the field when there are 'fishmen' to oppose them. But the Norman army will disintegrate into nothing if I spend my days doing nothing but tell you their virtues. Go home—and start behaving like other women!"

"And what is that behavior?" she asked acidly.

"I don't know. Take care of your children. Look after your kitchen. And leave the world to me."

Before she could say another word, he picked her up, deposited her in her saddle, and slapped her mare on the rump. The horse started off at once, and the Duchess's entourage, who had been waiting for her some yards away, out of earshot, hurried to catch up with her. If William had bothered to look at Matilda's face as she cantered off, he would have seen that she was deeply hurt. Her gesture was wasted, her warning had gone unheeded, and she thought that she would never understand him. Instead of seeing the transparent plot of Tostig and the Norwegian for its true worth he preferred to brush it aside.

Matilda's father had grown rich by preparing carefully for every possible contingency and being ready to meet any emergency, and she had been trained in a careful, painstaking school. Therefore, she had little sympathy for a man who refused to see beyond the end of his own complacent nose, and she could not be patient with someone who would see no viewpoint other than his own. It was no wonder, then, that she felt distinctly out of sorts and uneasy as she rode back to Rouen Castle.

What she failed to realize, however, was that William's brand of realism was as searching as her own. He had no faith in anyone but himself and trusted only those of his followers who best served their interests by serving him. He had become undisputed master of a territory almost as large as France because he had relied on his sword rather than on treaties, because he had never swerved or faltered in his pursuit of a goal once he had established it in his mind.

It did not bother him that the Norwegians were plotting with Earl Harold's brother, for he feared neither Tostig nor Harold Hardrara, and he had met too many foes on the field of battle to be upset at the prospect of a possible war with the Norsemen. There was not a ruler in Europe who would not find a pretext to pounce on Normandy if her Duke showed a weakness, and it was William's inflexible policy to maintain maximum strength at all times. Knowing he was invincible, he could sleep peacefully at night and was willing to let the world connive against him all it pleased.

And he was unconcerned over Matilda's inability to grasp his fundamental principle of statecraft; he did not expect her to know what he was doing, and he put her, together with their children, into a separate compartment of his life that was untouched by the constant tug-of-war between nations. Thus he was disturbed by his wife's attitude only when she invaded his sphere. Once she left him, each cog slipped back into its familiar groove, and he felt comfortable again.

Now, as he rejoined his seneschal, Matilda was

temporarily forgotten, and he did not even see the apprehension on the faces of those who had witnessed his latest domestic upheaval. Fitz Osbern, who had steeled himself for an outburst of ducal temper, was startled by his master's smile, and didn't know what to expect. "It seems to me," William said as he concentrated on the archers, "that we might increase our battle efficiency still more if we use three ranks of bowmen. Let's see if we can't work it out."

The clouds of dust raised by Matilda and her escort was plainly visible, but he was too absorbed to notice it.

Satisfied and pleasantly tired after their efforts, William and Fitz Osbern parted company at the end of the day just outside the Rouen town wall. The Duke, with only three horsemen accompanying him, was about to start for home when he remembered that a locket he had ordered for Gundrada was probably finished, and rather than send one of his retainers for it, he decided on sudden impulse to visit the goldsmith himself. And so the gates, which were usually closed at sundown, were opened for him.

As he rode through the narrow streets his subjects waved and called greetings to him, and he answered them in their own dialect, which was more informal than the language of the nobility. Most rulers would have hesitated before appearing in front of their people without the protection of at least a company of armed guards, but William's popularity was so great that he could have gone anywhere in his capital alone and even unarmed. The townsfolk respected him as a great captain and obeyed him because he was their lawful lord, the son of Duke Robert the Devil, but they liked him because they did not forget that on his mother's side he was descended from stock as common and sturdy as their own.

William, too, always remembered that his maternal grandfather had been a tanner, and he was careful, both literally and figuratively, not to trample on his subjects. He rode his great stallion slowly through the cobbled streets, giving the people ample time to clear out of his path, and when someone shouted a remark that a pompous noble would have considered too personal, he accepted it in the friendly spirit in which he knew it to be intended. He realized that his strength was based on the loyalty of the commoners, and he never condescended to them, just as he never dealt with them unfairly. When William meted out punishment to a wrongdoer, his sentence always won popular approval, for he thought as his people did, hence his verdicts were similar to those they would have given. He understood the artisans of Normandy; and that, he reflected, was more than he could say about his wife.

The goldsmith was neither surprised nor awed to find the Duke at his door, and when he offered refreshments to his guest, William insisted on drinking a small cup of the inexpensive red wine of the countryside rather than the treasured vintage which otherwise would have been produced in his honor. As he so often said, he preferred the simple, cheap wines because he had tasted no others during the lean years of his adolescence and early manhood.

His business concluded, he rode through the darkened town to the principal gate, and it did not once occur either to him or to his small escort to loosen the knives in their belts. William had nothing to fear from the people of Rouen or of any other city or village in Normandy; his enemies dwelled in other places. The stallion was eager to go home, William gave the mount his head, and the party cantered across the fields in the direction of the castle. They came to a farm that was heavily cultivated, and William, as careful of produce as the lowliest of his subjects, carefully led the way back to the road rather than risk harming a peasant's crops. The darkness was accented by a strip of woods more than a mile in length that ran parallel to the road on the left side, and the Duke, relaxed in the saddle, wondered why trees, particularly oak and poplar, always looked taller at night.

He was still musing when a movement inside the forest caught his eye, and before he had a chance to call out a warning to the three guards who were following him, a number of men swarmed out into the road. "There he is!" one of them shouted in English. "That's the one!"

The villains knew their business, and, moving with almost military precision, five of them blocked the path behind William, cutting him off from his retainers. The Duke would have spurred his horse to greater speed, but two of the attackers stretched a rope across the road and William had to pull his stallion to a halt. The man who had called out and who seemed to be directing the operation stood at one side of the road with a sword in his right hand, and in his left he held a white object, which he tossed at the horse's head. The stallion reared, and William, who hadn't expected the maneuver and had been busily drawing his own sword, was tumbled to the ground.

The enemy nearest to him sprang at him, a long knife raised high, and William barely had time to roll over, draw up his knees and then drive his booted feet into the stomach of his foe as the villain tried to drive his blade home. The attacker fell back, screaming, and the Duke jumped to his feet, gripped his sword, and took stock of the situation.

His soldiers could take care of themselves, but for the

moment they were unable to give him any help. Two of
them had been unseated and were fighting on the
ground; the third was still in the saddle but obviously
would not remain there long, for he was being attacked
both from the left and the right. Eventually three
trained Norman guards would certainly be able to dispose of five opponents, but until then William realized
he would have his hands full.

The leader, his sword extended, was approaching
cautiously, closely followed by a heavy-set brute who
was armed with a mace longer than those usually seen
in Normandy. And the man William had kicked was
out of action, temporarily at least; he was doubled up
on the ground, groaning in agony, and the Duke paid
no further attention to him. His mind worked clearly
and methodically, and it was enough to know that his
first task was to dispose of two would-be murderers.

"By God's splendor!" he said, and with characteristic
fury he leaped forward, his sword describing a wide arc
as he launched a violent attack.

Although his foes outnumbered him, they respected
both his reputation and his blade, and they retreated
several paces when he hurled himself at them. The
churl who carried the mace was the more cowardly of
the pair, and he stepped back into the protecting screen
of trees, but he came forward again when his compan-
ion said something to him in a low, sharp voice. He
moved reluctantly and tried to circle around the Duke,
but William, grinning broadly, merely shifted his position slightly and the villain jumped back out of range of
the renowned ducal sword.

The leader was far more difficult to handle, and
when William came at him a second time he held his
ground, parried a thrust expertly, and then slashed
wickedly at his tall target. In all probability, William

realized, the man was a renegade noble and was therefore extremely dangerous. Landless knights could be
hired to further any nefarious scheme, and this devil
had undoubtedly been promised a great prize in return
for skewering the one man who had ever been able to
outwit and outmaneuver Earl Harold.

"Salute!" William said, "William of Normandy, son
of Robert the Devil."

The knight did not reply, and the Duke certainly
expected no answer but had identified himself in the
proper manner in order to let his foe know that he
realized he was facing no mere man-at-arms and would
fight accordingly.

However, the first task was to eliminate the churl, for
a well-directed blow with a mace could split a head in
two, and the Duke had to be rid of this lesser menace so
he could concentrate on his more skilled opponent.
But in tactics of individual combat, as in his planning
of a general battle strategy, he always found it advantageous to keep his enemy off balance by concealing his
intentions until the last possible instant. He had re-
duced cunning to a fine art so early in his career as a
warrior that it was unnecessary now for him to map out
the moves he would make; he knew precisely what he
would do even as he moved forward.

Feinting twice at the leader of the assassins, he handled his cumbersome, heavy sword as easily as if it were
a light practice blade of the sort used by young, inex-
perienced boys. No man could hold his position in the
face of so fierce an assault, and the knight took three
steps backward. As he did, and before he could recover,
William turned on the churl. The burly villain knew
he was cornered and fought valiantly, lashing out with
the mace, which he held in both hands. Most fighting
men would have side-stepped, for his weapon was so

stout that it could have bent or even broken a sword. However, William had always taken calculated risks that others had been unwilling to hazard, and although some of his critics called him rash, he firmly believed that boldness provided a higher margin of safety than caution. And he had to be bold now if he expected to survive.

So he continued to press forward, straight into the face of the churl's counterattack. The mace missed his shoulder by no more than a fraction of an inch, and one of the nails imbedded in the club ripped a small gash in the fabric of his tunic, but he did not pause. Every second was precious, as the swordsman behind him would pounce at any moment, so he knew he had to put the churl out of the fight with a single blow. Timing was all-important, and he waited until the man had completed his downward sweep with the mace and was about to raise the club again. Then, but not until then, he struck.

The point of his blade penetrated the villain's throat, a geyser of blood spurted out, and the churl toppled over backward onto the ground. William's accurately aimed thrust had killed him instantly.

But there was no opportunity to rejoice; one enemy was dead, but the other was very much alive, and as the Duke withdrew his blade from the body of the churl, he raised it just in time to twist around and meet the rush of the knight. Steel clashed against steel as William barely managed to deflect the man's blow, and only agile footwork saved him as the knight struck a second time, before he could set himself for the onslaught.

At last he was able to plant his feet wide apart, to balance himself and to give as good as he received. Both swords were too heavy to permit the duelists much freedom of action, and as neither could move far in any direction without laying himself open to his opponent, it was customary in combats of this sort for enemies to trade blows, to take the brunt of the attack on their swords where possible and, when they could not, to let their armor absorb the shock. The Duke was wearing no protective coat of any kind, however, and hence he was at a disadvantage, for the knight was encased in a short tunic of chain mail and could take risks that William could not.

Even worse, the Duke's lack of armor meant that he had to parry every thrust successfully, for if he failed but once, he would surely be wounded severely, perhaps fatally. Therefore, in order to avoid being struck by the other's steel, he needed a perfect eye and would have to co-ordinate every movement unerringly, a feat almost impossible to attain in the early evening darkness. But he had no choice, and within the limited area of maneuver that was open to him he could do no more than try to set the tempo of combat and hope for the best.

Swinging his sword back and forth, first slashing, then thrusting, he quickly established a rhythm which the knight was forced to accept, and for several minutes metal beat ineffectually against metal. Every blow was jarring, and William's arms and wrists tingled, then ached, but he ignored these minor discomforts. His endurance, he knew, was greater than that of any other man alive, and if he could maintain the pattern he had set, the knight would eventually grow weary, and when he was tired he would become careless.

Somewhere behind him on the road the Duke's guards were fighting the ruffians who had attacked them, but William resolutely shut the sounds of their battle out of his consciousness, for he could permit nothing to distract him from his own struggle. Slowly, inch by inch, he and the knight moved from the center of the road toward the woods, and William maintained a gentle but inexorable pressure to force his opponent into the underbrush. There the knight might trip over a root or in some other way lose his balance, thus offsetting the advantage his armor gave him. The Duke was puzzled by the renegade's willingness to be pushed toward the woods; surely he was intelligent enough to realize why he was being led there, and no soldier willingly accepted a handicap.

The mystery was solved with blinding suddenness just before the knight was about to put one foot into a mass of partly trampled brambles. William heard a whistling sound, and almost simultaneously a knife buried itself in the trunk of a tree no more than a few inches from his head. The first knave who had attacked him, the man whom he had incapacitated with a kick in the stomach and had subsequently forgotten, had apparently recovered his strength sufficiently to hurl the blade at his unsuspecting target.

The man might be creeping up on him now, ready to strike again, but William, completely occupied in his duel with the knight, did not dare to take his eyes from his principal foe. The dilemma was a cruel one, and he didn't quite know how to proceed. Greater men than he had been killed by knives thrust into their backs, and the knowledge that death was very near goaded him almost beyond endurance. Life had never seemed more precious to him than it did right now: there was so much ahead, so much that he wanted to do in the future.

His desperation gave him added strength, and each blow he struck against the knight was shattering in its impact. Perhaps Earl Harold could have absorbed such punishment and given as good in return, and it was rumored that King Harold Hardrara of Norway was a duelist of prodigious strength, but no lesser being could continue to stand up against such a vicious attack. The knight tried valiantly, and for a brief time he continued to hold his own, but he was beaten and he knew it, and there was an expression of resignation on his swarthy face when a particularly heavy blow sent him reeling and knocked his sword from his hands.

At the same instant William heard a triumphant shout behind him, and one of his guards called out, "I got the scum, Lord Duke!"

The knave was sprawled on the ground, dead, and the three Norman soldiers, battered and bloody but still whole, came forward and seized the knight, who made no effort to flee. William, carefully wiping his sword on the clothing of the dead man, peered off into the night and thought he saw several other bodies down the road. He turned to the nearest of the guards, and the soldier grinned sourly.

"We killed two of them, Lord Duke. The other three got away. They ran like hares into the woods."

"That means we've rid the world of four out of eight," William replied. "Not too bad for one evening's sport."

"Five out of eight, Your Grace," another of the guards said, prodding the exhausted and crestfallen leader of the assassins in the ribs with the point of his dagger.

"No, only four," the Duke said quietly. "This vermin deserves hanging, of course, and someday he'll stand on a gibbet, but I'll let someone else have the pleasure of exterminating him."

The soldiers stared at him and the knight, unable to believe he had heard William correctly, looked stunned.

"Release him!"

The guards obeyed reluctantly.

"Go back to your master," William said, "and tell him I find his methods extremely crude. Tell him his lack of imagination is very disappointing."

The knight stared at him for a long moment, and then, seeing that he meant what he had said, scurried off into the woods. The guards, shaking their heads at the Duke's generosity, recovered the horses while William brushed dust from his tunic. Then, patting his stallion fondly on the head, he addressed his men.

"When we get home," he directed, "send a full squad back to this spot to dispose of the bodies. We don't want our lovely and clean Norman countryside cluttered with dead foreigners."

The tension was broken, and the soldiers roared with laughter, as he had known they would.

"Incidentally," he called over his shoulder as he climbed into his saddle, "I want nothing said around the castle about this little incident. Women don't understand the ways of men, and if my wife learned of our sport she'd be needlessly upset."

The guards nodded their approval of his wisdom, and the ride was resumed at a somewhat slower pace. William seemed to have put the bitter fight out of his mind, and when he hummed tunelessly as he led the way to Rouen Castle, his men could not conceal their admiration of him. Their expressions confirmed what his whole army already knew: he was the greatest leader on earth, and they would follow him anywhere.

When they arrived at the castle, protocol closed in on them: the Duke's arrival was heralded by three blasts on a trumpet, the guard of honor that had been awaiting his return stood at attention on the drawbridge and his escort dropped respectfully behind him. Torches were burning all through the main floor of the castle as

William dismounted in the entrance hall. He washed his hands and face in a bowl of water offered to him by a servant, then wandered into the great hall, saw that it was empty, and inquired as to the whereabouts of his family. He was told that Gundrada and the smaller children were at supper, so he decided to postpone the presentation of the locket until later in the evening, and he nodded approvingly when he heard that Gerbod was still at his studies with his tutor.

Mounting the dais and seating himself in the chair, he directed that the Duchess be informed of his arrival, then he accepted brief verbal reports from his chamberlain, his major-domo, and his treasurer. It was still some hours before he would be served his supper, so he asked that a loaf of bread and a head of cheese be brought to him to take the immediate edge off his appetite, and as he ate in solitary splendor, he remembered, for the first time, Matilda's visit to him in the field earlier in the day. He felt no more than a slight prickle of irritation as he recalled the incident, however; if she lacked the foresight and intelligence to see that the defection of Earl Tostig was good news, there was nothing he could do about it and nothing he really wanted to do. Facts weren't altered simply because Matilda was unable to see them.

He finished his light repast, washed it down with a cup of ale, and as he wiped his hands on his tunic, a lower-class habit he had never broken, he became aware of a powerful and unpleasant stench. Now that he thought about it, he had been bothered by it for several minutes, and he bellowed for his major-domo. "What's that smell?" he shouted as the man appeared at the far end of the great hall.

"There's nothing I could do to prevent it, Your Grace," the man stammered.

William was slightly nettled; only this evening he had felt pride in his subjects' lack of fear when they were near him, but the major-domo was very much afraid of him at this moment. "Has the chef burned a roast?" he demanded, identifying the odor as best he could. "Or have the tapestries in one of the rooms caught fire?"

"I—I really couldn't say, Lord Duke." The major-domo turned and fled.

"Come back here!" William called, and when there was no reply he jumped angrily to his feet. At that moment Gerbod appeared from the direction of the family dining room and his stepfather looked at him curiously, for the youth's face was flushed and he held a crumpled square of linen to his nose. "Now what in the names of all the saints is going on here?" William asked crossly.

"Good evening, Father." Gerbod's voice was thick.

"I thought you were at your studies."

"I was, sir, but the smell drifted up to my room and I came down to investigate it."

"Ah, then there is a smell. I was beginning to wonder if my imagination was playing tricks on me." The Duke sniffed again, then grimaced; the odor was growing stronger.

"It's real, Father." Gerbod began to edge toward the entrance hall.

"Just a moment, boy! What is it? I insist on being told what's responsible for this unholy——"

"Mother." Gerbod muttered the one word, then ran out.

As curious as he was exasperated, William stalked into the dining chamber, and, finding it empty, he moved through the passage to the kitchens, out-buildings he rarely visited. His chef and three or four other servants were huddled in one corner of the baking room, near the bread ovens, talking and gesticulating. They fell silent when they saw their master, and he brushed past them, following the scent that was becoming overpowering.

In the principal kitchen he stopped short; not in his wildest dreams had he ever seen a sight like that which confronted him now. His Duchess stood before him, still dressed in the gown she had worn when she had ridden out to the encampment. But over it was an apron, the first William had ever seen her wear, and in her right hand was a long wooden ladle. Four hearths sat along the far wall, and on each was a huge caldron; these, unquestionably, were the source of the stench. Two miserable servants were tending the fires, and it seemed to William that they were maintaining the fires at a low level.

Matilda's face was moist from the heat, several wisps of hair escaped from her braids, and she was so absorbed in moving from one vat to the next, peering inside and poking at the contents with her ladle, that she failed to see her husband. Thus William had a moment in which to recover from his surprise. She reminded him of his mother in the days when they had been poor and Harlotte had herself cooked all of their meals. He blinked his eyes, which were beginning to run, and cleared his throat. The two servants saw him, but Matilda continued to stir her brew.

"Woman," the Duke said, "I've never before seen you stand within ten feet of a boiling pot. What do you think you're doing?"

"Good evening, dear." Matilda brushed a strand of hair away from her face with her wrist, then turned to one of the servants. "Do be careful of that second caldron! The firewood is very dry, and I don't want such a high flame."

"Matilda!"

"Yes, dear?" She peered into the farthest vat.

"What are you doing?"

She turned to face him and smiled quietly. "Why, you told me to look after my kitchen, William. And I try to be obedient in all things."

"I didn't tell you to prepare a poison for me. Or for the household."

Matilda glanced at the servants, who had become very busy the moment they had heard a note of asperity in the Duke's voice. "You may leave the room," she said, and the wretches left hurriedly.

"Well?" William started toward the nearest of the bubbling caldrons, but the fumes drove him back.

Even a woman who had not been forced to suffer insults when she had merely tried to be helpful would have laughed, and Matilda made no attempt to conceal her merriment. Then she sobered quickly. "I'm sorry, dear. And I give you my word, no matter how nasty or unpleasant you've ever been, I've never wanted to poison you. Let me relieve your mind. I'm not preparing food." Something solid rose to the surface of one of the pots and she became busy with her ladle for a moment.

William had no intention of remaining in the kitchen any longer than was necessary to satisfy his inquisitiveness. "I don't like it out here," he said plaintively. "So will you please——"

"Of course. Do you remember telling me this afternoon that your archers don't wear chain mail?"

"What connection is there between my archers and this devil's broth? Of course they don't wear armor! It's too heavy for bowmen and would hamper their aim!"

"I see." Matilda's face brightened. "I didn't know the reason, but I see it now. They would be more efficient in battle if they had some sort of body protection, though. Isn't that right?"

"Yes. That's right. But I have no intention of staying in this damned kitchen and teaching you military——"

"Let me show you what I've done." She turned and picked up a small strip of tough leather from a table behind her. "This is the first one I treated," she said. "It's cured cowhide that I've boiled."

William took it and saw that it was pliable yet very strong; he drew his knife with the double blade and made a brief test. Only by exerting great pressure could he cut the leather or puncture it. "This has possibilities," he muttered.

"I thought of boiling it this afternoon, while I was riding home," Matilda said. "And now I'm treating some bigger pieces. I'll make them into tunics when they're finished, and then your archers can try them— but only if you think that armor of boiled leather would be useful, of course."

William looked at her in despair, but there was admiration in his dark eyes, too. "You're incorrigible," he said.

"I'm not sure how you intend that, dear, but I'll take it as a compliment."

They both started to laugh and soon tears were streaming down their faces. it was impossible to determine whether they wept for joy at having moved closer together or because the fumes from the caldrons made their eyes smart, but for the moment, at least, they both forgot the threat to their future posed by the Norsemen.

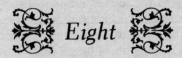 *Eight*

THE ATMOSPHERE at the breakfast table was convivial, for William was in excellent spirits, Matilda wisely voiced none of her worries, and the children were at ease. Gerbod became the center of attention when Adelize inadvertently revealed that she had seen him wooing a maiden with song, and as he had only recently begun to take an interest in girls, William teased him unmercifully. Matilda wanted to come to the boy's rescue, but instinct told her that he would resent rather than appreciate her help, so she remained silent and instead supervised the serving of a large platter of *faridan*, a dish consisting of beaten doves' eggs topped by finely chopped, smoked sole which had been baked in cream and seasoned with leeks.

William, who chuckled every time he glanced at his stepson's red face, made several vain attempts to discover the identity of the young lady whom Gerbod was courting, and then expanded his theme. "You won't take it amiss if I offer you some advice?"

"No, sir." Gerbod's embarrassment did not interfere with his appetite and he methodically consumed large quantities of *faridan*.

"Good, good." William winked at Gundrada, who was his principal audience as the other children were too young to understand what he was saying. "Your approach is all wrong, Gerbod. Oh, I know it's the fashion these days for young men to compose songs on

158

the virtues of their ladyloves, but the practice isn't sound. It's a mistake to put a woman on a pedestal."

Gundrada, who was fingering her gold locket, giggled.

"Be firm—that's the way to treat them. Don't spoil them, mean what you say, and they'll stay in their proper place." William took care not to look at his wife.

Matilda could stay quiet no longer. "Pay no attention to him, Gerbod. Your young lady will appreciate you all the more if the sentiments you express in your poem are true. There's nothing a woman likes more than to know she's admired and cherished."

"When you flatter them, boy, they develop false ideas of their own importance. And then you're going to have trouble." William's tone was bantering, as was Matilda's.

The conversation might have led anywhere, but little Robert, who knew only that Gerbod was a target, decided to intervene with a comment of his own. "Gerbod says he's going to be lord of Dover." His tone was accusing.

The Duke sobered immediately. "And so he is. Dover is the gateway to England, and I need someone there whom I can trust implicitly."

Robert could make no sense out of his father's words and pursued his own point relentlessly. "What part of England am I going to have, then?"

"You'll have none of it," William said severely. "As you've been told again and again, you'll be Duke of Normandy someday. So don't be greedy." He looked down the table at his second son, who was systematically spilling cream on his shirt front as he tried to eat his *faridan*. "It wouldn't surprise me if you become King of England someday, young man."

"And what will I become, Father?" Adelize asked.

Gundrada brought her cup down against the oak table so sharply that some of her watered wine spilled onto the wood. "I think you're horrid, all of you!" she said, looking remarkably like her mother when Matilda became angry. "All this talk of who's going to have this and who's going to have that is sickening! Normandy is still Father's and he's going to be King of England himself for a long, long time before any of you inherit anything!"

William beamed at her and held out his hand; she jumped up from her place and ran to him, and he kissed her fondly on the nape of the neck. Then, as the child sat down again, he caught Matilda's eye, and her expression puzzled him. She was pleased, he was sure of that, but she was tense, too, and guarded. "We have the finest princes and princesses in Europe," he said.

Matilda's face softened at once. "Yes, dear. We have."

At that moment they heard the sound of loud voices from the great hall but could not distinguish what was being said, and William frowned. The staff knew that he was not to be disturbed when he was having breakfast with his family, and he raised an eyebrow as he looked at Gerbod. The boy rose at once, frowning in unconscious imitation of his stepfather, and hurried off into the great hall.

"Quiet here in the name of the Lord Duke!" they heard him shout.

But the commotion continued, and although William and Matilda tried to resume their conversation, they could not. And the mood that had existed throughout the meal was destroyed. Adelize twisted around in her chair and tried to peer into the other chamber, little William had to be physically restrained from leaving the table, and Robert knocked over Gundrada's wine cup. Then Gerbod returned.

"There's a man outside who insists on seeing you, Father, and he won't give his message to anyone but you. He comes from Archdeacon Stigand of Canterbury, and he's landed from England just this morning. Judging from the looks of him, I believe him. He hasn't bothered to wash."

"Tell him to wait," Matilda said.

"Tell him to come in," William declared in the same breath.

Gerbod knew whose orders to obey, and he walked quickly to the arch. A tall, well-built young man followed him into the chamber, and William knew at once that the stranger, in spite of his short, multicolored tunic, was a soldier. His stepson quickly confirmed his guess. "Lord Duke and madam," the boy said stiffly, "permit me to present Captain Ethelric, chief of housecarls in Canterbury."

The Englishman's face was lined, there were dark blurs under his eyes and his hand shook as he saluted the Duke and bowed to the Duchess. Then he dropped to one knee, and he was so agitated that he began to speak in English. William tried to put him at ease after Gerbod peremptorily cut him off.

"Perhaps he speaks no French, and in that case you'll serve as our translator, Gerbod." The ducal tone of reproof was mild.

"I—I speak French, Your Grace," Captain Ethelric stammered. He looked up for an instant, and his eyes were terror-stricken.

"So much the better." William could never understand why foreigners were so often afraid of him. "Lord Gerbod tells me you're an emissary from the Archdeacon of Canterbury. I remember Stigand well from my visit to England some years ago." He did not add that his agents reported that the Archdeacon was two-faced and so afraid of being deposed that he

courted the favor of anyone and everyone who might be
able to help him keep his hold on his high office.

"His Eminence sent me to Your Grace as fast as it
could be arranged. I was able to leave just before the
ports were closed."

Although two huge logs were burning in the hearth,
a cold wind seemed to sweep through the chamber.
William and Matilda exchanged startled glances, but
said nothing and waited for the exhausted messenger to
continue as soon as he could gather his wits.

"King Edward the Confessor is dead, Your Grace."

"May God have mercy on his soul." William
gripped the arms of his chair. He knew that something
was amiss, for he should have been notified of his
cousin's death by a representative of the Witenagemot,
the council of English nobles. The closing of the ports
meant there was trouble, and the messenger was taking
care to address him as "Your Grace" rather than "Your
Majesty."

Ethelric's face worked and he tried to speak, but the
words would not come; he took a deep breath and tried
again. "Harold Godwineson has crowned himself King
of England."

There was a moment of dead silence, then Matilda
rose. "Children, leave the room," she said, and no one
spoke again until they were gone. Gerbod, whose position as William's equerry permitted him to remain, was
so overwrought that he forgot he was supposed to speak
only when someone addressed him.

"When did it happen?" he asked, and no one even
noticed his slip.

"Less than two days ago," Captain Ethelric said.

William's calm was incredible. With his own hands
he filled his cup with wine, and handed the goblet to
the grateful messenger. "You say he crowned himself?"

"Yes, Your Grace. Within two hours of Edward's death. He surrounded the King's house with a regiment of his own housecarls, and when the Confessor's body was carried out, Harold rode behind him wearing the crown."

"I see." A muscle twitched in William's jaw; otherwise he seemed impassive. "What of the Witenagemot? Have they given their approval to this rape?"

"Harold and his brothers control the council, Lord Duke. So the others had no choice. Besides, what could they do when five hundred housecarls armed with battle-axes surrounded the council chamber of the Witenagemot?" The outburst Ethelric had expected from William had not materialized, and he took courage. "The sons of Godwine have ruled England for years, Your Grace. Most of our lords have been champions of Harold's cause for a long time."

"No doubt." The Duke looked straight ahead, but saw nothing. "The weak seek only security, so they cling to the strong. That's as true in England as it is in more civilized lands. What of the northern earls, Edwin and Morcar—do they accept Harold as their sovereign?"

"They're like weeds in a wind. They bend in whatever direction is best for them. Harold knows that, and he needs their support. So he's giving up his handfast wife—begging your pardon, ma'am—and he's marrying their sister, Aldyth, in the hopes of binding them to him. Whether he can depend upon them or not is a question I'd hesitate to answer, Lord Duke."

William nodded and continued to look off into space. "You say Harold placed Edward's crown on his own head?"

"Yes, sir."

"When will his formal coronation take place?"

"This very week, Your Grace."

"So soon?" William's lips parted in a bloodless smile. "He's wasting no time."

Matilda, who had been sitting in a stunned silence, was about to ask a question but thought better of it. The color had drained from her face and she looked like one of the gray stone statues of ancient Norman rulers that lined the passageway leading to the castle chapel. But she remained alert to every nuance, and her eyes widened when she saw her husband's chin drop to his chest.

"What do the common people think of their—new King?" His voice was soft but cold.

"I've seen very little of the people, Your Grace," the Englishman replied evasively.

"You were in Canterbury. And from your description, you've spent time in London, too, before sailing to me." William was seemingly gentle but insistent. "You saw them in the streets. You heard their shouts. How do they feel?"

Ethelric knew he had to answer, and there was a quality in the Norman that compelled him to be truthful. "The people followed Harold in battle when he was an earl. They'll follow him anywhere now that he wears a crown."

"I'm not surprised." William lifted his head, and his dark eyes were piercing. King Edward had promised England to him, and so far the Archdeacon's messenger had mentioned nothing at all about the Confessor's will, which not even Harold would dare to disregard. "What of the late King's legacy?"

The Captain shook his head. "There was none," he said flatly.

"That's hard to believe. Edward was a careful man, and he certainly knew his country would suffer if he failed to leave a will.'

"I can't presume to guess what might be in the mind of a king, Your Grace. But I do know that Edward left no written will naming his successor." Ethelric paused almost imperceptibly. "Harold was at his bedside when he died. The only other person present was the King's wife."

"And she's Harold's sister. So any legacy that Edward may have left has been destroyed." William seemed to be talking to himself, and for a long moment he was unaware of the presence of anyone else in the chamber. Finally he turned again to the Englishman, and although a lesser man would have been scornful, there was no hint of malice in his voice as he said, "That brings us to the Church. What's the attitude of your master at Canterbury and of the Archdeacon of York?"

The messenger had apparently been told what to say on this point; at any rate, he spoke as though by rote. "His Eminence of Canterbury would be driven into exile if he failed to acknowledge Harold Godwineson as his sovereign. And it is his duty to remain with the people in their hour of need."

William nodded and his expression did not change; the hypocrisy of Stigand came as no surprise to him. And there was no need to ask what the lesser clergy thought, as Harold had cultivated their favor for years by encouraging them not to send their taxes, or "Peter's pence," to Rome, as was required of churches and monasteries everywhere in Christendom.

"I don't suppose you happen to know whether Harold has summoned all freemen to arms?"

"No, Your Grace. I don't. The Witenagemot doesn't confide its military plans in officers of my rank. But I'm sure of this—the new King will have no trouble raising an army if he finds it necessary to issue a call for men."

Matilda could keep silent no longer. "Harold took an

oath of allegiance to Duke William! How does he justify having broken his sacred word?"

"He doesn't, ma'am," Ethelric said politely. "And I don't imagine he ever will. It isn't the sort of thing he'd want to discuss. Of course his brothers have been saying for weeks that an oath taken under duress is no oath at all."

"But the people won't tolerate an oath breaker!" she cried.

Ethelric wearily ran his fingers through his long blond hair. "It isn't safe to call a king names, ma'am. I saw proof enough of that not half a mile from Edward the Confessor's house in Ludgate before I sailed. There was a man who was going through the streets shouting that Harold was an oath breaker. The churl had a French accent, so I guess that's what excited the people of the city, and——" He broke off abruptly as he realized that his story wasn't fit for feminine ears.

But William, who had been listening intently, seemed to be unaware of his wife's presence in the room. "What happened to the man with the French accent, Captain?"

"The crowd—quieted him, Your Grace."

"How?" the Duke persisted.

"They—tore him apart."

There was no more to be said, and William tapped his thumb ring on the arm of his chair to signify that the interview was at an end. He watched the messenger rise and back toward the door, then he raised a hand and spoke as though an idea had just occurred to him, which it had not. "Captain, if you would like to remain in Normandy, I offer you a place in my household."

Although Ethelric had anticipated no such gesture, his reply was immediate. "I am English, Lord Duke. I must return home."

William, honor-bound under the Code of Chivalry not to harm an emissary, accepted the situation. He had made the offer as a test, and he had been correct in his assumption that even an Englishman who was given an opportunity to join him would prefer to serve under Harold's banner. "Gerbod, attend to Captain Ethelric's needs, and see to it that he leaves Normandy unmolested. Anyone who harms him will be responsible to me."

Gerbod bowed, and his expression was troubled as he looked first at his stepfather, then at his mother. He muttered something under his breath to the effect that Dover meant nothing to him, that he would be content to remain in Normandy for the rest of his life. There was no response, and he reluctantly followed the English messenger out of the chamber. The Duke and the Duchess were alone.

Matilda stared at her husband, but he did not see her. "He couldn't have done it!" She was close to hysteria, and her hands trembled so violently that she had to rest them on the top of the table. "He swore to support you! He gave his sacred word before hundreds of witnesses!"

William did not reply.

"The Holy Father won't permit it! He won't allow a perjurer to sit on the throne, William! And no other ruler in all the world will recognize Harold, not one! I know what my father will say! So will the Emperor!"

There was still no response.

And Matilda's frenzy increased. "Even Philip of France won't dare send an ambassador to him! No king is so secure in his own right that he'll lend his support to someone who breaks an oath!"

William said nothing.

"That young English officer gave us a biased account

just now. We can't give credence to everything he told us. By his own admission he's a supporter of Harold's, so it's obvious he gave us as discouraging a story as he could." Matilda's voice became shrill. "I can't believe that even the English are such heathens that they'll accept a ruler who swore on a holy oath that he had become your vassal. If there are such things as justice and right in the world, as we've been taught to believe, then Harold's own people will throw him out. I wouldn't be surprised if they've done it already. They can't respect a man who breaks his word without a qualm. No one could!"

When she paused for breath there was no sound but the scraping of chair legs against stone as William slowly rose.

"Please, dear," Matilda begged, "tell me what you're thinking. I know you must be very angry and upset, just as I am, but we've got to decide what to do next. Harold has stolen a kingdom, and we need to be calm and farsighted as we've never been in all our lives."

William walked down the length of the table toward his wife, his hands at his sides, his face a mask. He moved without undue haste, and every step was deliberate. As he neared her she jumped to her feet, and when he halted before her they stood close to each other. Thoughts raced through Matilda's mind, but she could not express them now, for her panic was complete. Then, suddenly she read her husband's intent in his eyes and she shrank from him.

In the same instant William raised his right hand, and for the first time since he had married Matilda of Flanders he struck her. His open palm landed against her cheek, jarring her, but he did not bother to see the effect. Instead he turned sharply on his heel and, not varying his gait, walked slowly and ponderously out of the chamber.

Matilda was almost unaware of the stinging sensation in her face as she sank back into her chair. Her thoughts were disjointed, her body felt numb, and when tears filled her eyes she did not know it. Occasionally a servant approached the room but quickly disappeared again, and neither the ladies nor any officials of the court dared to come near the grieving woman whose interference had cost her husband a crown. Time lost its meaning for Matilda, and it was midmorning before she finally roused herself.

She felt old and bone-weary as she walked into the great hall, where she expected to find William. He was not there, but barons and lesser nobles were gathered in small groups, talking in low voices, their faces grave. Obviously the news had spread quickly. The chamberlain started toward the Duchess, but changed his mind and fell back, and she walked almost the length of the room before Fitz Osbern came up to her.

"It's true?"

"Yes." Her voice sounded metallic in her own ears.

"What does William intend to do?" The Seneschal tried to modulate his voice, but his hurt was too deep and his anger too great.

Matilda discovered that her cheek was sore. "He's told me none of his plans."

"I don't like this." Fitz Osbern's rugged, honest face reflected his concern. "He's barricaded himself in the armory and he won't see anyone."

"You say he's in the armory. Thank you." Matilda drifted past him to the stairs.

She was breathless by the time she reached the landing, and as she moved down the corridor the palms of her hands were moist. Perhaps William would refuse to admit her into his presence, but she had to try to see him and to reason with him. She stopped short when she saw two soldiers stationed in the corridor; beyond them, directly in front of the door to the armory was Gerbod, a naked sword in his hand. And Matilda needed to summon all of her remaining strength and courage before she could approach her son.

Gerbod flushed but stood resolute as he raised his blade and held it across the oak door. "By order of the Lord Duke, no one is to be granted entry," he said loudly, his voice quivering.

In the silence that followed Matilda could hear his uneven breathing. Gently but firmly she pushed his hand aside, raised the latch, and stepped inside the armory. Sunlight streamed into the chamber, blinding her for a moment, and she blinked several times before she saw William. He was standing at the far end of the room, methodically sharpening the long blade of his dagger on a whetstone that rested on a small table. As he stroked the stone with the steel, he studied a large tapestry that hung on the wall directly in front of him, and Matilda knew before she glanced at it that it was a very special tapestry, the map of England that she and her ladies had made for him three years ago.

William turned when he heard the door close, but when he saw Matilda he looked away from her and again devoted his attention to the map. His first reaction was one of shame, for he saw the red mark on her face where he had struck her; he had always felt contempt for men who beat their wives and had often expressed the opinion that anyone who struck a woman was a weakling and a coward. Yet he could not bring himself to apologize: his bitter despair permitted him no such conciliatory gesture.

And for the first time in his life he had wished he were someone other than the Duke of Normandy. Had he been born an insignificant knight, it was probable that he would have married a woman who loved him, but no ruler of a strong duchy could hope to find a wife who would be interested in him, or who would want anything other than the prestige and power she would acquire with her title of duchess. He should have taken a mistress instead of a wife, as his father had done, and he could understand now why his parents had never been married. Harlotte had loved Robert, and had cared nothing about the pomp of high office; had their son been wise he would have followed their example.

Instead he had stubbornly courted a woman who had cared nothing about him, who had made it plain that she did not love him. She had been the wiser, for she had certainly made no secret of her reluctance to marry him, and now he was paying for his mistake. Matilda's greedy cleverness had ruined them both; had he heeded his own counsel, Harold Godwineson would be dead and the crown of England would have been tendered to him peacefully as the rightful heir.

Worst of all, the perfidy of Harold in no way stifled or killed William's ambition. He still wanted to be King of England, and knew he could not be content to live the rest of his life only as Duke of Normandy. The odds against his achievement of his goal were almost insurmountable, and he realized that in the long months of struggle that stretched out ahead Matilda would always be a symbol of failure and frustration to him. Had she behaved as a wife should, had she remained quietly in the domestic background, he would not now be faced with the task of invading England with an army too small for such a purpose.

The knife scraped faster and faster against the whetstone, and William again became absorbed in his military problem. Even though his troops were the best in Europe, he could muster no more than seven thousand men, and Harold, who would be fighting on his own soil, could send at least twice that number into battle. But there was now no alternative to war, regardless of the bleak outlook.

"William." Maltida spoke his name repeatedly.

With a great effort he forced himself to concentrate on the immediate present. And although recriminations were a waste of time and unworthy of him, he could not resist lashing out at her verbally, just as he had been unable to prevent himself from striking her. "I shouldn't have listened to you, woman. Your meddling has cost me a kingdom that by rights is mine."

"We both did our best," she said, struggling to achieve a dignity she could not feel. "We couldn't know that Harold would break his oath."

"I knew." The dagger slid along the surface of the whetstone more slowly now. "There's the irony of it. I understand men. And I was sure Harold would be unable to resist the temptation when he thought he was safe."

"You wouldn't have broken your word."

"How can you be so certain?" He turned away from the map and faced her. "Who can say what a man will risk when boldness will win him the greatest prize on earth? I don't know what I'd have done if I'd been in Harold's position. It's a waste of time to speculate, and I only know that I'd like to be in his shoes now. They're resting on the dais of England."

"What do you think we ought to do, William?"

"We? We'll do nothing. You'll never interfere again as long as I draw breath. As for me, I'll declare war against Harold, of course."

Matilda knew little about military matters, but it was plain even to her that the Norman army was too small to subdue a whole nation. "There must be some other way—"

"There's no other way." William's voice was as cold as the steel in his hand. "Now, get out."

She might have been facing a stranger; looking into her husband's eyes, she saw no sign of personal recognition, and she thought that open hatred or contempt would have been preferable to this hard shell of indifference. He had not withdrawn from her, but had put her out of his life, and she knew him so well, or thought she did, that she was sure it did not matter to him that they had slept together and worked together, that she had borne his children and shared his tribulations.

And nothing she could say now would influence him; in a few short hours their marriage had disintegrated and only the façade was left. Matilda's pride was destroyed, and she crept out of the armory without another word.

William looked again at his map, then moved away from the tapestry so he could see it from a better perspective. The longer he studied it the more it came to embody all that was real to him, all that had meaning, and suddenly he lifted his knife and hurled it at the wall. The blade ripped through the fabric and clattered to the floor, leaving a jagged hole along the southern coast of England, where an invasion fleet would have to land.

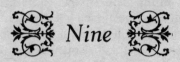

Nine

WHEN ABBÉ LANFRANC heard the news he left St.
Etienne for Rouen at once, although his monks urged
him to wait until after dinner. The roads were crowded
with travelers and his donkey was old, so it was early
afternoon before he rode across the drawbridge of the
castle. Nevertheless he gave careful instructions regarding the beast's care and watering before he asked to be
announced to the Duke and Duchess. The flustered
chamberlain informed him that neither was receiving
visitors; William was still in his armory, and Matilda
had secluded herself in her bower. The priest, neither
surprised or disturbed, elected to see the Duchess first,
and, waving aside the horrified, protesting officials and
servants, he made his way unaccompanied to the bower.

Matilda was seated in her chair, staring at the wall
opposite her and twisting a square of lace in her hands.
Her face was tear-streaked, and on her left cheekbone
was a mark that was turning black and blue. When she
heard footsteps she looked up, ready to order the in-
truder out, but when she recognized Lanfranc a dry sob
caught in her throat and shook her body. She started to
rise from her chair, but sank back again, and when she
tried to speak she could not.

The Abbé smiled at her. "Surely England isn't that
important to you—or to anyone."

"It is!" Matilda thought she was shouting, but her
voice emerged as a dry whisper.

"You won't be satisfied, then, until you're Queen?" he asked wistfully.

The Duchess nodded.

"And if it isn't to be?"

"I must be Queen of England," she said in a flat voice, "just as William must be King."

The Abbé ran his slender fingers up and down the length of the silver chain that hung from his neck. "I know no two people whose hearts and minds are united as yours are." He paused and his eyelids flickered delicately, then he added, "Together you can accomplish anything, no matter how difficult the obstacles that seem to confront you at one time or another."

"We're no longer working together, Father Lanfranc. William has made it very clear that he wants no more to do with me. He no longer wants me as his wife."

"Every marriage has its troubled times," he said, "and it's natural for a man to reject his wife when he believes that she has betrayed him. But love and time can soften his attitude."

"William no longer loves me," Matilda replied harshly.

"Oh? I can't agree with you—regardless of what he may have said—or done." The Abbé glanced for an instant at the bruise on her face. "I'd be better satisfied in my own mind if I were sure of your love for him as I am of his for you. Let's go to him and see if we can't work out this problem, shall we?"

"It's no use." She gripped the arms of her chair so tightly that her knuckles turned white.

A hint of amusement appeared in Lanfranc's eyes. "Suppose I were to tell you that out of the seeming defeat you and William have suffered can be fashioned the greatest and most enduring of victories. Would you still say it's useless for us to go to him?"

Matilda saw that he was not joking, and new vitality seemed to flow into her tired body. "How can it be done?" she demanded eagerly.

"We'll go to William," he repeated, and she needed no further urging.

They walked down the stairs together to the second floor of the castle, and the servants who saw them and noted the sharp and sudden change in Matilda wondered if some of the stories they had heard about Lanfranc might be true. Only a wizard, they whispered to each other, could transform a despairing duchess into a glowing woman so quickly. A young knight had replaced Gerbod at the armory door, and while he, too, had orders to admit no one, he stood at attention, saluted, and then himself raised the latch for the Duke's wife and his confessor.

William was seated at his worktable, one end of which was piled high with armor and weapons. He had cleared a space for himself, and was eating a solitary meal of cold meat and mead as he brooded over a sheet of parchment on which he had scratched a number of figures. He looked at Matilda, then through her, and his gaze rested on the Abbé. "I didn't send for you," he said rudely, not bothering to rise.

"The Lord sometimes comes to us even when we don't solicit His help, and we who try to do His work on earth try to follow His precepts," Lanfranc said firmly.

"Be good enough to leave, and take her with you." William had scarcely touched his food before they had come in, but now he picked up a lamb bone and made a pretext of eating a chunk of the meat.

"I haven't come in from St. Etienne for the purpose of turning around and going out again." The Abbé was not awed by William, and could not be cowed.

"Don't argue with me." William's voice was grating,

and he lifted his cup of mead to his lips. "I'm already bearing more than my share of vexations."

Lanfranc advanced to the table and rapped on it in the manner of a tutor disciplining a recalcitrant student. "William, you amaze me. Stop sulking."

"Sulking?" The Lion of Normandy made a noise that sounded remotely like laughter. "I'm trying to use what little wits have been left to me so I can repair the damage done by amateur bunglers!" He pointed the lamb bone at the priest. "You're as responsible for this situation as she is, you know. If you'd tended to your business of saving men's souls instead of encouraging the impractical notions of a romantic woman, none of this would have happened!"

"Did you expect me to encourage murder instead? Did you think I would approve when you planned the cold-blooded assassination of a man who was your guest?"

"If Harold had met with an accident as I planned originally, only one man would have died." William was annoyed at the need to justify himself. "Now hundreds will die instead, and a whole country will suffer. So spare me your platitudes—and your sophistry. When I've won England, I'll ask you to ring your church bells and to hold a special service so I can offer thanks for my victory. Until then there's nothing I want from you and nothing you can do for me."

Matilda, who said nothing, could no longer keep silent. "William, Father Lanfranc has something he wants to say to us. He has an idea—"

"I've had enough of other people's ideas to last me for the rest of my life." William let the lamb bone fall to his platter and shoved his chair back. There was rage in his eyes as he stood, and he flexed his fingers as he started around the end of the table toward his wife. "If you won't leave voluntarily, I'll have to throw you out!"

Matilda shrank from him, but before he could touch her Lanfranc moved between them. "I'm sorry it has come to this, but you'll have to throw me out, too," he said quietly.

William raised a heavy fist, but the Abbé did not move and met his fierce gaze coolly; gradually the Duke's wild anger ebbed and he dropped his hand wearily. "I've committed many sins, and I'll commit many more, but I can't strike a man of the cloth. You know it, Father, so you take unfair advantage of me."

"So I do," Lanfranc agreed calmly. "Every man uses the weapons at his disposal to achieve the goals that he believes necessary. You intend to issue orders that will send thousands of men across the English Channel, and they'll obey you, even though many of them will die. You'll take advantage of them because your rank gives you authority over them. Yet it hasn't occurred to you to wonder what they'll gain by winning England for you."

"My men will benefit, all of them! I'll give them land and houses——"

"They have fertile Norman land and comfortable Norman houses. But you'll take them with you to war because you want England." The little priest was unique in his ability to match William's ruthlessness.

"All right. What do you want with me?" Displays of emotion were a waste of time, as William well knew, and he had already given in to his feelings too often in one day. He would listen to whatever the Abbé proposed, and then he could return to his own calculations without fear of further interruption.

"May we sit down?" Lanfranc asked with a smile.

"If you insist."

At a nod from the Abbé, Matilda took the nearest chair and sat on the edge of the cushioned seat. She folded her hands in her lap and looked down at them demurely; no matter what might be said, she would remain quiet, she promised herself. William had no real grievance against Lanfranc, she knew, and he would be more amenable to reason if she remained in the background.

"Well? What have you to say? Please be brief, as my patience has already been sorely tried today." William walked to the table and took another swallow of his bitter mead.

The Abbé took his time as he moved to a far corner, picked up a stool, and placed it in front of the table. When he sat on it the Duke and Duchess could not see each other, and they both wondered if he had chosen the spot deliberately. His attitude gave no indication, however, for he placed his fingertips together and for a long moment he seemed lost in contemplation.

"When I gave up the practice of law to serve the Lord," he said, "I knew that mine would not be the usual life of a priest. And I was right. I have learned that I do His work by ministering to His children in a way I would not have chosen for myself. It is my strange lot to try to help a strong, intelligent man and his wife to maintain a balance, for when they are happy their people—my people—are content. When their relations are disturbed, their people—my people—suffer. And so I have come here today, not through my own choice, but because my duty demands it."

"No one else has ever called me an ogre to my face," William said smiling wryly.

Lanfranc ignored the interruption. "It will seem strange to both of you, whose ambitions are boundless, that I am not ambitious for myself. The pleasures of this world have no attractions for me, and when I contemplate the power of the Almighty, I find the authority of temporal rulers very puny. Be that as it may, my detachment enables me to see your problems from a somewhat different perspective."

"There's only one perspective, Father. Harold has stolen England from me, and I've got to take it from him" William's fist crashed on the table and the platter of meat slid away from him.

"So you must," Lanfranc declared, and smiled when Matilda looked startled. Reaching out, he took the sheet of parchment on which William had been scribbling, and he studied it, turning it in his hands, before continuing. "You're planning on using an army of eight thousand men, I see."

It was William's turn to be amazed. "How—"

"From your figures, of course." The Abbé tapped the paper with his forefinger.

"Yes, eight thousand," the Duke admitted grudgingly.

"You realize, of course, that you'll be denuding Normandy of men. There will be no one left here to till the fields or cut timber or tend cattle and sheep. Women can't perform such tasks."

"I'm well aware of it." William resented Lanfranc's ability to pinpoint the greatest weakness in his plans. "I have no choice but to take a risk, however. I'll need every man I can muster. Do you have any better ideas, Father? And don't tell me I can conquer England with prayer! A saint might do it, but God knows I'm no saint."

"As to your estimates on the size of Harold's forces, I'm afraid your sources of information are none too accurate." The thin, high head was bent over the parchment again. "You've made a notation to the effect that he has four thousand housecarls at his disposal. The actual number is closer to five thousand, or so I've been informed."

It annoyed William that someone else's sources

might be more accurate than his own; his agents were trained men, and one of their chief functions was to keep him up to date on the size and equipment of the English army. "Where did you get your data?"

Lanfranc waved his hand deprecatingly. "Does it matter? You might recall that my figures proved to be better than yours when you last fought Philip."

The Duke remembered very well; in fact he had been forced to dismiss two trusted spies, and the memory of the incident still rankled. "All right. For the sake of discussion we'll assume that Harold has five thousand professional troops on whom he can rely. But every man in my army, even the farmers and shepherds, will be real warriors by the time I've finished training them."

"I'm sure of it, William. You have a unique ability to make soldiers out of plowmen." The Abbé's compliment was sincere, but had been leading up to a point, and he made it deftly. "You'll still be badly outnumbered, of course."

"I've beaten bigger armies before, and I can do it again."

"But the odds against you in an English campaign will be enormous." Lanfranc looked again at the parchment. "You seem to indicate here that Harold can call up ten thousand freemen."

"I think he can."

"When the time comes, you'll discover that at least fifteen thousand English thegns will take up arms to protect their country."

"You may be right. I'm not particularly concerned one way or the other. A commander can never really count heavily on his part-time soldiers, which you may or may not know." William tried not to sound patronizing. "Farmers who join an army for a limited time are inferior warriors."

"I can't dispute the point," the Abbé said with a shrug. "But you might keep in mind that men who are defending their homes may display considerable vigor and bravery."

Most of the talk was beyond Matilda's grasp, but she listened carefully, and when she discerned that William was becoming increasingly uneasy she took heart. There was some purpose behind Lanfranc's insistent discussion of matters about which he obviously knew less than the most renowned general in Europe, and eventually his intent would become clear. In the meantime she was satisfied to let him pursue his devious course; he was the one person who was capable of restoring order out of chaos.

"I've listened to your counsel on political affairs, Father Lanfranc, sometimes to my regret," William declared. "But when it comes to war, I take no man's opinion. I'll take care of Harold's thegns in my own way."

"And that way will be very competent, I have no doubt," the Abbé said soothingly. "All the same, you will admit that your army of eight thousand is going to have a difficult time at best. You'll be fighting against a foe who numbers at least twenty thousand. And you surely can't pretend that you don't care, or you wouldn't have worked on these figures."

William reached across the table and took the sheet of parchment. "Of course I worry. Do you think my victories have been accidental? I leave nothing to chance that can be planned in advance!"

"Yet there's so little you can really plan in an invasion of a foreign land, isn't that true?" Lanfranc asked innocently. "The population will be hostile to an invader, and the supplies of food you can take with you will be limited. That means you'll have to live off the land, and foraging for eight thousand men is quite a problem, I'd imagine."

William leaned forward and his dark eyes glowed with anger. "If you're trying to discourage me from declaring war, you're wasting your time and mine!"

"A war with England is inevitable and has been ever since King Edward told you that you'd succeed him. In my opinion you'd have had to fight for your heritage even if you had disposed of Harold when you had the chance, but that's neither here nor there. I'm merely attempting—from the viewpoint of someone who admittedly knows nothing whatsoever of wars and armies—to demonstrate to you that your undertaking is very hazardous."

"I know all the risks." William sat back in his chair again.

"But you'll take peasants and herdsmen who are needed at home." The Abbé was gently insistent.

"I've already told you that I need trained troops! Come to the next council meeting, if you wish, and when you hear us planning detailed strategy, you may begin to understand why it's important to arm every man who's capable of using a weapon."

Lanfranc was unruffled by the Duke's exasperation. "The principle is already very clear to me," he murmured. "I know that you'll need every available man if you and Matilda are to sit on the throne of England."

William jumped to his feet, his face set in hard, unyielding lines. "She'll never be Queen of England, never!" he shouted.

Matilda pressed herself against her chair so he could not see that she was trembling.

"There was a time when I might have granted her a boon, but she's lost her chance for all time!"

The Abbé's expression indicated that he was supremely indifferent to the matter. "I wonder if I could trouble you for a bite of bread and meat. I left St.

Étienne without my dinner, and I find I'm growing hungry."

"Send for some food, woman." William glared at his wife.

"Oh, there's more than enough right here," Lanfranc protested. "Provided that you're finished."

"Help yourself." William discovered that he was still standing and he sat down abruptly. Having expressed himself emphatically on Matilda's future, the subject was closed. He watched the Abbé pick at the food, and he smiled grimly. From long experience he realized that the cleric had been trying to condition his mind, and he thought that Lanfranc was like a strolling player who nimbly produced certain musical effects on a lyre. But in this case the instrument was unresponsive, and he didn't care what ideas might be presented to him. The Norman army would of necessity invade England, regardless of the schemes that Lanfranc might try to persuade him to adopt.

At the moment the Abbé didn't look like one who was concocting a plot, however. He ate delicately, congratulated Matilda on the quality of the bread, and then smiled as though he didn't have a care in the world. "How wonderful it would be," he said blandly, "if you could command an army big enough and strong enough to insure a complete victory over Harold."

"I never indulge in useless dreams," William said, and his voice was cold. "I leave such pastimes to women. And to priests."

"Sometimes dreams can be made to come true. You may recollect a sermon I preached on just that very topic."

"I remember it," William declared derisively. "You told us have faith. Well, I put my faith in these." He tapped the armor at the end of the table.

"There are many kinds of weapons," the Abbé replied, his tone indicating that he refused to debate the point. "And I find it curious that honest men are most often the ones who don't use the swords that are offered to them. It's a strange form of self-imposed blindness."

"Crossing the river Thames is my province. I leave the river Styx to you, Father Lanfranc."

"At the moment I'm thinking about the Thames too. William, we have a magnificent opportunity, and if we'll just seize it——"

"I'll take England as best I can. I'll have no part of any magnificent opportunities."

Matilda spoke before she could stop herself. "Just listen to him, William! No one is asking you to do anything except listen!"

"I want nothing from you, William," the Abbé said hurriedly, before their ragged tempers erupted again. "Merely consider Harold's position for a moment. He's branded himself as an oath breaker, hasn't he?"

"But he's made himself King of England."

"The oath he gave was no ordinary pledge," Lanfranc continued. "It was administered by Archdeacon Gilbert, who represented the Holy Father. I'm sure that Pope Alexander will be grieved when he hears that Harold is a perjurer and a usurper."

"His grief can't be any greater than mine."

"I see a distinct possiblity of winning the approval and even the active backing of the Church for your campaign." Lanfranc did not raise his voice, but he spoke with increasing authority and conviction.

"Even if every cardinal and bishop on Vatican Hill prepares a declaration in my favor, I'll still have to defeat Harold in battle before England will be mine. And I mean no disrespect to the Church when I say that only a war will resolve the issue, Father."

Matilda, who had grasped the Abbé's meaning instantly, felt compelled to interrupt again. "But how much stronger you'll be if it's a holy war, William!" she cried.

He laughed unpleasantly. "A holy war, no less? As usual, you let your imagination run wild."

"Don't be too sure of that," Lanfranc cautioned soberly. "Pope Alexander has sanctioned campaigns against the Saracens. And he might be persuaded to regard a man who has broken a sacred oath as an infidel, too."

"And precisely what would I stand to gain?"

"Men," the Abbé said.

Matilda rose to her feet in excitement. "Of course! If the Holy Father will——"

"If!" William shouted. "I'm tired of 'if, if, if!'"

Lanfranc gestured sharply to Matilda, and she resumed her seat. "A manifesto giving you permission to wage a holy war," he said calmly, speaking as though there had been no new altercation, "would enable you to recruit men all over Europe, William. There are knights in Sweden who would join your cause, and peasants from Germany. Many nobles in the Italian states and in Spain are dissatisfied with conditions at home and would flock to your ensign. You could sail for England with an army double the size of the one you plan to take with you."

William clasped his hands behind his head, closed his eyes, and allowed himself to toy with the prospect. He had to admit that it was extraordinarily attractive, but he was determined to make no change in his own basic plan. He had erred when he had relied on the efforts of others, and by breaking the self-imposed rule that had guided him since he had been nineteen he now found himself in a position that a man of less determination would consider discouraging if not hopeless. He could not afford another mistake, and any distractions in the immediate future might be fatal to his cause. He knew, as Lanfranc and Matilda did not, that his barons were not required under the terms of their fealty to him to support him with troops, arms, or their own persons in any venture that would take them over open seas, so his most urgent task now was to persuade, bully, and cajole them into enlisting under his banner.

Hence he could not allow himself the luxury of wasting his time in hoping that his ranks would be enlarged by the enlistment of volunteers from other lands. The organization of the Norman army itself was of necessity his primary concern. He sat upright when Lanfranc coughed politely, and he looked long and hard at the cleric. "Your idea isn't without a certain merit," he said. "But I can't depend on it. I'll need to develop my campaign with the troops I have."

"But you'll have no objection to the dispatch of a mission to Rome?"

"Send one if you wish. It can do no harm."

"I intend to be a member of the party myself," the Abbé said. "I haven't visited Rome in many years. I'll prepare the necessary documents of authorization for your signature and seal."

"As you wish." If the priests wanted to amuse themselves by making a journey to the Vatican, they wouldn't be underfoot for some weeks. And that would leave him free to apply pressure to his barons without fear of interference from their chaplains, who might find moral grounds on which to base possible opposition to an invasion of England. "As you'll be representing Normandy, be sure your group is large enough to be impressive."

A light in the Abbé's eyes indicated that he was well aware of the real reasons for William's sudden concern, but he wisely refrained from comment. "You'll have no cause to be ashamed of your delegates, you may be sure," was all he said.

"Very well." William was about to conclude the interview, but he decided to clarify first his own stand beyond all doubt. "If you meet with any delays, I'm not going to wait for you. I'll sail for England as soon as I'm ready, so don't bother to send word back to me that if I'll be patient for another year all will be well."

Lanfranc had not expected the Duke to be quite so adamant; it would be a sign of weakness to reveal either misgivings or alarm, however, so he smiled instead. "How soon will you be prepared for your invasion?"

William took up a quill, dipped it in his ink jar, and made some hasty notes on a corner of the parchment. "I can see no reason why I shouldn't be ready in approximately five months. It could take me a little longer, but I'll sail in even less than five months if I possibly can."

"In other words, I have five months in which to persuade the Holy Father to lend you his support?"

"No, you have five months in which to get the Vatican's approval—and to bring me the recruits you've described in such dazzling terms."

Matilda sighed, but Lanfranc turned to her quickly. "Never fear," he said. "A great deal can be accomplished in five months."

She murmured something that William could not hear, and he shook his head sadly; if only he had realized that her childish optimism always clouded her judgment, his position would never have become so desperate. Rising, he offered his hand to the Abbé. "I wish you well, Father Lanfranc, but I must be honest with you. I'm convinced you'll fail." Then he looked straight at his wife, and his eyes grew hard. "I'll be going into the field soon to train my troops," he said. "Until then—I'm having my bed moved in here."

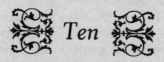 Ten

ROME, THE MOST COSMOPOLITAN of all cities, was
bored by visiting dignitaries. Kings and cardinals,
princes and generals from every part of the Christian
world had ridden through her ancient gates for centuries, and her citizens, accustomed to pomp and
power since the days of the Caesars, were accustomed
to seeing the great and near great. Hence the delegation
from Normandy, headed by Archdeacon Gilbert of
Lisieux, aroused little interest as it passed in stately
procession through the streets to Vatican Hill. Although the party consisted of three cardinals, five
bishops, and a score of lesser churchmen, what little
attention the Romans directed toward the group was
centered on the company of soldiers that had protected
the clerics from the vicissitudes of the highways. Even
Rome had respect for the Norman "fishmen."

At the Vatican the group was received with due
ceremony, and after being installed in suitable quarters
at one of the newer guest mansions, Archdeacon Gilbert, accompanied by the other cardinals and several
senior bishops, walked to the Pope's palace to greet the
ailing Alexander II. The rest scattered to visit churches,
see the sights of the city, and to renew their acquain-
tance with old friends, but Abbé Lanfranc was not one
of them. At his request he was conducted to a small
building set just inside the Vatican's walls, and although he was entitled to wear a bishop's robes he was
attired, as usual, in his plain black cassock, even for this
occasion.

After a brief wait in a bare reception hall he was conducted to a small office which contained no furniture other than a table and several plain chairs. And there, poring over a document, was a man as simply dressed as Lanfranc himself. Only his red cap identified him as a cardinal, and there was nothing in his manner that even hinted at his power. Archdeacon Hildebrand had been the real ruler of the Church ever since the health of the Pope had begun to fail, but his face was bland and his hazel eyes were innocuously pleasant as he extended his ring for the Abbé to kiss.

"I've been expecting you, Lanfranc, ever since the news arrived from London," he said.

"I'm glad I haven't disappointed you, Your Eminence." Lanfranc took the chair that was offered to him, and before he sat he shifted its position slightly so the sun would not strike his eyes.

Hildebrand noticed the maneuver and smiled; as a rule his visitors didn't become aware of the strategic position of the chair until too late. "You won't disappoint me, I'm sure. I've heard too many promising things about you."

They took each other's measure, and each liked what he saw. "Your Eminence needs no praise from me," Lanfranc said, and he, too, smiled.

"A glass of wine to settle the dust of the road?"

"Later, perhaps. Thank you. I've heard that you don't like to waste time on unnecessary social activity."

"Oh, you've taken the trouble to learn my habits, have you? I'm flattered."

"Normandy may be far from Rome, Your Eminence, but we hear many things. And we've been disturbed at word of the Holy Father's continuing illness."

The Archdeacon's thin mouth narrowed. "His Holiness's physicians tell me he'll continue to grow weak-er. With the world in such a disturbed state, it's too bad that we must further upset the balance by the need to elect a new Pope in the not too distant future."

"We in Normandy have been very upset at the pros-pect, as you can imagine." Lanfranc nodded sym-pathetically.

"You have three representatives in the College of Cardinals." Hildebrand was merely stating a fact.

"Yes, three, Your Eminence. Although we like to think we have five, as there are two Flemish cardinals as well. And as you know, Normandy and Flanders are united in virtually every sense of the word. Certainly we're united, and I speak here for all of our clergy, in our anxiety. It's our earnest prayer that the College will elect a new Pope who is strong and able and conscienti-ous."

There was a long silence, during which neither glanced at the other. "Each of your cardinals will vote according to the dictates of his own conscience, I pre-sume," the Archdeacon said at last.

"They're men of independence, to be sure," Lan-franc agreed. "But a rather unusual situation exists in Normandy and Flanders. A layman exerts a vast influ-ence over our clergy, owing to his extraordinary qual-ities of mind and spirit, and all of our priests—even our cardinals—have found that his decisions and judg-ments are almost always right. And so they're happy to let themselves be guided by him."

"I've taken an interest in William Bastard for a long time," Hildebrand said obliquely.

"He'll be delighted to hear it, Your Eminence. He's admired you for many years."

"Has he? I'm doubly flattered. I would have thought that he was too busy defeating his enemies to know much about us or what we do here."

"Duke William is a devoted and conscientiously loyal son of the Church, Your Eminence."

"Then much of the credit is due his spiritual adviser. I've been told that he leaves all matters pertaining to the Church in the hands of his counselor."

"I do what I can to help him, naturally," Lanfranc replied with a modest shrug.

"I've been interested in you, too. You wear your bishop's ring, but your habit is that of a simple monk. That's unusual."

"I follow the example of Your Eminence."

"Well said. There are so few who learn the futility of chasing shadows. It's the substance of power that fascinates you, eh, Lanfranc? No, don't bother to answer that. You wouldn't, anyway, just as I wouldn't." The Archdeacon chuckled, then grew serious. "No doubt you hope to become a member of the College of Cardinals yourself someday. Perhaps you even think in higher terms." He inclined his head in the direction of the Pope's palace, which could be seen through the nearer window.

"I have no personal ambitions, Your Eminence," Lanfranc said quickly. "And I certainly don't presume to think of myself in a class with someone like you."

Hildebrand observed him sharply, and finally was satisfied; the Abbé meant what he said, and had no intention of making himself a competitor for high office. "Your modesty does you great credit, Lanfranc."

"I shall treasure your compliment, Your Eminence. There are only two men in the world whom I admire. One will someday be a king, and the other—well, I shall do all that I can for both of them."

"You won't be the loser. Friendship is a rare trait in these times when every man seeks his own gain at the expense of others. If I were ever in a position of ultimate authority, I'd not be content until you wore a red hat." Suddenly the Archdeacon's attitude changed, and he became brisk. "What is the exact position of William Bastard with regard to England at present?"

"It's nebulous, Your Eminence. Nebulous and unsettled. He's been deeply hurt by the perfidy of a supposedly honorable man who swore on a holy oath to become his vassal."

"I'm frank to admit that Harold's callousness has shocked me too." Hildebrand didn't look like a man who could be shocked by anyone or anything.

"Then you can understand Duke William's feelings. He's determined to take England by force, although he deplores the need to make war. Unfortunately he has no other recourse."

"Unfortunately." Hildebrand stared up at the ceiling. "Why is he so eager to become King of England, Lanfranc? Normal ambition is always a spur, but William seems ready to go to greater lengths than most to achieve what he wants."

"England was promised to him by his kinsman, Edward. And William rightly refuses to be cheated out of what is his." The Abbé hesitated for a moment, then resumed more slowly. "There are other, less obvious reasons as well, Your Eminence."

"Oh?"

"Duke William is eager to add the votes of the Archdeacons of Canterbury and York to those of his Norman and Flemish cardinals when the time comes to elect a new Pope."

"A commendably filial trait." Hildebrand grew expansive. "The more I hear about William Bastard, the more I become convinced that he has the true interests of the Church at heart. As he is so devout, I dare say he

would be willing to take any advice the Holy Father
might deem fit to offer him on temporal matters."

"I have no authority to speak for him in any realm
except the spiritual, Your Eminence." Lanfranc knew
he was walking a tightrope as thin and taut as any on
which the jugglers in companies of strolling players had
ever balanced themselves. Archdeacon Hildebrand
had an appetite for power as insatiable as William's,
and had been trying for several years to gain a measure
of control over the temporal affairs of the states within
the Church's orbit. Therefore his desires clashed with
those of William, who would never permit any outsider
a voice in the government of a land he ruled.

"Would he oppose a worthy project which a new
Pope might propose, Lanfranc?" the Archdeacon asked
casually, screening his concern.

"I can't imagine a situation arising in which William
would be opposed to some new interpretation of
Church policy," the Abbé answered glibly.

"But he might not be willing to submit to higher
authority?" Hildebrand insisted.

Lanfranc realized that his whole scheme might
flounder unless he could convey a picture of a William
who was malleable. "I regret my inability to speak for
him in earthly matters. But you can judge his attitude
more accurately, Your Eminence, when I tell you one
of his principal motives in wanting to mount the English throne. Like us, he is worried over the laxity of the
Archdeacon of Canterbury in collecting Peter's pence
from the churches of the realm."

Hildebrand brightened at once. "I've never before
heard of a layman who shows such piety. So he grieves
with us! How heartening. Does he happen to know that
Stigand has ignored our requests—and we've made
many—to collect the taxes and forward them to us?"

"I've kept the Duke fully informed on the subject. And I can give you an absolute guarantee that when he becomes monarch of England, the churches there will pay their Peter's pence. Naturally I refer to their accumulated taxes that have gathered in the past as well as to their current obligations." Lanfranc had already worked out a carefully detailed plan for the collection of taxes from English churches and monasteries; his agents had sent him inventories of their riches, and he had decided to sell a portion of the gold and silver they had been hoarding for centuries. In that way the claims of the Vatican would be satisfied, and William could make a magnificent gesture at no cost to himself.

"I can speak only for myself and not for my colleagues," Hildebrand said quietly, "but I must tell you that I am increasingly impressed by William Bastard's petition. He has suffered a grave injustice."

"He has, Your Eminence. Would you care to see the actual petition?"

"That depends. He didn't prepare it himself, did he? I've been told he can read and write, and——"

"I wrote it for him. He's unfamiliar with the style of Church documents, and his Latin leaves much to be desired."

"Oh, if you've written it there's no need for me to bother. You've divided it into the usual preamble and twelve sections?"

"Of course, Your Eminence."

Hildebrand sighed gently. "This has been a most satisfactory meeting for me. I've rarely encountered anyone whose thinking so closely parallels my own."

"I'm overwhelmed by the kindness of Your Eminence."

"There's just one small detail that we may have forgotten. As Archdeacon Stigand is rather untrustworthy and Aldred of York is a very old man who really should retire to a monastery to preserve his health, it might be a wise precaution to appoint two new English cardinals as soon as William is crowned. Can we count on him to recommend men whom we know will cooperate with us?" The Archdeacon referred to the system whereby the Pope confirmed appointments made by kings; in the past several cardinals had put the interests of their sovereigns above those of the Holy See, and had consequently caused the Vatican great pain.

"I'm sure William would be pleased to nominate any reasonable candidates whom a new Pope might suggest to him." The Abbé stressed the word "reasonable."

"I won't be subtle with you, Lanfranc. He wouldn't insist on making that detestable brother of his a cardinal?"

"Under no circumstances will Odo ever hold any post other than his present one of Bishop of Bayeux," Lanfranc said firmly.

"Then we need say no more about him. But you'll agree that it's best to settle these points of minor dispute before they ever arise."

"By all means."

"Then," the Archdeacon declared, rising and smoothing his robes, "we have achieved a perfect accord. I'll ask His Holiness to summon a conclave, and the cardinals can debate the merits of William's claim for support."

The Abbé stood too, and although he should have been pleased at the results of the conference he was frowning. "How soon will the College meet, Your Eminence?"

"We move slowly here, so you mustn't be impatient, Lanfranc," Hildebrand said in a tone of rebuke.

The truth was preferable to any subterfuge. "William intends to invade in the spring, with or without Church approval."

"I see. In that case perhaps we can act with greater dispatch. Even so, the cardinals who live far away will need time to travel here." They moved together toward the door. "The French may prove troublesome, particularly the Archdeacon of Paris, but we'll have to worry about him when the time comes. I wish I knew of some way to avoid inviting the French, but I'm afraid there's no choice. So you and William Bastard will just have to take your chances."

"We'll do so gladly, Your Eminence. And I have no fear of the decision that the College of Cardinals will make, now that I know William's petition will be judged purely and solely on its worth."

In spite of the efforts of Archdeacon Hildebrand and the Norman clergy to speed the opening of the conclave, the princes of the Church journeyed to Rome at their leisure, and a month passed before enough of them had arrived at the Vatican to justify the calling of the meeting. The French archdeacons lived up to expectations by announcing that they were unalterably opposed to William of Normandy, and around them gathered a hard core of malcontents. Lanfranc, who remained in the background but observed every development, became increasingly worried as he came to realize that his unofficial understanding with Hildebrand was no guarantee of success, and his apprehension turned to consternation when he saw even those cardinals who usually sided with Hildebrand become rebellious under the influence of the vociferous opposition. It became evident that William, the most universally feared man in Europe, was also the universally hated.

It was some small consolation, however, to know that, through what was officially termed a clerical error, no notification had been sent to the English archdeacons. Therefore Harold would have no direct representation at the conclave, and no one could answer the charges of the Normans on his behalf. A number of archdeacons, notably the French, protested that the proceedings would not be fair, and they asked that the meeting be postponed until Stigand of Canterbury and Aldred of York could be summoned. The physicians who guarded Pope Alexander refused to allow their patient to read the indignant petitions, however, and those angry archdeacons who tried to plead with him personally in Harold's behalf were ceremoniously but firmly ejected from his sickroom and found it impossible to gain another audience with him. And Hildebrand, to whom Harold's supporters then appealed, declared that he himself would be willing to wait but that so many members of the College were anxious to return to their own archdioceses as soon as possible that a delay would work hardships on them.

And so the meeting was convened at the first possible moment. As secular affairs were to be debated, it was decided that an informal atmosphere would give the cardinals greater freedom of expression, and the dining hall of the Pope's palace, which had not been used during the years the Pontiff had been ill, was selected as the site. A vast room with high ceilings, it was equipped with two large hearths, in which fires were lighted to ward off the damp chill of the Roman winter. As not many rooms in the Vatican possessed such conveniences, most of the archdeacons had been suffering from the cold, and no one complained about the unusual place that had been chosen.

The Pope's gold and white throne dominated the

room, but it would remain empty, out of deference to him, and Hildebrand, who was to preside, deliberately chose a low-backed chair without arms for himself and had it set at the foot of the temporary dais on which the throne was raised. And his modesty placated the grumblers, who had tried to insist that Archdeacon Vincenzio of Milan, the senior cardinal in age and in years of service, should act as chairman.

It rained hard on the morning the conclave opened, and the blazing fires were so inviting that numerous priests and nobles who had no legitimate business in the dining hall found one excuse or another to warm themselves and had to be ushered out by sympathetic, shivering papal guards. The first officials of the conclave to arrive were two bishops who had perfected the art of writing rapidly; they were to keep a running account of the meeting, and their rank was deemed sufficiently high to gain them entry. Directly behind them was Abbé Lanfranc, who made his way into the chamber unobtrusively, and sat quietly. His presence was so unusual that some irate members of the Vatican staff called it illegal, but his credentials were signed and sealed by Hildebrand, and no one was in a position to question the authority of the Archdeacon. Lanfranc was present as an observer rather than as a participant, and anyone who was unfamiliar with the unique clerical situation in Normandy would have been surprised when Archdeacon Gilbert of Lisieux led his delegation and that of Flanders into the room.

All of the cardinals appeared anxious and harassed, but they relaxed when Lanfranc smiled and nodded to them, and they carefully chose seats near him; his mere presence seemed to encourage them. Gilbert, who was to present the petition that Lanfranc had prepared, re-read the document carefully, and once or twice he

seemed dubious of the wording. However, a quick
glance at the Abbé reassured him, and when his colleagues from other lands began to arrive, he assumed
an air of confident dignity.

Archdeacon Milhaux of Paris took a seat in the front
row, to which his seniority did not entitle him, and his
cohorts took chairs behind him. The Spaniards sat on
the far left, and the Germans, with whom they were
engaged in a theological dispute, took places on the far
right. The others did not seem to care, and as long as
they were not too far from the pleasant heat of a hearth
they were content.

Papal guards closed the doors and Archdeacon Vincenzio opened the meeting with a prayer; then he
called on Hildebrand, who had donned his red robes
for the occasion, from the rear of the hall. Smiling
affably, the most powerful of the cardinals walked to his
chair at the front, and, as was to be expected, he opened
his address with a few remarks expressing his sorrow at
the inability of the Pope to attend. Then, without
further preamble, he briefly outlined the facts with
which every man in the chamber was already familiar.
Harold Godwineson, he said, had crowned himself
King of England, and William of Normandy claimed
the throne for himself. Hildebrand carefully refrained
from expressing any opinion of his own, and his lofty
tone further conveyed the impression that his attitude
was one of scrupulous impartiality.

He called on Gilbert of Lisieux to present William's
case, and the primate of Normandy read the petition in
a deep voice rich with emotion and passionate conviction. He spoke steadily for the better part of an hour,
and not once did he falter as he presented two principal
points: William, he declared, was the rightful heir to
England, and Harold, his vassal, had sinned against

God and man by breaking his sacred oath and seizing the country.

When Gilbert finished and sat down, a stir went through the assemblage, and Hildebrand allowed the College some little time to discuss the Norman arguments among themselves. Ordinarily Harold's spokesman would have made a rebuttal, but no one was either prepared or authorized to speak for him, and not even the French wanted to arouse William's wrath against their country and their monarch by becoming open champions of the usurper's cause.

When the talk began to ebb Hildebrand made a signal to two of the papal guards who were stationed just inside the nearer entrance, and they came forward at once. They were carrying a roll of cloth, and when they opened it at the Archdeacon's bidding it was seen that they held a huge flag of silk, embroidered in gold with an ornately designed cross and trimmed with scores of gems. They held the banner aloft, and Hildebrand, who was watching his audience closely, waited until the curiosity of his fellow archdeacons was satisfied. Then he spoke softly.

"His Holiness blessed the ensign that has been unfurled before you," he said. "It was made at his direction, and only this very morning he blessed it. His Holiness has expressed the desire that it be carried in battle as the personal standard of Duke William Bastard. Archdeacon Gilbert, will you accept the banner and give it to the Duke?"

"I accept it gladly," Gilbert replied, unable to conceal a broad smile. The flag was carefully rolled again, and when the guards brought it to him he held it as though it were made of the most fragile substance imaginable.

Hildebrand, who continued to show no emotion,

reached inside his robes and drew forth a tiny box of chased gold, which he grasped firmly between his thumb and forefinger. "His Holiness has also directed that Duke William Bastard be shown some sign of his personal high regard, and it is his desire that I present this relic to Archdeacon Gilbert as an indication of his favor for the cause of truth and justice. In the box," he added as the cardinals strained to see it, "is a locket containing a hair of St. Peter."

There was a stunned silence, and Gilbert of Lisieux was so overcome that he almost dropped the tiny casket when it was handed to him.

For a long moment no one moved; then, as Hildebrand was about to resume, Milhaux of Paris jumped to his feet. "We have not yet voted on this matter," he cried. "But we are being placed on record as patrons of William of Normandy. I must protest, my lord Archdeacon Hildebrand! This procedure is irregular, and my conscience will not permit me to accept it in silence!"

Hildebrand stood slowly, and although his face remained impassive, his voice was loud and clear when he spoke. "My lord Archdeacon Milhaux! Do you have the temerity to question either the wisdom or the motives of His Holiness?" His tone was incredulous. "Are you better fitted than Alexander II to read and to know what is in the hearts and the minds of men?"

Confused and abashed, Milhaux sat down.

"Does any other member of the College wish to express a view?" Hildebrand glanced briefly at each of the malcontents in turn, and when no one moved he sighed. "Our course of action is clear, then. Duke William Bastard of Normandy is a faithful son of the Church. Harold Godwineson of England, to his everlasting shame, is a perjurer, an evil man who deserves neither the support nor the comfort which the Church offers to her children. A bull of excommunication has been prepared for the signature and seal of His Holiness. Does any member of the College offer valid reason why the bull should not be signed by His Holiness?"

Milhaux was red-faced, and he would have struggled to his feet again had not the Archdeacon of the county of Burgundy whispered in his ear. Apparently he saw the futility of making another gesture, and he subsided.

Hildebrand nodded pleasantly. "I will convey word to His Holiness that the College of Cardinals entreats him to excommunicate Harold Godwineson from the Church."

He sat down quickly, Vincenzio of Milan came forward again and offered another prayer, and the conclave ended. The Norman archdeacons could not hide their jubilation as their colleagues crowded around to offer congratulations, and even the French, trying to repair the damage in their relations with William, insisted that Gilbert convey to him their best wishes for his success. The locket was examined with reverent interest, the banner was unfurled again for the admiring inspection of the princes of the Church, and expressions of good will were extended to the Norman delegation by the prelates of every land.

The doors were thrown open, and word quickly spread through the Vatican and then through Rome: William was authorized to conduct a holy war against an outcast. Never within the memory of living men had the Church taken such drastic action, and the few English priests and pilgrims who were in the city realized that they would have to depart for home at once, as men everywhere began to damn the infidel Harold so vigorously that his compatriots fell under a cloud too.

Lanfranc, the architect of the victory, seemed to be

the least affected by it, and, slipping out of the dining hall, he quietly gave instructions to the officers of the Norman escort troops to prepare at once for the return journey to Rouen. Then he made his way past excited crowds to the cell in which he had been sleeping and packed his few simple belongings. He was just completing the task when footsteps sounded in the stone corridor outside and he glanced up from his labors to see Archdeacon Hildebrand, still dressed in his ceremonial red robes, standing in the frame.

They smiled at each other but did not speak; there was no need for words between them, for they alone realized the magnitude of their triumph and the delicacy of maneuver that had been necessary to achieve it. And that knowledge was satisfying to them. Their work was done, and the future depended on William and his men-at-arms.

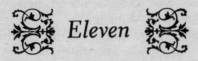

Eleven

The ATMOSPHERE AT LILLEBONNE, the ducal headquarters, was simple, martial, and exclusively masculine. There were virtually no comforts and the castle,
one of many that William owned, was cold, drafty, and
barren. So it was natural that a man who had grown
accustomed to gracious living should think of home
and, occasionally, of his wife. William had paid only
one brief visit to Rouen since Abbé Lanfranc's departure for Rome, and although he had been pleased to see
the children, he and Matilda had been uncomfortable
in each other's presence, and he had been relieved
when his sojourn had ended and he had rejoined his
army. He felt freer when he and Matilda were separated, and it was convenient to tell himself that circumstances made the present situation unavoidable; all
this was true, but he found it easier to contemplate her
virtues from a distance, for the barriers that had grown
between them made life under the same roof unbearably complicated.

He had almost no time for contemplation of domestic matters, however, as his attempts to raise an army
occupied practically all of his waking moments. And as
the weeks passed he gradually came to realize that he
was facing a crisis so grave that his whole plan for the
invasion of England was in peril. His nobles were
reluctant to answer his call for help, and in spite of his
strenuous efforts over a period of a month they remained so lethargic that his entire corps still numbered

less than three thousand men, the vast majority either
his own household troops or the retainers of Fitz Osbern and Robert of Mortain.

It was plain that the Norman gentry, who had always
been quick to respond when their own land was in
danger, had no appetite for costly foreign adventures,
and William knew that unless he acted promptly and
decisively he would be forced to abandon his project.
Even worse, his authority in the duchy itself would be
weakened, and some of the bolder landlords, who
would interpret his lack of initiative as a sign that he had
passed the peak of his powers, would rebel. After spending several sleepless nights wrestling with the problem,
he came to the conclusion that attack, as always, was
preferable to defense. And so, not bothering to consult
his advisers, he summoned all of his nobles to Lillebonne for a *parlement*, or meeting, at which all could
speak their minds freely without fear of punishment or
retaliation.

English spies filled their reports to the usurper in
London with good tidings: the opening of the conclave
was twice postponed, for the great men of Normandy
took their time obeying their Duke's summons, and
most came to the council only after the Seneschal sent
squadrons of his own cavalry around the countryside to
make a census of those who were tardy. The nobles,
seeing there was no escape, rode at last for Lillebonne,
and so did the prelates, the wealthy merchants, and the
shipowners William had honored with invitations.

Primitive living conditions did little to brighten the
mood of the gathering, and all but a few barons and
favored counts, who were given accommodations in
the cramped castle, were quartered in tents of thin silk
erected on the castle green. Everyone was cold, and as
the kitchens were inadequate, all but those who had

brought their own cooks and provisions with them were a trifle hungry, too. And William, who was deliberately observing none of the social amenities, made a deliberate show of his strength; a more timid man might have been conciliatory, but he stationed a battalion of his own infantry on guard duty at all times, and just before the meeting opened he paraded all of his regiments just outside the castle keep.

And when the landowners, more than two hundred in all, finally gathered in the great hall, their surliness was as obvious as the chill in the room. No tapestries hung on the walls of heavy stone, the fire in the hearth was insufficient to warm men who had been shivering for days, and the hard-packed earth floor was bare of all furniture, so the gentlemen attending the *parlement* had to stand. There was only one chair in the great hall, located on a dais, and in it sat Fitz Osbern, who, according to the traditions of his office, was to act as chairman.

His introductory remarks were brief and pungent. The landlords knew why they had been summoned, he said, and they burrowed their chins in their fur collars while surreptitiously grasping their money pouches with numb fingers beneath their long wool cloaks. All had grown wealthier during William's prosperous reign, and no gentleman of substance wanted to part with even a portion of his gains.

William entered the great hall on a prearranged signal from his seneschal, and, clad only in his usual leather tunic and wool breeches, he mounted to the dais, waved aside the chair that Fitz Osbern offered him, and began to address the assemblage. He had prepared no speech in advance, for he did not consider himself an orator, but he had often inspired his soldiers on the eve of battle, and he relied now on his own enthusiasm for his cause to fire the imaginations of the *parlement*.

He reminded the nobles of the oath that Harold had taken, he spoke of the justice of his claim, and he explained in some detail that although no vassal was required to take part in an expedition across the sea, all who accompanied him would share in the riches of England. Each man's share would depend on the size of his financial contribution and on the number of his retainers he led into the army; England was a large country, a country overburdened with wealth, and there was plenty for all. He ended on an impassioned patriotic note, recalling past triumphs and dangling the bait of future glories, then he stood back and waited for the inevitable applause and cheers.

The quiet in the great hall was deafening.

William was too experienced a campaigner to show his surprise, but he made no secret of his displeasure and, with his hands planted on his hips, he scowled at his audience. Every man there had enjoyed his largesse, every man had become the lord of vast new properties as the borders of Normandy had expanded, and the lack of gratitude angered him. Staring coldly at the *parlement*, he directed his gaze first at one noble, then another. The domain of Hugh Montfort had doubled, Roger Beaumont was now a count, Walter Giffard had a magnificent new castle, Roger Mont Gomeri was wealthier and more powerful in his own right than many reigning dukes. but not one could meet his eyes, not one stirred.

Only his own quick thinking prevented an ugly situation, and William turned to Fitz Osbern with a feigned smile. "Lord Seneschal," he said, "I shall withdraw so the discussion won't be hampered in any way by my presence."

Stalking from the dais, he shouldered his way

through the silent crowd, and the great men of the duchy moved aside to give him passage. His sudden gesture was unprecedented, and he felt rather than saw a shift of sentiment in his favor, especially on the part of the younger, more militant lords. The gentry didn't realize it, he thought, but they were remarkably like their own peasant: all Normans responded to the unexpected, provided it was audacious.

Several junior officers were gathered in the entrance hall, but they left hastily when their Duke appeared, and he was alone in the bare chamber. He could not be seen by anyone in the great hall, but he could hear what was being said, and he paused to listen to the debate. It would be as well not to wander too far, he told himself; he trusted Fitz Osbern's ability to handle the *parlement*, but if emotions soared too high he might find it necessary to reappear.

Several nobles started to speak at the same time, and one voice was louder than the others. "I've supported William Bastard in four wars, and I'll support him again—but only in Normandy!"

There was a wild shout of approval, and the Duke closed his eyes and concentrated. Unless he was very much mistaken, the speaker was Olifaunt Fitz Browne, whose wife was ambitious for a promotion in the peerage. Fitz Browne would have a long wait before he would be created a count.

The cheers died away, but the Seneschal could not maintain order, and to William, standing with clenched fists in the entrance hall, the clamor sounded like bedlam. And, unfortunately, it was no longer possible to identify the dissidents, for too many tried to claim the floor simultaneously.

"Not even Charlemagne was strong enough and wealthy enough to invade England!"

"What would happen to our homes if we leave? Our

manor houses would crumble and our wheat fields would rot!"

"Normandy is a poor country. I'll give the Bastard my men and my life, but I wouldn't follow him to England!"

"Our taxes are too high now! He's trying to bleed us to death!"

William had to exercise all of his self-control to refrain from rushing back into the great hall, but he knew better than to court disaster. If he were patient, the nobles would rid themselves of their resentments, and, like common soldiers, they would feel better after they had been allowed to grumble. Then, but not until then, would they be malleable.

Gradually the tumult subsided, and William heard the voice of his seneschal. "That was edifying," Fitz Osbern said sardonically. "As I sat here listening to you, I wondered if I might be in the wrong place. I wasn't sure if this was a Norman *parlement* or a meeting of the English Witenagemot."

The Duke grinned quietly as a low murmur rose and fell in the great hall. Fitz Osbern had taken control, and was handling the mob as deftly as he could have done himself.

"As I watched your exibition, I found that I missed a number of familiar faces. None of the Talvas family is represented here today, for example. You remember Baron Hugh of Talvas, I'm sure. He was a distant kinsman of yours, Mont Gomeri, if my memory is correct. You may recall that Duke William was forced to execute the whole Talvas family for treason. Lord Busac of Eu isn't here, either—may his soul rest in peace. Nor is Count William of Arques, who unfortunately forgot the loyalty he owed his liege lord.

"But I have no wish to dwell on the past and the dead

in the presence of the living. I'm sure that every man here realizes that Duke William is his sovereign, and that the Duke's power over all of us and over all of our possessions is absolute. There's no question of that in anyone's mind, is there? I thought not.

"The Lord Duke, as every one of us has reason to know, is liberal in his rewards to those who are faithful to him. But I know him well enough to tell you that he'll be deeply disappointed in anyone who is niggardly or delinquent in supporting this project that is so close to his heart. And it has been my observation that truly wise men always make strenuous efforts to keep in Duke William's good graces. We never know, do we, when we might need his help or want his friendship?"

There was a stir in the hall, then Robert of Mortain cried, "We're all his loyal followers, Lord Seneschal! Tell him for us that we'll go anywhere he may lead us!"

William had heard enough, and slowly mounted the stairs to the room in which he slept and did most of his work. The masterful skill Fitz Osbern displayed did not surprise him, but he was mildly startled by young Robert's political acumen. Not many men understood that it was as important to know when to speak as it was to have in mind a precise concept of what they were going to say, and Robert deserved encouragement. The western half of Cornwall, perhaps, or the rich farm lands of Mercia might be an appropriate gift to a half brother who had injected the right note into the *parlement* at exactly the right moment.

Weapons were piled onto plain wooden benches in the stark bedchamber, a litter of maps and parchment covered the chairs, and even the Duke's bed, which was no more than a crude pallet near the hearth, held its share of helmets and war gear, shipbuilding plans, and estimates. William swept a pile of documents from the nearest chair to the floor, then sat down and for a moment buried his face in his hands. He must be growing old, he thought, for in spite of the intense cold he was perspiring, and he told himself severely that as recently as four years ago he wouldn't have been so shaken by a near rebellion of his nobles. But that wasn't quite true: the reduction of Maine and the war against Anjou had been comparatively minor operations, and even his campaigns in France had been simple, though strenuous.

The task of invading England was greater than anything he had ever undertaken, and the noble who had called out that the Emperor Charlemagne himself had lacked the resources to conduct such a war had struck close to the mark. In a sense William couldn't blame his lords for their reluctance; it was possible that some of them secretly believed him to be mad. The Danes and Norwegians who raided the eastern coasts of England had never tried to capture the entire island, and although many men had dreamed of such a grandiose project, only Julius Caesar had translated fantasy into reality.

But William was prepared to gamble his wealth, his duchy, and his own life, and he smiled as he reflected that he was known as a leader who would not take unnecessary risks. No one knew how much the conquest of England meant to him, and no one realized to what lengths he was willing to go in order to accomplish his aim. An ever-mounting fever had been burning in him since he had visited Edward the Confessor in London so many years ago and had been promised the throne, and now the fire was all-consuming.

He remained cautious, however, in spite of his compelling recklessness that urged him to plunge deeper into his venture, and when Gerbod appeared in the door to tell him that the Seneschal sought an interview with him, he nodded calmly, as though only a routine conference was in prospect. Fitz Osbern's expression was bland too, as he entered, but his poise was not as great as his master's, and his eyes glowed when he looked at William.

"I've been delegated by the *parlement* to assure you that your lords are loyal to you, without exception," he said.

"Very comforting. Have they voted yet to support the invasion?"

A look of mock dismay crossed the Seneschal's lean face. "You may find this hard to believe, but I was in such a hurry to tell you of the fidelity of the lords that I completely forgot to put the question to a vote."

William laughed and gripped his friend's hand. "You'll have your choice of earldoms, I swear it."

Fitz Osbern sat on the edge of a bench and stared out into space reflectively. "Shall we make it triple the usual levies and contributions?"

The Duke considered the matter for several seconds, then shook his head. "That would be unfair, I'm afraid. Besides, it isn't practical."

"True."

William sat up in his chair, cupping his hands, and shouted for Gerbod. And when his stepson appeared, he issued a series of concise instructions. "Send in three of my best clerks, men who can write quickly and legibly. Send them to me at once, and tell them I want them to record every word that's spoken here. Then go down to the great hall and send the lords here to me—one at a time."

The Seneschal chuckled and slapped his knee. "You're going to see them individually?"

"As they're so loyal, they deserve private audiences,"

the Duke replied dryly. "And I think we'll find that each man's sense of fealty will increase in direct proportion to his isolation from the others. Oh, Gerbod— hand me that list of vassalage duties before you start. And when you go into the great hall, you might send up Olifaunt Fitz Browne before all the rest. He's the first I'm going to honor."

Gerbod hurried out, the clerks came in and took seats on a bench at the rear of the chamber, and William, after studying the leather-bound parchment book he held, handed it to the Seneschal, who moved and stood at his side. After a brief wait Fitz Browne, a heavyset, dark man entered and dropped to one knee. William thought that he looked pale, but refrained from comment.

"Olifaunt Fitz Browne," the Seneschal said in his best official voice, "it has been the custom, under the terms of your vassalage and that of your ancestors, for your house to provide twelve men-at-arms and forty pieces of gold as your measure of support for each war which the Lord Dukes of Normandy have seen fit in their wisdom to fight."

"That's right, Lord Baron." Fitz Browne wasn't sure which made him the more uneasy, William's cold glare or the Seneschal's fierce scowl.

"I'm sure," the Duke said impersonally, "that you'll want to give me twenty-four men and eighty pieces of gold for the glorious expedition against England. I know of no better proof of your undeviating loyalty to me, Fitz Browne. I'm right, am I not?"

"Absolutely right, Lord Duke," the unfortunate noble declared earnestly.

"Splendid!" William's tone did not change. "Naturally you'll join the expedition yourself?"

"Certainly, sir."

"You clerks are making a note of all this? Good."
William rubbed his chin. "As I recall, your wife's
family owns a shipyard at Caen, Fitz Browne. I'm
certain she'll want to demonstrate her devotion by
providing us with a vessel large enough to accommodate fifty men and ten horses. She won't disappoint me,
I hope."

"Never, Lord Duke!"

"I knew I could rely on you." William shook the
hand of his vassal with warmth and vigor, then dismissed him, and, after a brief exchange of triumphant
glances with Fitz Osbern, turned quietly to Gerbod,
who was standing just outside the arch. "Well!" he said
with enthusiasm. "Who's next?"

While tribute was being exacted from the nobles in
greater or lesser degree, depending on their rank and
wealth, the Seneschal sent a full battalion of his own
household troops to Arques under orders to return with
the person of Count William. Not only was the Count
the highest-ranking lord who had failed to respond to
the summons to Lillebonne, but he was also a kinsman
of the Duke. An example had to be set, there was a
lesson to be taught, and Arques was a natural selection
for an uncomfortable role.

The nobles had been asked to remain in Lillebonne
for an extra day, but they had no idea of what was in the
Duke's mind. Nor did the Count, who had been held
in a small room at the rear of the castle, even suspect
what was in store for him until he was escorted under
heavy guard to the torture chambers located deep in the
cellars. There, in a cavern lighted by flickering torches
of reeds, he found his namesake waiting for him, with
all of the assembled nobles nervously grouped behind
the Duke. None of the lords carried arms, but two rows

of soldiers lined the walls, and these men, all of them members of either William's or Fitz Osbern's own guards, carried swords in their belts and held javelins at their sides as they stood stiffly at attention.

The Count, whose glance flickered from his master to a trio of masked men in black grouped around a thick post set into the stone floor, was perspiring heavily as he bowed to the Duke. "Lord Cousin," he said in a voice that shook, "it's a joy to see you again, even in such unusual surroundings."

"You made your joy very plain when you ignored my demand that you come to Lillebonne," William said icily. "Do you suppose we have nothing better to do these days than to send two hundred of Fitz Osbern's best men to bring you here?"

"I was detained, Lord Cousin," the Count stammered. "I had every intention of coming to you— indeed, I was going to leave Arques in another day or two—but urgent business detained me, and I couldn't——"

"Enough!" the Duke shouted, and in the dead silence that followed he turned and briefly inspected the nobles behind him. "What is about to happen to William of Arques could have happened to any one of you. It isn't yet too late. In fact, I can guarantee that any lord who forgets his obligations to his liege and who is willfully disobedient in time of war is certainly going to receive the same treatment."

William was not by nature a cruel man and he usually avoided the excesses in which so many other rulers indulged, but in his opinion there was no alternative to the course of action he had set for himself in the present situation. His eyes glittered in the torchlight, his mouth was compressed into a thin, hard line, and a vein stood out at his left temple. Even his usually ruddy complexion appeared to have turned gray, and those of the older men present who had known his father thought his resemblance at this moment to Duke Robert was remarkable. And, remembering why William's predecessor had been called "the Devil," they shuddered.

"Here my decree," the Duke said, turning back to Arques. "The castle at Arques and all lands of the county are now ducal property. From this time forward they will belong to the Dukes of Normandy."

William of Arques cried out in anguish and wrung his hands.

"Your son," his master continued, "stupidly followed your example and did not appear to bend his knee before me. Because of his youth I have taken pity on him, and have sentenced him lightly. He has merely been banished forever from Normandy, and has already been escorted to the French border."

Several of the nobles began to mutter to each other under their breaths, but Fitz Osbern glowered at them and they fell silent again.

"I have learned," William went on in a metallic voice, "that your daughter was in large part responsible for your stupid disobedience. It was she who encouraged you to rebel, and she must pay in full for her folly. Last night she was taken from Arques to Caen, and there she was given to the keeper of a large military brothel. Why do you weep, you stupid man? You should rejoice in the knowledge that she will no longer give ruinous advice to dolts, but will spend the rest of her days providing pleasure for the loyal soldiers who fight willingly for Normandy and their Duke."

William of Arques sobbed, and then there was no sound in the chamber but the crackling of the burning reeds.

The sovereign of the duchy took a single step forward. "This place lacks some of the conveniences of Rouen, so I'm willing to spare you unnecessary pain. I offer you the right to meet me immediately in personal combat."

On the surface the offer sounded eminently fair, but no man could hope to survive a duel with the Duke, and the Count trembled violently. "I couldn't raise my hand against my liege," he said. "Our grandfathers were brothers, and in their name I beg you to be merciful."

"You'll get exactly what you deserve." William nodded to the masked men in black.

They seized the Count and shackled him to the post, with his hands secured fast behind him. Then one of the executioners moved to a corner and returned with a curiously-shaped length of iron; one end had been sharpened to a point and the other had been fashioned into a pair of pincers. When the Count saw the instrument he began to babble semi-coherently, and the Duke had to raise his voice to make himself heard above the sound.

"Put out his eyes," he said calmly.

The executioners obeyed, and the Count's screams vibrated against the thick stone walls. The nobles looked pale, but the Duke was unmoved as he watched the operation closely. His expression indicated neither approval nor disapproval; he obviously took no pleasure in the torture, but it did not disgust him, either. His purpose was to teach his lords a lesson they would not forget, and personal considerations did not move him.

"If the prisoner makes any more noise, pull out his tongue," he declared, and the Count made a desperate effort to stifle his cries.

There was a stir in the throng, and the nobles shifted

about uneasily. All of them knew of cases of members of the gentry who had been executed for treason, but never had anyone heard of one of the elite being tortured merely because he had been derelict in his obedience to his liege, and William's harsh and uncompromising severity frightened even the bravest of them.

"Now," the Duke said, "cut out his heart." He drew his own sword and handed it to the chief executioner, a gesture that was lost on no one. Several of the nobles started to move toward the stairs that led to the sane daylight above, but William halted them with an abrupt gesture. "This execution is being held for your instruction, my lords," he said flatly. "Anyone who leaves now will take the place of the Count of Arques at the stake."

The departing nobles hurried back into the chamber and forced themselves to watch the masked executioner perform his grisly task. The Count achieved a measure of courage at last, and he died with dignity, but a few of the lords had to close their eyes when he gasped and expired. It was unnaturally quiet in the dungeon, and when William spoke again his voice seemed to fill the room.

"Feed his heart to the vultures and take his body to the forests as a feast for the wolves."

Several in the assemblage wanted to protest, but did not.

William's expression was reminiscent of the rock that workmen cut out of Normandy's granite quarries as he watched the executioners remove the chains from the Count of Arques and carry his body away. When only the living remained, the Duke stepped up to the stake in the center of the chamber, and, with a torchbearer on either side of him, he turned to his nobles.

"My lords," he said softly, "the greatest task in all

history is ahead of us. We must not fail in that task. The price of failure is death, as you have all seen. And any who are remiss in their duty to Normandy will pay that price. It is too late now to turn back, and this post awaits any who falter." His tone changed and became conversational. "The council is adjourned until further notice. I'm sure you'll all be prompt when it next convenes."

No one moved, and William strolled toward the stairs, where Fitz Osbern was waiting for him. "Lord Seneschal," the Duke said, "be good enough to give me your company at dinner." There was a deathly hush below as they mounted the steps together.

Every county in Normandy sent double its quota of fighting men to Lillebonne, and within a month of the meeting of the *parlement* a city of tents had been erected on the right bank of the river Seine. Many of the soldiers were veterans of William's previous campaigns, but even the most experienced were exhausted by the Duke's training schedule. He was undeterred by the cold and snow, indifferent to the complaints of those who had never in their lives worked so hard, and he forced every unit to drill incessantly, from sunrise to dusk, seven days each week. The lazy were flogged, repeated offenders were branded, and even officers who shirked their duties were punished. The son of one of the western barons was beaten with a metal rod before the entire army because he had fallen asleep while in command of a sentry post, and a wealthy young count was sent into banishment for refusing to lead his squadron in a simulated cavalry charge after having spent ten hours in the field earlier that same day.

The army took shape gradually, and it became evident to even the most ignorant peasant boy that he was a member of an elite band, an organization that made up in discipline and stamina what it lacked in numbers. Barons slashed at each other with swords, counts hurled steel-tipped spears at targets until their arms ached, and each night, after the common soldiers had stumbled to their straw pallets, every officer was required to ride to the castle, where Fitz Osbern, Mont Gomeri, and other generals delivered a series of lectures on battle tactics.

It was the custom for a commander in chief to retire and take his ease during a period of training, but Duke William remained with his troops, and no one labored harder. He appeared everywhere, and no effort was too great for him, no task too menial. He ran beside chain-mail bearers to show them how best to protect their masters, he demonstrated the most efficient method of armoring a horse; and he thought nothing of standing in knee-high snow and mud to sharpen a blade on a stone. Men who had never caught more than a glimpse of him in all their lives soon became so accustomed to his presence that they took him for granted; he joked in rude country dialects with farm boys, he dipped his fingers into iron stew pots with youths who had a short time before led the peaceful lives of shepherds, and he exchanged coarse banter with townsmen who liked to think of themselves as worldly sophisticates.

His strength was prodigious, and nobles ten years his junior discovered that they were no match for him in test jousts. They learned, too, that there were sharp limits to the spirit of equality that he encouraged during the day. When they encountered him during the evenings at the castle, he demanded rigid politeness and an observance of the most formal etiquette, and no one was permitted to forget that his word, his least desire, was law. He was seldom seen after dark, however, for he made it a practice to dine with merchants, travelers, and sailors who had visited England, and he spent countless hours with half-closed eyes, listening to descriptions of the land he would invade.

Late one morning he was in the hills beyond Lillebonne, personally testing a new catapult, when a messenger arrived from the castle, and Gerbod, whose principal function was to see that the Duke was not unduly disturbed, conferred briefly with the man. William, paying no attention to the conversation, hoisted a large rock into the catapult, then joined the six men of the machine's crew. They pulled together at the ropes, the catapult arm was released, and the stone soared high into the air. The Duke watched it with satisfaction as it crashed into a sapling more than fifty yards distant, and only then did he become aware of his stepson, who stood beside him.

"I think you'll want to know, sir, that Abbé Lanfranc has returned from Rome."

"Has he?" William wiped his grimy hands on his tunic and started to turn back to the catapult.

"He's at the castle," Gerbod added hastily.

"Here—in Lillebonne?"

"Yes, sir. He's waiting to see you. And Bishop Odo is with him."

William laughed and slapped the boy on the shoulder. "That means they've brought a good report from Rome. If the news had been bad, Odo would have ridden straight for Bayeux. Unfortunately—for Odo—I have too much on my mind to see him at present." He beckoned to the messenger, who hurried forward. "Tell the Abbé I shall join him shortly. Let him understand that I'll receive him privately. And tell my brother Odo—Oh, make any excuses you like. Catapults are more important to me these days then the stories he'll tell of his successes in Rome."

As the messenger rode off to do his bidding, William again directed his attention to the catapult crew, and not until the men had mastered the art of loading the cumbersome weapon rapidly did he consent to return to the castle. Then, with only Gerbod beside him, he rode toward the river. His tunic was smeared with mud, there were dirt smudges on his face, and the fabric of his cloak was soggy, but it didn't bother him that he looked more like a brigand than a reigning duke, and as they neared the castle he was happily telling Gerbod of several refinements he was planning in the art of siege warfare. English town walls were low, he said, and even manor houses of the greatest nobles were virtually defenseless.

He was still thinking of catapults when he dismounted in the entrance and walked into the sparsely furnished great hall. Two people were standing close to the hearth; the nearer was Lanfranc, and for a moment he thought that Odo, who never knew when he was unwelcome, had stubbornly insisted on remaining. Then he recognized his wife, and stopped short. Gerbod, who had obviously seen his mother from a distance, had diplomatically retired in anticipation of a storm.

Matilda saw William and hurried to him, and he could tell by her expression that she was greatly excited. She lifted her face to him and he kissed her, but his lips were cool as they brushed against hers. She had no business coming to Lillebonne, he thought irritably, and eventually she would be sure to comment on his untidy appearance. She delighted in telling him that the Duke of Normandy—and future King of England—should never look like a ragged plowman.

His greeting to Lanfranc was warmer, and he discovered that he was genuinely pleased to see the cleric. "Well, Father," he said, "you've gained weight in your travels. Did Archdeacon Hildebrand set a bountiful table or was your nourishment spiritual?"

The Abbé laughed and said something inconsequential, but Matilda could not wait for the usual exchange of polite amenities. "William, the Holy Father has given you his blessing. And Harold has been excommunicated!"

"Congratulations, Father Lanfranc." William felt no sense of elation, though it was comforting to know that Hildebrand, who rarely supported a losing side, had faith in him. "How large a payment of Peter's pence must we make after we've taken England?"

Lanfranc smiled in quick appreciation of the Duke's perspicacity. "I'll give you the full details, if you'd like them."

"You might tell them to me a little later, when there's more time. At dinner, perhaps. You'll stay to dinner too?" he added politely to his wife.

She either ignored his indifference or was too overwrought to notice it, and throwing open her long wool cloak with an embroidered collar, she brought out a tiny gold box and offered it to William. "Father Lanfranc has allowed me to carry this. It's a special gift to you from the Holy Father—a hair of St. Peter!"

"A very interesting curio," he murmured, turning the little case over in his hand.

If his lack of enthusiasm dampened Maltida's fervor, she gave no sign of it as she picked up a furled banner that had stood propped against the stone wall. Unrolling it carefully, she held it up for his inspection. "This," she said breathlessly, "is a papal banner from His Holiness and the College of Cardinals!"

"It will be an inspiring token, I'm sure. Thank you very much for it, Father Lanfranc, and please convey my thanks to the Vatican. My troops will enjoy knowing they're fighting with the blessing of the Holy See." William tried hard to inject the right note of sincerity into his voice. The Abbé had been successful by his own standards, and it would be cruel to hurt his feelings, just as it would be impossible to make him understand that wars were won by armed men, not by pretty flags.

Lanfranc smiled quietly. "I hope you'll find it useful," he said complacently.

Matilda, as eager as a child, waved the banner back and forth. "Don't you understand?" she cried. "You've been authorized to fight a holy war against an outlawed criminal. You have the official sanction of the Church! Our—your claim to the throne of England has been recognized legally, and every ruler in Europe must either support you—or at the very least remain neutral—unless he wants to be excommunicated too."

Her husband looked at her closely; in her agitation her cloak had come open, and under it he saw her smoothly fitting gown of fine blue wool. He had no way of knowing that she had chosen it with great care because it had a wide neck that framed her shoulders and throat, nor did he remember that he had once complimented her on the scarf of emerald-green silk that swathed her waist, diaphragm, and hips. He merely thought that she looked remarkably attractive, that he could hardly hold her to blame for her enthusiasm and that it had been a very long time since they had slept together.

"I understand perfectly," he replied, and his voice was surprisingly courteous and gentle. "I'm grateful to Father Lanfranc for his efforts on my behalf, and I hope

that I'll someday be able to offer him a suitable reward.
Now, if you'll both pardon me, there are about two
hours left before dinner, and a cavalry squadron is
waiting for my inspection. I'm afraid I can only offer
you plain fare—unless you find some way to make
different arrangements with the chef, as long as you're
here, Matilda."

Before she could utter an impatient retort, the Abbé
stepped forward and slipped his arm through William's. "We'll walk out into the courtyard with you, if
you don't mind," he suggested. "There's something I'd
like you to see."

The pole attached to the papal banner was long, and
Matilda was unsure how to carry it, so the Duke took it
from her. He was still holding it as they emerged from
the entrance hall of the castle, and he was astonished
when a large group of mounted men on the green
began to cheer when they saw it and him. Some wore
armor, some were more lightly clad, and William
identified a score of different types of helmets, shields,
and swords. The presence of these strangers on his
property was incomprehensible to him, and he turned
to Lanfranc for an explanation.

"They're gentlemen who want to join your expedition," the Abbé said when the tumult subsided. "Some
are landless Italian knights, a few are German, and
some are French."

"How—"

"Naturally Archdeacon Gilbert carried the papal
banner aloft on our journey home from Rome, and
these fine lords and knights were attracted by it. As its
fame spread, men actually sought us out and insisted
on coming with us. I imagine that by this time most of
Europe has learned you've been authorized to conduct
a holy war. Oh yes—there's one little detail. As these

gentlemen came to me, I assured them that you'd make specific individual arrangements with them which will guarantee them a precise portion of the spoils of war, depending on their own rank and on the number of men-at-arms they bring with them."

William forgot his dignity completely as he enveloped the priest in a bear hug. "Father Lanfranc, you've given me the sword that will win me the greatest of victories!"

"You'll be victorious because it is the Lord's will, not because you wish it," the Abbé replied when he recovered his breath.

The Duke stood very still for a moment, his mind racing. The possibilities that the Vatican's approval had opened to him were just now blossoming in his mind, and they staggered him. Matilda said something to him, but he did not hear her, and he started to pace up and down, a sure sign that he was concentrating. Suddenly he stopped and shouted for Gerbod and three other equerries; they came running to him, badly frightened by his tone.

"Tell those knights out there that I'll receive them this afternoon, one by one, and conclude agreements with them!" he commanded. "Send the Seneschal to me, and tell Mont Gomeri I want him to prepare fifteen—no, twenty—small troops of cavalry for courier purposes. I want them to travel to every kingdom, every duchy, every county with the news of the holy war, and I want them to offer a fair share to all those who'll join me. Tell Baron Robert to make immediate plans to enlarge the encampment. We'll need several times the space we now use. And send word to all shipyards that we'll need every boat they can build between now and summer!"

The equerries dashed off, and he was about to re-

sume his pacing but could not because Matilda stood in
his path. He was vaguely annoyed at seeing her, and it
did not occur to him that she was waiting with increasing impatience for her share of praise and congratulations. "Have you offered any suggestions to that
unimaginative chef of mine yet?" he demanded. "The
barons and Abbé Lanfranc are going to be hungry for
their dinner after we hold a war council, and so am I! It
isn't every day we're given an opportunity to double or
even triple the size of our army. So see to our dinner,
will you?"

The worst of it, Matilda thought, was that he was not
being malicious; he meant every word quite literally.

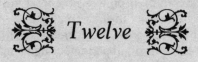

Twelve

SPRING ARRIVED EARLY in 1066, and with the advent
of warmer weather the army moved from Lillebonne to
St. Valéry, a fishing village on the English Channel, its
principal attribute a magnificent natural harbor. The
shift was advantageous to Duke William, for he could
train his rapidly growing army and at the same time
supervise the building of his invasion fleet. And as the
area around St. Valéry was sparsely settled, the presence of so many men created relatively few problems
for the few local inhabitants.

Each day recruits from all over Europe arrived, and
William, refusing to delegate authority to his lieutenants, interviewed each noble and each knight personally; all agreements with these adventurers bore his
seal, too. In return they pledged themselves uncondi-
tionally to support his enterprise, and they soon learned
that they had to pay a price for the prizes of war they
were seeking: they were required to subject themselves
and their men-at-arms to Norman discipline, and they
discovered that Roger Mont Gomeri, to whom their
training was entrusted, was a harsh taskmaster.

Some of the foreigners wanted to form their own
units and others thought that their rank entitled them to
posts of command, but their desires were ignored and
they were without exception assigned to regiments and
squadrons whose personnel was predominantly Norman. It was obvious that, although William was delighted to accept the volunteers, he was placing his trust

only in his own generals, and the outsiders were compelled to discard their previous habits. Only Norman tactics would be used in the campaign.

By the time the army numbered sixteen thousand men, the problems of preparing enough ships to carry such a mammoth force became paramount, and the Duke spent several weeks conferring with builders, offering bonuses to them, and sending agents into every North Sea port with orders to purchase any vessel that would remain afloat long enough to reach the shores of England. He interrupted these labors only to hang three German knights who, following their native customs, had relieved the boredom of camp life by pillaging in the neighborhood. The foreigners in the army understood at once, and no further lesson was needed to teach them that Norman homes, Norman property, and Norman women were inviolable. There was no repetition of unpleasant incidents.

From time to time rumors reached William's headquarters that the Norwegians, too, were making progress in their preparations for an invasion of England, and the officers who gathered each day to confer at the Duke's pavilion were afraid that the Norsemen, whose fighting prowess was legendary, might strike first. William laughed at his generals' fears, however, and he let it be known that he was indifferent to the strength of King Harold Hardrara and to the cunning of the outlawed English Earl, Tostig. The Norsemen, he announced loudly, were pagans, and their cause could not prosper; privately he confided to Fitz Osbern that Harold Hardrara could not muster more than three or four thousand men at the most, and that any attacks he might make would of necessity be in the nature of scavenger raids rather than serious attempts to conquer the whole of England.

No attempt was made to curb the exaggerated stories

about the Norwegian plans that occasionally swept through the encampment, however. As William explained to his aides, the threat of competition helped to keep the spirit of the mongrel army at a high pitch. Similarly, the troops were kept busy at all times, for it was William's theory that an idle soldier might have time to think, and anyone who pondered long enough was certain to arrive at the conclusion that it was suicidal folly for even a trained and superbly equipped force of sixteen thousand to attempt the conquest of an entire country. However, no one except the barons of the inner war council realized that the Duke was tortured by doubts of success, and like him they expressed the greatest of confidence in public.

Whenever William felt insecure over the future, and he was too intelligent not to measure the hazards he faced, he prescribed the same treatment for himself he had devised for the army, and he worked at a pace that left the most vigorous of his lieutenants unable to keep up with him. No quarrel between knights was too small for his attention, changes in the training schedule of the archers had to be approved by him before they could be put into effect, and he made it a point to take at least one meal each day with the soldiers. It was his habit to arrive unheralded just as a unit was about to eat, and if the food failed to meet his standards, the officer in charge was certain to reprimanded.

Somehow he found the time to administer the affairs of the Duchy of Normandy, too, and civilians to whom he had entrusted positions of responsibility in Rouen, Caen, and Bayeux visited his headquarters almost daily. His barons were less fortunate, for there was no one who could relieve them of the burden of their own affairs, and the Duke reluctantly but wisely granted them leaves of absence so they could return to their homes for brief periods. He himself could not afford such a luxury; there were too many things he had to do, and too few hours in which to do them, so he remained permanently at St. Valéry.

As a consequence life at Rouen Castle was insufferably, monotonously dull. The only men in the household were the middle-aged guards who provided a token security force, and the Duchess's ladies, deprived of male company, complained loudly to each other of their misery. The children were a problem too; Gundrada sulked most of the time, and for no visible reason Adelize lost her appetite and little William succumbed to a series of head colds. And Robert became impossible after a tutor made the unfortunate error of informing him that he *was* now the senior male representative of the ruling house in the capital. The boy became overbearing, and for two days was so rude to everyone that his mother was finally forced to administer a spanking of such severity that he needed a special cushion at mealtimes.

Abbé Lanfranc was a frequent visitor at the castle, and through him Matilda gleaned some idea of the army's growing strength and of her husband's many activities. Once each month Gerbod came home for a day and a night, too, and gave her glowing accounts of all that his stepfather was doing, but she rarely had any direct word from William himself. As she so often told herself, he might as well already be in England. But she knew better than to complain, and she endured her dreary existence with such a show of high spirits that her ladies were amazed.

She enjoyed only one break in the dreary routine, and that proved to be a nuisance. A Swedish count, Einar Gustaffson, joined the army, and as he brought more than three hundred of his retainers with him, William wrote one of his infrequent letters to Maltida, instructing her to entertain Gustaffson's wife. The

Countess was a harridan who found fault with everything and everyone, her three-week visit was a nightmare, and when she finally left Matilda was happy to sink back into the blank of living through one day while waiting for the next.

Late one afternoon that was indistinguishable from those that had preceded it the Duchess sat alone in her bedchamber, rubbing oil into her face. It had been sent to her as a gift from Athens, and although she found its odor unpleasant, she had decided to try it for want of something better to do. She had just finished washing her hair, and it hung in damp strands over the collar and shoulders of the old faded wool dressing robe she had been wearing of late. Her movements were slow as she massaged the oil into her cheeks, her forehead, and at the corners of her eyes, and she deliberately was thinking of nothing; it was easier, she had discovered, to pass the time when she emptied her mind.

Suddenly she was roused from her near stupor by the blast of a trumpet at the drawbridge, but it nevertheless sounded three times before its significance dawned on her. Then, as she heard the cheers of the elderly guards, she knew that William had returned unexpectedly, and she jumped to her feet in a frenzy. It was like him, she reflected bitterly as she hastily pinned up her hair and slipped a silk turban over her head, to give her no advance warning of his arrival.

His voice boomed in the entrance hall below, but Matilda, who had yearned for its sound, was in no mood to appreciate it now. Her fingers trembled as she threw off her dressing robe and snatched a gown from her cupboard. She was in such a hurry that she couldn't take time to select a dress that she knew would please William, and there was no time to summon one of her serving maids to help her, so she dislodged the turban and had to adjust it again.

There were joyous shouts at the foot of the stair well as the children raced to greet their father, and their laughter, mingling with his, floated up to the frantic Duchess. Kicking off her old slippers, she pulled on her stockings so quickly that she ripped a small hole in the top of them, and she took the first pair of shoes she found. They were green, and her dress was blue, but there was no opportunity now to find clothes that would match.

William was roaring a greeting to several of the servants he knew and liked and the children were still making a frightful din when Matilda, who had been desperately wondering whether there was a side of beef in the kitchen larder, suddenly remembered the oil on her face. She looked around for a towel but could find none, so she caught up the first piece of cloth she saw. It happened to be her dressing robe, and it was fortunate that the material was soft. She barely had time to wipe away the last vestiges of the Athenian oil and stuff the robe into a shelf of her cupboard when William arrived at the door.

"I'm home," he announced.

Matilda simulated amazement and gasped. "What a shock! You're the last person on earth I expected to see!"

He advanced across the room to her, and there was something in his step, or perhaps it was his expression, that made Matilda think that in spite of all his bluster he was at times unaccountably shy. She felt a trifle timid herself, and as she stood for his kiss she thought that their long separation was responsible; they had been apart for so long and their lives had been so different that they were almost strangers. William's kiss was gentle, and he held his wife in his arms for a long moment; his tenderness surprised her almost as much as it pleased her.

He took a step away from her and looked her up and down. "What's that on your head?" he asked gruffly.

"It's called a turban, and it comes from Persia. Do you like it?" If he insisted that she remove it, she would be lost, for her hair was nothing but a tangle of damp curls.

He grinned and shrugged. "If it pleases you, I have no complaints."

Matilda concealed her relief artfully. "How long will you be home, dear?"

"Until the day after tomorrow." William sat down on the edge of the bed, tested the softness of the mattress without quite realizing what he was doing, and smiled. "I've been taking care of most government matters from St. Valéry, but I need to hold meetings with the chamberlain, the treasurer, and Lanfranc, so I decided it would be simpler to spend a day and a half in Rouen."

"I wish you'd told me you were coming."

"I didn't know it myself until I made up my mind just before I left."

His tone was defensive, and Matilda knew she had taken the wrong appraoch. "All that really matters is that you're here. I've missed you, darling."

"I've missed you, too."

They gazed at each other steadily, and Matilda thought that there was at last a truce between them. It was even possible that his hard core of bitterness had melted; he was always happiest when he was in the field with his army, so perhaps he had forgiven her for what he still believed to be her blunder. Lanfranc had assured her that, even if William had murdered Harold when he'd had the chance, an invasion of England would have still been necessary, and she had thought on numberless occasions that someday she would force her husband to see the truth. Now, however, she discovered that she no longer cared; if there was peace between them, she was willing to forget old scores.

"I wish you'd do something for me." William stood abruptly.

After he had been with his troops for a time his manners were often rather brusque, and Matilda wondered if she was blushing. "Of course, dear, anything."

"I know you're rather strict about the children's schedules, and ordinarily I agree with you. But it won't hurt them to have supper with us just his once, will it?"

"Indeed it won't." The attempt to sound cordial cost her an enormous effort, for she realized that the barrier that separated her from William still existed.

"Good!" he said heartily. "I've missed them, too, you know."

"Yes, I'm sure you have," she murmured, following him to the entrance and into the corridor because he gave her no alternative. "Is everything going as it should at the encampment, William?" she asked in a desperate effort to detain him, to keep him to herself for a little longer before she was forced to share him with the children.

"I'm satisfied," he replied, continuing to walk toward the staircase. "We have occasional difficulties, to be sure," he added indulgently. "The Spanish cavalry can't learn the principle of making mass attacks, but they will. I've turned them over to Taillefer to tame."

She stared at him, and her sense of bewilderment, of being completely out of touch with all that he was doing became greater. "Taillefer—the juggler, the minstrel?"

"I've knighted him," William said as they reached the bottom of the stairs and started into the great hall. "War often brings out the best in a man." he stooped to pick up Adelize, who raced to him, and soon all the children were surrounding him.

Each clamored for his attention, making further adult conversation impossible. Matilda noticed that as always William favored Gundrada, and she had to curb an absurd feeling of jealousy as the family moved toward the dais. Robert promptly seated himself in his father's chair, which amused the Duke; had he spent more time at home lately he would have sent his son flying. Little William tried to pluck his father's dagger from its sheath, all the children were speaking and shouting simultaneously, and the result was pandemonium. William sat down, Gundrada and Adelize immediately settled themselves on his lap, and for the first time in many months he looked younger than his thirty-nine years.

Then someone hurried into the chamber. The Duke and Duchess looked up at the same instant and saw Gerbod, his boots dusty, the dirt of the road still on his hands and face. He greeted his mother with a quick, perfunctory kiss, then saluted his stepfather. And William smiled at him quizzically.

"I thought you were going to stay at St. Valéry while I was away. You had some work of a rather special nature that was going to keep you busy, if I remember correctly." It was better, in front of Matilda, to mention nothing of Gerbod's romance with the daughter of the local lord there; the boy had begged him to say nothing and William respected his confidence, especially in the light of his suspicion that Matilda might become upset when she realized that her eldest son had become a man.

Gerbod's eyes expressed his appreciation of the Duke's discretion. "I've come to bring you word of an incident that took place at St. Valéry not an hour after you left."

Matilda was dismayed at the thought that even this brief visit would be cut short. "You can't go back there tonight!" she cried.

"Suppose you let me hear what's happened first," her husband said. "What is it, Gerbod?"

"Robert of Mortain has captured a spy, and not one of the ordinary ones this time, either. He's an extremely intelligent man who speaks fluent French and seems to have a thorough knowledge of military organization. I suspect he's at least a knight, and Robert thinks he may even belong to the English nobility."

Matilda gasped and was about to say something, but William cut in before she could speak. "How much has the man seen and how much does he know?"

"We're not sure, sir." Gerbod glanced at the younger children and hesitated for a moment before continuing. "Baron Mont Gomeri was in favor of applying—persuasion to find out just how much information the man did gather, but the Seneschal wouldn't permit it."

"I've thought for a long time that Fitz Osbern has been growing soft!" Matilda declared indignantly. "Why shouldn't he put a spy to the torture?"

"Why should he?" William asked tolerantly. "As the man has been captured, he can do us no harm. The English have indulged in some rather barbaric practices when two or three of my representatives have fallen into their hands, but I see no need for us to follow their example. I hope to civilize the English, not reduce myself to their level. What's being done with the spy?"

"Nothing, Father. The Seneschal is waiting for word from you before he disposes of the case."

Perhaps Matilda's frustrated loneliness was responsible for the emotion that surged up in her, or it might have been her husband's tone of reproof when he had contradicted her. All she knew was that she felt wildly angry. "I hope you'll have the fiend put on the rack!" she cried.

William gazed at her in mock sorrow. "You were a cultured young woman when I first brought you here from Flanders." He paused, and there was a serious vein beneath his heavy humor as he asked, "Is that what you'd do with a spy?"

"Hanging is too quick and too easy a punishment. I don't believe in leniency when there's so much at stake!"

"You still have a great deal to learn about government and war—and people." William addressed her quietly now, and without levity. "If you have nothing better to do, it might interest you to come to St. Valéry with me and see how I handle the matter."

"I have nothing better to do." Matilda was elated but she could not keep the bitterness from her voice.

"That's settled, then. Gerbod, you'd better eat some supper, and then ride straight back to the camp. Tell the Seneschal to hold the prisoner under close guard until I arrive the day after tomorrow, and be sure that my pavilion is made ready to receive your mother. Her Grace is going to be taught a lesson in statecraft."

The departure of the Duke and Duchess was marred by only one minor unpleasantness. While the horses were being saddled, William, who had devoted himself to the children at breakfast, looked at his wife's dress of deep gold-colored velvet and frowned. "Is that what you're wearing?"

"Yes, is something wrong with it?" Matilda was irritated, for she had selected her gown with great care. The honey-colored silk sleeves of her undertunic fitted her wrists closely, and she had thought that the costume was an eminently sensible one for the journey.

"Those black velvet laces on the sides," William declared, pointing. "What is it the priests call them?"

"Gates-of-hell," Matilda replied, and laughed. "I

really am surprised at you, dear. I never would have dreamed you'd be a prude about my *chainse* showing through the laces."

It was his turn to laugh. "I'm a prude, am I? You're going to ride through an army camp, not make a gracious appearance before your subjects in your own home. I was merely trying to think of you and your sensitivities, that's all. You've never been near thousands of men who haven't seen a woman in months. I can tell that you have more than one lesson to learn today!"

He moved off and mounted his stallion before Matilda could thank him for his consideration. She would have gone upstairs and changed her clothes had there been time, but William was impatient to leave, so she had no choice but to allow her groom to help her into the saddle. William was uncommunicative for the better part of an hour after they rode across the drawbridge of Rouen Castle, but the sun and the wind, the disciplined precision of the cavalry escort, and the obvious pleasure of other travelers at the sight of the ducal party restored his good humor.

During the remainder of the journey he rode at Matilda's side and chatted with her, and although he talked about nothing of significance, he had not treated her with such kindness in so long a time that she felt almost as though he were courting her anew. Color rose in her cheeks, her eyes began to shine and by the time they reached the outposts of the encampment she once more justified her reputation for beauty.

As William had predicted, there were more men gathered in the area than Matilda had ever before seen. They saluted the Duke but they cheered the Duchess, and Matilda could not help but wonder if her costume was in any way responsible for their enthusiasm. She felt distinctly uncomfortable as she saw soldiers and officers alike eye her hungrily, but she waved and smiled regally as her mare carried her past the vast sea of tents, and not even William, who glanced at her from time to time was struck by her aplomb, guessed that she was suffering from acute embarrassment.

Several of the barons were waiting at the ducal pavilion, a billowing tent of silk with a wooden floor, and Matilda found that she was as pleased to see them as they were to greet her. They and their wives had been important to her for years, and she was surprised to discover that she had missed them. Fitz Osbern's heartiness, disguised by a thin veneer of urbanity, Mont Gomeri's aggressiveness, and the ambitious alertness of Robert of Mortain were almost as familiar to her as her own husband's temperament. Only now did she fully realize how events had swept past her and had left her stranded behind the thick piles of Rouen Castle's masonry.

William was curiously indulgent and made no objection when his barons lingered at the pavilion; ordinarily he would have accused them of loitering and sent them back to work, but he apparently recognized their need for feminine companionship, and he permitted them to present several foreign nobles to the Duchess, too. He smiled to himself when his standard-bearer planted Matilda's personal ensign beside his flag and the papal banner in the front of the pavilion, and only Gerbod, who had come to recognize all of his moods, knew that he was waiting for something and was not merely pampering either Matilda or his generals. The Lion of Normandy was aptly named; there was a ferociously feline streak in his nature when he was about to pounce.

The English spy was brought to the pavilion, and to

the astonishment of Matilda and the barons William
greeted him with the utmost courtesy. The Duchess,
already prejudiced against the man, took an instant
dislike to him; he was blond, slender, and tall, and
something in his manner reminded her of Brihtric, the
Cornish lord who had been indifferent to her charms
prior to her marriage to William. The spy's sardonic
blue eyes chilled her, and when he bowed to her she
thought that, if William had brought her here so he
could hang the man for her entertainment, she would
enjoy the spectacle.

"Gentlemen," the Duke said cheerfully, "Her Grace
is paying her first visit to St. Valéry, and I'm sure she
wants to see the encampment, the ships in the harbor, the training fields, and the arsenals. Our guest
from London has probably seen some portions of our
camp, but he was unfortunately detained before he
could make a real tour of the place. So I suggest that we
act as guides, both for Her Grace and for our English
guest."

The barons thought he was joking and laughed
heartily; then, one by one, they came to the conclusion
that he was serious, and they fell silent. Matilda was
uncertain that she had heard her husband correctly,
and the spy looked bewildered, having expected immediate execution when he had been led before the
Duke. Now, for some unfathomable reason, he was
being offered a brief respite from death, and he was the
first to speak. "I'm very pleased to accept your invitation, Lord Duke," he said.

"I'm sure you are," William replied with a chuckle.
"Remove this man's bonds at once, and saddle a horse
for him. And bring up a mare for Her Grace, a gentle
one."

He walked out into the afternoon sunlight, and the

others, still perplexed, followed him. Fitz Osbern, who thought he knew his master, cast a surreptitious glance of inquiry at Matilda, but she could only shrug her shapely shoulders as she followed her husband into the open. Within a few minutes the party was mounted, and William immediately took on the role of principal guide.

"At our last muster," he said, waving toward the great mass of tents that spread out in every direction, "the army numbered approximately sixteen thousand five hundred men. Is that figure correct, Seneschal?"

"It's closer to seventeen thousand now," Fitz Osbern muttered, looking uneasily at the spy.

They moved slowly through the camp, and occasionally William stopped to ask a soldier about his previous military experience his reaction to the prospect of invading England, and his opinion of his immediate superiors. The replies demonstrated clearly that here was an army of confident, experienced veterans who were eager to test their skill and courage against the enemy. The spontaneity of the troops' enthusiasm was obviously unfeigned, and the spy was impressed.

His eyes widened even more when William led the way into the fields, and Matilda, who knew nothing of the war, was dumfounded. The energy of lords and knights, men-at-arms, and churls was apparently inexhaustible; a mock battle was arranged, and the cavalry and infantry fought with such disciplined vigor that the Duchess was sure there would be hundreds of casualties. The calculated savagery was unlike anything she had ever witnessed, and although the sun was hot she began to shiver.

William blandly exhibited his warehouses, hastily built wooden structures in which arms, clothing, and blankets were heaped, and he proudly showed the spy a large pile of maps; these, he explained, were being painstakingly reproduced by a corps of friars so that every senior officer would land in England carrying on his person a complete portfolio of the countryside.

The harbor, which they inspected shortly before sundown, was an awesome sight. Scores of craft rode at anchor, and dozens more were being constructed on the shore. Builders hammered at skeleton hulls, painters and calkers and sailmakers by the hundred were at work, and as the party watched, a new vessel was gently hauled down the beach and floated. The barons, openly apprehensive because the Englishman had seen so much, remained close to him with their hands on the hilts of their swords, but William smiled and remarked cryptically that the spy would not run away because escape was unnecessary.

When the tour was completed they returned to the pavilion, where flares were lighted and Matilda was ensconced in a cushioned chair. William called for refreshments, and when they were provided he raised his cup of mead to the Englishman. "I believe I've shown you everything worthy of notice," he said.

"If there's more, Lord Duke, I wouldn't care to see it." The spy was depressed, partly because he was overwhelmed by the display of strength he had witnessed, partly because his own end was drawing near.

"Do you have any questions?" William asked solicitiously. "If there's anything you don't understand we'll try our best to explain it to you."

"No, it's all clear to me. Too clear." The Englishman closed his eyes for a moment.

"Then you'll have no trouble giving Harold a full description, I'm sure." William turned to the Seneschal, who stood beside him. "See to it that this gentleman is given a seaworthy fishing skiff, well provisioned. And send an escort in two of our own ships into the Channel with him. As for the rest of you, I suggest that you remain close beside him until he sails for home. If he should be killed—or harmed in any way—the general whose troops are responsible for the outrage will be relieved of his command."

The Duke's words were received in stunned, disbelieving silence. The barons wanted to protest but said nothing when William stared at each in turn, and Matilda was so shocked that she became momentarily speechless. And so it was the spy who was again the first to reply. "You're giving me my life—and my freedom?" he asked incredulously.

"I am. But only on condition that you give Harold a complete account of everything you've seen here. Let him see me and my army through your eyes, so he'll know that his days are numbered."

The gesture was so audacious, so breath-takingly defiant that Fitz Osbern grinned, and soon all the barons roared their approval. Boldness was a virtue, bravery won wars, and they were followers of the most fearless and courageous leader in Christendom. They were still laughing and shouting as they escorted the Englishman into the night, leaving the Duke and Duchess alone in the pavilion. And Matilda, who had not spoken a word, gripped the arms of her chair.

"That was nothing but sheer bravado!" she cried.

"Really?" The smile faded slowly from William's lips.

"You showed the Englishman your strength and then set him free for only one reason. You wanted to insult me. Your vanity was hurt the other night when I said he should be tortured to death. You thought I was interfering in something that was none of my business, and so you made a mad gesture just to spite me. You had to risk all that's at stake to thumb your nose at me."

There had been a time, William thought, when such an outburst would have angered him, but now he knew better. Like all women, Matilda could see problems only in terms of personal issues. It was an effort to explain his conduct to her, and he wondered briefly why he bothered. "I've seen too many men die to believe in killing for its own sake. If I'd put the spy to death, I'd have gained nothing. It was to my advantage to let him live. Harold will hear of my preparations and will be afraid. All England will whisper the story of my clemency, and the way will be prepared for victory before I've struck a single blow. You see, Matilda," he added, his voice hardening, "I have confidence in my army. And I have confidence in myself. I know my capabilities, and my faith in myself is unlimited. I'm sorry you don't share that trust. It's too bad—for both of us."

He turned abruptly and walked out into the night, leaving Matilda alone in the military pavilion that was so alien to her.

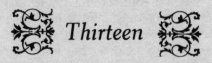 *Thirteen*

LATE IN MAY the last sails and oarlocks were fitted into place and the invasion fleet was ready to sail. In June the army completed its training, two hundred Bavarian war horses arrived and were armored, and the forges of the swordsmiths glowed day and night. By the end of the month the generals reported to Duke William that preparations would be completed within a week's time, and he relaxed his strict regulations sufficiently to permit the wives of officers to join them at St. Valéry. His own wife was among the first to respond, although he had issued no specific invitation to her.

And then, early in July, the winds failed. A hot midsummer sun shone down on the encampment each day from a cloudless sky while the army waited, patiently at first, then with growing restlessness, but still there was no wind. Prayers were offered morning and night, and some of the Germans and the Scandinavians, who were pagans, made secret sacrifices to their gods. The horses began to grow fat because of lack of exercise, and the soldiers, forced to subsist on a diet composed chiefly of rye bread and herring, became thin. The men were bored, and their martial fervor melted away beneath the hot sun; they grumbled and gambled, and each day there were fights and knifings.

August came, and still there was no wind. Provisions became slimmer and the barons pauperized Normandy for months to come by sending to their own storehouses for barley and rye to feed the hungry troops. The papal banner wilted listlessly on its staff, and the soldiers inevitably began to mutter to each other that God did not favor their enterprise. England, just across the Channel, seemed very far away.

By the first of September the foreigners were so discouraged that they started to desert, and the Duke made no attempt to hold them to their vows, knowing that men who had lost the will to fight would be useless to him. The fever of disaffection spread rapidly, and within a few days more than two thousand of the adventurers vanished, leaving a scant fourteen thousand would-be invaders in St. Valéry. Then the Norman troops, who had until now remained loyal, spoke openly of returning to their homes if there was no wind that day. None appeared, and a time of supreme crisis was at hand.

Everyone wondered what William Bastard would do, and even some of his own nobles predicted that he would voluntarily call off the whole enterprise rather than lose face by allowing his entire force to disintegrate. While the army speculated, the Duke ate a gloomy supper with Matilda, his barons and their wives, and then, taking no one into his confidence, he rode unaccompanied down the beach and stared out at the idle ships in the harbor.

It was late when he returned to his pavilion, but Matilda, who had been in bed for several hours, sat up as soon as she heard his footsteps. He did not look at her as he lighted a single taper, and his eyes were those of a lonely man who carried a great responsibility that could be shared with no one. His face was pale, almost waxen, and from the way he stood Matilda knew how he would look when he grew old.

"Are you all right, dear?"

"Certainly." He turned to her but seemed to look past her.

"After you left tonight we heard a rumor that Harold Hardrara and Tostig have already sailed. Do you suppose it's true?"

"I don't know." William's lips twisted in a wry smile. "It would be strange if Thor and Wotan have conjured up a wind for the Norsemen when the Lord God Almighty has denied me even a gentle breeze."

Matilda peered at him anxiously. "Count de la Warde said that Hardrara has enough men to conquer all of England. You don't suppose that's possible, do you?" There was no reply, and she felt a wave of panic. "Where would Hardrara find so many men?"

"I don't know." William stood with his hands clasped behind his back and continued to stare at the silken wall of the tent.

"What are you going to do?" There was a note of hysteria in her voice.

"I don't know." He was silent for a long time, and then he said abruptly, "Go to sleep."

Matilda obediently closed her eyes, but her fists were clenched and her body was tense. She felt a sense of failure so great that it suffocated her; now, of all times, she should be of help to William, but her mind would not function, and she thought that the dream of conquest was ended. The army would be disbanded, Harold would keep England, and she would not blame William if he sent her off to a convent for the rest of her days.

Somewhere in the camp a soldier was playing a zithern and another sang to its accompaniment. The music was stickily sweet and the words were simple and sentimental, but there was honest yearning in the man's voice as he plaintively recalled the joys he had known in his little cottage. Matilda could not shut out the sound, and her lashes were wet; she opened her eyes and saw that her husband had not moved.

"William," she whispered. "Please. What are you going to do?"

"I don't know."

Had he spoken with any emotion, even discouragement, Matilda would have been relieved, but his tone was flat. Always practical, he was wrestling with his problem in the only way he knew, and while he weighed and balanced facts, his army was crumbling. Matilda had to bite her lower lip to prevent herself from screaming, but after a time she grew calmer and toward dawn she slept.

When she awoke she saw at once that William's side of the bed was untouched and she looked at the place where he had stood through the long hours of the night, but he was gone. She dressed hurriedly in a severe dress of dark gray linen, and when an attendant came in with a small loaf of barley bread and a mug of watered wine for her breakfast, she could not eat. The man was humbly sorry, but he did not know where His Grace had gone, and Matilda completed her toilet in a fraction of her usual time, then hurried outside.

Gerbod was standing near the pavilion with two chevaliers when she emerged, and all three were talking animatedly. When the knights saw her they bowed and moved away with more haste than dignity, and Gerbod walked quickly to her. "Good morning, Mother," he said with a nervous smile.

"Good morning, dear. Do you know where your father has gone or what he's doing to——"

"I'd advise you to stay inside the pavilion today," the boy interrupted, taking her arm. "It's going to be very warm, and the dust is worse than ever."

Matilda wrenched free and glared at him. "It's no warmer than it's been any morning in the past two weeks. And you know I loathe being told what to do!"

"Mother, you really should——"

"And if you won't tell me where your father is, I'll find him myself!"

She walked away rapidly, so disturbed that she paid no particular attention to where she was going. Gerbod, she reflected grimly, was becoming more like William every day, and it gave her a small measure of satisfaction to note that he made no attempt to follow her. The camp seemed strangely deserted, and she felt a stab of uneasiness despite the reassuring thought that she had slept late and that the men had gone off to the fields for a mock battle. Then she heard raucous shouts somewhere in the distance.

She was so agitated that she immediately imagined that the army was disbanding; drawing closer to the sound, she realized that it came from the main entrance to the camp, and her fears seemed to be confirmed. She lifted her skirts and started to run, but as she came within sight of the gate she stopped short and wished that she had never come. A long row of covered, mule-drawn wagons was lined up outside the camp, and from the nearest of them stepped the most brazen young woman the Duchess had ever seen.

The girl wore only a single garment, a kirtle of thin, flame-orange silk, and the dress, if it could be called that, was wrapped about with braid in such a way that every line of the wench's body was clearly revealed. Her loose, flowing hair gave her an abandoned look, her shoes of scarlet silk had long, pointed toes, and she wore pendant earrings of cheap brass. Swaying slightly from side to side, she walked through the gate, and even at a distance Matilda could see that her lips were smeared bright red and that her eyelids were painted blue.

The shouts became louder, and the Duchess

realized that hundreds of soldiers were crowded inside
the gate. Horrified, she watched as a number of men
beckoned to the girl, who paused, studied the crowd,
and then smiled at a burly cavalryman. He ran forward,
picked her up, and carried her off. Unable to move,
Matilda thought she had descended to the hell that
Abbé Lanfranc so often described in his sermons: trollop after trollop sauntered through the gates, and all
were shameless, wicked beyond Matilda's ability to
imagine depravity. Skirts clung to thighs and knees,
some necks were so wide and loose that they gaped
open, and many kirtles left one arm and shoulder
provocatively bare. And without exception the
wenches wore scarlet shoes with pointed toes.

Matilda was revolted, but she could not tear herself
away from the spectacle, and when someone touched
her arm she screamed before she realized that William
was looking down at her, his eyes stony. "Gerbod said
you'd walked in this direction. Come away." His big
hand gripped her upper arm and he began to lead her in
the direction of the pavilion.

It was difficult for Matilda to catch her breath, and
she could not keep up with her husband's long strides.
But her indignation was boundless, and at last she
found her voice. "How could you permit such a thing,
William?"

"Permit it?" He made a strange rasping noise that
remotely resembled a laugh. "Damnation, woman! It's
on my direct orders that every brothel in Normandy has
been emptied."

"Damnation, indeed!" She had to trot to match
his pace. "I've never seen such a disgusting spectacle!"

"It isn't here for you to see. Just remember that
nobody asked you to come to St. Valéry. The place for a
good woman is at home, where she'll be sheltered. But

if you insist on living in the field, then you've got to be prepared to face life as it is, not as you'd like it to be." William was firm but did not raise his voice.

"Did you see their shoes?" she demanded irrelevantly. "Every single one of them is wearing dreadful scarlet slippers with long toes—just like Satan's!"

"Of course," he replied reasonably as they arrived at the pavilion. "They're trollops." Shaking his head, he pointed to a chair, gently pushed her into it, and then stood over her. "You're to stay there! All day! Under no circumstances are you to leave this tent!"

"You mean I'm to give my tacit consent to———"

"You're to obey my orders, Matilda! I'm very pleased to find that you're so ignorant about men, and I intend to keep you ignorant. When you hear about Mabel Mont Gomeri's near escape a few minutes ago, you'll be very happy that you stayed here. The chief difference between you and Mabel Mont Gomeri's near escape is that she knew what she was doing."

He turned and walked out, and before he drew the silken curtains of the entrance together, Matilda caught a glimpse of a file of ducal guards moving into place in front of the pavilion. She was literally a prisoner, and would have to endure the degradation that William was bringing on her, on himself, and on Normandy. Through the long hours of the day the sounds of wild carousal filtered in to her in spite of all her efforts to shut them out. Men shouted and laughed coarsely, women shrieked, and the Duchess thought the terrible orgy would never end.

Although she had no appetite, she forced herself to eat a solitary supper, but her cheeks burned and she could not rid herself of the thought that William, her husband and the father of her children, had deliberately pandered to the worst in men in a desperate effort to hold his army together. No prize, not even England, was worth such debasement.

Exhausted, she retired as soon as she had finished eating, but she did not fall asleep until long after the sounds of the debauched revels had ceased and quiet had once again enveloped St. Valéry. When she awakened in the morning, William, who had conferred with his barons until long after midnight, was already shaved and dressed.

"There's still no wind," he said by way of greeting, "so we'll have to make our own." He grinned at her as though the previous day's disgraceful episode had been an unimportant incident. "Get ready as soon as you can, will you? And wear that dress with the belt like mine. I want you to come with me this morning."

Matilda sat up and brushed her curls away from her face. "Isn't it dangerous for me to go out?" she asked frigidly. "With all those women——"

"They're gone. I permitted them to come here for one day only. This is an army camp, not the site of a pagan festival. Now hurry. Everything depends on the outcome of what we do today." Never had he seemed so self-confident.

He left before she could reply, and Matilda had no choice but to follow his instructions. Several years previous her dressmakers had fashioned her a simple gown of green linen, principal feature a deep, natural-leather corselet which fastened with twin gold buckles. The girdle had amused her because it was a refined, feminine version of William's heavy hide belt, but she recalled distinctly that he had been faintly annoyed when she had first worn it. She sighed over the perversity of men as she buckled the corselet into place, and after a quick breakfast she came into the open.

The drooping flags, lifeless in the still air, reminded

her anew of the gravity of Normandy's crisis, and she managed to smile for the benefit of the officers who stood about in small groups, frowning and looking at the sky. The weather, of course, was their principal topic of conversation. William, who had been pacing up and down restlessly, looked at her corselet, grinned broadly, and came to her at once.

"We're going to take a walk," he said, and offered her his arm.

Two equerries fell in behind them, and they strolled a short distance to a large tent that was sometimes used for staff meetings. Some thirty men in armor were gathered inside, and Matilda saw at once that they were among the leading foreign nobles who had attached themselves to the expedition. They were lounging on benches, and they rose to their feet, reluctantly, it seemed, when they saw the Duke, who entered first. Then Matilda came in, and they politely removed their helmets.

Count Einar Gustaffson of Sweden came forward, kissed the Duchess's hand, and was about to launch into a flowery speech, but William cut him short. "I've asked you to meet me here for a specific purpose," the Duke said, his tone amiable and deceptively soft. "It has come to my attention that all of you are planning—or at least contemplating—leaving the army. If I've been misinformed about any of you, accept my apologies and be good enough to leave the tent, as this little conference does not apply to you."

Some of the nobles struck defiant poses, others looked down at the hard-packed earth, but no one left.

"My lords, I make no attempt to hold you to your promises. However, if any of your retainers would like to remain in my service, there is a command which you might recommend to them. Her Grace has a great zest

for the expedition, and as you can see, she is prepared to
take the place of any lord who might be suffering from a
spasm of cowardice."

William touched Matilda's corselet lightly with his
fingertips, and the foreigners, following the motion of
his hand, gazed hard at her. Suddenly she understood:
no one could fail to note the similarity of her girdle and
William's belt, and he was deliberately shaming the
wavering nobles, but with a sense of humor. They
could leave, but a mere woman would replace them.
Matilda immediately realized the brilliance of William's strategy, and she stood proudly, letting the officers stare at her. To her infinite relief the foreigners'
defiance crumbled, and they began to smile sheepishly.

Gustaffson, whose title gave him seniority, again
stepped forward. He knew, of course, that he had been
maneuvered into a corner, but he had been touched on
the raw core of his honor and had to accept the inevitable. "We would be less than men," he said with a
courtly bow to the Duchess, "if we deprived Her Grace
of the security of her home and the companionship of
her children. So it is our hope that she will be compassionate and will let us serve in her stead."

There had been a time when Matilda would have
replied at once, but now she was less sure of herself. It
was William, not she, who had planned this delicate
move, and she looked at him, wanting his guidance.
He used her hesitation to drive home the lesson to the
defecting nobles and pretended to consider the request
for a moment before nodding slowly.

"My thanks, Lord Count," Matilda said gravely,
playing her role with dignity. "Before you sail I'll give
each of you a favor to wear into battle on my behalf."
She had brought a number of scarves to St. Valéry, she

thought, and if she cut them in half, there would be enough.

The adventurers cheered and loudly proclaimed their renewed loyalty to the Duke's cause. William made no attempt to curb their exuberance, and after shaking the hand of each he gave his arm to Matilda and they walked out, smiling regally. They moved out of earshot of the men in the tent, then William halted and laughed.

"That ridiculous belt was finally of some use," he said.

Before Matilda could respond, he beckoned to a common soldier and the man came running to him. Deeply tanned, with large hands and close-cropped black hair, the churl was indistinguishable from thousands of others, but to Matilda's amazement her husband called the man by name.

"Well, Vilan," he said, speaking in the impossible dialect of the Conteville district, "how are things since your trip home? Your swine has recovered from her distemper?"

The soldier dropped to his knees in the dust. "Thanks to the mercy of the saints and the kindness of your worshipful self, she is well." It was difficult for Matilda to understand his accent; in spite of the years she had spent in Normandy she still could not master the bewildering variety of local speech patterns.

"And Colette?" William asked. The Duchess was so surprised by his ability to remember intimate details of the lives of ordinary people that she wasn't sure whether he was referring to another animal or the soldier's wife.

"She prospers, great Duke," Vilan said, smiling broadly and showing several gaps in his gums. "Soon there will be a little one." Matilda couldn't tell whether he was expecting a piglet or a child.

"God be with you," William declared heartily, help-ing the man to his feet and slapping him between the shoulder blades. "Name him for St. Valéry."

"Colette and I have already decided, great Duke, that he will bear your name." Deeply embarrassed, Vilan bobbed his head and hurried away.

William watched him for a moment, then he turned to his wife and his manner changed. "My thanks for your help this morning," he said impersonally. "I imagine you can find your way back to the pavilion alone. I have a few things to do, and I dare say you'll be busy too."

He walked away from her, and Matilda, hurt by the casual abruptness of his leave-taking, stood and watched him as he started off in the direction of the harbor. For the first time she noticed that scores of soldiers were moving in the same direction, and to her amazement William greeted one after one by name, and he spoke to each in the man's own local dialect. She had heard his lords discuss his phenomenal mem-ory and his versatility, but she had never before seen so clear a demonstration of the qualities that made his men follow him blindly, and she felt a twinge of guilt. As Lanfranc had so often told her, it was a wife's duty to understand and appreciate her husband.

After William disappeared from sight, Matilda started back toward the pavilion, but the sound of drums and cymbals arrested her attention and drew her toward the beach too. The slow, measured beat of the drums was an unusual tempo and anything but martial, and although she was curious she knew she should be discreet, so she headed toward a sand dune that over-looked the harbor from a distance. She guessed that William was providing some sort of diversion for the troops and she wished that he had told her what was happening; it always irritated her when she was kept in ignorance.

The soft sand filled her shoes and made the climb difficult, but when she reached the summit of the dune she saw what seemed to be the whole army lining up in formation, facing toward the sea. A company of musicians at the water's edge played a mournful dirge, a group of monks unrolled a long strip of purple carpet down the length of the beach, then William, flanked by his barons, arrived and took a place in the front ranks.

Matilda had not seen the entire army gathered together in one place, and the sight of fourteen thousand men who were united in high purpose was as awe-inspiring as their potential massed destructive power was terrifying. It occurred to Matilda that she had always taken for granted William's ability to command the army; men fought wars, and it was natural for the wife of the mighty Duke of Normandy to expect victory at the end of every campaign. But now, with the regiments standing in ranks as solid as the trees of a forest, she felt a faint sense of the responsibility that was William's permanent burden; when he was strong and cunning, his men triumphed, and when he erred they died.

The drums beat louder, the trumpets blared, and the crash of the cymbals became deafening; Fitz Osbern bawled an order, other officers repeated it, and the soldiers bared their heads. Then the music stopped abruptly, and in the silence that followed Bishop Odo of Bayeux walked slowly onto the carpet, followed by at least twenty other priests and monks. Directly behind Odo were four friars carrying a silver casket, and Matilda instantly recognized it as the coffin of St. Valéry, which she had seen in the local church. Some of the troops bowed their heads and others dropped to their knees in the sand and prayed as the procession moved slowly along the carpet. Toward the rear two monks held high a square silver box containing various sacred relics of St. Valéry, and Matilda began to appreciate William's cleverness in utilizing every conceivable means to raise the sagging spirits of the army.

It was very quiet on the beach after the priests had gone. Then a crudely built platform was carried to the center of the area, William mounted it, and the units closed in around him in a compact circle. Matilda could hear the tone of his voice but not his words as he began to exhort his men, and she could see enough of the expression on their faces to judge their reactions. He spoke quietly, earnestly at first, and the army listened soberly, perhaps grudgingly. Gradually his tempo increased, his gestures became broader, and Matilda could tell that he was capturing the attention of officers and men-at-arms alike.

William had often told her that he was an inferior orator, and she had always believed him, particularly after she had heard a few of the stilted addresses he had delivered at state functions. But the beach from which the invasion of England was to be launched was his element, and he seemed to play on the emotions of the audience he knew so well with the skill of a minstrel plucking at the strings of a harp. Sometimes he paused after a remark, and the army roared with laughter as one man; then he said something else, and a low growl, animal-like in its ferocity, swept through the throng and caused Matilda to shudder involuntarily.

His voice became more and more insistent, and the troops, unable to stand still any longer, shuffled and stamped, brandished daggers, and shook their fists above their heads. Even the barons were swaying and moving about, and when William, his voice challenging, shouted something defiant and pointed his sword in the direction of England, there was pandemonium. A parade was immediately organized, with William marching at its head, and although the demonstration seemed to be spontaneous, the operation was so smooth that the Duchess realized it had undoubtedly been organized well in advance.

Matilda's legs trembled and there was a weakness at the base of her spine as she made her way down the sand dune and back to the pavilion. William, she knew, had just won a battle as great as any he would be called upon to fight in England. Through sheer intellect and understanding of human nature he had bound his wavering army to his cause and to his person; when he had stood alone and all had seemed lost, he had triumphed against odds that would have crushed anyone less than a Caesar or a Charlemagne.

It struck Matilda that she was seeing him for what he truly was for the first time since she had known him. When he had come to court her in Flanders, his crude manners and lack of social polish had clouded her vision, and after her marriage to him her own soaring ambition had further distorted her views. She had always assumed that people followed William out of habit simply because he was a reigning duke, but she knew now that he commanded respect, obedience, and adulation because he possessed rare qualities of leadership.

And she, who had secretly believed herself to be his superior, was the most fortunate of women. He had been generous where other men expected their wives to do the giving; unlike other rulers, who misused their high positions and took mistresses, he had been undeviatingly faithful to her. He had treated her children as his own, and he had been almost too lenient when she had been capricious or headstrong.

In brief, she knew that he loved her. But she was

certain that he was unaware of the depth of her own feeling for him, and she realized that Abbé Lanfranc had been right when he had said that she was raising barriers that would destroy her marriage. But it was not too late, and she made up her mind to tell William all that was in her heart as soon as she saw him.

She would word her thoughts carefully, she told herself as she arrived at the pavilion, and she expected to have the rest of the day in which to compose herself. But William, ever unpredictable, stalked in only a short time after she sat down, and she started to talk at once nervously. "I saw your ceremonies at the harbor. I couldn't hear much, but I saw it all." That wasn't what she had intended to say at all.

"It went very well, as I expected it would," he replied in a tone of mild satisfaction. "I'm glad you're here. There's something I want to discuss with you."

"I have something to say to you, too." Matilda felt unaccountably hesistant when he raised his eyebrows. "I'm sorry I was so shortsighted yesterday. And I want you to know how much I admire the way you've drawn the army back to you." She had never found it so difficult to express herself.

William shrugged and began to rummage in a large leather box that stood at the foot of the bed. "To an outsider it all seems more involved than it really is. But I've been on so many campaigns that I ought to know what I'm doing by now." He was not being modest, but was stating facts as he saw them.

Matilda saw her opportunity for a graceful opening. "I should be old enough to know what I'm doing, too, but sometimes I'm not so sure." She was exaggerating, of course, and didn't expect him to take her literally, but it was an excellent start. "It seems to me that we've been drifting farther and farther apart. Don't you agree?" There was no answer; he continued to search for something in the box and a wave of annoyance washed over her feeling of sentiment and obscured it. "William, are you listening to me?"

"It ought to be right here on top somewhere," he muttered.

She sighed and decided to try again on a slightly different tack. "Every marriage has its trials," she said, speaking loudly and firmly, "and we've been wrong to let our mistakes in judgment influence our feelings for each other. I'm free to admit that I'm more to blame than you." That wasn't quite accurate, of course, but it was the first time she had ever voluntarily confessed to an error and she felt rather proud of herself. "But now, when you're about to leave at any time, it's more important than ever that we understand each other. Isn't that true?"

"Here it is," he said, and brought out a scroll of heavy parchment.

"What I'm saying is vital to both of us."

"Here's something really vital," he replied. "I had this prepared weeks ago. I was going to wait until I sailed to give it to you, but after all these delays we won't have much time at the last moment." He paused, then extended the scroll to her, and his face was solemn. "In my absence you and Abbé Lanfranc will govern the country." She did not answer, and he raised his voice. "You'll be Regent of Normandy. It's the first time in hundreds of years that a woman has ever been given such an appointment. I debated with myself for a long time, but I can think of no one better qualified for the post."

"Thank you," Matilda said faintly.

"Not at all. You deserve it, and I trust your loyalty." He studied her, and then he frowned. "I thought you'd be pleased. It's an unprecedented honor. And it's what you've always wanted."

"Yes, I'm very pleased. But I wish that you'd listened to what I——"

"Good! It's settled, then. Just remember that all state documents will need Lanfranc's signature in addition to your seal. And if anything out of the ordinary comes up, you can always write to me. But I'm not worried about you. I'm sure you'll do well. You're a remarkable woman, Matilda—in some ways."

A trumpet sounded not far off, and William started at once toward the entrance. "I've summoned a rally of nobles and knights," he declared, and left the pavilion quickly.

Matilda's fingers were cold as she picked up the scroll, unrolled it, and glanced through it. The powers that William had delegated to her were absolute; she would rule the duchy while he was away, with Lanfranc to help her, and her authority would be limitless. Here at last was all she had ever craved, far more than she had ever imagined she would achieve. She would reign in her own name, her decisions would be binding on the people, and her place in history was assured. Barons and counts would obey her, the ambassadors of kings would defer to her wishes, and when she spoke the whole world would listen to her.

Until a short time ago the appointment would have elated her, and nothing else could have given her so much satisfaction. But now the triumph was meaningless, and she let the scroll fall into her lap. Life, she thought, was unbearably ironic at times; tribulation and loneliness had taught her that all she really wanted was William's recognition of her as a woman, but all he saw was the hollow image that she herself had created. The scroll slid to the floor, but Duchess Matilda, Regent of Normandy, the mightiest woman of her century, could not see it through her tears.

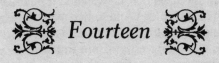

Fourteen

THE EVENING BEGAN inauspicously, in the same dull
pattern that had become routine. At dusk the bored
nobles and their ladies gathered at the ducal pavilion,
and as every possible topic of polite conversation had
been exhausted on previous nights, no one had anything either stimulating or interesting to say. The
women, whose wardrobes were limited by the primitive
conditions, looked at each other's familiar dresses, and
the barons started to drink more than was good for
them. Everyone had heard of the Duchess's appointment as Regent, and she quietly accepted the congratulations of her subjects, knowing full well that the ladies
were envious and that the great lords disapproved. No
one dared to voice an objection to her husband's decision, of course, so on the surface all was serene.

William accepted a small silver cup of spiced wine
from a servant and briefly debated whether to turn his
back on the company; with a sigh he decided it was his
duty to make the best of the situation, which was
rapidly becoming intolerable. If his followers could
maintain a pretense of cheerful optimism, he could not
let them see how he really felt, and he turned to them
with a fixed smile on his face. Mabel Mont Gomeri,
who had been watching him, saw that he was now in a
receptive mood, and she immediately crossed the pavilion, intending to tell him the story of the latest scandal
she had unearthed.

At that moment William glanced over her shoulder

and saw the silk of the pavilion wall ripple slightly. Then it billowed, and as he stared at it he crushed the silver cup in his hand. Wine spilled over his fingers and a few drops splashed onto the startled Mabel's skirt, but the Duke was aware only of the fluttering silk of the tent. A film of perspiration appeared on his forehead, his blood pounded at his temples, and the cup, still dripping, fell to the floor.

"The wind!" he shouted. "By God's grace, the wind!"

Dignity was forgotten as William, followed by his barons, dashed out into the open, and the ladies were alone in the pavilion. A breeze, gentle but persistent, had appeared from the southwest, and there were clouds overhead, drifting slowly in the direction of the Channel—and England. The great nobles all started to speak at once, and men all over the encampment, realizing that there was a wind at last, milled around in front of their tents, pointed at the sky, and cheered.

Ignoring the hubbub, William stood motionless, his head erect and his eyes unseeing. He let the breeze play on him for a few moments, then he spoke in a voice barely above a whisper. "Let the embarkation begin," he said. "We sail tonight."

Fitz Osbern bellowed for his trumpeters, the barons hurried off to supervise the activities of their own commands, and the camp became the scene of ordered bedlam. Tents were dismantled and packed, horses were led aboard the waiting ships and all manner of supplies were stored in holds and on the decks of the vessels of the invasion fleet. The embarkation had been rehearsed many times, but scores of last-minute problems developed, and most decisions were ultimately referred to the Duke. He settled questions promptly, as fast as they arose; a squad of soldiers absent without permission on a drinking bout would be left behind, a Hungarian count would be allowed to take a cumbersome cooking stove to sea in spite of the vehement objections of the unlucky Norman sea captain charged with the responsibility of transporting the Hungarian, and a young Norman knight who was disconsolate when he was forbidden to take his pet hunting dog with him appealed in desperation to his liege lord and was indulgently granted the right to keep his pet.

William paced tirelessly from one end of the harbor to the other and back, observing everything, correcting errors, and prodding the inept. The wind freshened and he was feverishly impatient to sail, but he knew that any display of tension on his part would cause repercussions in the ranks, and he maintained a surface calm that was remarkable. He gave orders to his officers in low, quiet tones and raised his voice only to joke with the common soldiers; with his own hands he hoisted sacks of turnips and onions onto a barge when the men who were loading the raft moved too slowly to suit him, and twice he intervened personally to settle disputes between cavalry commanders who were indignantly demanding precedence in shipping for their horses.

The night was dark and lighted torches flickered in the wind as the final preparations were completed. One by one the barons came to William and reported that their commands were ready, but he was not satisfied and continued to roam the harbor until he saw with his own eyes that every ship in the invasion fleet was prepared to weigh anchor. Then, at last, he walked briskly to the spot where a small boat was waiting to take him to his flagship, the *Mora*, which sat far out in the harbor. His own staff had already gone on board, and the sailors in the boat rested on their oars, gazed at the sweet Norman soil, and wondered if they would ever see it again.

A contingent of the middle-aged guards who would remain behind stiffened and saluted as William approached the water, and beyond them he saw Matilda, who was patiently watching for him. She was alone, and she looked unexpectedly small and fragile to the Duke; he realized that he had not thought of her during the hectic hours of the long evening, and when he smiled at her his lips and face felt stiff.

"You haven't eaten anything tonight," she said as he drew near to her.

He had been afraid she might become sentimental, and her crisp tone relieved him. "Oh, there's plenty of time for that." He laughed but stopped when he saw that her eyes were suspiciously red.

"I've sent a meal onto the *Mora* for you. Gerbod took it out, and the chef will keep it warm for you."

"So Gerbod is on the ship." That accounted for her tears, of course; mothers always wept the first time their sons went off to war.

Matilda gazed up at her husband and a wave of loneliness swept over her. Her blunder had made the invasion of England necessary, and if William died she would be as responsible as if she had killed him with her own hand. She wanted to tell him how she felt, and she desperately needed the comfort and reassurance that he alone could give her. But in years past, when he had gone off to fight a campaign, it had been their custom to part casually, and she could not force herself to break the habit pattern now. "I've packed your new armor on the top of the big leather box," she said.

William wished he could rid himself of the absurd

notion that she was defenseless and weak. She was the most competent and self-sufficient woman in Christendom. "On top of the big leather box. I'll remember."

She decided she had to tell him that she loved him, that she didn't care whether he conquered England or won new glories on the battlefield. All that mattered was his safety.

"Say good-by to my mother for me, and tell her I'm sorry I didn't have a chance to see her again." William failed to observe that his wife's lower lip was trembling. "When you hold court, be sure you give the foreign ambassadors favorable reports on my progress, even if you haven't heard from me. And don't be afraid to use the prisons. A few shortsighted merchants and land-owners may try to test your strength, and you'll find that if you deal firmly with the first to cross your will, the others will give you no trouble."

Matilda nodded, unable to trust herself to speak, and knew she could not bring herself to tell him what was on her mind.

The sailors in the little boat shifted in their seats, and William thought that if he had forgotten any last-minute instructions it was too late now even to try to remember them. He could not keep the army waiting any longer. Taking Matilda into his arms, he kissed her, and when she clung to him he became uncomfortable and gently disengaged her hands. "Take care of yourself and the children. And of Normandy." Annoyed at the huskiness he heard in his own voice, he walked quickly to the boat and stepped into it.

The soldiers on the ships cheered as he was rowed past them; he removed his helmet and waved it, then he turned toward the shore and raised his arm in farewell to Matilda. She stood close to the water's edge, with the torches behind her, so her face was in the shadows and he could not see the tears that streaked her cheeks and stained her gown.

The *Mora* was equipped with a lantern of special brilliance which was suspended from the mainmast, and the captains of the other ships in the fleet were under orders to stay within sight of the beacon at all times. Even the most skilled sailors found it impossible to comply, however, for there were no horses on the flagship, and she cut through the water at such a fast clip that she soon outdistanced the more heavily burdened vessels. Some members of the Duke's staff were disturbed, but William cheerfully directed his captain to slacken sail and wait for the other ships to catch up. In the meantime, he said, he was hungry; sea air always gave him an appetite.

One of Matilda's best banquet cloths was spread over the long table that had been placed amidships on the deck, the chef and his assistants became frantically busy at the iron stove they had set up in the stern, and William sat back in a chair of heavy oak and beamed at Fitz Osbern, Bishop Odo, and Gerbod, his traveling companions. The light cast by the lantern was incredibly bright, and Odo, who had snatched the seat on his half brother's right, blinked and shaded his eyes.

"William, isn't there some way to dim that lantern?" he demanded.

Fitz Osbern and Gerbod exchanged significant, covert smiles. Odo, they knew, had been unaware of the lamp's existence until he came on board the *Mora*, and as always he was ready to decry anything for which he could claim no credit. William, however, was not amused. "Trust a churchman to lose sight of practical values. We want the fleet to find us, not sail on to

England without us." He glanced up at the lantern, and his spirits rose; solid achievement invariably pleased him. "It burns whale oil," he told the Bishop, "and the sides are made of shaved marble from the quarry at Caen."

"Very interesting," Odo muttered, folding his plump hands in his lap and peering at the chefs.

"We can thank the Seneschal for it. How many were made for you before you were satisfied?"

"Twenty or thirty," Fitz Osbern replied.

Odo was about to make a caustic comment, but at that moment the chef brought a savory roast to the table, and his helpers followed him with silver dishes filled with a variety of delicacies. The Duke helped himself liberally, the others did the same, and there was silence as the party enjoyed its long-delayed supper. Each was busy with his own thoughts, and those of William soon became obvious. "Have any of you ever tried English sea cabbage?" he asked. "It's tasteless, I can tell you."

Odo gazed fondly at a tiny new turnip, which had been broiled in butter and sprinkled with chopped chives and parsley. "This is almost as good as I eat in my palace at Bayeux."

The Seneschal, who had been staring out at the dark sea, did not look up. "I'm very fond of little peas cooked in wine. My wife has them prepared for me at least once a week." His eyes softened and he smiled at a private memory.

Gerbod, who had been pensively quiet ever since the *Mora* had sailed, glanced at the Duke. "We're all partial to *dilligrout* at home, aren't we, Father?"

William did not hear the question. "The English also eat wild parsnips, which they boil. The last time I was there I was astonished to find them at Edward's table. They won't be served at mine, I assure you."

"We'll just miss the autumn crop of carrots at home," Fitz Osbern said.

"And the apples." For once Odo felt no sense of competition.

"It won't seem like autumn without apples." Gerbod laughed a trifle shakily.

William finished his joint and threw the bone into the sea. "To my way of thinking, food is important as an indication of a people's standard of civilization," he said, wiping his mouth on his sleeve. "Julius Caesar first brought parsnips to England, but when the old Roman culture died out, the barbarians were so lacking in imagination they could think only of boiling. But they'll learn. The best method of educating them is to set an example for them, of course." He looked around the table, waiting for someone to reply, but his companions continued to muse.

Rising abruptly, he walked to the high prow and peered off into the night. He could not expect the others to feel as he did, for they were only his minions. England, lying only a few miles away in the dark, would belong to him, not to them, and he could not blame them for dreaming of the secure world of yesterday, just as he could dwell only on the kingdom that he would claim tomorrow.

An hour or two after midnight the fleet caught up with the *Mora*, and shortly after dawn land was sighted. The warriors ate a light breakfast, donned their armor, and the captain of the flagship, who was familiar with the whole English coast, altered his course slightly and headed for Pevensey, a sheltered harbor large enough to accommodate the hundreds of ships that followed the *Mora*. Green fields and elm trees, a sandy beach fringed with grassy slopes, and a rolling countryside dotted with oak and beech gave England a surprisingly peaceful appearance, and as nearly as the observer in the crow's-nest of the flagship could judge, not one native was on hand to witness the arrival of the man who proclaimed himself the rightful successor to King Edward.

The invaders, who had been certain they would plunge into battle immediately, swarmed ashore unopposed, and after the light infantry had been formed on the beach and several squadrons of cavalry had lined up behind them, William was rowed across the harbor. Fitz Osbern and Odo had already landed, and they stood now with his other generals, waiting to welcome him. The occasion, he thought, was one that probably required a touch of lasting oratory, and he wished he had prepared some appropriate remarks. He tried to compose something suitable, but the few ideas that occurred to him were pallid. Giving up the effort, he grinned at Gerbod, who sat opposite him in the boat.

"How does your armor feel? Mine is so new that the leather is still stiff."

Gerbod's reply was lost in the cheers of the soldiers on the shore, and those who were still on board the ships crowded against the high bulkheads to witness the historic moment. The papal banner and the Duke's own ensign were unfurled, twenty trumpets sounded a fanfare; and the army stood at attention. Two members of the ducal guard pulled the boat up onto the ground and stood aside; William rose, and his officers raised their swords in salute.

He stepped over the side of the boat and placed his feet on the soil of England. He supposed that he should be thinking some noble sentiment that could be related to the chroniclers in due time, but his new armor hampered his movements and spoiled his pleasure. Irritated, he tried to compensate for his feeling of clumsiness by taking large strides as he walked toward his generals. Unfortunately the leather on his suit of chain mail was so unyielding that William, the Lion of Normandy, lost his balance and pitched forward onto the ground.

Gerbod, who was following him, was at his side in an instant, and Fitz Osbern left the ranks of the barons and hurried forward. William felt an urge to laugh loudly, as he would have done had someone else fallen; he hated pomposity, and the fact that he himself was the victim of the situation in no way detracted from its humor. One look at the Seneschal's grave face sobered him, however, and he realized that a strained silence had settled over the troops. Although he was contemptuous of superstitions, he knew that his soldiers and the majority of his officers believed firmly in signs and omens, and the absurd incident could create alarming repercussions. Unless he acted quickly and decisively, virtually every man who had seen him stumble would be convinced that the expedition was doomed to failure.

Digging his fingers into the earth, he grasped two large chunks of soil, and when Gerbod and Fitz Osbern helped him to his feet, he held his hands high over his head. "Here is an omen of success!" he shouted in a voice that carried to the farthest ranks and floated across the bay to the ships. "I have taken England with both of my hands!"

A sustained roar of approval greeted his words, and the din was so great that no one heard him tell Gerbod to fetch his old suit of armor at once.

An advance guard of light cavalry fanned out into the

countryside in search of information, and when the entire army had landed, William rode at the head of the long column, fourteen thousand strong, down the old Roman road that led to London. The men were under strict orders not to molest the natives, and after a time a few English faces began to appear at the side of the road. Most were timid and darted away after catching a brief glimpse of the invaders, but some were boldly curious, a few were actually defiant, and one white-bearded old man shook a gnarled staff at the troops and sang something in a hoarse, tuneless voice.

William, who was amused, asked his stepson to translate the words for him, but Gerbod, who spoke English fluently, wisely pretended not to have heard the old man. The little rhyme had contained a scurrilous attack on William's mother, had compared her to Jezebel, and had branded her as an abandoned strumpet. As even the most subtle derogatory reference to Lady Harlotte sent the Duke into a violent rage, Gerbod knew better than to let him know that even the peasants of England had been taught exaggerated stories about Duke Robert the Devil and his baseborn mistress, who had borne him a son.

Late in the afternoon the army arrived in a wooded section near the tiny village of Hastings, and here William decided to pitch his camp. The terrain was favorable, and from a hill on which he set up his headquarters he commanded the approach to London; equally important, he could defend the position with ease, and by deploying his troops on all sides of the slope he made it virtually impossible for the English to launch a surprise attack against him. Sentry outposts were established, and the Duke and his seneschal, inspecting the defenses, declared themselves satisfied.

They retired at dusk to William's silken tent at the

crest of the hil, and there they settled down to await reports on the state of affairs in the country. The knights commanding the advance guards of cavalry had brought word that they had encountered no opposition anywhere, and although they had ridden over an area extending twenty-five to thirty miles inland, they had not seen one English soldier. This perplexed William and worried Fitz Osbern, for they knew that, even though Harold's housecarls, his professional soldiers, might be in London, his local levies of freemen had been under arms for several months.

The barons were concerned over the lack of news too, but William, who always became calm when others were upset, advised his generals to eat hearty dinners and sleep soundly. There were scores of Norman agents in England, he said, and by this time many of them had undoubtedly heard that he had landed in the country, so some of them would certainly arrive at the bivouac the following day. Until then there was nothing to do but wait, and the Duke rejected all speculation as a waste of time.

The soundness of his reasoning became apparent shortly before noon the next morning, when a man dressed in the multicolored, short-skirted garb of the English gentry rode up to the outposts, showed the sentries his thumb ring, and was promptly admitted to William's presence. The Duke chose to receive his spy in private, with only Fitz Osbern and Gerbod in attendance; William had always supervised his espionage system himself, and even under special circumstances he was reluctant to give his barons an opportunity to question his personal agents.

The "Englishman" would have dropped to one knee on the dirt floor of the tent, but William, seeing that he was exhausted, embraced him, offered him a chair, and poured him a cup of wine. "I might have guessed you'd be the first to come to me, Richmond," the Duke said. "You look as though you've had a long ride."

The agent, a younger brother of the lord of the manor at Eu, where William and Matilda had been married, drank his wine thirstily. "I've been on the road all night and all morning, Lord Duke." There was pride in his Saxon-blue eyes as he added, "It pleases me that I'm the first to bring you the news."

Fitz Osbern, who had been trying to control himself, gnawed his lower lip. "It will please us when we hear what you have to tell us."

"God is truly on the side of the Normans," the spy declared. "Harold has just fought a great battle against the Norwegians at Stamford Bridge."

"Where is that?" Gerbod asked, forgetting to keep silent.

"Near the town of York, in the northeast, and be quiet!" his stepfather said. "What happened, Richmond?"

"The battle was fought four days ago, and Harold won a great victory, but at a fearful cost. King Harold Hardrara and the outlawed Earl Tostig landed at the mouth of the Humber with a tremendous army, and Harold marched north against them with his housecarls. The Norwegians were careless, and Harold took them by surprise. The King of the Norsemen is dead and so is Tostig. It's said that Harold killed them both with his own hand, but I can't swear to it that he did."

"No matter. It's an excellent story and will help to give the English people confidence in the usurper." William sat down and nodded thoughtfully.

"So Hardrara is dead. Well. I've got to admit that I'm impressed," Fitz Osbern said in a musing tone. "He was a great warrior."

William was interested only in the living. "Where is Harold now?"

"He was celebrating his victory in York when he received word of your landing. He and his housecarls are now marching back south to London."

"When did they start?"

"Yesterday afternoon, Lord Duke," Richmond said, drinking more wine.

"How is that possible? We just landed yesterday morning!"

"Bonfires were lit at posts that had been set up in advance all over the country. As soon as the men at one station got the news, they lighted their fire and passed the word along."

The Duke exchanged a significant glance with his seneschal. "I've said all along that Harold is clever, and I'm right. Bonfires. I must remember the technique. Is he planning to fight me, Richmond?"

"I don't know, Lord Duke. His housecarls suffered heavy losses at Stamford Bridge, and he'll need replacements before he can wage war again."

"Who fought with him against the Norsemen?"

"His brother, Earl Gyrth."

A faint smile appeared at the corners of William's mouth. "What of his other nobles?"

"Earl Waltheof fought at Harold's side, but he contributed no troops of his own."

"I see." The Duke tapped on the arm of his chair for a moment. "Gerbod, bring our guest some sausage and bread. What of the northern earls, Richmond? I find their names strangely missing from your account."

A slow grin spread across the spy's tired face. "Morcar and Edwin are cautious men, Lord Duke. And wily. They sent word to Harold that they hadn't been able to reach Stamford Bridge in time to join him.

His casualties would have been far fewer if they'd been at his side, that's sure. Harold must be very annoyed with them, although no one knows for certain."

Fitz Osbern laughed and slapped his knee. "I can't blame him for being angry. Didn't he give up his mistress and marry the sister of Edwin and Morcar just to win their support?"

"He did, Lord Seneschal, but the earls aren't the sort who'll help a man simply because he's their brother-in-law. They're looking out for their own interests—as the English nobility always do."

William glanced up as Gerbod re-entered with food for the agent, and he absently helped himself to a chunk of sausage. "I can see that I'm going to have to teach the lords here that a country is only as strong as its king. But that's a lesson they'll learn a little later. Right now it's to our advantage to let Edwin and Morcar try to play both sides at the same time. They command about six thousand men between them, if I remember correctly."

"More or less, Lord Duke."

William straightened in his chair and looked across the tent at his stepson. "Gerbod, how would you like to see the English countryside?"

The boy came to him eagerly.

"Richmond, where are the earls at present?"

"At Winchester. Harold gave them a fine house there when he married Lady Aldyth, and they've used it as their base ever since."

"Can you conduct Lord Gerbod to them there?"

"Of course, sir. He'll need to wear the change of clothes I carry in my saddlebag, though. Otherwise I won't be responsible for his safety."

"Are Normans so unpopular in England these days?" Fitz Osbern demanded, bristling.

"They don't think very highly of us, Lord Seneschal," the agent replied. "Harold looks like a king, and he's made himself popular with the people."

"I've always said that he's a natural leader," William muttered, and for the first time in several months he felt a surge of old resentments against Matilda.

"What instructions do you have for me, Father?" Gerbod asked hastily, seeing the Duke's eyes become cloudy and realizing the cause.

"Tell the earls I'm sending a member of my own family to them as a sign of my high esteem for them. Flatter them. You'll know what to say—you're better at that sort of thing than I am. Tell them that if I'm forced to do battle with Harold, I don't expect them to become our active allies. I merely request them to remain neutral. It would be too much to expect Englishmen to fight against other Englishmen. What's more," he added in an aside to Fitz Osbern, "we couldn't really count on them." Rising, he put his hand on his stepson's shoulder. "Remind the earls that Harold has been excommunicated by the Holy Father. There isn't a real Christian in England, of course—in my opinion they're all heathens. But we've got to give Edwin and Morcar a reason for deserting their brother-in-law, a reason that sounds logical and convincing. Their troops could mean the difference between victory and defeat."

"I understand, Father," Gerbod said, his eyes glowing. "There's more than one way to win a battle."

"Exactly." William gazed at him quizzically and spoke in a tone that was open to a variety of interpretations. "It's obvious from the way you think that you're Matilda's son."

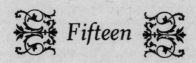

Fifteen

"WHEN ARE WE GOING to fight the English?"

Every day the soldiers asked the same question, and every day their officers, unable to provide an answer, were forced to evade the issue. During this period Duke William Bastard was strangely inactive and took no one into his confidence; indeed, he spent most of his time sitting in his tent and receiving the reports brought to him by men whom the army assumed were his spies. Each morning he made a brief inspection of his defenses, and on such occasions the troops noted that he was singularly cheerful, but the men could not share his good humor.

They had expected to be sent into battle as soon as they had landed in England, but five days had passed without action and without sign of an enemy. They began to wonder if they were really waging war against Harold Godwineson, and they told each other that for all practical purposes they had been better off at St. Valéry than they were at Hastings. There were more trees here, and the weather was a trifle cooler, but their movements were restricted to the perimeter of the camp, and the sentries, who were members of the Duke's own household guard, permitted no one to leave the bivouac area. Even the great lords were restricted in their movements, but William ignored their complaints and the Seneschal merely told them to exercise patience.

On the afternoon of the fifth day the Duke summoned his barons to a meeting, and they came to him eagerly, dressed in their armor and ready to march at an hour's notice. When they entered his tent, however, they saw that he was dressed in a tunic, and from the cooking odors that drifted in from the rear of the pavilion they knew that his chef was preparing an elaborate supper for him. It was therefore plain to them that the situation would remain unchanged in the immediate future, and their ardor for battle quickly cooled. They became surly and belligerent as they filed into the tent, and although they saluted William with the respect due his rank, none of them returned his welcoming smile. They removed their helmets, sat down on the benches that had been provided for them, and glanced at each other surreptitiously; among the many rumors that had been heard in the camp was one to the effect that the Duke had struck a bargain with Harold, and had agreed to call off the war in return for the gift of a vast tract of English land. They could not quite bring themselves to believe that the story was true, but they nevertheless hoped to hear William disavow it and set their minds at rest.

The Normans in the group, knowing their liege lord of old, would have proceeded cautiously, but Langbein of Bavaria, a fiery German baron, was less discreet. Glowering, he held his helmet under his arm and pointed the forefinger of his free hand at the Duke. "I was told you were holding a meeting," he said. "I've fought in many wars, and when a commander brings his generals together in the field, it is usually called a council of war."

William, who might have taken offense, chose to be amused. "We've been known to call them that too."

"Is this such a council?" Langbein demanded.

"If you insist on giving it a name." William was

aware of the mood of the barons and felt their tensions, but it suited his purposes to be vague for the moment. He had been far busier in recent days than they realized, and as he wanted their approval of the action he had taken, he was trying to lead up to his point slowly, in order to give them time to digest the news. "A council of war is usually very stiff and dignified. As you've been with us for only a short time, Langbein, you probably don't realize that we're always very informal and express our opinions freely."

He knew, and so did the Normans, that his statement was something of an exaggeration. Any general could say what he pleased, it was true, but only on condition that he did not contradict the Duke. Ordinarily no one would have challenged William's remark, but Roger Mont Gomeri had been deprived of excitement for so long that he discarded what little sense of tact he possessed. "Langbein is wondering whether we're in England to fight a war!" he declared bluntly. "I'm wondering the same thing, and so are all the rest of us."

William smiled broadly and decided to change his tactics; he would meet candor with candor. "I hope to avoid a war if it's at all possible," he said quietly.

The barons muttered and shifted in their seats.

"I always believe in achieving my aims with the smallest expenditure of effort and the least loss of lives," the Duke continued smoothly. "Roger, you must remember the first time we fought old King Henry of France. You objected when I sent him several offers of friendship before we met him in battle, but you may recall that my letters confused his nobles, upset his troops, and gave us the chance to beat him with only three regiments."

"Then you've been in touch with Harold," Mont Gomeri replied accusingly.

"Yes, I have." William held himself in check with an effort. "He's arrived back in London, and——"

"We should have marched to London ourselves." Bishop Odo, who liked to consider himself a military strategist, seemed to think he could interrupt the Duke with impunity. "Then we'd have been there before Harold returned from the north."

"I'm trying to win England, not lose it." An edge crept into William's voice in spite of a slight warning cough from Fitz Osbern. He had too much on his mind to explain military fundamentals to a pompous churchman, but as Odo had raised a point, he thought an answer was required. "The English would have shut the gates of London in our faces, and we'd have been forced to lay siege to the city. That would have given Harold time to raise a new army and attack us from the rear. A march on London would be the most stupid move we could make."

He looked pityingly at Odo, then grinned at the generals, and they showed that they shared his sentiments by glancing contemptuously at the Bishop. "Harold," the Duke said, "is in a very difficult position. He lost approximately half of his army fighting the Norsemen, and he's having no easy time rounding up levies of freemen to replace housecarls who were killed and wounded."

Fitz Osbern nodded. "So we intend to make him come to us," he told the nobles. "His men are tired after the long march from the north, and they're not in condition to fight again so soon. That's why we've stayed at Hastings."

Langbein and Mont Gomeri were dissatisfied. "By staying here," the German declared ponderously, "we give Harold time to reorganize."

"We could spend the whole winter in this damned

country before anything happens!" Mont Gomeri added.

"You're mistaken," William said crisply. "I've written to Harold and offered him an honorable peace." The barons looked at him in consternation, but he was unruffled. "I've given him an opportunity to keep his oath, and if he does, I've promised in return to make him Vice-King under me."

"No!" Robert of Mortain shouted, and the others echoed his indignant cry.

"Yes!" William said firmly, and stood. "Just what is a vice-king? Do any of you know?" When they were silent his tone became condescending. "Neither do I, and neither does Harold. He'd be no more than another earl among many earls. The price is a cheap one to pay for the conquest of a country. If he accepts, England will be mine the moment I get his letter of acceptance. And we won't lose the blood of a single man!"

The generals were unhappy, but they did not dare to oppose such a reasonable plan too strongly, and only Mont Gomeri had the courage to lift his voice again. "Suppose Harold keeps you waiting. Suppose he neither agrees nor refuses. What then? You'll be giving him time to rebuild his army."

"You know me better than that, Roger," the Duke replied. "Have I ever given an enemy the chance to gather his full strength?"

"No, you haven't. But——"

"All right. I have no intention of forgetting everything I've ever learned about war, I can tell you that. Harold has been posing as the champion of the English people, and I'm going to give him an opportunity to make good his boast. In brief, my lords, I'm going to make it impossible for him to delay his decision. Two

columns of our troops will roam through the countryside, beginning tonight. They will destroy crops,
burn and pillage in any way they please. If a man sees a
woman he likes, he may take her. I place only two
restrictions on the columns. Churches and shrines are
not to be touched, and the soldiers are to be reminded
that we're fighting a holy war. Also, the houses of the
nobility are not to be destroyed. You, my lords, will be
taking possession of those very properties yourselves in
the near future, and I'm sure you'll want your new
homes to be given to you in good condition."

The language of bloodletting was one that the barons
understood, and everyone started talking simultaneously. The generals were experienced, expert raiders
who had terrorized most of Europe at one time or
another, and they were content to leave the art of
diplomatic maneuver to the Duke and his seneschal.
Such sedentary pursuits taxed their faculties, but they
needed no instruction in the use of the sword and
firebrand. Enthusiastically voluble, they made so
much noise that William had to rap on the arm of his
chair with the hilt of his double-bladed dagger in order
to make himself heard.

"My policy seems to be acceptable to you," he said
dryly.

They jumped to their feet and roared their approval.
While they demonstrated, a young knight on the staff
of the ducal household guard appeared at the entrance
to the tent and signaled to Fitz Osbern, who slipped out
unobtrusively.

William waited patiently for the cheers to subside,
then he addressed the group again. "I've been wondering to whom I should give command of the raiding
columns." He silenced a fresh clamor by holding up his
hand. "You yourselves have helped me to decide.

Baron Langbein will ravage to the northeast, Baron Mont Gomeri will ravage to the northwest. It's been my experience that restless generals command restless troops, so the exercise and diversion will be as good for your men as it will be for you."

The Seneschal hurried back into the tent, and from his expression William knew that he had learned something of importance, but that he was reluctant to reveal it before the others. "Mont Gomeri, Langbein—I charge you with the responsiblility of keeping your men in check. I want no tortures and no unnecessary cruelty. Remember that the people you'll be attacking are about to become my subjects. If there's nothing further to discuss, the meeting is adjourned."

The barons crowded around the two lucky raiders to offer congratulations, but Fitz Osbern was in no mood to allow them to linger indefinitely in the tent. Councils of war usually ended on a social note, and it was customary for the Duke to serve cups of wine to his lords; on this occasion, however, the Seneschal wasted no time on the amenities. "His Grace grants permission for you to take your leave," he said, and the barons, although mildly surprised, saluted and left.

"Well?" William asked as soon as he and Fitz Osbern were alone.

"Gerbod has returned from Winchester."

"With what news?"

"I don't know. Young Arundell had the presence of mind to take him into the tent of the captain of the guard until we got rid of the generals."

William hurried to the entrance and beckoned to the knight on duty outside. "Send Lord Gerbod in to me at once."

In a few moments his stepson, wearing a scarlet and yellow dress cut in the style of the English gentry, stepped into the tent. The boy, self-conscious in his outlandish attire, grinned sheepishly. He would have dropped to one knee, but William grasped him by the elbows and then embraced him. Now that Gerbod was back, the Duke could admit to himself that he had been worried for the past four days.

"It's good to see you, Son," he said huskily, and Fitz Osbern, embarrassed by the show of emotion, turned away for a moment.

"I've been in no danger, Father." Gerbod, anxious to prove his manhood, was overly casual. "The earls were very kind to me the whole time I was with them."

Fitz Osbern moved back to the center of the tent. "What word do you bring us?"

"I'm not sure, Lord Seneschal."

William forgot that he was a father and became the commander in chief. "Will Edwin and Morcar remain neutral, or will they march with Harold against us?"

"They didn't say. They were careful not to commit themselves."

"You did as you were bidden, I hope, and reminded them that Harold is under a ban of excommunication."

"Yes, Father, I did. I even told them in detail about the day Harold swore to accept you as his overlord. Earl Morcar was very curious and asked me scores of questions about the ceremony. I told him everything I could remember, and he seemed to be quite impressed."

Fitz Osbern hooked a thumb into his broad belt and tapped his forefinger against the leather. "Edwin and Morcar must have given you some indication of their intentions," he said irritably.

"I wish I could be more specific, Lord Seneschal, but they didn't."

"Did you ask them for a straight answer?" William was annoyed too.

"Yes, I did." Gerbod, who was perspiring, shifted his weight from one foot to the other. "They were so vague the first night I was there that I finally came out with a direct question. Earl Morcar walked over to a window and looked out of it, so I couldn't see his face. Earl Edwin, who seems to be the head of the family, just smiled at me, but he didn't answer. He didn't say a single word, Father."

"This is exasperating." William looked at his seneschal. "What do you make of it, Osbern?"

"So far it's open to any interpretation we want to give it. Did the earls send any message to His Grace, Gerbod?"

"Oh yes. When I left they both made long, flowery speeches. The sort you always make to foreign ambassadors, Father, when you don't really want to say anything."

William smiled in spite of himself.

"They sent a gift for you, too. It's out in my saddlebag. A heavy silver bowl with Edwin's crest on it. Judging by the weight, the silver in it is valuable, but the workmanship is crude by our standards. English silversmiths are rather primitive."

"I'm familiar with local craftsmanship, thank you," the Duke declared peevishly. "Tell us how you were treated, and we may be able to get a better idea from that. Did they keep you under guard or give you the impression at any time that they were holding you as a prisoner?"

"Not for a moment," Gerbod replied firmly. "For one thing, their houses are very strange. I was amazed to see that Earl Edwin doesn't live in a castle, as our barons do. His house was surrounded by no more than a narrow moat and a wooden palisade, which he built to discourage thieves. And the whole house was flimsy. A few of our bombards would destroy it completely."

"We're also familiar with English architecture," the Seneschal interjected. "Tell us how they behaved toward you, Gerbod. That's all that interests us."

"I was an honored guest, Lord Seneschal. The first night I was there, they gave a banquet for me." The boy grinned broadly at his memory of the affair. "Most of the things they served were really inedible, although I had to pretend to like everything, of course. They had roast crane and boar's head—and those boiled parsnips you told us about, Father."

William raised an eyebrow at Fitz Osbern. "Roast crane and boar's head. They only serve those delicacies when they're trying to win favor. You're sure they didn't set up a guard over you, Son?"

"I'm positive. I was free to come and go as I pleased. When Dorella showed me around Winchester, there were just the two of us, and not one soldier even——"

"Who is Dorella?" William asked quizzically.

Gerbod reddened, hesitated, and took the plunge. She's a girl Earl Edwin—uh—made available to me. But she's no ordinary trollop," he added defensively. "She's very pretty and sweet and—"

"When you write to your mother," the Duke interrupted, "be sure you don't mention the wench. It will all be my fault if you do, and she'll say that she never should have let you come away with me in the first place." His eyes twinkled, but he sobered as he turned again to Fitz Osbern. "They certainly gave him a royal treatment, I must say."

"It could be significant." The Seneschal pondered

the matter briefly. "On the other hand, it could mean absolutely nothing."

"And there seems to be only one way that we'll find out," William said. "If we're forced to fight Harold, either Edwin and Morcar will join him to crush us, or else they'll absent themselves and give us a chance. Apparently we won't know until the last, but there's no way to avoid the risk."

Fitz Osbern laughed unhappily. "Did it ever occur to you that our grandfathers lived and died without ever leaving Normandy? Think of the trouble we'd have saved ourselves if we had stayed at home."

"True." William nodded reflectively, brightened, and winked at his stepson. "But think how dull life would have been. Nobody remembers the names of our grandfathers, but we aren't going to be forgotten. By the time we're through we'll either be known as the greatest conquerors since Charlemagne or the most reckless madmen since Nero. But one way or the other, we'll make our mark on history."

Roger Mont Gomeri methodically devastated several counties in Sussex, and Baron Langbein, although less orderly, wreaked havoc in Kent. Refugees clogged the roads to London, Winchester, and Exeter, and numerous delegations of landowners raced to the capital, where King Harold sat in almost continuous session with his Witenagemot, and begged him either to make peace or to drive the invaders out of the country. Families fled from their homes and either hid in the forests or sought sanctuary in overcrowded churches and monasteries, all normal trade and farming ceased abruptly, and the Norman terror stalked England.

William privately regretted the upheaval and the

inevitable loss of English lives, and whenever the marauders committed outrages that would influence public opinion in France, the Italian states, and other civilized nations, he sharply reprimanded the barons who were conducting the raids. But he had good cause to be satisfied with his basic strategy, for his spies reported to him that all England was clamoring for decisive action. There was dissension in the Witenagemot, according to the Duke's agents; some of the nobles were urging Harold to fight, while others, principally those whose estates had been ravaged, counseled him to make peace at any price.

When the usurper continued to hesitate, William reluctantly concluded that his provocative acts had been too mild, so he decided to intensify them. To the dismay of his lieutenants he announced that he would lead a column of raiders himself, and although he knew he would be courting personal unpopularity among the English, a development he had heretofore tried to avoid, he answered the objections of his staff with the logical argument that Harold could not fail to respond to such a blatant challenge. If he did, his own people would discard him, but it was unlikely that he would continue to sit still when he learned that the Duke himself was ravaging the realm.

The expedition was organized quickly, for every day of additional rest was helpful to the weary housecarls. And William knew, too, that the defenders' best strategy was to let the Normans wear themselves out in futile raids and then attack them piecemeal, after the fashion of the savages who lived in the mountains of northern Spain. Certainly the Duke would have devised such tactics had he been in his enemy's boots, and he realized privately that if Harold were to conduct a war along such lines, the invaders would be fortunate to escape across the Channel with one third of their forces intact.

But the Duke was confident that his exasperating scheme would force the Englishman's hand and either cause him to accept William as his sovereign or bring him to Hastings with as many men as he could muster. William was relying heavily on his own judgment of character, and, knowing that Harold was impetuous and proud, he figured that the usurper was incapable of remaining idle for a few more weeks and losing an opportunity to achieve the glory that would be his if he won a pitched battle.

After a night of hasty preparation the raid that was to goad the English into action was ready, and at dawn William led two hundred picked cavalrymen out of the encampment and rode north and west through Sussex. Every man in the unit was a veteran, and care had been taken to include soldiers from the divisions of every general and every independent commander. The barons had clamored for the privilege of accompanying their master, and Fitz Osbern had insisted that he be allowed to take part in the raid. But William had turned a deaf ear to all of their pleas. The Seneschal, he had explained, would succeed him if the expedition should end in disaster, and the lives of the others were too valuable to risk for the sake of a day of excitement.

From the ranks of his own staff the Duke had chosen only Walter Giffard, a man of great personal integrity, as an aide, and at the last minute the woebegone expression on Gerbod's face had melted his opposition, so he had allowed the boy to come too. His stepson rode directly behind him now, carrying his personal banner as he cantered across the open countryside.

Everything about the raid was unorthodox, but nothing in the planning was accidental. No scouts preceded the column or traveled on its flanks, for William wanted to be sure that as many natives as possible saw that he himself led the expedition, and then carried the word to Harold in London. The men were lightly armored, for they could maneuver more rapidly when they were not encumbered, and their safety depended as much on their speed as on their daring. Each soldier carried only a loaf of hard bread and a ration of dried meat in his saddlebag, and even William had brought no delicacies for himself to appease his hunger, much to the horror of his chef.

It was the Duke's intention to strike at a region that had previously been spared, and as he had privately informed Giffard, who was acting as his second-in-command, he would permit the raiders to indulge in any atrocity short of murder. Dead victims were silent victims, and the outing would be pointless if Harold failed to receive a stream of firsthand accounts from compatriots who had felt the wrath of William of Normandy.

Here and there the unit passed gutted farmhouses, charred barns, and dead cattle, all evidence that Mont Gomeri and Langbein had done their work well on previous raids. In fact there was no sign of life anywhere, and it gradually dawned on William that the inhabitants of the region had all fled, making it necessary for him to ride farther afield than he had expected in order to accomplish his purpose. So he stepped up the pace of the column, but it was almost noon before frightened faces appeared for an instant in the doors of homes and young men could be glimpsed riding madly in every direction to warn their neighbors that the devils from Normandy were abroad.

Several avaricious knights wanted to stop when they saw houses sufficiently substantial to contain riches worth plundering, but the Duke permitted no pause. It was his idea to strike but once, and to attack a community large enough to insure that every resident within many miles of the place would be touched by the tragedy. The watery sun was directly overhead before he found such a village, and he brought his column to a halt on the top of a gently rolling hill overlooking it. He and his knights dismounted and gazed down at the houses nestling in a valley below them, and for a moment or two no one spoke.

"We'll attack first and stop to eat later," William said thoughtfully. "We'll fan out into a semicircle and move on the village in a single unit."

Three or four of the knights quickly agreed, but Giffard, who stood shading his eyes with a mailed hand, shook his head. "I wonder if we haven't picked the wrong place, Lord Duke. Even from here you can see them bustling around down there. They've had word of our coming, and they're making ready for us."

"So much the better," the Duke replied. "If we meet a show of opposition, some of the valiant defenders will be among those who hurry to London and tell Harold how bravely they fought against us. We couldn't ask for more."

"I'm not so sure, sir. Do you see how many houses there are? The place is almost big enough to be a town."

Some of the knights scoffed, but William silenced them with a wave of his hand. "How many people would you estimate are living in the village, Walter?"

"That's hard to say, Lord Duke. I've been told the English crowd together like animals." Giffard studied the houses for a few moments. "I'd guess there must be six hundred people in the place. Maybe seven hundred."

"Perfect for two hundred Normans." William had

listened to the argument, and after weighing it had rejected it. His mind was made up, and he walked back to his horse.

At his command the unit gathered around him, and he explained the simple tactics to the men, and then added a few further instructions. "Kill only when absolutely necessary," he said, "and spare the children. My name is going to be black enough after this day's work, and I don't want it said that I eat babies. Keep out of the church, and don't harm the priests. Take what you want out of the homes provided you only steal what you can carry comfortably. I won't permit anything to delay our journey back to Hastings. And destroy everything in sight, particularly the houses. Have I made myself clear?"

There was a rumble of assent, then one young cavalryman in the rear called out eagerly, "What about the women, Lord Duke?"

William shrugged and concealed his disgust. "Take them; if you must, but don't dally with them. There's a job to be done, and we've got to be back at our camp by nightfall." Since his first venture into the field he had been forced to control his impatience with soldiers who looked on wartime as an opportunity for excesses of every sort. To him war was a science, an art, that was waged in part because of the natural desire of a leader for greater power and in part for its own sake. He felt little sympathy for those who were chiefly interested in satisfying their appetites, but this was one occasion when the lust of his men was almost welcome. The more lurid the stories the natives took to London, the sooner Harold would either capitulate or fight.

Gerbod blew a single blast on his trumpet, the troops formed on either side of the Duke, and at another signal they started down the hillside toward the village. William's personal standard fluttered in the autumn breeze and he deliberately held the column to a walk so that every inhabitant of the community would have a chance to see it and to identify it. Then, when he was no more than five hundred yards from the nearest houses, which sat on the opposite bank of a little brook, he spurred his mount to a gallop.

The cavalrymen needed no further encouragement, and the raiders swept down on the English village in a scythelike arc. William brandished his own sword, but he had no intention of using it against helpless civilians; if a local knight rode out against him, he would happily meet the man, but he liked to think that he had never raised his hand against those who could not defend themselves, and he had no intention of changing his policy or his habits now.

Loud screams and protesting wails filled the air as the attack began, the villagers scattered, and their dogs, scurrying out of the path of the horsemen, barked loudly. Young women who ordinarily were fleet of foot allowed themselves to be caught, but their mothers ran away in genuine terror. Bright fires began to dot the landscape, and plumes of thick, black wood smoke rose into the air as the houses started to burn. To William's surprise, only a few middle-aged and elderly men appeared to put up even a token resistance, and they were quickly cut down. He did not like the development, for it probably meant that the men of military age had gone off to join Harold Godwineson, and if similar conditions prevailed throughout England, the usurper would be in a position to take to the field with a very large army.

That was a problem for the future, however; at the moment there was nothing to do but allow the raiders to complete their immediate task. As some of the individual scenes were unfit for the eyes of a young boy, William stationed Gerbod at the entrance to the church with orders to let no one enter the place, and then he roamed around the village to make sure that none of his men went too far in the outrages they were committing.

After an hour of pillage and rape the column was reassembled, and when the Normans started their long ride back to Hastings they left a ruined village behind them. The men were inclined to dawdle so they could discuss in detail the adventures they had enjoyed, but William maintained a rapid pace. His mind was racing ahead to the moment that the refugees would arrive in London. It was possible that the messenger he had sent to Harold would return with word that the usurper had capitulated, but it was more likely that the English would choose to do battle with him. In any case, a decision would soon be reached, and the prospect that this period of interminable waiting would soon end relieved him. He and Harold were much alike, he thought wryly: they both hated inactivity.

The route to Hastings was principally across open country, but there was a short cut through a forest, and although the Duke normally would have avoided any terrain that might be a trap, he decided to push through the woods. His unit had encountered so few natives on its ride out of Hastings that he felt fairly secure, and even more important, he was anxious to return to his headquarters.

The sun had disappeared behind leaden clouds when he rode down the path that took him into the forest, and he smiled to himself as he sniffed the familiar odor of pine. The smell always reminded him of his boyhood, and he thought that it wouldn't be long before he began to feel at home in England. The climate was cold and damp compared to that of Normandy, but there were compensations, many of them.

The smile faded suddenly from his face when a heavy spear came hurtling out of the trees and struck him in the chest. Fortunately its force had been partly deflected by a branch of an oak tree, so he was uninjured, but the point became entangled in a loop of his light chain mail, and the shaft dangled across his chest. Other spears were thrown from both sides of the path, and in the uproar that followed William realized that he had allowed his raiders to be ambushed.

This was not the time to permit himself to feel chagrined, however. He had to extricate himself and his men quickly, and as he swung himself from his saddle to the ground, he roared an order for his troops to dismount. They were perfect targets so long as they remained on their horses, and they would suffer the added disadvantage of a loss of mobility. Walter Giffard, and four or five others rushed forward to surround their liege, but William waved them away.

"Never mind me," he shouted. "Form at arm's length. The first squadron to the left—you take them, Giffard! The second squadron, follow me to the right!"

The Normans obeyed unhesitatingly, and when they plunged into the underbrush a fresh shower of spears greeted them. Here and there an invader dropped, wounded, but no man paused because a friend had been struck down, and direct contact was quickly established with the enemy. The invaders advanced cautiously, ready to fall back if necessary, for there was no way of determining how many of the foe might be lurking in the forest. And William understood now why there had been no young men in the village when he had attacked it. They had planned this counterstroke carefully, and he blamed himself for what he consid-

ered a gross lack of military foresight. He had out-
guessed so many enemies in so many battles that his
failure today to divine the intentions of the English
was, in his opinion, his own fault.

If his agents had misled him as to the whereabouts of
the English army and if he was surrounded by Harold's
housecarls, he would have to retreat, and he would be
lucky to escape. If, on the other hand, he was merely
being ambushed by a band of aroused villagers and
their friends, the ecnounter could be regarded as an
incidental skirmish. Certainly the next few minutes
would tell him precisely where he stood, and he moved
forward slowly, his sword raised, peering past every
thick oak trunk and every furry pine.

A hail of arrows halted the Normans for a moment,
but William called on his troops to advance again, and
without waiting for them to respond he plunged into a
tangled thicket of brambles. It was so dense that it made
a perfect hiding place, and as he had suspected, two
fair-haired Englishmen were crouched behind a wall of
bushes. One of them fired an arrow at him, but it fell at
his feet, and when the other threw a spear he caught it
with his free hand as he continued to push forward.

Even if they had been heavily armed they would
have been no match for him, and he made short work
of them with his sword, finishing them off before a pair
of his cavalrymen could crash through the brush to join
him. Examining the bodies at his feet, he was encouraged. Neither of the dead Englishmen was in uniform,
and their rough clothes, their lack of supply pouches,
and their thin-soled sandals all indicated that they were
independent avengers, not members of Harold Godwineson's army.

There was no need to fall back, and it might even be
possible instead to wipe out the entire native force.

William issued a new series of orders and instructed his troops to take as many prisoners as they could. For the next quarter of an hour the Normans searched the forest diligently, meeting opposition in occasional flurries but encountering no serious difficulties. No more than eight or ten of the cavalrymen were wounded, and none was seriously hurt, but the English suffered heavily. It was impossible to estimate how many of the peasants escaped, but at least a dozen were killed, and twenty-three others were captured.

The prisoners were all brought before the Duke, who had gone back to his stallion and was standing at the horse's side, thoughtfully chewing a chunk of bread when the natives were herded onto the path. He studied them, and knew almost at once that any leniency he might show would be misinterpreted. The blue eyes that returned his gaze were insolent and blazed with hatred; if he spared them now in the hope that they would be loyal to him when England became his, he would merely be storing up trouble for the future.

Gerbod tried to question the prisoners, but they refused to answer him, and either turned their backs on him or spat onto the ground at his feet in contempt. William, who was watching the scene intently, shook his head in wonder at the stubborn pride of the English, and one of the peasants caught his eye. The man knew a single word of French and spoke it loudly.

"Bastard!" he said.

Several of the troopers would have struck the wretch down with their swords, but William halted them. Then he laughed, and the sound was so harsh that even his own men shivered. He walked slowly up and down the line of prisoners, his lips pursed, and then he turned suddenly to Walter Giffard.

"Geld them" he said. "If a few clucking capons flap

their wings at Harold, they might help persuade him to stop delaying and make up his mind one way or the other. Gerbod," he added to his stepson, "tell these prisoners I want them to give Harold a message for me. His choice is now very clear. Either he'll be true to the oath he took, or his England will soon be a land of eunuchs."

The raiders arrived back at the Duke's headquarters shortly after dark, and William relaxed, confidant that his unpleasant day's work would bring results and that the issue would be resolved without delay. Harold's freedom of action had been narrowed, and he would now either capitulate or accept the challenge of his archfoe and do battle at once.

The Duke did not have long to wait, and thirty-six hours after his return to his encampment his faith in human nature was rewarded. In midmorning on October 11 his emissary to Harold, a monk from Fécamp who had often performed services of a confidential nature for Abbé Lanfranc, arrived back at Hastings. Several of the barons, who had been making it their business to remain near the ducal tent at all times, asked to be allowed to hear the report of Dom Hugues Maigrot, and William graciously granted their request. Nothing was to be gained by secrecy now; as Harold had given his answer, the question of war or peace had in actuality been decided.

The great lords formed in a semicircle behind William, and their faces reflected their strain as the monk, his robes dusty and his sandals caked with dirt, entered the tent. He crossed himself, and the barons, remembering his calling, followed his example. Then he walked stiffly toward William, and several of the barons smiled in spite of the tension of the moment, for it was obvious to them that Maigrot, who usually traveled on his own feet, was sore after his long ride on the spirited stallion Fitz Osbern had loaned him.

William, who had dealt with members of religious orders for many years, knew the value of a slow and gentle approach; if he tried to deal with the messenger as he would with a military courier, the man would simply become flustered and would give a garbled report. "Welcome, Father Maigrot," he said easily. "You appear none the worse after your journey."

"I'm much the worse, thank you. That great beast of the Seneschal's has jarred every bone in my body. I try to tell myself that the Lord has His own ways of making mortals do penance for their sins, but I can't believe I've ever erred so gravely."

The Duke concealed a smile behind his hand. "And how did you find affairs in London?"

"I've always contended that the English are heathens, Your Grace, and I have proof now that my beliefs are right." The monk forgot his aches, and his placid expression became indignant. "London is a huge city of at least thirty or forty thousand persons. Yet I've seen more churches in a Norman town of only five thousand! The new church and abbey that Edward the Confessor built at West Minster just outside the city looked interesting, but I was given no chance to stop and examine the place. So I know only what I actually saw with my own eyes, and what I saw shocked me. The few churches there are in the town are small and dark, and I was astonished at how few people there were in them, day or night. I'm not one to cast stones, but I can't help feeling that the Archdeacon of Cantebury is very lax in his discipline and his administration. Abbé Lanfranc will be eager to hear all I've learned. He asked me to send him my pertinent observations, you know."

Of all those gathered in the tent only Bishop Odo even pretended to care whether the churches of London flourished. The barons began to mutter, but William silenced them with a curt gesture. Then he turned back to Maigrot with a serene smile. "What of your mission?" he inquired, prodding quietly. "You found Earl Harold, I presume."

"To be sure, Your Grace. I was taken to him at once. He's living in King Edward's old house on Ludgate Hill, and although I couldn't verify the rumor, I was told that he's forced his sister—King Edward's widow, you know—to move elsewhere. The members of the clergy to whom I spoke all agreed that she's a saintly woman and that she was a fit companion for her late husband."

"And Harold?" William made up his mind never to send a churchman on a diplomatic mission again. Priests were apparently unable to realize that brevity was a virtue.

"The Holy Father," Dom Hugues Maigrot declared in ringing tones, "showed great wisdom in excommunicating him. Harold is a most ungodly man!"

"So we've had reason to suspect," William replied wryly. "You presented my offer to him?"

"I did, Your Grace, in the presence of his earls and other nobles. He sat on Edward the Confessor's throne, he was dressed in splendid cloth of silver and on his upper arm was the royal bracelet of King Cnut. It was a pagan spectacle that took my breath away!"

"How did Harold respond to my offer?" William's voice was still calm, and the barons marveled at his unusual display of patience.

"He listened carefully, Your Grace," the monk said. "His eyes never left my face, but I couldn't tell what he was thinking. It's my personal opinion that he's made a compact with Beelzebub to help him conceal his reactions, but that's neither here nor there."

"Indeed it isn't," William declared pointedly.

"When I finished speaking," Maigrot continued, "he sat very still for some time. Then his face flushed, and before I quite knew what was happening, he leaped out of his chair and struck me across the face."

There was a stunned silence, and the generals stared at each other in amazement. It was a flagrant abuse of the code of chivalry to mistreat a diplomatic courier who traveled under a flag of truce. The barons had accepted Harold's renunciation of the oath he had taken under duress, for they would have behaved under similar circumstances just as he had, but his extreme discourtesy to a messenger was such a shocking demonstration that the Normans could only conclude that he had abandoned all honor.

"You're sure of what you're saying to me, Father Maigrot?" William, who had always thought of Harold as being much like himself, could not believe he had heard the monk correctly.

"I'm very sure, Your Grace. Harold's brother, Earl Cyrth, and Earl Waltheof—both of them fine young men endowed with many of the best Christian virtues—took hold of him and forced him back into his chair. They apologized profusely to me, and they asked me to extend their sincere regrets to you."

The Duke made no attempt to curb the anger that welled up in him now. "What did Harold do while they apologized to you?" he asked huskily.

"He would have struck me again, but they kept hold of his arms, and I withdrew from the hall."

The barons began to shout, and the voice of Robert of Mortain was louder than all the rest. "Death to the usurper!"

They took up his cry, but they grew quiet again when William rose slowly and turned to face them. Even Fitz Osbern, who had known him in all his moods, had never seen him so enraged; his face was pale, his lips were bloodless, and the pupils of his eyes had shrunk to the size of spear points. "Harold has chosen war, and he shall have war," he said in a cold, hard voice. "Either I will kill him or he will kill me. And by God's splendor, I mean to become King of England!"

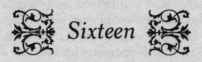 *Sixteen*

ON THE MORNING of October 12 Harold marched out of London at the head of a column of his magnificent housecarls and battle-seasoned thegns, veteran farmer-soldiers from Wessex and churls who had fought in many past battles. Bringing up the rear was a long, straggling line of freemen, ill-trained and poorly armed but filled with enthusiasm and determined to repel the invaders. The English army moved rapidly, and by the following day it had covered the sixty-two miles from London and pitched camp six miles from Hastings on a hill later to be known as Senlac.

William's spies and observers, whose activities were being coordinated by one of the most conservative of Norman generals, Baron Alain Fergant, began to send back a stream of reports to the Duke. Harold had selected a site that he could defend with comparative ease behind him was a deep forest, which would prevent the Normans from attacking his rear, and there were woods on his flanks, too. These he strengthened with ditches, and the observers were unanimous in expressing the opinion that the ground over which the Normans would be forced to move if they chose to attack was at best difficult terrain. The slope leading to the summit of the hill was irregular, the ground was broken by numerous depressions and a score of bogs would hamper the movements of horses and foot soldiers.

In spite of the obstacles that presented themselves,

however, there was no question in William's mind. He would attack. As he pointed out to Robert of Mortain and Count Eustace of Boulogne, more than one third of his force was made up of cavalry, while the English, for reasons no one could understand, had no horsemen at all. Hence the Normans would be throwing away their basic advantage if they failed to take the offensive.

Shortly after noon the barons were called to a conclave, and William calmly announced that, according to the best information available, the English army numbered somewhere between fifteen thousand and twenty thousand men. He went on to explain that this superiority was offset in part by the Norman cavalry and in part by the professional incompetence of Harold's freemen. Most of the lords accepted his estimate of the situation phlegmatically, but then questions were raised about the intentions of Edwin and Morcar. The corps of the northern earls was made up of experienced troops, at least half of whom were mounted, and if they should come to Harold's aid the invader's chances of victory would be slim.

William, who had privately been discussing the problem with Fitz Osbern and Alain Fergant only a short time before the council had convened, shrugged indifferently. He was neither a soothsayer nor a prophet, he said, and it was impossible for him to make any predictions regarding Edwin and Morcar. He would attack Harold the following morning, and if the usurper received reinforcements by that time, the Normans would simply have to fight all the harder. It would not be the first time, he remarked lightly, that his army would be going into battle against an enemy that outnumbered it by a ratio of two to one.

In order to stifle any further discussion of this delicate subject he sat down, and Fitz Osbern promptly took his place. The Seneschal promised to keep the generals informed of any new developments, and he said that by the end of the day an announcement would be made regarding the order of battle and the assignment of the coveted posts of top command. Everyone present looked eagerly at the Duke, but he pretended to be immersed in thought; actually he had already decided how his forces were to be arrayed, but was deliberately delaying telling the barons his final plans. There was no better way to avoid jealous arguments.

Alain Fergant rose and gave the generals a detailed description of English weapons and armor, and then, with the aid of two young observers who had just been over the ground, he drew a rough sketch of the proposed battlefield. The barons asked a number of questions, and after their curiosity had been satisfied, Fitz Osbern read a brief ducal decree. From this time forward no man was to be permitted to leave his own immediate bivouac area, discipline was to be rigidly enforced and neither soldiers nor officers, regardless of rank, were to drink either wine or stronger spirits.

The lords then looked at William again, expecting him to adjourn the meeting, but instead he reached inside his tunic and drew out a folded square of parchment, which he held aloft. "I know that all of you would be sorely disappointed if the battle failed to take place," he said casually, "but it's only fair to warn you that we may not fight at all. I've written a communication to Harold, challenging him to individual combat and offering to let the issue be decided personally between us."

Even the Seneschal had not heard of the proposal, and the barons could only stare at their master in horror. When they had absorbed the shock they began to protest, and then, one by one, they demanded the right to take his place against the usurper. Those who had witnessed the Duke's friendly jousting match with Harold at Rouen Castle thought he was risking too much, and everyone agreed that he could not place the entire expedition in jeopardy by taking such a chance.

William smiled as he listened to their arguments, then he stood and walked to the entrance, where Walter Giffard was on guard. "Walter, take this to Earl Harold at once, under a flag of truce, and bring me his reply," he said, and turned back to his barons. "I appreciate your concern for me, but I choose to exercise the prerogatives of my position as your liege. I ask no man to do for me what I can do for myself."

There was nothing more to be said, and the generals filed out of the tent. The afternoon passed slowly, and the busiest men on both sides were the spies. Several of Harold's agents were captured, but William, following the precedent he had set at St. Valéry, treated them courteously, had them shown around his camp, and surrounded them with protective cordons of horsemen when he sent them back to the English lines.

In midafternoon Walter Giffard returned from the enemy headquarters with a brusque rejection of William's challenge. The usurper had refused to entertain the idea of individual combat, but two of his brothers, Earl Gyrth and Earl Leofwith, had begged for the chance to substitute for him. The Duke, who listened carefully to Giffard's account, thought more highly of Gyrth and Leofwith and sent word to his generals that both were to be watched carefully during the battle.

Twice there were flurries of excitement when word was received that Edwin and Morcar had led their troops into the English camp, but both times the stories proved to be false, and the Seneschal gave strict orders that no such rumors were to be allowed to circulate unless they were first verified. It was also said that the enemy, who were still moving into position, were drinking heavily, and that the Wessex farmers and the freemen were the worst offenders. William gave little credence to the accounts, thinking that his spies were merely trying to say things that would please him, and he dismissed the matter from his busy mind.

At dusk the invaders ate supper, and shortly after dark the Seneschal summoned the barons to his own tent to announce the order of battle to them. The Duke purposely absented himself from the meeting so that those who found his decisions displeasing would have no chance to appeal to him. On the left, Fitz Osbern said, would be the men of Flanders and Maine, Anjou and Brittany and Poitou. They would serve under the command of Baron Alain Fergant, and no one could object to his selection, for he had fought with distinction under Robert the Devil before pledging his allegiance to William, and he was the most experienced commander in the army.

On the right would be the foreigners, and as this mixed group came from so many lands, the Duke had created a joint command for it, apparently on the theory that no one man would be competent to direct the independent, hard-bitten adventurers. Roger Mont Gomeri was to be one of the leaders of this wing, and the barons were satisfied with his appointment, for they knew that he was as ruthless as the most conscienceless of the hirelings. His co-commander would be Eustace of Boulogne, and only the most astute of the barons saw the wisdom of his appointment; Eustace, a suave and wily diplomat, could be counted on to smooth the ruffled feelings of Danes and Germans, Hungarians and Italians when they were given assignments that were odious to them.

In the center, the Seneschal said, would be the Norman hard core, and every lord stiffened, hoping desperately that he would be called upon to lead the "fishmen" and thus win everlasting glory. But another surprise was in store for the generals: His Grace, the Seneschal said, was going to command the Normans himself, knowing that they would obey and follow him as they would no one else. Fitz Osbern did not add that through this maneuver William was neatly avoiding bitter and endless controversy among his lieutenants. The less than enviable task of co-ordinating the activities of all three units was to be performed by the Seneschal himself, with the assistance of Robert of Mortain, and Fitz Osbern reminded the barons that any order he might give them carried the weight and authority of a direct ducal command.

The meeting broke up on a note of surprising amicability, the generals retired to their tents, and the camp settled down for the night. The weather was unseasonably warm, but there was a hint of autumn in the air, and the men who would wear armor the following day consoled themselves with the thought that the heat would not be unbearable; the moon came out, the stars appeared, and the farmers in the army knew that the sun would shine on the hills and ridges around Hastings in the morning.

William received a report telling him that the last of the English troops had taken their places in Harold's bivouac area, and observers who had been roaming around the countryside brought word that they had seen no sign of Earl Edwin's corps anywhere. Hence it was likely that the Englishmen from the north would not arrive in time to participate in the opening of the battle; whether they would appear later and make their presence felt was still open to conjecture.

The Duke ate in the open with members of his staff, then he retired to his tent and confessed his sins to the Auxiliary Bishop of Coutances, after rather obviously spurning the offer of Odo, who had proffered his aid as a spiritual adviser. The camp grew quiet, and William, sitting at his worktable of rough pine, tried to write a letter to Matilda by the light of a sputtering candle. But the words he put on paper were stilted, he found he could not express his thoughts adequately, and he gave up the effort. There was nothing, he reflected, that he could say to his wife that she did not already know, and long before a letter could reach her the battle would be either won or lost. It did not occur to him to wonder whether or not he loved her, just as it had never crossed his mind to be unfaithful to her. Unlike most of his lords, he had never bothered to philander; Matilda was his wife, and consequently no one else interested him. He would have been faintly surprised had anyone told him that his attitude was unusual.

He allowed himself the luxury of thinking about her for a few moments; he grinned as he recalled the day he had rolled her in Flemish mud, and the lines of his mouth softened as he remembered the first nights and days of their marriage. It was unpleasant to dwell on her meddling before and during Harold's visit to Normandy, and as he knew from experience that he would become angry unless he exercised self-discipline, he put her out of his mind and went to bed. Nevertheless she appeared in his dreams that night, as did his mother, and neither Matilda nor Harlotte had ever seemed lovelier.

The camp began to stir more than two hours before daybreak on the Ides of October, and when Gerbod came into his stepfather's tent, carefully shielding a lighted candle, he saw that William was wide awake and staring at the rippling silk overhead. The boy, who was completely dressed, tried to smile and made a valiant effort to conceal his nervousness. "Good morning, Father," he said. "The chef will have your breakfast for you very soon."

"We'll eat together, shall we?" William rose from his pallet, and then, as Gerbod watched him, he washed, shaved, and dressed by candlelight.

Servants appeared silently with more candles, and as the Duke was pulling on his boots the chef carried in a steaming bowl and set it in the middle of the wooden worktable. William sniffed appreciatively and raised an eyebrow at Gerbod, who flushed and smiled. "I ordered if for you last night, Father."

"*Dilligrout*, eh?"

"I thought it would remind you of home."

"It's just what we need. There's nothing like going into battle on a full stomach." William began to eat heartily, but he saw that Gerbod had no appetite, and he glanced across the table with guarded eyes. "I was thinking about you this morning before you came in to wake me up," he said. "Would you mind very much if I sent you with the priests and the others who aren't going to take part in the fight today?"

Gerbod, incapable of speech, could only gape at his stepfather.

"Your mother would like it better that way," William continued uncomfortably. "I'm afraid she'd be very much upset if something happened to both of us."

In the long silence that followed Gerbod clenched his fists. "You've accepted me into the ranks of knighthood," he said at last in a choked voice, "and you've acknowledged my right to help and support you. I won't let you deny me the privilege that's mine. You can't do it, Father."

William sighed and ladled more *dilligrout* into the

boy's bowl. "Well, I tried. I did that much for your mother, I tried. Eat your breakfast before it gets cold."

Vastly relieved, Gerbod began to consume his meal rapidly. Outside the sounds of battle preparations became louder and more insistent; trumpets blared, men shouted, and there was an increasing metallic din as the horses were armored. William, to whom such confusion was no novelty, ate slowly, savoring his food, and he did not bother to look up when one of his aides raised the flap and stood in the entrance. He would have no privacy from now until the end of the battle, but he had long ago learned to perform several functions simultaneously.

"Sir, Taillefer begs permission to see you for a moment. I told him you were at breakfast, but he—"

"Who?" The Duke speared a chunk of sausage.

"Taillefer, the minstrel you knighted."

William considered the request briefly. "Send him in, then."

A tall, broad-shouldered man in armor, his conical helmet under his left arm, entered and saluted. "Lord Duke," he said, "I've served you longer than anyone in the army except Lord Seneschal. And I pray that you reward my many years of fidelity by granting me the honor of striking the first blow at the enemy."

The Duke looked up from his bowl and saw that the former minstrel was serious. Sentiment and heroics in war were amateur concepts that annoyed him, and he frowned. "I can't think of a better way to get yourself killed," he said curtly.

Taillefer shrugged, and in the candlelight his eyes looked enormous. "You've never been a juggler, Lord Duke. Songs will be sung in your honor and chronicles will be written about you for generations to come. I was once a minstrel, but you made me a knight, and today I

have my chance to repay your faith in me. Whether I
live or die doesn't matter. But perhaps someone will
include a verse about the juggler in one of the songs
they'll sing about you, and that will be enough for me."

William stood and held out his hand. "There was a
time," he said, "when the world paid little attention to
me, you know. I was a bastard, I was a fugitive who hid
in forests, and no one thought I had the wits or the
strength to win my inheritance. Permission is granted,
Taillefer. You may strike the first blow." He watched
the knight's departure, and Gerbod was unable to interpret the strange expression in his eyes.

Breakfast was soon finished, and with the help of
several servants William donned his armor, taking care
to wear the suit of chain mail that had seen prior
service. Then he emerged into the fresh air of early
morning and mounted his great Spanish stallion. His
knights fell in behind him, his churls handed him his
sword, mace, and shield, and he started off down the
hill to join his troops, who had already assembled and
were awaiting him. He had given the knights of his staff
the right to select one of their own number to carry the
papal banner, and a young Norman named Toustain
held high the great flag of azure emblazoned with a
cross of gold. Beside him was Gerbod, carrying the
ducal pennant, and when the little cavalcade appeared
the army was called to attention.

Bishop Odo celebrated Mass, the men received
Communion, and then it was time for William to
address his comrades-in-arms. The first streaks of light
were appearing in the sky, and the men peered through
the gloom, trying to see him. Those who did not know
him expected the usual harangue delivered by commanders just before a battle, but William did not in-

tend to make a speech. Standing in his saddle, he gazed out at the long, straight rows, and for an instant he was shaken by an emotion he could not identify. Then he took hold of himself.

"May God help us!" he cried, and signaled to his trumpeters.

The household guards formed in the van, the Duke's personal entourage surrounded him, and the march toward the English position six miles away was begun. Walter Giffard brought word that Edwin and Morcar had not yet been sighted, the Seneschal reported that all elements of the army were ready for combat, and the column swung onto the Hastings road that led straight to London. Dawn broke when they had ridden no more than two or three miles, and when they arrived at last at a spot that someone identified to the Duke as Telham Hill, the early morning mist was vanishing.

The invaders needed an hour or more to reach Telham Hill and form their battle lines, and while they gathered William rode to the crest of the eminence with his principal lieutenants to study the enemy. The sight that greeted him was far from encouraging: the terrain over which his troops would have to move was indeed rugged and broken, and the English had taken up their position on a natural ridge part of the way up the opposite slope. Harold's men were formed in a huge semicircle, with the superb housecarls in the center and the flanks drawn back to meet the forests on either side.

The English, who were waiting for their foe, stood close together with their round shields overlapping, and their short, heavy javelins and sharp battle-axes gleamed in the early morning sunlight. It was plain that they were planning to fight a completely defensive

battle, and that their strategy was based on the hope that
the Normans would destroy themselves in vain attempts to batter down the wall of shields.

The Duke and his generals were silent for a time, and
then William raised his voice. "Where is Harold?"

Alain Fergant pointed to a banner slightly to the right
of the English center; even at a distance the figure of a
fighting man, outlined in gold and jewels, could be
seen on the pennant. "There, Lord Duke."

William stared out across the field at his enemy, and
his face was dark. He admired Harold for his abilities,
and in many ways thought more highly of him than of
any other man he had ever known. But the world was
too small to contain both of them, and before the sun
set one or the other would die. But now, for a brief
moment, he could look back as well as forward, while
the battle waited.

The generals could not guess the thoughts that raced
through his mind, but they knew he looked pensive,
and they stood quietly, respecting his mood even
though they did not understand it. At last his face
cleared, and when the lines around his mouth and eyes
set in hard, familiar lines, they smiled at each other;
this was the William they knew, this was the William
they would follow anywhere.

"Mark well the place where Harold stands," the
Duke said.

Fitz Osbern was better able to divine his feelings than
were the rest. "We've already marked it."

Roger Mont Gomeri laughed coarsely. "I'll bring
you his head on the point of my sword, Lord Duke."

"You will not." A rare, brittle note crept into William's voice. "He's mine. The issue that stands between
us is one that only Harold and I can settle. Because of us

many people have already suffered. Because of us many more will die before nightfall. So you will leave God-wineson to me."

"We hear you, and will obey," Alain Fergant replied, and the others nodded.

"So much for the usurper." The Duke shifted in his saddle and carefully studied the disposition of the English troops. He raised his nose-guard to give him a better view of the field, then lowered it again. "Osbern!"

The Seneschal rode to his side. "What do you make of them, William?" he asked in a low, confidential tone.

"I couldn't quite believe that Harold has no cavalry, but it's obvious from his use of the old Roman formation that he hasn't. However, we're going to have no easy time of it."

"True. And the ground won't help. He couldn't have found a site that suited him better."

"We'll need to soften that human wall." The Duke raised his voice so the others could hear. "Our initial attack will be made in three parts, each following closely on the heels of the one preceding it. The archers and slingmen will strike first. Behind them will come the crossbowmen and the infantry. Then the cavalry will smash into the English formation. If there are no questions, join your commands. Fergant! Mont Gomeri! Send me a signal when you're ready!"

The generals cantered off, the Normans formed behind the crest of the hill, and the tension mounted as the archers and sling throwers moved forward and crouched on the downward slope. After a wait that seemed interminable a messenger brought word from Baron Fergant that his troops were in place, and a little

later Baron Mont Gomeri sent similar word. William
shaded his eyes for a last look at his Normans, then he
told Toustain and Gerbod, "Dip your banners!"

They obeyed, and the trumpets sounded the attack.
The English stiffened, but to their astonishment a
single man in armor came riding up the hill toward
them, singing a song in honor of Charlemagne as he
repeatedly threw his sword in the air and caught it with
the dexterity of a professional juggler. Taillefer shouted
a challenge to individual combat, and the shield wall
parted to allow passage to one of the few English knights
who was mounted. While both armies watched, the
Saxon and Taillefer crossed arms; the minstrel knight
cleverly outmaneuvered his opponent and killed him
with a deft lance thrust. The Normans and their allies
cheered, and a second Englishman rode out to accept
the gage. Taillefer used his sword this time and the
defender swung a battle-ax as they circled around each
other, then Taillefer feinted, slashed wickedly, and
toppled a second opponent.

There was a stir in the English lines, and William
smiled broadly as he watched the exhibition. Nothing
he might have planned could have been so beneficial to
the spirits of his men or so harmful to the enemy. Then
his grin faded abruptly: a third Englishman rode out
from behind the shields, recklessly headed straight for
Taillefer, and killed him with a single stroke of a
battle-ax.

It would be fatal to give the men time to think, and
William again ordered the trumpets to sound. The
archers leaped to their feet and ran toward the enemy,
halting in unison to fire, then dashing forward again.
Behind them, in a solid mass, came the infantry, and
when both had approached close to the foe and then
moved aside to leave the field clear, the cavalry thun-

dered up the slope. But the English refused to panic, and they were not impressed by the charge; perhaps no one had ever told them that the Normans were invincible, and they struck back vigorously, killing and wounding scores who came within range of their javelins and axes.

To the dismay of William, who was watching the assault from Telham Hill, the Bretons on his left flank weakened and began to retreat. The men from Flanders, many of whom had never fought before, lost their heads and started to run, and the troops from Anjou followed them. Only the veterans from Maine held firm, but they were too few in number to stem the tide, and their comrades swept them toward the rear too. The English, scarcely able to believe that the enemies they had feared were so vulnerable, so human, began to shout jubilantly, and the freemen and farmers on Harold's right promptly forgot their strict orders to hold their positions at all costs. Thinking that victory was already within their grasp, they broke out of the tight, semicircular formation and pursued the retreating foe.

Scores of individual combats immediately developed, and it was painfully clear from the command post that the English, amateur soldiers though they were, had the advantage. They were the attackers, and the troops of Alain Fergant were so disorganized that their units were broken up and those who could not flee fast enough were slaughtered, one by one. There was a stir around the banner of the fighting man, and William, across the field, could almost feel Harold's elation. It was incredible but true that the battle might be ended almost before it had begun, for all would be lost if the contagion of fear spread to the rest of the Norman army.

Unless Fergant's corps rallied and made a stand at

once, the entire flank would crumble, and William, waiting to see no more, galloped madly toward the panicky Bretons. His staff, taken by surprise, followed him, but he outdistanced them and was in the midst of his auxiliaries before his knights could reach the bottom of the hill.

Rally! Rally!" he roared, and his voice was so urgent that the men heard him in spite of the din.

Not bothering to see if anyone was following him, but hoping desperately that he would inspire the troops by his example, he pushed toward the English freemen, slashing left and right with his sword. Enemy spears sounded like ominous hail as they fell against his shield and bounced off his stallion's armor. But he was indifferent to the deadly shower and seemingly gave no thought to his own safety as he rode straight into the charging ranks of Harold's farmer-soldiers. Some of the enemy, recognizing him, redoubled their efforts to strike him down, but he seemed to lead a charmed life, and wherever he rode he left trampled bodies in his wake.

The hard-bitten infantrymen from Maine were the first to recover, and they dashed after him in twos and threes to resume the fight. Their resistance slowed but did not halt the English advance; however, there was now a hard core around which to form, and William cut a path to the Maine banner and there, with the aid of three knights, he organized the equivalent of a battalion into a line. Then, as Harold's men threw themselves against this wall, the Duke cantered into a mass of confused troops from Anjou. Using the flat of his sword, he beat them back into formation, and their officers, ashamed of their own failure, followed his example, and they were so energetic in their attempts to compensate for their previous inadequacy that he could not help but smile.

When he saw the men from Anjou moving into solid ranks, he knew he was needed in their midst no longer, and moved off toward the milling, frightened Bretons. By this time his own knights had joined him, and he commanded them to drive the Bretons toward him. Then, snatching a spear from a stumbling foot soldier, he used the weapon as a club to force the frightened men into formation. He swore and cajoled, threatened and pleaded, half standing in his saddle as he rode restlessly back and forth.

Meantime the infantrymen from Maine and their cohorts from Anjou brought the English freemen to a halt, and the Bretons, taking heart, moved to join them. The men from Flanders and even the little contingent from Vexin came back into the fray. The tide of battle changed, the English were sent hurtling back across the field, and William, still muttering angrily to himself, retired to his command post to survey the scene.

The near-disaster had been a sobering experience, and Baron Fergant hurried to the Duke in order to apologize, but William cared nothing about the past. All that mattered to him was the smashing of the enemy formation, and he told his equerries to pass the word that he would lead the "fishmen" himself in an attack on the center of the English line. The knights knew it would be useless to dissuade him, and the approving roar of the Norman cavalry was sufficient indication that the Duke knew his countrymen and realized that his proposed gesture would be the best tonic he could feed them.

They formed in a column eight abreast behind him,

and with his banner bearers beside him he rode down
Telham Hill, up the opposite slope, and galloped
straight toward Harold's banner of the fighting man.
The housecarls were sturdy and courageous, and certainly they were as dependable as any soldiers on earth,
but no human beings could withstand the impact of the
Norman cavalry, and the wall of shields split open. The
attacking knights struck right and left with their swords
and maces, the housecarls gave as good as they received, and what had begun as a concerted drive de-
generated into a series of individual combats.

William, swinging his mace like a scythe, cleared a
path for himself as he drove toward the banner of the
fighting man, around which some fifty knights and
housecarls had formed a protective cordon. A man in
heavy plate armor came out to meet the Duke, and for
an instant William thought that his opponent was
Harold. Then he saw that the face beneath the helmet
was that of a younger man, and when he heard the
housecarls shout, "Gyrth! Gyrth!" he knew that he was
going to fight the young Earl who was reputedly the
most courageous and wise member of the family of
Godwine.

A trial of strength with Harold himself would not
only have been more satisfactorily conclusive, but it
would have been less of a physical strain for a man of
thirty-nine to fight someone approximately his own
age. Gyrth was at least twelve years junior to the Duke
and in the prime of young manhood, but William did
not hesitate, and, grinning behind his nose-guard, he
pushed ahead. He was mounted and Gyrth was on foot,
which gave the Norman an advantage, but the Earl
made the odds more nearly equal by hurling a spear
accurately and with great force; the point penetrated

the forehead of the Spanish stallion, and the beast stumbled and dropped.

William fell heavily to the ground, but he rolled over, regained his feet and picked up his sword in time to meet Gyrth's wild charge. The Englishman swung his heavy battle-ax as though it weighed no more than a javelin, and William, who had lost his shield when his horse had been killed, had to fend off the blows with his sword alone. Several Norman lords and knights would have come to their master's assistance, but William ordered them to keep their distance, and Gyrth likewise refused help from two eager comrades.

Gradually the Duke shifted to the offensive, and after feinting and thrusting several times he felt a surge of confidence. Gyrth was as powerful as Harold, but he was less clever, and his sole advantage, aside from his youth, was his round shield, which he shifted nimbly to absorb the shock of the blows being rained upon him. William knew that he had to finish off the Earl quickly; in a long combat Gyrth would wear him down, and there was always the danger that some English freeman or churl who was not bound by the code of chivalry would find the Duke of Normandy an irresistible target for a well-placed arrow or javelin.

And so the tempo of the combat increased as William slashed wickedly at his opponent, aiming first at Gyrth's face, then his neck, then his sides, where he wore no armor. The Earl fought valiantly, and, regardless of his opinion of the Duke as a political antagonist, his expression mirrored his admiration for William the swordsman. They beat at each other mercilessly, neither giving nor receiving quarter, and at last William's experience, cunning, and prodigious strength brought him victory. With a bold stroke that would have been sheer recklessness in one less skilled, he drove the point of his great sword through the Earl's throat, just above his armor, and Gyrth fell to the ground dead.

Housecarls and English nobles immediately came at the Duke, but his own men were ready for just such a maneuver, and, surrounding him, they led him off, fighting their way inch by inch to safety. Someone gave William another horse, one of his equerries handed him a shield, and from his new vantage point he saw that the attack had been less than successful, for the English were still holding their own. He ordered his trumpeters to sound a withdrawal, and the Normans drew back for the second time.

The defenders closed the gaps in their wall of shields, and all was as it had been before the assault. Losses on both sides had been heavy, and William learned for the first time that Leofwith, another of the sons of the Godwine, had been killed too. But Harold still lived, and the issue of the day had not yet been decided. The knights on the ducal staff begged William not to risk his life again, but he ignored their advice and led charge after charge in person, rallying his men, inspiring them by his example and encouraging them when they faltered.

He lost his second horse, then a third, but he himself remained unscathed, and the Normans became convinced that he was under divine protection. He roamed the field constantly, bolstering his line, shifting units and noting even the slightest change in the disposition of his forces. His energy seemed to be inexhaustible, but when the day wore on and afternoon came, even the most devoted of his followers began to grow tired. The English remained confident and defiant in spite of the battering they had received; their wall of shields was solid, and behind their line was the banner of the fighting man, with housecarls ten deep surrounding it.

The time had come, William thought, to revise his strategy, and, retiring to the summit of Telham Hill, he called a council of war. He listened to the ideas of his barons, and he showed remarkable patience as he explained his reasons for rejecting their suggestions, one by one. Then he turned to his seneschal, who squatted beside him, reflectively chewing a blade of grass.

"Osbern," he said. "do you remember our experiments with archers? If we can't smash the wall, we'll go over it."

"You're right." Fitz Osbern smiled, and his teeth looked very white against the background of grime and dirt that streaked his face. "The archers should direct their arrows in an arc, over the shields."

"They won't do much damage that way," Roger Mont Gomeri objected. He stood leaning against a tree, and appeared to be less fatigued than anyone present, with the exception of the Duke.

"We'll confuse the enemy," William said. "And remember that they're as tired as we are. Now, I want you to recall what happened this morning when the Bretons became panicky, and I mean this as no insult to you, Fergant. The housecarls held their places, but hundreds of Harold's men broke out of formation and chased after us. I propose that we tempt them now with a false retreat. We'll annoy them and make them angry by shooting our arrows in a curve. Then we'll pretend to run away, and they might forget their orders and come after us."

There was a silence broken only by the distant shouts of the bowmen on both sides, then, in a nearby tree a bird, blithely unconscious of the human carnage,

chirped incongruously. Fitz Osbern ran a hand
through his short hair. "Let's try it. We have nothing to
lose and everything to gain."

New instructions were given to the archers, who took
up positions on the flanks and directed their darts over
the shields of their enemies. The English could not
protect themselves without moving, and as they were
forced to remain in place they were helpless against this
new type of assault. The shrieks of the wounded and
dying mingled with the angry shouts of the survivors,
and William, seeing his strategy succeed, sent his cavalry at the line again and again. The horsemen hurled
their javelins over the wall, then rode quickly away,
and this maneuver was repeated for the better part of an
hour.

Then the entire Norman strength was massed, and
the combined cavalry of William, Fergant, Mont
Gomeri, and Eustace rode toward the English at a
full canter. To the defenders this charge must have
looked like a final, desperate assault, and they held
their positions grimly, ignoring the continuing shower
of arrows that fell on them. The attackers tried to break
through but could not, and as they turned away they
seemed to panic. Breaking up their formation, they fled
down the hill, every man apparently interested only in
saving his own skin.

The English, who had been goaded beyond endurance, could hold back no longer, and they pursued
their enemies ferociously. William's horsemen quickly
halted their retreat, formed themselves into squadrons
again, and methodically slaughtered the defenders. It
was the turn of the English to run now, but they were
unable to reach their former positions, for Fitz Osbern,
leading one thousand cavalrymen, cut them off, and

the English had no choice but to stand, to fight as best they could, and to die.

The housecarls, true to their traditions, rallied as best they could and formed a far smaller wall of shields around the banner of the fighting man, but it was only a question of time before they, too, would be cut to pieces. The Normans would have charged them, but William, cautiously cool even in the moment of supreme crisis, directed that the successful tactics just employed should be repeated. The archers were called forward again, and they sent their arrows flying in arcs over the stout shields of the housecarls.

The cavalry stood ready, and when a terrible cry was raised by the Englishmen, the Normans knew that one of the arrows had struck Harold. The defenders were obviously demoralized, and Fitz Osbern led his horsemen in a final charge. The housecarls fought like madmen, but there was no stemming the Norman tide now, and the invaders swarmed over them, smashing the remnants of their shield wall. Harold, although wounded by an arrow that had penetrated an eye, still lived, and when the Normans discovered that he was merely wounded, they surged toward him. His men took two lives for every one they lost, but their gallantry was futile, and four Norman nobles, among them Eustace of Boulogne and Walter Giffard, thrust their swords into the usurper.

And so, shortly before sundown, Harold Godwineson, the last of the Saxon kings, was killed.

According to precedent and all reasonable rules of warfare, his death should have ended the battle, but the English, refusing to recognize the indisputable fact that they had been beaten, fought on. Their resistance was no longer either organized or unified, but they would not stop, even after they saw their companies and regiments crumble away. Many fled into the forests, and when a squadron of the invaders tried to pursue them, the Normans fell into the man-made ditch that had been dug the previous day. Scores of Englishmen reappeared, threw stones and javelins at them, and wiped out the entire unit.

Bands of Saxons ranging in size from two men to fifty continued to harass the Normans, and William was forced to assign at least one third of his tired force to eliminate these pockets of resistance. The rest of his army spread out over the battlefield, removing the bodies of the dead and stealing valuables. The officers, unable to curb their men, made no effort to maintain even a semblance of discipline, for the victory was complete, and the jubilant troops deserved a reward.

William, accompanied by several of his barons and equerries, climbed on foot to the hill where the English headquarters had been located, and he stood silently for a time, looking out into the gathering night and wishing he could stop thinking about Harold.

"Edwin and Morcar have missed their chance!" Robert of Mortain said exuberantly. "They'll appear any day now to swear their fidelity to you."

"Yes, I suppose they will." William nodded absently, then raised his voice. "Tomorrow we must try to find Harold's body. I don't want him buried in a common grave with all the others."

Gerbod approached and touched his arm. "There's nothing more that can be done tonight, Father. Shouldn't we go back to our own camp?"

"No," William said. "I'm going to spend the night right here. My tent can be brought to me."

His officers, recognizing the stubborn note in his voice, looked hopelessly at each other and knew better than to plead with him. But Fitz Osbern dared to speak when the others did not. "It isn't safe for you. There are still Englishmen roaming about the countryside."

"I was unharmed all day, wasn't I? Nothing will happen to me tonight. I want to stay here, and I will!"

"Very well, if you insist. I'll throw a guard around the crest." The Seneschal paused then added dryly. "I can't argue with the man who has just become King of England."

"By God's splendor, so I have!" His Majesty's voice cracked and he looked at his lieutenants with unseeing eyes; then, unutterably weary, he sat down on the ground, removed his helmet, and buried his face in his hands. Afterward some claimed that he wept, while others said that he offered a prayer of thanks.

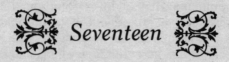 *Seventeen*

WHEN EDWARD THE CONFESSOR had lived on Ludgate Hill, the King's house had been a meeting place for clerics and holy men, and visiting bishops, traveling monks, and foreign Church dignitaries had congregated in the modest, sparsely furnished hall. During Harold's brief tenancy few had been admitted except members of the family of Godwine, and the atmosphere had been distinctly warlike. The people of London, accustomed to judging the tone of a reign by the visitors who came to the house, stood patiently outside the wooden palisades from dawn to dusk, stared past the stolid, expressionless Norman sentries, and were unceasingly astonished.

Of course generals bustled in and out regularly, but William's callers included men from every walk of life, and, for the first time in the memory of even the oldest inhabitants, baseborn commoners were summoned to appear before the new King as frequently as were the nobles. Merchants and tradesmen, priests and fishermen and farmers were led before William Bastard, who urged them to speak their minds without fear, and who questioned them closely on living conditions, taxation, and a bewildering variety of related subjects.

He dealt leniently with those who accepted him as their King, but his legions were constantly on the move against those who rebelled or failed to swear fealty to him, and his columns of merciless Normans roamed incessantly from the North Sea to the English Channel

to the Irish Sea, stamping out pockets of insurrection.
The curious who loitered daily on Ludgate Hill were
impressed by the crisp discipline of the invader's military commanders, but what awed them the most was
the seemingly inexhaustible energy of the new King.
He began to receive visitors shortly after daybreak
each morning, and tapers burned far into the night in
the room that was quickly identified as his bedchamber. And so the rumor spread that His Majesty was
endowed with more than human strength.

William heard the stories and tried to smile at them,
but he was too tired; there were so many things to be
done, and so few hours each day in which to do them.
Some members of his entourage had seen the great
victory at Hastings as an end in itself, but the battle had
been a mere beginning, and even the less contempla-
tive barons were learning that it was far more difficult to
govern a country than to conquer it. William devoted
all of his time and thought to the organization and
administration of his new realm, but there were moments when he wondered if he would ever succeed in
reducing the chaos and establishing some measure of
order in the kingdom. Edward had never bothered to
rule, Harold had been too busy defending himself to set
up any system of efficient government, and William,
knowing a throne was only as secure as the man who sat
on it made it secure, labored unceasingly.

Now, as he dressed one morning in November, he
thought that he was always weary, even after a heavy
night's sleep. Perhaps the English climate was at least
in part responsible, he told himself; London was damp,
the walls of the King's house were thin, and he secretly
longed for the solid, dry comforts and thick masonry of
Rouen Castle. His chef brought his breakfast into his
chamber, and he ate moodily, reflecting that either the

cook had lost his touch or else the food available on the
island was inferior to the Norman variety. Matilda, he
knew, maintained a high standard in the kitchen by
conferring frequently with the chef, but William had
no idea what she said to the man, and as his own
attempts had merely frightened the cook but had not
improved the cuisine, he had decided to leave well
enough alone. Besides, there were far more important
matters to consider.

A tap sounded at the door, and Bishop Odo, who was
serving as chief secretary to the King, entered with a
leather-bound ledger under his arm and a sheaf of
parchment documents in his hand. William exchanged greetings with him, and then sat back and
finished his mug of breakfast ale while Odo sorted the
papers and laid them out on a table. It had been a
mistake, William told himself, to have given Odo a
high ecclesiastical appointment; as a bishop he was less
than a success, but he had a real aptitude for secretarial
work. William had appointed him to his present position principally to keep him close at hand where he
could neither meddle nor allow his own boundless
ambitions to create complications, and although Odo
hated the word, he was perfoming his functions brilliantly.

"A messenger has arrived from Count Eustace at
Dover," he said. "The rebel garrison will surrender
within the next twenty-four hours, provided that you'll
grant clemency to the troops that have fought against
you. Eustace wasn't sure what your policy would be, so
he's awaiting instructions. You'll want to see the messenger yourself, I suppose."

"I haven't time. Tell him the leaders of the rebellion
are to be hanged." William finished his ale and wiped
his mouth.

"Ah." Surprise, then pleasure showed in Odo's eyes.

"The troops are to be granted a full pardon, if they'll swear allegiance to me."

"You're making a mistake there, William. It seems to me——"

"I know how it seems to you, Odo. You never miss an opportunity to tell me. For the thousandth time, let me remind you that I'm King of England, and that you aren't. If you had your way, you'd kill every native."

"I certainly would!" The Bishop faced his half brother insolently.

"Well, I have no intention of maintaining a huge Norman garrison in this country permanently. I'm trying to win over the English, not alienate them." A deep frown appeared on the royal brow. "Did you ask the messenger about Gerbod's safety?"

"Naturally," Odo's tone became openly contemptuous. "It's ridiculous the way you worry about that boy."

"I happen to be responsible for him. He's my stepson, in case you've forgotten it."

"No more than you've forgotten that I'm your half brother. Oh, I'll grant that you've given me two or three very nice churches, and I'm fond of that monastery in Sussex that you presented to me a few weeks ago, but as your nearest of kin I'm entitled——"

"You were going to tell me how Gerbod is faring." William stood, and the huskiness in his voice was warning to the Bishop not to push him too hard.

"Lord Gerbod enjoys excellent health," Odo replied sulkily. "Two days ago he led a charge against the invaders, and showed great gallantry. Even the enemy cheered him."

"Good! Then they'll accept him without question as lord of Dover." William wandered to the table and began to examine the papers. "Is there anything here that requires my immediate attention?"

"Earl Morcar has written from Cumberland, asking

permission to come to London and swear his fealty to
you. He says he would have appeared with his brother
last month, but he's been ill."

A most convenient illness. He was waiting to make
sure there wouldn't be a spontaneous uprising that
would drive us out of the country. Permission is
granted. Set a date for the ceremony. He can ride here
in four days, so make it early next week."

"The throne I'm having carved for you won't be
ready by next week."

"Then I'll sit in any chair that happens to be in the
house," William said in exasperation. "Winning the
allegiance of Cumberland without the loss of a single
man is more important to me than delaying a ceremony
for the sake of unnecessary pomp."

"I don't happen to believe it's unnecessary."

"No you wouldn't." William picked up a sheet of
parchment and studied it for a moment. "The supply of
stones for my tower is running low. I don't want the
work stopped, so you'd better send to the quarries at
Caen for more."

"Is there any reason we can't use local stones?"

"There certainly is. Norman builders are erecting a
Norman tower for me, and I want them to use materials
they know."

Odo shrugged and then smiled maliciously. "If I do
say so, William, you're inconsistent. How can you talk
piously about winning the freindship of the English
people when you're building a defense tower right in
the heart of London that's going to be bigger and
stronger than any of your castles in Normandy?"

"It so happens that I don't believe in taking chances
when it's possible to avoid them," William answered
with dignity, seeing nothing illogical in his attitude. "It
may take a little time before the savages here accept me

completely. Until they do, I prefer to be safe. And what's more, I'm more comfortable in a tower than I am in this kind of a house. The English ideas of ventilation and heating are primitive."

The Bishop saw he had not scored and was forced to drop the matter. "There's a ship from Rouen that cast anchor in the Thames last night. I know it carried letters."

"Where are they?"

"Your equerries were sorting them in the hall as I came up."

The King of England felt unexpectedly homesick. He started at once toward the door but stopped short. "Was Abbé Lanfranc on board?"

Odo, white-faced and glowering, blocked his path. "I didn't know you had sent for him."

"You know it now."

"May I inquire why he's coming here?"

William barely resisted the impulse to shove the rotound figure aside. "I need his help. It would be a waste of time for me to abolish the old Witenagemot and form a new council until the archdeacons and bishops who will sit on it have been appointed and confirmed in office."

The Bishop cleared his throat and puffed out his chest. "It so happens that a member of your immediate family is in a position to offer ecclesiastical advice."

"Offer it to Lanfranc, then. He'll take it or reject it, as he sees fit."

Odo struggled unsuccessfully to conceal his dismay. "He'll have the authority of an archdeacon of Canterbury."

"Yes." William reached past him, opened the door, and walked out into the narrow corridor.

"You're actually going to replace Archdeacon

Stigand?" The Bishop was forced into an undignified trot as he tried to match William's rapid pace.

"I'm not replacing him. The Holy Father will do that. The fact that I consider Stigand to be a two-faced scoundrel is totally beside the point, because I'm just a layman and I don't pretend to understand anything but temporal affairs." William started to descend the stairs. "It's enough for me that the Holy Father and Archdeacon Hildebrand believe Stigand to be unreliable."

Odo, close on his heels, was breathing down the back of his neck. "Mother," he said, "would certainly be proud to see one of her sons become Archdeacon of Canterbury."

William turned for an instant and smiled blandly. "Mother is already very proud. After all, her eldest son has become a king, and no woman can ask for more than that."

Reaching the foot of the stairs, he gave the Bishop no opportunity to reply and walked into the hall, where several of his generals, the members of his personal staff, and a handful of English nobles who had sworn to support him were waiting for him. Everyone stood respectfully as he entered, and he was about to wave them into their seats again when he saw Matilda's handwriting on a yellow-sealed roll of parchment that one of his aides held out to him. Changing his mind, he cleared the room, permitting only his old companions, Fitz Osbern and Mont Gomeri, who had also received letters from home, to remain. Then, seating himself in the simple chair of polished oak that had been Edward the Confessor's, he broke the seal and unrolled the scroll slowly, as though to demonstrate to his companions that he felt no eagerness to read a routine communication from Matilda.

But the others were too engrossed in their own letters

to pay any attention to his reactions. Mont Gomeri, who was now entitled to be called Earl of Wessex, labored slowly over the parchment in his hand, spelling out each word; Fitz Osbern, to whose many titles had been added that of Earl of East Anglia, was smiling broadly as he scanned his letter, and it was he who finally broke the silence. "Do you remember that mastiff you gave me two years ago, William? My wife writes that she's had a litter of four pups. One of them has gone to your children as a gift. I imagine Matilda mentions it to you."

"I haven't come to that part of her letter yet," King William muttered. "She's had to devote quite a bit to an official report in her capacity as Regent." He did not look up.

It was quiet again, then Mont Gomeri laughed loudly. "Mabel gave a little party last week. There were about thirty at the feast, most of them older people, of course, what with all of the men here in England. She says they drank half the wine in my cellars, and for the next day and a half she kept finding the sleeping bodies of guests all over the castle. It must have been a real party. I'm sorry I missed it."

The Seneschal's eyes glowed, and he slapped his knee enthusiastically. "My wife has sent me two crocks of good Norman apple butter. We'll have some of it for dinner today! That will take away the taste of the damned English bread we've been eating."

William nodded absently and continued to read, his face stiff.

"My son," Mont Gomeri said, "got into an argument with a butcher's apprentice in Falaise, and the butcher's boy blackened his eye and made his nose bleed. I hope Mabel had enough sense not to have the apprentice whipped. Roger needs to learn how to defend himself with his fists." He continued to scan his letter painfully, syllable by syllable.

"Here's what I've been waiting for," Fitz Osbern said. "My family will join me in time for Christmas. My wife has told the children about it, so that makes it definite. She never goes back on her word to them."

"Mabel hints that she'd like to come over," Mont Gomeri replied, "but I'm going to write her that I'll go home to Normandy for Christmas. It's a good time to be home."

William's left boot tapped rhythmically against the rushes on the floor, but he continued to say nothing, and finally the Seneschal glanced at him anxiously. "Is everything all right at Rouen Castle, William?"

"The wheat harvest dropped only 31 per cent, which is far less than we thought it might."

"That's fine." Fitz Osbern was interested in family news, too, but refrained from further comment. It was inconceivable that Matilda could have written a completely impersonal letter, yet from the expression in his master's eyes he was none too sure. And this was not the time to break his self-imposed rule never to interfere in the private relationship of William and his wife.

"She also says that since our victory Rouen has been filled with foreign ambassadors. The Duke of Burgundy sent a special envoy to offer his congratulations, and Philip of France wants to negotiate a new trade agreement with us."

"Wonderful." The Earl of East Anglia and first baron of Normandy averted his gaze.

"There's also a full account of the current tax situation, which is rather complicated. Lanfranc helped her with that portion of the report, she says. You'll want to read the whole document when you have a chance." William rolled up the scroll again and tossed it to his seneschal.

Fitz Osbern was too blunt a man to dissemble. "There are certainly parts of this that are personal, so if you'll tell me what sections to avoid, I'll——"

"Her Grace has sent me a detailed report on her regency, Osbern, no more and no less." The absurd notion crossed William's mind that he envied his lieutenants. His achievements were greater than those of any ruler since Charlemagne, and he knew that his place in history was secure for hundreds of years to come, but he was dissatisfied. He knew better, of course, than to expect warmth from Matilda, but the lack of it hurt all the same.

On the afternoon that Abbé Lanfranc arrived from Normandy, the King paid him the high honor of riding to the docks to greet him, and the Londoners who witnessed the event knew at once that the little man in the rusty black habit was a personage of consequence. William embraced him and did not permit him to drop to one knee on the stones of the quay, and the great generals of the conquering army bent their heads low as they kissed Lanfranc's ring. A large number of Norman nobles were waiting at the King's house to pay their respects to him, and a delegation of English clergymen, headed by the Bishop of Winchester, called within a few minutes after his arrival, too.

But the equerries explained that the Abbé was closeted in private audience with the King, and that under no circumstances could they be disturbed. The atmosphere in the house was tense, everyone was certain that matters of the highest policy were being settled in the King's chambers, and only in the room that had once been Edward the Confessor's reading hall was there an aura of serenity. William, grinning as he paced up and down, looked fondly at his guest.

"I'm glad to see you, Father, he said for the fifth or

sixth time. "There's so much for you to do that I scarcely know what to tell you first."

"You've lost weight, I see," the priest replied as he sat and smoothed his robe.

"A little, I suppose. The food here is almost inedible." It was bad enough to be forced to eat the meals he was served, but discussing them was senseless, so William dropped the subject. "I won't really become master of the English until spiritual as well as temporal discipline has been established. You'll be shocked at what you find, Father. There's corruption everywhere, and the parish priests are so haughty and independent you'd think they were members of the College of Cardinals. The bishops make and break laws to suit themselves, and the archdeacons are impossible. They agree to everything I say to them, but they're all looking for a chance to stab me in the back."

"Your hair is turning gray," Lanfranc observed mildly.

"Some districts have been paying very heavy taxes—including your Peter's pence—but others have escaped completely. It's little wonder that we conquered them. Their lack of order and efficiency is disgraceful."

"We'll have time to look into the situation," the Abbé remarked gently. "Judging from the smudges under your eyes, you haven't been sleeping as you should."

"I get all the sleep I need," William answered defensively, paused, and then asked the question that had been on his tongue from the first moment he had met Lanfranc. "You undoubtedly saw my family before you sailed. They're all in good health?"

"Excellent. Adelize is cutting a new tooth, I believe."

The King passed his hand across his brow. "And Gundrada is well?"

"She was radiant when I last saw her. She's beginning to discover that there are young men in the world, I believe."

William stopped pacing and stood very still. "No one may court her without my permission. I hope her mother realizes that."

"Oh, she does." Lanfranc was watching him closely.

"Good." Relieved, William dropped into a chair and locked his hands over a knee. "I recommend that you see Archdeacon Aldred of York first. He's the most pliable member of the high clergy here, and as he's none too intelligent, you'll learn more from him than you could from any of the others."

The Abbé ignored his comment. "You haven't yet inquired after Matilda." He spoke carefully to insure that no note of rebuke crept into his voice.

"I had a long report from her only a few days ago." William did not realize that his tone had become bitter. "She was so crisp and businesslike that I could tell she was in the best of spirits. It's plain, very plain that she enjoys her sense of autonomy." He laughed harshly. "She modeled her report to me on the messages that the Empress Irene used to send to the Senate in Byzantium. I really must show it to you."

"I've already seen it. And I can assure you that it isn't the letter she wanted to write."

"Is that so?" William's eyes were veiled.

"She has received direct word from you only once since you came to England, you know. About a week after your victory over Harold you sent her a brief account of it, and at the very end you told her that Gerbod was in good health. But you mentioned nothing whatsoever about yourself." The faint smile vanished from Lanfranc's lips, and his voice became firm. "She merely tried to send you a reply in the same general style."

The King's heavy fist smashed on the arm of his chair. "By God's splendor," he roared, forgetting in his anger that he was taking the name of the Lord in vain in the presence of his confessor, "I haven't been spending a holiday here. I've sent a dozen or more messengers to her since I've been in England. But I've been too busy to write love letters to her!"

"Matilda has been rather busy too, you know," the Abbé responded unsympathetically. "She knew nothing about government when you made her Regent, and she's worked day and night. Your instinct for leadership and administration is so highly developed that you apparently lose sight of the fact that others may not have the knack at all."

"So she's learned it isn't as easy as it appears," William murmured.

"What's more, she's been responsible for the children and she's had a large household to supervise. She's done her work competently and without complaint, and you should be proud of her, William."

The conqueror of England said nothing.

"Seeing you and the way you look, it strikes me you should send for her."

"Why?" the King demanded roughly. "What has the way I look to do with sending for Matilda?"

"You're tense and tired and overworked," Lanfranc declared bluntly. "You need her."

"That's damned nonsense." William stood and glared at the frail priest. "I need no one! I never have and I never will! Of all the insane rubbish I've ever heard——"

"I wonder if it has ever occurred to you that Matilda might also need you," Lanfranc interrupted softly.

"She has power. That's all she's ever wanted or needed." William laughed savagely. "With all due respect to you and to your calling, Father, I've been married to the woman for a long time. And I tell you flatly that she never has and she never will need me."

"With all due respect to you as a man and as a husband, you're mistaken." The Abbé stood and yawned delicately. "I'll be grateful to you if you'll have someone show me to my room. Sea travel always upsets my stomach, and I find I'm rather exhausted."

After he had gone, William remained alone and stood for a quarter of an hour at a high window, staring down at the houses of London. The neat influence of the Romans had vanished centuries previous, and the narrow, twisting streets and the houses crowded together without reason or planning annoyed William. London was as cluttered and disorderly as his own mind, and he hated the unaccustomed feeling of uncertainty that both depressed and confused him. One of his equerries, knowing that no one was with him, came into the chamber but left again silently when William seemed unaware of his presence.

The ramparts of the mighty stone tower that Norman builders were erecting were strangely comforting, and the thick blocks of gray Caen stone were a reminder to the King that his roots were in his own land. Blinking for a moment at the uncompleted tower, he sighed heavily, turned away from the window, and picked up a small ivory bell that sat on the table. He rang it vigorously, and its sound was still reverberating when Odo bustled into the room, his round face lined with concern.

"Everything is settled, I suppose," he said breathing heavily.

"What's that?" On sudden impulse William drew his knife and thrust the longer blade into the scarred wood of the table top.

"You've told Lanfranc that you're going to make him
Archdeacon of Canterbury, and you want me to write a
letter to Hildebrand for you. Well, I won't do it. I've
been acting as your secretary purely as a favor to you,
but I have my own dignity and my own standing to
think about. You can't expect the Bishop of Bayeux to
request the Vatican to give a tremendous promotion in
rank to his rival. It would put me in a ridiculous light,
and I——"

"Sit down," William said.

Odo, Bishop of Bayeux, sat.

"I want you to send a letter in my name to my wife."

"Certainly!" Odo opened his ledger, dipped a quill
into a jar of ink, and smiled. The red hat of Canterbury
had not yet been assigned to the little Abbé, he thought,
and there was still a chance that he might win the
most powerful post in England next to the crown itself
for himself. He would write to Lady Harlotte and enlist
her support; William had never yet been able to reject a
plea from their mother.

"Tell the Duchess," William said, breaking in on his
reflections, "that I desire her presence here in London
at the earliest possible moment."

The Bishop raised his eyebrows, but said nothing as
he scribbled in his ledger.

"Tell her it is my wish that she bring the children
with her. Living conditions will be less comfortable
here than in Rouen, but I want her to understand that it
is important for the people of England to see the entire
family of their new sovereign. That sort of thing creates
an aura of solidity and will give my new subjects confidence in my regime. I want the Duchess to know my
reasons, so define them clearly for her."

Odo nodded and wrote furiously. Finally he glanced
up, his face bland and his eyes innocent. "You'll need

to appoint a new regent for Normandy, of course."
Lady Harlotte might need time to secure the Canterbury position for him, and in the interim there could be nothing he would like more than to act as Regent for Normandy.

"Tell the Duchess I'll name a new regent after I've discussed the matter with Fitz Osbern and Lanfranc."

The Bishop bent his head over the parchment so his half brother could not see his disappointment.

"Be sure to stress that I dislike inconveniencing Her Grace, but reasons of state give me no alternative." William paused and pondered. "Prepare the letter for my full signature as King of England and Duke of Normandy. I want no doubt left in Matilda's mind that this is anything other than an official request."

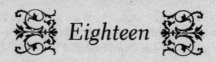 *Eighteen*

THE WITENAGEMOT, for hundreds of years one of the most sedate and decorous of councils, was in an uproar. Norman barons who now owned vast estates in their new land, foreign adventurers who had been granted resounding titles, and native English lords who had sworn to support the conquering monarch were bound together in a joint cause, and they raised their voices in a half-score of languages as they shouted and cursed. Norman and Englishman and Italian and Swede all suffered together, and they forgot their jealousies and hatreds as they glared at King William, who was carefully polishing his helmet on his sleeve as he sat at the head of the long council table.

Of all those in the room only Fitz Osbern and Lanfranc were calm, and they leaned back in their chairs, relaxed, and waited for the storm to die down. At last the great lords exhausted their supply of expletives, and William glanced at them coolly. "As I was saying, I am instituting a new policy, effective immediately. From this time forward, all land in England, every acre of it, is the property of the crown."

Again the storm broke loose, and this time William stood. Count Eustace and Robert of Mortain fell silent when he glared at them, and Earl Waltheof of Northampton, one of the most prominent of the English nobles, looked sheepish. Giulio of Tuscany stared at the floor, Earl Edwin bit his thumbnail and Roger Mont Gomeri tried to smile but found the effort too great.

"Members of the nobility will be the King's caretakers, and will guard his property for him. They will use it as their own, and the crown will take no more than a just and reasonable tax from them. I'll decide eventually just what the rate of taxation will be, and I feel sure that all of you have confidence in my fairness." William gazed hard at each of the lords in turn, and when no one replied he smiled. "Thank you. None of you will find the new policy a hardship I know."

"May I make a brief comment, Your Majesty?" Lanfranc sat forward in his chair at the far end of the table.

"The Lord Archdeacon of Canterbury is always free to say what he pleases," William replied graciously.

Lanfranc settled his new red cap firmly on his head. "It occurs to me that the lords have a right to know Your Majesty's reasons for this policy." He turned to others and smiled soothingly. "England was disunited before King William's reign. Without a sense of national unity, any country will perish, and His Majesty appointed the Earl of East Anglia and me to recommend ways and means of building our English strength." He nodded to Fitz Osbern, who indicated his agreement. "It will become apparent to all of you, my lords, that there is no better method of achieving this unity that we all want than through the medium of placing all land under the name of the crown."

The door opened and Gerbod came into the room. William, annoyed at the interruption, jumped up. "What are you doing here? I thought you were in Dover."

"I was, until this morning. Mother is here," the boy said in a low voice.

"In London?" William knew that everyone at the table was listening, and his irritation grew.

"Yes, sir. Right here in the house. I rode up with her and the children." Gerbod spoke even more softly, so no one else could hear. "The equerries didn't dare interrupt you, so I came in. Father, she said to tell you she wants to see you as soon as possible. I think she's rather upset because you weren't on hand to greet her when she arrived."

It was typical of her to appear at an inopportune time and then become angry because he failed to dance attendance on her, and William had to struggle to curb his annoyance. To say the least, it was an inconvenience to suffer an interruption just when he was forcing his key nobles to accept an increase in his power at their expense, and any delay now might be dangerous. If they had a chance to think, their recalcitrance would surely become greater. "Have someone show your mother around the house," he said to Gerbod, "and tell her I'll join her when I can." Turning away abruptly, he resumed his seat at the head of the long table.

Gerbod, who had been about to reply, changed his mind and left hastily. The reunion of his mother and stepfather was going to be stormy, and he wished himself elsewhere. His own little citadel of Dover was a peaceful haven, and he decided to return there at the first possible opportunity.

Fitz Osbern waited until the door closed, then he nimbly picked up the discussion where it had been dropped. "We're all in agreement on His Majesty's new policy, I know," he said, and continued to speak rapidly before anyone else could protest. "Our next task, and it's a difficult one, is to find out precisely what lands there are to determine their exact boundaries. I'm not sure of the extent of the earldom I hold, and I know the rest of you are in the same quandary I am. So we're going to initiate a survey, a census, in every shire in England."

"An undertaking that extensive will require years of work," Earl Morcar said, impressed.

"We intend to be in the country for a long time to come," the Seneschal replied tactlessly.

The new Archdeacon of Canterbury intervened smoothly. "The census will be very useful for Church purposes, too, so I'll be grateful for your co-operation."

"And there are times," William added, "when every one of us wants and needs the help of the Church. What's more, my lords, you'll find that your own positions will be strengthened."

"How?" Roger Mont Gomeri demanded bluntly.

"I shall hold you responsible to me," the King said vigorously. "In the same way, each of the lesser nobles will come directly under the jurisdiction of his immediate overlord."

"It will be much like our system of command in the army, Roger," Fitz Osbern declared helpfully. "You'll be the absolute and final authority in your own sub-realm. That is," he continued, as though the point he was about to make was barely worth mentioning, "your decisions will be subject to the King's approval or veto. Naturally."

"Naturally," William echoed.

"Perhaps," Archdeacon Lanfranc said softly, "you'd like to discuss the idea among yourselves for a few minutes."

"I'm sure that won't be necessary," Fitz Osbern interjected. "The merits of the plan are so obvious that any delay now would be a waste of everyone's time. I propose that we put his Majesty's idea to a vote."

William smiled blandly. "As you say, Osbern, the

positive values of my policy are plain. So I wouldn't insult the superior intelligence of my Witenagemot by asking for a vote of confidence. Instead, I suggest that anyone who objects make his views known to the rest of us. Do I hear any protests?"

He looked slowly up and down each side of the table, and the barons and earls, who might have had the courage to express their convictions in company with others, remained discreetly silent. It would have been simple enough to raise a hand for an affirmative or negative vote, but no man wanted to stand alone against the ruler who had become the most powerful sovereign of his age. Every lord present knew that he had been outmaneuvered, of course, but there was no longer a choice; the nobles would have to make the best of the situation.

"I commend you on your wisdom," the King said, and shifted in his chair in such a way that his chain mail rattled. "From this hour forward, all land in England is the property of the crown. If there is nothing else to be brought before the attention of the Witenagemot, I'll welcome an adjournment.'"

"I propose such an adjournment," Fitz Osbern responded promptly, and William, nodding pleasantly, stood, and walked quickly out of the room.

The Norman guards stationed outside the door saluted, and the King made a mental note to form a regiment of housecarls in the near future. He would use his own men, to be sure, but he would change their uniforms, and his English nobles and other native visitors would not be subjected to constant reminders that they were being governed by foreigners. It would be wise, he reflected, to adopt as many local customs and habits as his Normans could tolerate; English clothes, to be sure, were outlandishly barbaric, but he would encourage his nobles to grow their hair longer, in the native style. As a personal concession he might raise a mustache. He realized he would have to set an example, and a mustache would probably be the least trouble.

One of the English servants was sweeping the corridor with a broom, and William hailed her. "Where is my wife?"

The maid replied in her strange tongue, and, seeing that the King didn't understand, she pointed toward the stairs and then, badly frightened, scurried away.

William started to mount the steps two at a time, but deliberately slowed his pace as he neared the landing. He wondered why he was in such a hurry, and after pondering briefly he concluded that he was anxious to see the children. He had certainly missed them, and he stood for a moment at the top of the steps, listening for the sound of their voices. But he heard nothing, and the corridor was empty except for another serving-woman, who was scrubbing the floor with a stiff brush. After a moment of indecision he started off to his own bedchamber, and when he reached it he stood in the open frame and peered inside.

Matilda, her back turned to him, was putting clothes into a chest with the help of her personal maid. Something about her appearance startled William, and as he looked at her he decided that she looked much smaller than he had remembered her. He had always pictured her in his mind as a tall and rather stately person, but she was actually small-boned and petite. Perhaps her dress was responsible for the illusion of fragility that she created: he had never seen it before, and the thin, pale blue wool was very dainty and feminine.

The maid saw him first, and, hastily curtsying, left the room by a side door. William entered the chamber, and Matilda, hearing his footsteps, whirled around. She was even lovelier than he had recalled her, and although her face showed the effects of her journey, she was still the most beautiful woman he had ever known. Her red-gold hair was shining, and when she saw him a touch of color appeared in her cheeks.

"I expected to hear the children," he declared, and felt irritated at himself. It was an inane remark, and not what he had intended to say at all.

"I've had them served an early supper. They had very little to eat today, and I wanted them to have a hot meal." Matilda was angry at herself, too. She had imagined this meeting a score of times, and the last thing she had expected to discuss was the children's appetites. Nevertheless she heard herself pursue the topic relentlessly. "They wanted to see you, but you took so long in coming to us that I had to feed them."

William advanced across the room and kissed her before replying, and for a moment, as their lips touched, they almost established a rapport. But they had too much on their minds, and the gulf that separated them was old and deep. William released her and stepped back. "My time isn't my own these days."

"I'm sure you must be very busy." She looked at him with the expression he had never been able to interpret, then she sank to the floor in a full curtsy. "My congratulations on your magnificent victory, Your Majesty."

Her movements were so graceful that he could not help but admire her; however, he was unable to make up his mind whether her gesture was sincere or whether she was mocking him. So he confined himself to a terse, "Thank you."

Rising, Matilda studied him, and although she had been warned by Lanfranc that he looked tired, she was still unprepared for the deep lines she saw in his forehead and at the corners of his eyes. She lifted her hand to touch his face, but withdrew it without accomplishing her purpose. William was so austere and remote that she could not bring herself to indulge in an intimate gesture on her own initiative.

He was aware of her intent, and when she first hesistated and then changed her mind, he frowned. It was as he had anticipated: as an individual he meant nothing to her, and had significance in her eyes only as a symbol. Now that he was King of England, she was almost afraid of him, and because he was hurt by her withdrawal he could not resist rubbing salt in what he believed to be her wound. "When you first rejected my proposal of marriage to you, I dare say you never thought I'd someday wear a crown."

She had no idea why he was raking up such an old dispute and could only think he was seeking grounds for a fresh quarrel. But she had no wish to bicker with him; on the contrary, she wanted only to comfort him, to cradle his head in her arms, and hold it against her breast until the signs of fatigue and worry disappeared from his face. "Is everything going as it should?" she asked tentatively.

"I have a great many problems, but I'm handling them." William's tone was brisk, but when he unbuckled his armor and threw it onto a small bench his shoulders sagged. "Did you enjoy your journey?" he inquired politely, sitting on the edge of the bed.

Matilda turned away quickly and busied herself at the clothes chest before she answered him. After all these years he certainly knew that sea voyages invariably made her seasick, and if he chose to be facetiously indifferent, his conduct was inexcusable. "We had a miserable journey, thank you," she said tartly. "I was sick all the way across the Channel, Robert climbed the rigging and almost fell overboard, and I had to send Gundrada into the cabin because she insisted on flirting with one of the young knights in our escort. Adelize and little William had a dreadful argument and had to be forcibly separated. And when we arrived in Dover——"

"What knight dared to make advances to Gundrada?" William asked in a low, intense voice.

"I really can't remember his name," she snapped. "Does it matter?"

"It does!"

"There was no harm in the incident. But I was frightfully ill. And the roads between here and Dover were no help. I do hope you're going to have some decent roads built!"

"You've returned to normal by now, I see," he remarked dryly.

Matilda refolded a gown that required no further attention and carefully slipped it into a drawer. "I've improved slightly, if that's what you mean. But only slightly. William, I was shocked at the slovenliness I saw when I arrived here. This house was just filthy."

Now he understood why the serving-women had been cleaning so energetically, and he grinned. "To be honest with you, I hadn't noticed whether the place was clean or dirty."

"Well, I certainly noticed! And I've started to do something about it! I must say, I didn't think you'd receive your wife and children in a house that looked like a pigsty."

"One or two matters that have been somewhat more important to me have been occupying my attention, as it happens." It was stupid to argue with her on the day of her arrival, but she expected too much.

"And the kitchens! It's no wonder you look as though

you've been starving! I told that chef a few things he won't forget. I don't know why it is, but you always let servants take advantage of you."

It was pleasant to know that the quality of the food was going to improve, and William sighed. He had truly missed Matilda, and he wished there were some way he could tell her how he felt without sounding awkward. But they had been unable to communicate for so long that he didn't quite know how to begin, and so he said nothing.

She immediately misinterpreted his silence and thought he was showing her that he disapproved of her criticism. As a matter of fact, she wondered if perhaps she had gone a trifle too far. To her own surprise, she was discovering that she was actually in awe of him, partly because of his new rank but principally because he had overcome so many seemingly insurmountable obstacles to win his crown. William was indeed the great man that all Europe proclaimed him, and Matilda was so afraid he had risen too far above her that for an instant she wished she could turn the hourglass upside down. If there were some way to make the sands run in the opposite direction, she would go back to the day when he had rolled her in the mud. How differently she would have behaved through the years if she had known what she now knew. She wished that he would drag her from her horse again, but she realized that those days were gone.

It was imperative that she find some common denominator, and as only his work seemed to have meaning to him, she thought she should ask him about it. After all, he had neglected her and the children after a separation of months because he had been presiding over a meeting of some sort, so if she showed an interest in what he was doing she might be able to strike a spark.

"The countryside seemed very peaceful as we rode here today," she said tentatively. "Has all the fighting died down?"

"There's still scattered resistance in Northumberland and on the Welsh border." He propped himself on one elbow and regarded her quizzically.

"But none of it is serious?"

"Any form of warfare is serious, but there's nothing too extensive for me to handle. Sooner or later I'll have to teach the Scots and the Welsh a lesson, but there's too much to be consolidated here first, so it will be another year or two before I'll really be in a position to move against them."

"You're going to keep a Norman army here all that time?" Her strategy was proving successful, and she felt relieved; he was talking freely and without restraint now.

"I'll keep the Normans here as long as I think they're needed," William said. "But sooner or later I intend to incorporate English troops into my army. They're superb fighting men, and with the proper training—that Fitz Osbern will give them—they'll be able to hold their own against anyone."

"They fought well against you at Hastings?"

"Magnificently," he said curtly. She knew better than to try to draw him out on the subject of the battle, he thought bitterly. It was his inflexible rule never to discuss details of military operations with any woman; the subject was not suitable for feminine ears, as he had told her repeatedly after every war. If she chose to be absent-minded, he would need to remind her forcibly that he was not going to lower his standards simply because her curiosity was insatiable.

"And the English nobles have sworn their allegiance to you?"

"Every earl who survived the battle has taken the oath. So have the bishops."

"Lanfranc will replace the English bishops with his own people, I suppose." She knew very well what the new Archdeacon's plans were, for she had received a letter from him just prior to sailing, but she was keeping alive the discussion.

"You'll have to ask him his intentions. I've given him autonomy." William supposed that she had a right to know what was happening in England, but he was growing restless. "I think I'll go to see the children."

"I'd rather you'd wait until they're through, if you don't mind. They'll get so excited that they won't finish their supper if you go to them now."

"I do mind, but I'll do as you ask." William sank back on the bed and glanced across the room at her. He felt a sudden urge to see Matilda with her hair loose rather than in the tight braid she wore, but the notion struck him as being rather foolish. "Is there anything else you'd like to know?" he asked gruffly.

"Only what you want to tell me." There was a great deal she wanted to hear, she thought. She wished he would tell her that he had missed her, and more than anything else she wanted to know if he still loved her. So far there was nothing in his attitude to indicate his feelings one way or the other.

"There is something, as a matter of fact."

"Yes, dear?" Matilda crossed the room and stood before him.

"I don't want you to feel offended at the attitude of the English toward you. None of them will call you 'Your Grace,' and they'll never use your title of Duchess."

"I see."

She looked crestfallen, precisely as he had anticipated. "They'll always refer to you as Lady Matilda. It's their custom, and as I'm trying to encourage our people to adjust as much as possible to local habits, you'll have to put up with the situation as best you can. Do I make myself clear?"

"Very clear." Matilda retreated to the far side of the chamber and took a pile of underclothes from a packing box. She didn't want William to think she was sulking, because she wasn't. It was ironic, but she didn't care what the natives called her, just as she no longer felt deep concern over matters of state. William would govern the country, as was fitting and proper; her sole concern was her husband himself, but she didn't know how to indicate to him that she had changed in the past year. She wasn't actually too sure of what it was that had happened to her, so it was difficult to put her feelings into words, even to herself. All she knew was that ever since Harold Godwineson had stolen the crown, she had been weighed down by a sense of responsibility for all that had subsequently happened. She saw things in their right perspective now, but it would be useless even to try to tell William that she was a different woman. She would have to show him by her actions, but she didn't know whether he'd give her the chance.

Neither of them spoke for several minutes, and William, watching her unpack, reflected that she was actually neither fragile nor delicate. Unfortunately she was the same Matilda she had always been, and right now she was showing signs of boredom. That was how she always reacted when she didn't have one of her long, firm hands on the reins of government. Standing, he started toward the door. "The children must be finished by now."

The door opened and closed, and Matilda continued to take clothing out of the chest.

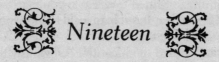

Nineteen

LONDON SHIVERED in the raw January wind, the streets were icy, and the cold penetrated into every building. The King's house on Ludgate Hill was not spared, and as the new tower of heavy stone would not be ready for occupancy until sometime the following year at the earliest, the royal family was forced to spend the winter in the perpetually chilly wooden structure. The King's wife clad her children and herself in furs, which His Majesty scorned for a time, but he changed his mind after catching a head cold, which made him miserable for a week. His new tunic was beaver-lined, and although it added to his bulk, he enjoyed the luxury of spending his days in comfort.

He sat now in his workroom, the collar of his tunic raised and his hands plunged deep into fur-lined pockets as he conferred with the Archdeacon of Canterbury. Lanfranc, indifferent as usual to the elements, was concentrating his full attention on the business at hand. "I've melted down the gold and silver plate, the statues and the ornaments that I've taken from the churches. And I find there's more than three times as much as I need to pay the Vatican's Peter's-pence taxes."

William raised a heavy eyebrow. "Does that include taxes for past years, too?"

"It does. And there's even more gold and silver left in the churches than I expropriated!"

"Amazing how greedy the English clergy had become, isn't it?" William pondered the matter for a moment, then grinned. "What do you plan to do with the gold and silver that remains after you pay the Holy See, Your Eminence?"

Lanfranc smiled significantly. "Obviously that great a sum shouldn't be idle. There are too many uses to which money can be put these days. I've discussed the problem with my bishops, and they agree that the English Church, as a whole, can use half of the total remaining amount to very good advantage."

"And I'll send a company of my new housecarls to your palace tomorrow for my half share," William replied casually, disposing of the subject. "I wish you'd sit closer to the hearth."

Lanfranc was wearing only a robe of thin red wool, but he shrugged and did not move. "There's another matter I want to take up with Your Majesty. Advices from Rome indicate that the Holy Father's health is fading rapidly, and it's probable that the College of Cardinals will be forced to convene sometime this spring."

"That means you'll want to appoint a new Archdeacon of York in time for the election."

"Exactly. Have you any suggestions, barring Odo?"

"I'll leave the choice completely in your hands. When the time comes, will you want me to write Philip of France and the Emperor, suggesting that their archdeacons follow the lead of our English, Norman, and Flemish cardinals?"

"Thank you for the offer, but it won't be necessary. Our prestige, yours and mine, is so great that the moment I cast my vote for Hildebrand, the College will elect him Pope by acclamation."

"The extent of our power never fails to amaze me."

William paused and stared at the hickory logs burning in the hearth. "Some people would call me very fortunate, I suppose. They judge me by my success, no doubt."

Lanfranc gazed at his troubled eyes and looked away again. "It's true that you've become the most famous ruler in Christendom, William," he said, creating an opening in the event that the King wanted to unburden himself.

"I suppose I am." William absently picked up a sheaf of parchment documents and let them fall to the table again.

It was plain that he had no intention of saying anything more, so the Archdeacon had to seize the initiative. "I'm still your priest, you know."

"Yes, I know" William couldn't bring himself to mention the difficulty that was vexing him.

"Of course, if it's something you want to bring up in the confession box——"

"No, nothing like that." The King stood, walked to the window, and drew aside the tapestry that covered the opening. He gazed out at the bleak city for a few moments, then pulled the decorative wool drape back into place and resumed his chair. "When do you think you'll start your journey to Rome?"

Lanfranc ignored the question. "Your appearance has improved considerably since Matilda came on here from Rouen."

"Has it?" William did not realize that his tone revealed a deep bitterness.

"Unquestionably. You've regained the weight you lost, the color in your cheeks has improved, and your face is far more relaxed," the Archdeacon said blandly.

"Then it's fortunate I waited until she arrived to pose

for the artist who is taking my likeness for the new coins." William was becoming so aroused emotionally that he lost sight of personal dignity and subtlety.

"Few women could move into an alien land and take hold so quickly in new surroundings."

"She performs her duties admirably." William was too upset to see that Lanfranc was guiding him and that he was starting to speak more freely.

"I'm pleased that you recognize her virtues, William." The Archdeacon was firm but compassionate. "She's a woman of great integrity and many talents. The English respect her as your consort, but they're developing a genuine affection for her as a person. She has become a valuable asset to you here."

"Very valuable."

"As always she's a good mother."

"I've never had any complaints against her as a mother." A royal boot began to tap restlessly against the floor boards.

"And there's no better housekeeper anywhere. The house is spotless, the servants are working as they should, and if the dinner I was served yesterday is any criterion——"

"Yes, she knows how to bring out the best in the chef, I'll grant you that. And daily living is more comfortable than it was. Not that I require soft living, you understand," William added hastily. "I've slept on the bare ground many nights when I've been on a campaign, and I can do it again without considering it a hardship."

"I'm sure you can." Lanfranc looked straight at the King and raised his voice. "Then what's wrong?"

"You haven't said anything about her as a wife, I note. She fails as a wife!"

"Why?" the Archdeacon demanded.

William was so provoked that he lost all sense of caution. "Because she doesn't love me, that's why!" he shouted. "And when a woman doesn't love her husband, she's no wife!"

Lanfranc knew he was mistaken but made no attempt to contradict him. "Perhaps the shoe is on the other foot. I wonder if you love Matilda."

The royal chair crashed over backward as His Majesty jumped to his feet. "That's the most asinine remark I've ever heard you make, Father! Of course I love her!"

The Archdeacon stood, picked up his short cloak, and buttoned it slowly. "How long has it been since you've told her how you feel?" he asked in a tone as deadly as it was quiet, and without waiting for a reply he walked out of the room.

William stared at the closed door, and when an equerry came in to announce his next visitor, he scowled so fiercely that the knight forgot his mission and backed out. Lanfranc, the King told himself, was a meddler who, knowing nothing about marriage, delighted in putting a man on the defensive. How much simpler it would have been, William thought, to give the post of Archdeacon of Canterbury to Odo than to a sour busybody. In all justice he had to admit that Lanfranc wasn't at the root of his troubles, of course. Women, not the Archdeacon, were responsible, but he couldn't concentrate on his work as he should when he realized that Matilda was telling her confessor self-pitying tales that were deprecatory to him. And his sense of frustration increased when he remembered the letter he had received yesterday from his mother, bemoaning the fate of Odo, whose heart, she had said, had been broken because he had not been promoted to the rank of first archdeacon of England.

A man was at peace with himself only on the battlefield, William reflected, and he wondered if there was any possible truth to the story of Adam and Eve. In any event, Adam should have known better. Consoling himself with the thought that had he been in Adam's place he would have left well enough alone, William walked out of his workroom. The antechamber was filled with visitors, all of whom stood and bowed deeply when he appeared, but he was unconscious of their presence as he hurried past them and started up the stairs.

He found himself moving in the direction of the room his wife was using as her bower, and although he had no clear idea of why he was going to her, he increased his pace. Lanfranc's question had stung him, he had to admit, and a vague plan that had been in his mind for several weeks began to take firm shape. He knew good from bad, right from wrong, and he needed no one to guide his behavior. He had been a model husband through the years, and it was no fault of his that Matilda didn't love him, but if further effort on his part was required, he was willing to make it. He might not be able to achieve happiness, but at least his conscience would be clear.

As he approached the landing he came face to face with Gundrada, but to the girl's astonishment he scarcely noticed her, and the expression on his face as he neared the bower sent a surge of jealousy through Gundrada. Several people were inside the room, and William, unobserved, paused on the threshold and looked in. Matilda was speaking to a group of five men, and the King recognized three of them as Norman builders. The others, Englishmen, were strangers to him.

"You'll feel as I do after you've inspected the house,"

she was saying in the crisp tone that William knew so well. "The builder who designed the interior plumbing here for King Edward was brilliant, and you'll do well to profit by his example."

"I'm sure we will, Lady Matilda," one of the Englishmen said unctuously.

"See that you do," she replied, "because I want every house and castle built for the nobility from this time forward to be similarly equipped. We want to set an example for the rest of the world in everything that we do."

She was so earnest, so passionately sincere that William had difficulty in keeping a straight face as he walked into the bower. "You'll please me by pleasing Lady Matilda," he told the builders. The men, awed by his presence, started backing toward the door even as they bowed to him, and a moment later he was alone with his wife.

"I hadn't finished my meeting," Matilda complained.

William looked after the builders. "They were afraid of me," he said sadly. "Everyone on the face of the earth seems to be afraid of me these days." Shaking off his mood, he turned. "Get your cloak. I want you to come with me."

"I can't possibly go out now," she protested. "I'm taking my English lesson in a little while, then I've scheduled a meeting with a number of ladies of the local nobility. I'm hoping to know them better, and it wouldn't do to have them arrive when——"

"Get your cloak," he repeated.

Matilda sighed, went to a cupboard, and drew out a fur-lined cape. To her surprise William gallantly held it for her while she drew on ermine mittens, but she knew better than to ask questions. When he gave orders in that rasping, slightly booming tone, he expected to be obeyed. They walked silently to the door of the inner courtyard, and while they waited for horses to be saddled, a page hurried off for the King's sword, cloak, and hat. A squadron of the new housecarls formed in the yard, William gave instructions to the captain in a low voice, then he helped his wife to mount before vaulting into the saddle.

The gates were opened, the sentries on duty saluted, and when the little cavalcade rode out, the people pulled off their headgear at the sight of the monarch. Then they realized that Matilda was with him, and they cheered her; she looked at William anxiously, fearful that her popularity would annoy him, but he was smiling broadly, and in spite of the snow flurries in the air she felt warmer. They rode in silence for several minutes, with half of the escort in front and the rest behind, and the hoofs of the horses clattered on the icy cobblestones. Then William pointed off to the left.

"Those are the law courts and the offices of the lwayers," he said. "I've been told the English call them inns, which is ridiculous, but I'll not change their custom. On the other side, right up ahead, are the military barracks, and just past them is the palace of the Archdeacon of Canterbury."

She refrained from saying that they had dined with Lanfranc only two days previous, and that she now knew her way around London.

"If you'll look down the river you'll see the new tower."

Matilda could see it daily from the windows of her bower but didn't comment. William seemed to be making an effort on her behalf, and although he was banal and clumsy, she had no intention of discouraging him.

"There are the peasants' markets, where the farmers bring foodstuffs to sell," he declared, indicating a row of low sheds with a sweep of his hand.

She had been to the markets twice with the chef in order to familiarize herself with local edibles and their prices, but she nodded as though she was learning about the city for the first time.

The King chuckled when he saw a large house, surrounded by a low wooden wall and a narrow moat. "You might not believe this, but that's actually a nobleman's home. Earl Waltheof maintains it for his visits to the city."

"How quaint," Matilda murmured.

"Quaint? It's dangerous. A man of rank ought to protect himself with thick walls and proper defenses. Not that I don't approve of the interior plumbing too," he added.

"You don't object to my giving instructions to the builders, then?" she asked.

"Certainly not. I'm always in favor of improvements."

For the next ten minutes he continued to point out sites of interest, and Matilda listened and looked politely. Finally, as they came to the city wall and rode out into the countryside beyond it, she found the courage to speak up. "Where are you taking me, William?"

"You'll see." He forced a smile.

"There's something on your mind that seems to be bothering you, dear."

"Is there?"

She knew that he was too honest to lie and was seeking to evade an answer with a rhetorical question. "You don't care to discuss it with me?" She could always tell when he was ill at ease, and she was worried about him.

"There's nothing to discuss—at the moment." He rose in his saddle and pointed ahead. "We'll be at West Minster in a few minutes."

"West Minster?"

"Edward built a very impressive new church and abbey there. I want you to see them."

Surely he wasn't taking time out of a busy day to show her the sights, and Matilda wondered briefly if he had drifted so far from her that he was intending to confine her in the nunnery attached to the church. Kings had been known to dispose of inconvenient wives in such a manner, but after an instant of panic Matilda recovered. William was too direct to deal with her in a roundabout manner, and had he intended to be rid of her, he would have told her as much, and in so many words.

"There's something I'm planning, and I need your advice," she said. "My ladies and I are going to make a tapestry showing your whole relationship with Harold Godwineson. We'll illustrate the battle in detail, too."

"That will be nice," William replied politely.

"I know that you're too busy to give us a full account of what happened in the battle, but Odo has promised to help us."

"Odo will have won the battle singlehanded by the time he finishes telling you bout it." William could not resist a chuckle. "What advice do you want from me?"

They arrived at the church, where workmen were completing the task begun under Edward the Confessor; nothing had been done to finish the edifice during Harold's short reign, and one of William's first acts had been to order the builders to resume their operations. The church, with its abbey and nunnery, was as large and impressive as any in Normandy or France, and he was anxious to use it as a national cathedral.

Matilda smiled at the masons and carpenters who

tugged off their caps as she dismounted, then she devoted her full attention to her husband again. "Every man of note has a special name to distinguish him. There was Henry the Bold of France, and Philip the Brave——"

"My father," he said dryly as he offered her his arm and started toward the church entrance, "was called Robert the Devil, in case you've forgotten it."

"No. I haven't forgotten." She was sure the voices of their sons would never become tight with hatred when they spoke of William.

"I've been called the Lion of Normandy since I was about twenty. I think that's good enough for your tapestry."

"It's no such thing. You've done what no one, not even Charlemagne, has been able to accomplish since Julius Caesar took possession of all England, and I think you need a name that people will remember."

"Whatever you want." They arrived at the heavy oak doors, which a workman opened for them, and they walked into the uncompleted church. Snow had drifted in through the high window openings and lay in little piles in the nave, but even in its unfinished shape there was a grandeur to the building that could be matched by few cathedrals, and William, his mind on the idea that had led him to bring Matilda here, was thinking of matters far more important than her tapestry.

"I've decided," she said, daintily skirting around a heap of snow, "to call you the 'Conqueror.' That is, if you don't object."

"Please yourself." He glanced at her briefly, and somewhat to his surprise saw that she intended no sarcasm. He would have imagined that the plumbing in Edward's house would have occupied her far more than thinking of an appropriate new name for him.

"Then I will." She had hoped he would realize how

much loving care had gone into her selection and that through it he would begin to see how much she loved him, but at times he seemed to be incredibly obtuse.

"The builders," he said, "assure me that they'll be through here in another three months. So I plan to hold the coronation here, probably around Easter. Perhaps a little sooner, if Lanfranc has to go to Rome around then."

"I knew nothing about the coronation." Matilda tried not to sound hurt.

"Didn't you?" he asked, hoping his voice sounded innocent. It was impossible for her to have had any inkling of his plans, for he had just formed them today. "I took the crown rather informally, you know, and I think a full religious ceremony will lend the right touch. I want everything done legally, and with the proper amount of pomp. It will be good for the English, it will help to bind my own nobles to this new land, and it will make it easier for me to control the foreigners to whom I've given titles."

"That's very wise, dear." It occurred to Matilda that he seemed excited by the prospect, and she thought it strange that he should find so much pleasure in the anticipation of a coronation when ceremonies had always bored him. Remembering how he had objected when she wanted a big wedding, she tried to curb a feeling of faint pique.

"*This is* the only church I've seen in the country that's big enough to accommodate all of my nobles and knights and the whole of the English gentry, too. I'll put them all over there," he continued, gesturing, "and they can watch the whole ceremony without any difficulty. How does that strike you?"

Increasingly surprised, Matilda thought that she

never would have dreamed that the purpose of this visit was to discuss the details of his coronation. "I'm sure you know best," she said.

"Well, it will be convenient for them to walk, one by one, to the spot where I'm now standing. I'll have my throne here, and they can renew their allegiance to me."

"I see."

William paused, and when he spoke again his voice was unaccountably husky. "As I say, the King's throne will be right here." He moved three paces to the left and stopped. "And here," he said very slowly, "will be the Queen's throne."

Matilda couldn't believe she had heard him correctly. Her eyes became misty, and she had to struggle to choke back a sob.

"As soon as Lanfranc has crowned me, he'll then crown you. Choose any goldsmith you like to make your crown for you. But don't let him spend too much," he added, cautious even now. "Jewels would be too ostentatious, as my crown is made of iron, so don't give the designer a free hand."

Still unable to reply, she looked up at him; her tears dried and her eyes began to shine. They had traveled a long road together, a hard road, and they had both made mistakes too numerous to recall. But their major errors were in the past, and could not be repeated. Matilda knew now, as she never had before, just how deep and permanent was her feeling for William. Her main purpose in life, from this moment forward, would be to open his eyes so that he would become secure in the knowledge that she loved him. She would not have believed it possible, but the fulfillment of her greatest ambition no longer satisfied her. It was pleasant to know that she would become England's first Queen, but her marriage meant far more to her than did the exalted rank.

William, startled by the intensity of her gaze, became embarrassed. Now was the moment for him to tell her how much she meant to him, but he could not; he was a soldier, not a minstrel who sang glibly of love. "You're probably wondering why I've changed my mind," he said, trying to sound casual. "Well, I've established a measure of order, but England is still seething, and a queen will help to give my regime an air of stability. We badly need something real and solid for the whole country to use as a model, and you'll set the example. Do you understand what I mean?"

"Yes, dear. I understand. Perfectly." Matilda smiled at him tenderly, took his arm, and walked out with him into the open. William the Conqueror, King of England, Duke of Normandy and Brittany, Count of Anjou and Maine, Lord of Vexin and Grand Constable of Jersey, the greatest man of his century, did not yet know that he had won his greatest triumph and had vanquished his wife. Matilda's hold on his arm tightened, and they approached the waiting horses for the ride back to London.

Don't Miss these Ace Romance Bestsellers!

———— #75157 **SAVAGE SURRENDER** $1.95
The million-copy bestseller by Natasha Peters,
author of Dangerous Obsession.

———— #29802 **GOLD MOUNTAIN** $1.95

———— #88965 **WILD VALLEY** $1.95
Two vivid and exciting novels by
Phoenix Island author, Charlotte Paul.

———— #80040 **TENDER TORMENT** $1.95
A sweeping romantic saga in the
Dangerous Obsession tradition.

Available wherever paperbacks are sold or use this coupon.